HANDYMAN

Forge Books by Jean Heller

Maximum Impact
Handyman

HANDYMAN

Jean Heller

A Tom Doherty Associates Book
New York

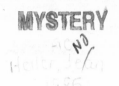

HANDYMAN

Map by Cristina Martinez

A Forge Book
Published by Tom Doherty Associates, Inc.
175 Fifth Avenue
New York, NY 10010

Forge® is a registered trademark of Tom Doherty Associates, Inc.

Library of Congress Cataloging-in-Publication Data

Heller, Jean.
Handyman / Jean Heller.
p.   cm.
"A Tom Doherty Associates book."
ISBN 0-312-85818-3 (hardcover)
1. Women journalists—Florida—Tampa—Fiction. 2. Serial murders—Florida—Tampa—Fiction. 3. Tampa (Fla.)—Fiction.
I. Title.
PS3558.E4758H36   1995
813'.54—dc20   95-34734
                      CIP

First edition: November 1995

Printed in the United States of America

0 9 8 7 6 5 4 3 2 1

For Dorothy and Bob,
who probably thought they taught me better.

ACKNOWLEDGMENTS

There's always a lot of technical support that goes into a book like this. Most valuable to me were the following:

Curt E. Lau, an expert in all the technical systems in modern office towers, showed me places I didn't even know high-rise buildings had, and explained things I never dreamed I'd want to know, in ways I could readily understand.

Major Gary Terry of the Hillsborough County Sheriff's Office, who tracked down the real-life serial killer, Bobby Joe Long, lent invaluable support to my efforts to learn how an investigation of that nature works.

Jack Espinosa, spokesman for the Hillsborough County Sheriff's Office, helped me with key operational details.

Jeffrey Wartman, MD, gave generously of his time to help me understand how lightning acts and the physical damage it can inflict.

Brooks Buck, DVM, counseled me about what no one would have expected from a certain breed of dog.

Jan Glidewell, my good friend and colleague at the *St. Petersburg Times,* gave me critical support, as well as information about important aspects of Florida criminal records.

My agent, Roslyn Targ, eased my mind when elements of this story left me wondering about my sanity.

Melissa Ann Singer, my editor, suggested major improvements.

And, as always, Ray Stephens, was generous to the extreme in his support, his time, and his understanding.

Jean Heller

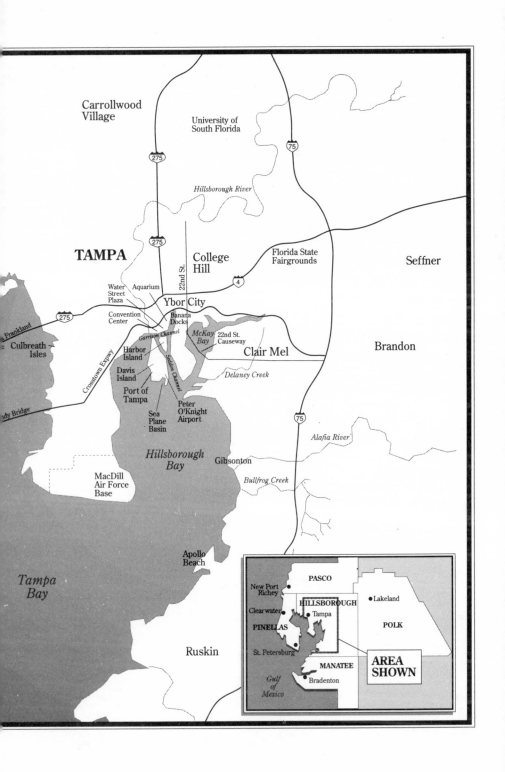

Hey, girls, gather 'round.
Listen to what I'm puttin' down.
Hey, baby, I'm your Handyman.

I'm not the kind to use a pencil or rule.
I'm handy with love, and I'm no fool.
I fix broken hearts,
I know that I truly can.

If your broken heart should need repair,
then I am the man to see.
I whisper sweet things, tell all your friends,
they'll come runnin' to me.

Here is the main thing I want to say:
I'm busy twenty-four hours a day.
I fix broken hearts.
Baby, I'm your Handyman.

PART
ONE

1

What happened to me?
  Head aches. Shoulders hurt. Feel sleepy.
  Can't move!
  Has there been an accident? Maybe I shouldn't try to move. If I'm hurt, moving could make it worse.
  I'm a doctor. I should be able to figure this out.
  Have sensation. That's good. I'm not paralyzed.
  I'm lying on a hard surface . . . arms pulled down . . . My God, it feels like I'm tied!
  Legs raised and spread. It's an examining table. My feet are up in the stirrups.
  I remember!
  The noise in the other office. Went to see what it was. The window was open. Something . . . somebody . . . hit me.
  What's on my leg?
  Something's moving up my leg.
  He's going to rape me! That's why he has me tied up this way. Somebody has broken in and he's going to rape me.
  Got to stay calm, think straight. I should keep my eyes closed. Don't look at him. Don't be able to identify him. If I see him, he might think he has to kill me to protect himself.
  He's cutting through my panty hose.
  What's he using? Scissors? A knife? Oh, God, don't let him be a madman with a knife!
  He's on the other leg now.
  What the? . . . That's crazy! . . . He's humming.
  I know *that song.*

*   *   *

THE Handyman knew she was conscious. He could see her eyes moving under the lids, the way they do in REM sleep, or when somebody's trying to fake sleep and doesn't know how. Or maybe she knew how, but was too frightened to think straight. It was wonderful. Exactly what he wanted. She had barely regained consciousness, and already she was terrified. He had removed her blouse and her skirt before he bound her, and he started cutting away her panty hose as she began to wake up, so her first sensation would be of someone messing with her lower body.

He intended to draw the ritual out for a long, long time, until she had no more tears to shed, no more voice to scream, until she was incoherent with pain and unspeakable terror, and then he would bring her back so she could comprehend one more thing, one final act.

It was time to begin. He had laid open her panty hose to the waistband; now it was time for her panties. He inserted the tip of his blade under the elastic of the right leg hole, carefully keeping the flat edge down, against her skin. He paused and looked at her. Did she get it yet? Did she know what was happening to her?

With a quick, short thrust, he stuck her in the lower belly. Not deep. Not deep at all. But it was enough to snap her eyes open.

She was tough. He saw her resist the impulse to look at him and fix her gaze on the textured ceiling as she yelped and then moaned, as much in fear as in pain. But it was exactly what he wanted, and the thrill rippled through his abdomen.

"Yes!" he told her. "Scream, bitch!"

His words got her attention. She glanced at him and as quickly looked away. A light perspiration broke out on her forehead.

"So you were faking it," he said with a smile that changed only his mouth. "I knew it. You might as well look at me. You want to see the last lover you'll ever have, don't you?"

"No," she said, her tone of defiance surprising him. "I'm not going to look at you. I don't want to be able to identify you."

"You think that might stop me from killing you?"

"Yes."

"Wrong. It won't matter a bit. I'm gonna kill you whether you look at me or not."

"No! Please!" The defiance was slipping.

"Oh, that's good," he said, moving his knife ever so slightly, not pricking her again, but reminding her it was there. "I love to hear you beg."

Her lip quivered.

"Are you going to cry?" he asked in a tone of happy surprise.

Maybe she wasn't so tough after all. "I want you to cry. I want to hurt you. I want to punish you. Opal knows what to do. She's gonna slide under your panties and cut through them on the way to her next port of call. If you think she hurt you last time . . ." He let the thought trail off. "We're takin' it real slow, Opal and me. Headin' north, cuttin' cloth, and keepin' time."

Now the knife was cutting directly up the center front of the panties. As the rend lengthened, the cotton opened. When he found what he was looking for, he stopped the knife's advance.

"Well, lookie here," he said with vicious glee. "We've come to the belly button. Let's see what Opal can do here. Right in the center, Opal, deeper than the first prick, but not too deep. Don't want to do any damage yet, just a world of hurt."

He shoved the point of his knife about a quarter inch into the small circle of folded skin. Her whole body jerked, and she screamed. As the scream died, she trembled violently. He grinned, the nastiness of the expression commanding his entire face.

"That's a good scream," he said. "But there's nobody around to hear you. Just me, your Handyman. Opal and me are gonna make you scream a lot."

"Please, don't do that," she begged.

"What? This?"

The stick was a little deeper this time.

She screamed again, her head thrashing from side to side. Then she began to sob.

He grinned again.

"We love hurtin' you," he said. "We're gonna hurt you bad, and you're gonna scream and cry and beg. It makes me so hot. Beg, bitch! Plead with me!"

She did. "Please, don't do any more. I can't stand it. Please, for God's sake, stop!"

He laughed. He was becoming seriously aroused, not at the prospect of rape, but at the prospect of inflicting more pain.

"That's only the beginning," he promised.

He walked around to the side of the examining table, so he could bend well over her and look her straight in the eyes. His face came within inches of hers, and he saw her flinch. He guessed she smelled the strong odor of alcohol on his breath. He was slightly drunk, and he hadn't bothered to try to cover it up. He was always slightly drunk when he killed—well, okay, maybe more than slightly. He found courage in bourbon bottles. It took courage to kill. If he didn't get drunk, he wouldn't be able to go through with the killing, and Opal would be angry, indeed. He killed to win approval from Opal. When he satisfied her, she would let him stop. It was the only way she would ever let him find peace.

"Once we've unwrapped you, I'm going to dedicate you to Opal," he said, still in her face. "Would you like to meet Opal? She likes you very much. Here."

In a hand encased by a surgical glove, he held up his knife so she could see the haft, inlaid with luminescent blues and greens and gold flecks with a blush of pink. He turned it so its bloody point swept close to her face, and he saw the horror fill her eyes. The weapon must look huge to her. Hideous and terrifying.

"It's purty, ain't it?" he asked. "You like purty things? I bet you like them rainbow crystals. I know you got one hangin' from the rearview mirror in the convertible car you drive. You got 'em hung all around your house, too? Betcha do. Always flashin' in the sun, makin' rainbows on the walls and the ceiling. You think it's real purty, don't you?" He got low to her face again. "Did you ever know I *hated* them damned things? Is that why you hung 'em all over, cause you knew how much I hated 'em, flashin' in my eyes all the time? You're gonna pay for it now, bitch. You're gonna pay for everything."

"I don't know what you're talking about!" she said desperately.

"Oh, sure you do. Hey, you know what I did with all them crystals from your house? Buried 'em. Buried 'em where you'll never find 'em."

"Please! I don't . . ."

"Shut up!"

She began struggling in her bonds. But escape was impossible. Her bare feet were tied to the table stirrups and her wrists were bound to the base of the table with thick bands of latex, the tourniquets lab technicians wrap patients' arms with to make veins stand up for drawing blood.

He bent low to her again, deliberately expelling his reeking alcohol breath into her face.

"Opal's gonna have her way with you," he said in softly menacing tones, "and in return, you're gonna give your heart to the Handyman. I'm gonna win your heart for Opal, sure thing."

She took several deep breaths, trying to steady herself, to stop the trembling.

"Why are you so angry with me?" she asked.

He didn't answer.

"Do I know you? Were you a patient? I'm sorry. I don't remember you. Have I done something to you?"

"Shut up!"

He was through talking. He was back between her legs, working again with his knife on her clothes. He had cut through the right leg of her panties when he pricked her the first time. Now he cut through the left, so the only thing keeping them on was the elastic at the waist. He would take care of that very soon. From now on he would let his actions speak for him.

She studied his face. She thought perhaps she could find a way to appeal to him, to connect with him. For all his savagery, he didn't have a cruel face. It was almost a gentle face, a slightly feminine face. Maybe she could make him listen to reason.

Her eyes widened, and the realization struck her like a hammer in the chest. With absolute certainty, she knew who he was.

But why had he come for her? The papers said he chose prostitutes and homeless women. Vulnerable women.

No. The last one wasn't a prostitute. She was . . . she was a school-teacher.

And now he'd come for her. A doctor.

Her throat was parchment dry. She thought there must be no hope after all. She began to cry softly, and he began to sing. His voice sounded very far away. It was the same song he was humming when she regained consciousness. It sounded familiar then. She recognized it now; she could have sung it with him.

> *If your broken heart should need repair*
> *Then I am the man to see-e-e.*
> *I whisper sweet things, tell all your friends,*
> *And they'll come running to me-E-e-e.*

So sharp was the knife it cut through the waistbands of her panty hose and underpants with barely a tug. It slid over her abdomen and up to the base of her bra.

"It gets even more fun now," he said absently, talking to himself as much as to her.

With a single motion, he slid the knife under the bra, between her breasts, and with a sharp upward jerk, cut cleanly through the fabric. Gently, being careful not to prick her this time, he inserted the point under the left cup and flipped it up and off her, leaving her breast exposed and the ruined undergarment hanging over her arm. He ran the flat of the blade over her nipple and smiled to see it harden in fear.

He repeated the ritual on the right side.

"Oh, yes!" he breathed. "We're in a hurtin' kinda mood."

He placed the blade between her breasts, flat against her sternum.

He paused only a moment, then plunged it in, deep enough to scrape the bone at the center of her rib cage. When he withdrew the weapon, blood bubbled from the wound.

He heard her sharp intake of breath, and then a frantic scream that chilled even him. It rose in a crescendo, held a moment, then died abruptly as she lost consciousness once again.

"HOLD still!" he barked at her.

She groaned softly and tried to turn her face from the source of the sting in her nasal passages. The intrusion was disturbing her sleep, and she didn't want anything to disturb her sleep. She didn't remember why she resisted, but she desperately didn't want to wake up.

"I said, hold still!" he repeated.

She stopped resisting. She did as he ordered because the pain in her body brought back the vivid memory of what caused her to pass out. She opened her eyes and looked up into his face and saw him smile.

"Very handy, these little things," he said, holding something in his gloved fingers for her to see. "Handy, like me."

She recognized the ammonia capsule. Smelling salts. He must have gotten them from the supply closet down the hall. She wondered what else he'd taken from the closet. Drugs to give him courage to go through with this, maybe? Were there any drugs in the office that could be described as backbone in a bottle? She couldn't recall, but she knew she wasn't thinking straight. On the other hand, what did it matter?

There was nothing she could do about any of it.

She realized he'd left her side. She raised her head tentatively and looked around the small examining room for him, but he was gone. She had one brief rush of hope that he was gone for good, but logic told her to be realistic. Wherever he'd gone, he'd be back.

Her gaze was drawn back to her body. Blood leaked from the knife wound on her sternum and trickled down her ribs. A tiny pool of blood was congealing in her navel. The place he'd pricked her on the lower abdomen was barely visible. How could something that hurt so much appear so insignificant?

God, but she looked vulnerable, with her clothes laid open and her feet tied high in the stirrups. She let her head fall back and tried to regulate her breathing. She didn't want to cry again. That's surely what he wanted, to see her acknowledge his absolute power over her. If she could possibly help it, she wouldn't give him the satisfaction.

She tried to remember if there was anyone who might come to the office at night. Police? No, no hope there. They were used to driving by and seeing lights on late. It had been that way for several months, since she'd started staying after hours, while it was quiet, to study for her surgery boards. The cleaning crew! Maybe. At her request, they made her the last stop of the night, so they didn't disturb her studies. They usually got in around nine P.M.

What time was it now?

When she heard the noise in her partner's office, she had looked at her watch and it was . . . what? . . . 6:40. She went into the room and saw the window open. Then she saw somebody move, and he hit her, and the next thing she knew, she was waking up on an examining table with the intruder systematically cutting his way through her clothing. If she was unconscious then for, say, half an hour, and for a couple of minutes just now, it couldn't be much after 7:40, 7:45.

If her calculations were correct, it would be more than an hour, maybe an hour and a half, before the cleaning crew showed up. She doubted he would wait that long to kill her.

She allowed herself to groan. She hurt so much.

Again she wondered where the intruder had gone. What was he doing?

She thought of Andy and had to fight back tears. He would blame himself for her death. He never called her at the office in the evening because he didn't want to interrupt her studies. He called her at home, later. But when they found her dead, he would wonder: If he had called, would he have recognized something was wrong and been able to act to save her? She hated the thought that he would blame himself. She hated that now they would never have a chance to marry, never have a family. She wanted children so badly. But it wasn't going to happen.

Mentally, she kicked herself. Why was she giving up hope? Her chances weren't good, but they were alive, as long as she was.

His voice jarred her.

"Ah, you look chipper enough to resume," he said. "This sort of thing goes better with bourbon, so I went out for a couple of belts. I also thought I'd pick up some more of these smelling-salt things. I think we're going to need a lot of them before we're through for the night."

"No more," she said softly.

"There has to be more," he replied. "I don't like my woman falling asleep on me. When you're asleep, I can't watch your eyes. I like to watch your eyes. I don't like it when you close them. I'm going to have to punish you for that."

"Wait!" she said desperately. "Tell me what you want. You don't have to kill me for it. I'll give it to you willingly. I'll even enjoy it with you. Tell me what it is! Sex? Rough sex? It's all right. I'll do it with you. Just tell me what you want!"

"I don't have to tell you. I can take what I want."

"Please don't do this!"

"You're trembling. That's good. We're getting where I want you to be. You'll lose all control soon. You're completely open to me, you know. You should raise your head and take a look at yourself. Your legs are spread wide, your back is arched, your tits are reaching up to me. That's a vulnerable point for you, ain't it? It is for all women. It scares you to hear me talk about your tits like this, don't it? Of course it does. By the way, Opal likes to cut tits. She's going to cut yours underneath. Maybe she'll even cut 'em off. She'll glide through your flesh like a hot knife through butter, and she'll be so happy . . . Terrifies you, doesn't it? Good!

The point of the knife penetrated the base of her right breast at the center of her chest and blood spattered his blue jeans. Although the penetration wasn't deep, her shriek sounded like the scream of a mortally injured wild animal. He grinned wickedly at her torment as the knife traced the base of her breast all the way to her armpit.

"Oh, yes, scream!" he urged. "You've never known such pain. But don't thrash around so much. You're making it tough for Opal to keep a neat line. Opal doesn't like not being neat."

He withdrew the knife and surveyed its work. Blood cascaded down her side along the entire length of the wound.

"There," he said, satisfied with his work. "Maybe I better use one of them smelling-salt capsules. You look like you're gonna leave me again. I won't let you leave. Not until I'm ready. When I'm ready, you'll leave for good."

She had stopped screaming, and her bloody chest heaved as she tried to get her breath.

"It's time for Opal to move to the other side," he said. "Wouldn't want your left tit to feel left out." He laughed. "Left tit . . . left out. Get it? That's funny."

The knife dipped into her flesh again, and it went deeper this time. This time the spattering blood blotched his shirt and dripped onto his shoes. She tried not to scream, but she was rapidly losing control. Her grip on reality was sliding away. For an instant, she thought she was in Andy's bedroom, and he was trying to rouse her from a nightmare. The intruder's voice brought her back to the bloody office.

"You got a good set of pipes," he said. "I never heard anybody scream that loud before. It's excitin' me more than I can tell you. Good job, Opal. A matched set of sliced tits. I love it."

She was perspiring heavily, partly from fear, partly from exertion. The sweat was leaking into her wounds, layering her pain, doubling the agony. For the first time, she found herself hoping for a conclusion to the ordeal. She wanted it to be over, even if it meant her death. Death, at least, would be an escape from the torture.

He was singing again. The sound seemed to come from far away.

> *Here is the main thing I want to say-a-yea:*
> *I'm busy twenty-four hours a day-ay.*
> *I fix broken hearts. I know that I truly ca-a-an.*

"You want me to hurry, don't you?" he asked. "You want to get this over. Well, too bad. We ain't gonna hurry."

He laid the knife down lengthwise along the center of her chest, so the blade covered the puncture wound over the sternum.

"Look how hard your nipples are," he said gleefully. "I'm gonna play with 'em a little bit. Then maybe I'll cut 'em off. Hmmm? Yes, I felt you cringe. I expected it. The others did, too. You're disgusted to have me touch you, aren't you? Well, you shouldn't be. I'm as good a man as the next. Your nipples are hard. They want me. I knew they did. All those days and nights I watched you, I knew under your blouse, inside your bra, your tits wanted me. And your heart. I'm gonna win your heart tonight, bitch. I'll steal your heart, and I'll add it to my collection."

He bent close to her face. "What's that you said? Your voice is weak. I can't hear you."

She whimpered between gasps for air, "Please don't hurt me anymore."

"But I want to," he said. "I control you, bitch. You are powerless beneath me. I have broken you. I dominate you. I can do whatever I want to you now, and you can't do one damned thing about it. How's it feel? How's it feel to be laid out like the whore you are, and for me to take you and take you and take you? Any time, as many times as I want. I am your god. You are nothing."

His eyes glazed over.

"I am on cruise control now," he said. "I am automated. I am going to ruin your nipples."

He pinched them, then pinched harder. He twisted and pulled and pinched again. She was sobbing quietly, with no strength left to resist.

"Beg me to stop," he demanded. "Please beg me! Beg me to stop. This is our foreplay, bitch. I mean it to hurt you."

"Can't . . . stand . . . any more," she whispered. Her eyelids fluttered.

"Oh, sure you can," he said. "We can both stand more. More and more and more and . . ."

His arousal had reached peak intensity. His erection pressed painfully against the zipper of his bloody denims.

"I think it's time, my dear," he said hoarsely.

He plucked the knife from her chest and bent over her again. She felt his fingers probe the left side of her neck, pressing into the flesh. He apparently found what he was looking for. Quickly, and without warning, he stuck the knife point in deeply at the place where his fingers had been. She gasped. He duplicated the action on the right side. Through the expanding haze of pain and blood loss, she sensed more than she knew that he had punctured the carotid arteries. Every time her heart beat, the wounds spurted her blood onto the examining room floor. Her own heart was now conspiring to kill her. How long would it take to die? It depended on how large the cuts were. She suspected they weren't very big. He wouldn't want the ordeal to end soon, or easily.

He moved between her legs.

"I'm gonna slide my fingers up in there and see what you've got to offer, bitch," he said to a victim now only barely perceiving him. "You're not reactin'. What'sa matter? Can't feel new pain over the old pain? Well, let's get a little rough and see what you think about it." He scraped the ends of his gloved fingers hard along the walls of her vagina, pressing deeply into her flesh. "Ah, you're feelin' it now, aren't ya?"

In fact, she was aware of his fingers inside her, but she only barely felt him clawing her flesh. But the next pain was so intense, it crashed along her nervous system and reached her brain almost instantly.

"Let's see how you feel about Opal doin' some business down here," he said, as the knife dipped to her crotch and cut her quickly. "One . . . two . . . three." He counted off the cruel wounds and laughed sadistically.

She screamed and sobbed in long spasms of sound from deep within her chest, a cornered, wounded animal in its death throes. Despite her growing weakness, seizures convulsed her lower body. Her hips bucked uncontrollably, trying to dislodge the agony. Existence became a red-hot haze of tortured nerves.

"Now you're hurtin' my eardrums," he said. "I don't think you should be bangin' your head against the table like that. You could hurt yourself."

He had reached the point where he could put off the inevitable no longer. He opened his belt, unzipped his pants, and freed himself.

"You might wanna hold your head up and watch the rest of this, bitch," he said. "You ain't never gonna see nothin' like it again. Yeah. I'm ready. I'm good and ready. I'm ready and good. You watchin' this, Opal? You seein' this real good?" He pried her open with his fingers and plunged in. "There, bitch, take it all at once!"

He buried himself deep inside her and remained motionless for a few seconds. "You want me to pull out?" he asked. He did, only to slam into her again. And again. And again.

But she was beyond the point of feeling anymore. She was dizzy and disoriented. And she was cold. The blood loss was taking its full toll. She was slipping into shock.

She could feel the blood jump from the cuts in her neck every time her heart beat, and at the moment her heart was pounding. She realized something else, too. He was timing his strokes to coincide with those blood spurts.

How grotesque, she thought. A joint ejaculation.

Then his rhythm changed. He was singing again. And his strokes were coming in time with his song.

> *Here is the main thing I want to sa-a-ay:*
> *I'm busy twenty-four hours a day-ay.*
> *I fix broken hearts, baby.*
> *I'm your handyma-a-an.*
>
> *Come-a-come-a-come-a-come-a-come-come,*
> *Yeah, yeah, ye-e-e-e-ah.*

He finished explosively.
   The song died away.
   Her life ended.

HE stood there for several moments, wallowing in his triumph, his chest heaving from the exertion and emotion. But as his heart rate began to slow, the mood began to slip away. He was revulsed at the sight of her torn body; the wounds he'd inflicted were still seeping blood. The power was draining from him faster than it ever had before, and he reached out to take it back. He picked up his beloved knife, the one he called Opal after his dead mother, and began to attend to the details. His confidence stabilized, and sweet peace returned, although not at the extreme level he'd felt as his rape escalated to ejaculation.

"This is for you, Opal," he said softly.

When he finished twenty-seven minutes later, his hands and his knife were awash in blood, but he smiled at the quality of his work.

"Here's another heart for you, Ma," he whispered. "It's another heart I've fixed. I'll leave it right out here where you can see it. You didn't think I was man enough, but I told you I could do it. Who's your best handyman, Ma, huh? Who do you love?"

His voice sounded satisfied, but already he could feel the old depression creep in and pry away the outer edges of his ecstasy.

He very badly wanted a drink.

He left the examining room door open and set out to scout around the offices. He snatched up the brown bag holding his bourbon bottle from the spot where he'd left it on the hallway floor, leaned against the door frame and took a long pull. The bottle and the bag became smeared with blood from his gory gloves, as did the door frame from his blood-soaked clothes, but he didn't notice. An ounce or so of the brown liquid splashed onto the vinyl tile floor. He didn't notice that, either. He took another pull and savored the burn in his throat and the warmth in his gut.

He thought he could still salvage the evening's adventure if he found the right souvenir. He identified the suite that had been hers without a problem, let himself in, and switched on the light. His glove left a bloody smear on the switch.

He looked around carefully. There were so many things from which to choose, he was tempted to take several. But that would be wrong. That would be greedy. He needed only one item of hers. But it had to be the right one.

He circled the office twice before narrowing his choices. It was between her framed medical school diploma and the photograph on her desk of her with a smiling young man standing on the bow of a sailboat. After a time, he took the photograph. He slid it inside his shirt, glass side out so it wouldn't get smudged against his skin, still clammy from exertion, although the frame became blood-smeared as soon as he picked it up, just as everything else he touched in the offices bore grisly reminders of the work he'd done this evening.

He returned to the other suite.

He slipped out the window through which he'd come and vanished into the night.

2

"I can not fucking *believe* this!"

He was dressed in gray slacks, a long-sleeved blue shirt, and a red-on-blue silk tie. Even during the hottest weather he wouldn't wear short-sleeved shirts. He hated the way they looked ("Like I should be selling used cars," he told his wife). He made something of a concession to the sweltering temperature/humidity combination by rolling the long sleeves to mid-forearm, a look he liked a lot. Muted authority.

A light sheen of perspiration on his face glistened under the glare of nearby street lamps and the pulsing wash of rotating emergency lights from six Hillsborough Sheriff's Office units and one lone, unneeded ambulance.

Captain Benjamin Britton had been at home eating a late dinner with his wife and two boys when his phone brought the gut-wrenching news of the nightmarish carnage found by a cleaning crew at a doctor's office in Carrollwood Village. The shock sent one charwoman to the hospital.

Britton smashed his fist into the door frame of his unmarked car.

"Damn it to hell!" he swore softly, so only the homicide detective at his side could hear. "What was her name?"

"Tentative ID is Marilyn Erlich, thirty-two, a doctor of internal medicine," said Nick Estevez, the first detective on the scene and the man who'd rousted Britton from his evening meat loaf. "We gave a general description to her partner who confirmed the probable ID. She was studying to be a surgeon. That's what she was doing down here so late, studying."

"Again and again and again and again, and we're no closer to him than we were after Mabel Brown," Britton said.

"Except the victims are getting older," Estevez noted.

"Then why aren't they any smarter?" Britton snapped. "Why do

they keep letting this guy get close to them? The first ones, the homeless girl and the prostitutes, them I can understand. They don't think
about this stuff. But a teacher? A *doctor,* for chrissake?"

"It wasn't a matter of *letting* him get close this time," Estevez said.
"Looks like he got in through an unlocked window on the blind side of
the building."

"I repeat, they're not getting any smarter," Britton said, frustration
casting a hard edge on his voice. "If you're smart, you don't leave a
window unlocked when there's a serial killer running around loose. If
you're smart, you don't leave a window unlocked any time, and especially not in a medical office."

"The educated ones, they think they're not vulnerable," Estevez
suggested. "We tell 'em it ain't so, but they don't believe. I got a
week's pay says they'll believe now."

"Not a good bet," Britton replied glumly. "Some of them never
learn."

They were silent for several moments, staring at the front of the
typical suburban medical building that had become a house of horrors. Pete Sisko, the sheriff's chief spokesman, stood in the grass by
the parking area, away from the building, so television and still cameras trained on him wouldn't pick up the doctors' names spelled out in
gold-toned metallic letters by the front door. The photographers
would get shots of the building anyhow, but Sisko didn't want to
make it any easier. He was fielding questions from the early wave of
reporters. "No, I don't have a positive identification yet," he was saying.

Sisko, too, had been home, and deep into his second stiff Scotch,
when the call came. He'd pulled off his T-shirt and put on a dress shirt
he left open at the throat and a jacket. On the air, seen only from the
chest up, he would appear fully clothed for his official late-evening
duties. Full-frontal, however, he looked ridiculous, wearing the shirt
and sport coat over a pair of rumpled cargo shorts and heavily worn
Topsiders without socks. "We simply don't know yet if this is the
work of the serial killer," Sisko told the reporters. "We aren't dismiss-
ing any possibilities. . . . I'm sorry I don't have anything more for you
at this time. . . . We won't know the cause of death until the medical
examiner has had an opportunity to examine the body. . . ."

"You wanna go in, see it before the ME gets here?" Estevez asked.

"Not really," Britton said, wiping perspiration from his upper lip.
The humidity was thickening by the minute, and the mid-August
night was suffocating. It had been bad all summer, but this was the

worst. He sighed. "How much death do I have to look at in one lifetime?"

Estevez shrugged. "That's why the citizens pay you the big bucks."

Britton glared. "You're funny, man. I'm not in a mood for funny." He sucked in a long, deep breath and expelled it slowly, a technique his wife, Laura, had taught him a year earlier when she was into relaxation therapy and tried to get him interested, too. She'd given him the whole course. Slow, deep breathing was all he remembered of it. He nodded toward a white Mustang convertible, sitting alone in a corner of the parking lot. "That belong to the doctor?" he asked.

"I think so, yeah," Estevez replied.

"Organize a canvass of the neighborhood. Find out if anybody remembers seeing any other vehicle in the lot late. And you might as well start the search for the surgical gloves."

"Long shots," Estevez suggested.

"They're all long these days," Britton replied.

When Estevez returned, they circled the brick-and-stucco building. All four sides were bathed in official headlights and spots. Finding where the killer gained entry was easy. It was a double-hung window pushed all the way open. The screen lay in the sparse Bahia grass where it fell when it was yanked from its anchors.

"You're sure it wasn't forced?" Britton asked.

"The window? No," Estevez repeated. "Go figure."

"Is this the victim's office?"

"No, her partner's. Nadine Winfield, specialist in obstetrics and gynecology. Said she couldn't remember the last time she had the window open, so she didn't know how long it had been unlocked. It's possible somebody else, one of the cleaning people, maybe, opened it and forgot to relock it, or opened it to make it easier to come back looking for drugs later. Insurance company's gonna love it."

"And maybe a member of the cleaning crew is the killer," Britton suggested. "Find out what service supplies the crew and who's on it. Is there a regular team that comes here, or do they rotate? I want names and addresses for everybody who's cleaned this place this year."

"All the members of the crew that found the body have alibis. They've been with each other since four o'clock. This office was still open at four. Probably lots of people around. The killing had to be later."

"Then find out if anybody ever cleaned here who wasn't on the job tonight."

"I'll get somebody started on it right now," Estevez said.

While Estevez was gone, Britton searched the window frame with his flashlight for signs of scratches or scuffs that might help identify the killer's clothing or shoes, anything that might be a lead. He was tempted to feel for evidence, too, but he knew better. He kept his hands away to avoid tainting latent clues, if there were any, which he devoutly wished but doubted. He did find a smear of something that looked like blood, an indication that the killer left the building this way. But likely the blood belonged to the victim. Whoever this guy was, he left powerfully little for the police to follow. And that was strange. From all Britton knew of the typical serial-killer profile, the murderer's disgust with himself grew roughly in proportion to the length of his list of victims. And as his revulsion grew, so did the desperation to be caught and put out of business. The desperation often led to carelessness, and carelessness meant clues. But this man wasn't following the pattern.

"Anybody called on this brilliant Dr. Winfield?" Britton asked when Estevez returned.

"Yeah. She lives two blocks away. Bobby Brown talked to her by phone then left to pick her up, bring her back here. When the ME says it's okay, we can take her in and go over the scene, look for things, you know, out of the ordinary."

Britton shook his head. "Well, she won't have to look very far, will she?"

BRITTON, Estevez, and the medical examiner arrived at the front door at the same time.

Britton thought Jerry Lowensdorf had become a medical examiner because he looked and acted like someone who should be: gruff, short, squat, and rumpled, with salt-and-pepper Brillo for hair, and black-rimmed half-glasses he slowly polished with an old handkerchief when he needed a moment to think. Lowensdorf growled as he pushed past the detectives and entered the doctors' waiting room.

"You saved me from a pitcher of martinis and a good book, Ben," he said to Britton. "Don't know how I'll ever repay the favor. Where's the body?"

"Down the hall, second door on the left," Estevez replied. He and Britton followed Lowensdorf into the building.

Nothing in the waiting room appeared amiss. But there were bloody footprints on the vinyl floor midway down the hall. Always a bad sign, Britton thought.

Lowensdorf called back over his right shoulder and pointed at the stains. "Don't step on these," he ordered, as though he were talking to two police cadets.

The officers didn't react; that was just Jerry. Everybody got testy when there were six—now probably seven—unsolved but definitely related murders on the books.

Lowensdorf disappeared through the second door on the left. The cops stopped outside the room. Britton was looking at something else on the vinyl floor.

"Hello," he said, squatting down next to it. He pulled a handkerchief from his pocket and reached toward a small puddle of brown liquid. Estevez peered over Britton's shoulder as the captain touched the puddle gingerly and brought the stained cloth to his nose.

"Hmm, whiskey," Britton said. "Bourbon, I think."

"Not standard issue in any doctor's office I've ever been in," Estevez offered. "I might go more often if it was."

"So our killer's a bourbon drinker," Britton continued. "That narrows our potential suspects a bit. Not by much, but it's more than we had five minutes ago." He looked up at Estevez. "Make sure the lab people pick this up and get it analyzed. We might get lucky and get a brand name."

"What if it's a house brand?" Estevez suggested bleakly.

"It'll still fit some distiller's grain formula," Britton said. "Don't make things harder for us than they have to be."

Britton stood and noticed the bloody smear on the door frame.

"The killer probably stopped here after the deed was done to have a celebratory drink and got blood all over the wall," he guessed. "His clothes must have been a mess."

Estevez just grunted.

Britton peered into the examining room from the doorway. He had steeled himself for it, but the scene still caught his breath. They were looking at the young woman lengthwise, her naked legs pointed toward them. Her feet were still banded to the stirrups, her arms still tied to the table. She was fully exposed and her torso had been laid open from her neck to her navel. Britton thought she didn't look human anymore.

"Jesus," he whispered. His breath caught in his throat, and he felt a stinging in his eyes he fought to put down. Beside him, he saw Estevez swallow twice, hard.

Lowensdorf was circling the examining table, carefully stepping over pools of blood congealing on the floor, tilting his head to look at the body one way, then another, frequently whispering notes into a small tape recorder.

One of his assistants had arrived and was taking photographs, lots of photographs. Britton wondered if the scene was easier to view through a camera lens.

"Is it number seven, Jerry?" he asked, getting his voice back.

"I'd almost swear to it, yes," the medical examiner replied. "Lots of similar elements. He tortured her before he killed her. He used a knife, very sharp, like before. There's no evidence he used a gag—no bruising or other marks around her mouth—and she probably screamed a lot. If this building was closer to the others in the neighborhood, somebody mighta heard her and called for help. It's a damned shame."

"Cause of death?"

"Probably blood loss. There's a puncture wound on each side of the neck, right over the carotids, where runners and Stairmaster freaks monitor their pulses. He wanted her to go slow. After she was dead, he opened her up the same way he opened the last one, only more so. And he's graduated again."

"What do you mean?" Britton asked.

"Surgery," the ME replied. "He's a cardiac man, no less."

Lowensdorf was pointing to a place on the blood-soaked table beside the dead woman's head. There was a large lump there, something shiny and reddish brown. Britton had to lean into the room and look hard to make out what it was. When he recognized it as a human heart, he felt bile rise in his throat.

"Oh, Christ," he said softly. "Hers?"

"Probably so. She seems to be missing one from the usual place."

Britton was incredulous. "What'd he do, rip it out?"

"Uh-uh," Lowensdorf said. "Cut it out, nice and neat. Regular surgical genius, this lad. His mother would be proud."

NADINE Winfield was a nearly total basket case. The detectives who sat with her in her office tried to be solicitous, but it was difficult when every question they asked triggered a wave of new hysteria and self-loathing for neglecting to check the lock on an office window.

Detective Bobby Brown, who brought her from her home and broke the news about the brutal death of her partner, tried to diffuse the guilt.

"Look, Dr. Winfield, anybody can forget a thing like that. People do it all the time," he said softly. "And what if you hadn't forgotten? What if you *had* locked it? A pane of glass isn't going to stop somebody who's determined to get in." He didn't mention iron bars might have done the trick, however. When you're trying to protect a doctor's office in a drug-crazed era, iron bars are not an overreaction.

"Then it should have been me, not Marilyn," she sobbed, plucking a tissue from a dispenser on her desk, dabbing at her eyes, blowing her nose and disposing of the soiled paper in a wastebasket before plucking another from the dispenser. It was a ritual, Britton thought. She would say something, start to cry, then go through the Kleenex routine. This was the fifth time he'd watched her do it. The routine never changed.

"Serial killers pick their victims in advance, Doctor," Britton said. "He didn't want you. He specifically wanted Dr. Erlich. He probably spotted her several days ago, maybe several weeks or months ago. We might never know why he picked her. Something about her set him off. Maybe it was the way she looked, the way she walked, the way her voice sounded. It could be anything. Chances are he's been stalking her ever since, creating the fantasy he acted out here tonight. No offense, but probably the only time he even thought of you was figuring out what obstacles he had to overcome before he made his move. You were an obstacle to him, nothing more."

The doctor began crying again. "Marilyn was younger and prettier," she said from behind her eighth tissue. She blew her nose again. Britton shook his head in frustration. There was no getting through to this woman. She was in shock.

"That has nothing to do with it, ma'am," he said. "This wasn't a sex crime; it was a crime of violence. Given your specialty, you of all people should understand that about rape, the difference between sex crimes and crimes of violence. What Dr. Erlich looked like was important only because it might have fit his fantasy."

She looked at him quizzically. "What did you say your name was?" she asked.

"Benjamin Britton."

"Wasn't there a famous musician by that name?"

"Composer. He spelled it with an e-n."

"Oh."

The woman's mind was wandering. Britton cleared his throat and tried another tack. "Doctor, do you think you're up to viewing Dr. Erlich's body, to make a positive identification?"

"Here? Now?"

"Yes, ma'am. Or later, down at the morgue. That might be easier, although since you're a doctor, I thought . . ."

"Just because I'm a doctor doesn't mean I'm devoid of human emotion, Captain. I hardly want to see Marilyn as she is."

"Then later, perhaps, at the morgue."

"Perhaps. I don't know."

"Would you at least be willing to take us on a tour of these offices, to determine if anything's missing or out of place?"

She rose stiffly. "Where do you want to start?" she asked.

"How about the back of the complex," Britton suggested. "We'll work our way forward. I'm especially eager to see Dr. Erlich's suite."

"Why?"

"We'll know when we see it, ma'am."

The smashed supply closet door was easy to spot. The killer had put his foot to it directly beside the lock and mangled the door frame.

"Can you tell if anything's missing?" Britton asked.

The doctor reached in to turn on the overhead light.

"Don't touch the switch!" Britton barked, and the doctor started. Britton regretted his tone, but his message was urgent. He tried to explain. "If the killer turned on the light, there might be fingerprints on the switch," he said. He leaned into the closet and pushed the switch to the up position with the tip of his pen. The light illuminated a bloody handprint on the wall plate. Britton couldn't see any hint of the ridges and whorls of fingerprints. Most likely the killer was already wearing his trademark surgical gloves when he broke into the closet.

He motioned for the doctor to take a look.

She glanced in tentatively, as though a monster from her childhood might be lurking there. She gasped when she saw the palm print.

"Can you tell if anything is missing?" Britton asked.

"I wouldn't know for sure without a complete inventory," she said. "The only thing that looks amiss is the box." She was pointing to a spilled container on a middle shelf. The contents didn't look to Britton like pills. She saw his confusion. "Ammonia capsules," she explained. "For patients who feel faint."

Britton nodded. "Or to keep torture victims from passing out. That looks like blood on the box, too. The killer came in here after the torture had begun."

He rued the words as soon as they left his mouth. They set the doctor off on another crying jag. He changed the subject. "Dr. Winfield, I'd like you and your office staff to do a complete inventory of this closet in the morning, please. I'll assign one of my detectives to assist you and take your report."

"Certainly," she replied softly.

They left the closet standing open, although Britton used his pen again to turn the overhead light off. The next stop was the lunchroom.

The coffeepots were off and clean. The refrigerator hummed satisfactorily. The microwave was quiet. The bottle in the watercooler was full. And the sink was spotless. But the trash from the day hadn't been emptied from the tall wastebasket. Britton took a quick look inside. Coffee grounds. Microwave food packaging. An empty milk carton. Nothing at all resembling a clue.

"Marilyn . . . Dr. Erlich's office is across the hall," Nadine Winfield said.

Britton nodded grimly. He and Estevez followed. The light was on, and the three of them stood in the doorway peering in. There was another bloody smear on the light switch wall plate. But nothing else appeared amiss. They moved inside.

"Take your time, Doctor," Britton said. "I want you to look around carefully. Sit in the chair where you normally sat when you came in to talk to your partner. Sit in different chairs. Sit in her chair. Be very observant, but also let yourself feel familiarity with things around you. We want to know if anything doesn't look right or doesn't feel right."

"What are you looking for?" she asked.

"Anything and everything," he replied. "Ah, especially anything that might be missing. Serial killers generally like to take souvenirs."

The doctor gasped, and her hand flew to cover her mouth. "Why?" she asked through her fingers. Her eyes were wide with astonishment and fixed intently on the detective. "That's so . . . sick . . . so . . . *disgusting*."

"No quarrel there," Britton said. "They take souvenirs so they can relive the event. They'll look at the souvenir and remember the chase, the confrontation and capture, the excitement, the arousal, and, finally, the murder. For a serial killer, the replay can be quite satisfying. Then, after some period of time, it gets less and less so, and that's when they start trolling for new victims. Strangely enough, it's a pretty clear pattern with most serial killers. If he came in here hunting souvenirs, he might have left some evidence. If you can identify what he took, it will give us something to tie him to the crime when we find him."

"Do you think you'll ever find him?" she asked. "There've been so many killings, and you don't seem to know much about this man."

Britton cleared his throat and rubbed an index finger across his upper lip. "Well, we do know some things about him from previous killings," he said. "But they aren't things we've made public, and we won't until the case is solved."

"I see," she said.

Bobby Brown came in.

"Crime-scene people just got here," Brown said. "They're gonna lift prints in case the killer touched something before he put on his gloves. Even if he did, they're gonna have a deuce of a time finding anything we can use. How many people go through a doctor's office like this in a day, anyhow? Thirty? Forty?"

"When you count mothers with their kids, wives with their husbands, husbands with wives, friends with friends, and other assorted combinations, at least twice that, maybe three times," Nadine Winfield said.

"Wonderful," Brown muttered. "Just wonderful." He turned away to deliver the good news to the fingerprint team and spotted the blood on the light switch. "He was in here," Brown said.

"So we saw," Britton replied.

The doctor shrank from the wall and turned back to Britton. "I don't want to be here," she pleaded. "I don't think I can stay."

Britton smiled kindly. "Do the best you can," he said. He cupped her elbow in his hand and, with gentle pressure, urged her to get on with it.

Reluctantly, she moved to a chair in front of the massive, cluttered desk. "May I sit if I don't put my hands on anything?" she asked.

Britton nodded. He watched as she settled herself down gingerly. She crossed her hands demurely in her lap and seemed to be trying to keep her elbows off the arms. Her head was lowered slightly, so when she looked at the walls, she had to raise her eyes and peer over the tops of her glasses. She assiduously avoided looking anywhere near the bloody wall switch. Britton thought she looked like a whipped puppy.

And why shouldn't she? She was helping look for clues to the identity of the man who butchered her partner on a medical examination table a few feet away. He felt a sudden surge of sympathy for her.

"Take your time," he said gently when she turned and looked at him with pain on her face.

She lifted her hand and pointed away from herself, to a spot on the wall next to the desk. "There," she said.

Britton and Estevez both looked where she was pointing and saw nothing.

"What?" Estevez asked.

"There," she insisted. "The diploma."

Both cops saw the certificate from the University of Michigan School of Medicine, matted in beige and fitted inside a lustrous fruitwood frame, but there wasn't anything unusual about it, except it wasn't hanging straight.

"I'm sorry," Britton said. "I don't see what you're talking about."

"The di-*plom*-a," Nadine Winfield said forcefully. "It's crooked."

"So it is," Estevez replied. "So what?"

"Marilyn didn't have many, uh, idiosyncrasies, but, well, it was an office joke about stuff on the walls," she said. "She was always going around straightening everything. Not just in her office, either. The reception area, the cashier's cubicle, *my* office, all the examining rooms, the *lunchroom*, for heaven's sake. I was with her once, talking to a patient I was taking on a referral from her, and we were in examining room one, I think, or maybe it was two. Oh, well, it doesn't matter, does it? We were talking to the patient, and Marilyn stopped, got up, and started fiddling with a landscape print on the wall. She asked me and the patient to tell her when it was straight. The patient thought it was funny. We all did. It was very Marilyn. But that's why I especially noticed the diploma. She'd never have allowed it to stay crooked. She'd have seen it the second she walked into the room."

"How do you suppose it got crooked?" Estevez asked.

"How do I know?" the doctor replied. "Answers are your department. Maybe it wasn't balanced right on its wire and slid by itself. Or maybe somebody touched it. But the cleaning people never got this far tonight, and Marilyn wouldn't have left it that way. So . . ." She let her voice trail off as though to tell the detectives they should be able to deduce the rest.

"We'll have it dusted," Britton agreed, squinting at the frame. "Actually, there's some blood here. Good work, Doctor. Anything else? Do you notice anything *missing*?"

"Not that I see," she said. She got up and began to move slowly around the office, her eyes darting over everything. When she arrived behind the desk, she looked for a moment as though she wanted to sit in Marilyn Erlich's big chair, but changed her mind. Instead, she stood beside it and very carefully scanned the cluttered surface before her. Her eyes appeared to take in and stop on each item. Britton saw a slight frown crease her brow, but he wasn't certain if it was concentration or recognition of something. Very deliberately, she began to retrace her visual path. She sucked her breath suddenly.

"Andy's gone," she said cryptically.

"Who's Andy?" Britton asked.

She pointed decisively to an empty spot on the desktop. "Andy was right there, and now he's gone," she said.

"Who's Andy, Dr. Winfield?" Britton asked again, more sharply this time.

She looked up at him abruptly. "Oh, I'm sorry," she said. "Of course, you'd have no idea. Andy is . . . was, Marilyn's fiancé. He's a dean of something at USF, the reason she came to this area to practice. They were supposed to be married pretty soon, right after she took her surgical boards. There was a picture of them together on his sailboat right here on her desk." She pointed to the empty place again. "It was Marilyn's favorite picture. They loved to sail, and Andy has a good-sized boat, close to forty feet, I think. But the picture's gone." She paused and tears welled in her eyes. "Oh, God," she sobbed, "does Andy know? Who's going to tell Andy? Poor Andy. This will devastate him."

"I don't doubt it for a minute," Britton said.

IMPROBABLY, they found Andrew Christopher's address and phone number, as well as his phone and address at the University of South Florida, on Marilyn Erlich's Rolodex. It was strange, Nick Estevez suggested, because who needed to keep their fiancé's addresses and phone numbers on file? Wasn't that something you'd remember?

"The card probably dates back to when she was still in Michigan, and he was down here," Britton said. "She probably never bothered to throw it away."

"So who gets to make this house call?" Estevez asked.

"Send a couple of uniforms," Britton said. "Have them bring Christopher down to headquarters. I'd like to talk to him, and we might need him to identify the body if Dr. Winfield doesn't come around. Either way, I don't want anyone who was close to her to have to see her until she's cleaned up."

"Nice of you," Estevez said.

"Hell, I didn't want to look at her until she was cleaned up," Britton said.

"But that's why the taxpayers give you the big bucks," Estevez reminded him.

"So you've said before," Britton replied as he left the room. Then he turned back. "I want the full team in for a meeting early tomorrow morning, seven-thirty, usual place."

"Lowensdorf might not be finished in time," Estevez said.

"Then he'd better bring a note from his mother," Britton replied cryptically, and disappeared through the doorway.

*   *   *

WHEN Ben Britton returned to his office at the sheriff's headquarters on Eighth Avenue in Ybor City, Sheriff Armand Romano was waiting for him. Romano wasn't a happy man. Britton didn't blame him, although he hated being the target of Romano's anger when he knew he was doing everything humanly possible to track down the killer, and Romano knew it, too. But the sheriff was facing a reelection battle to head a department so far unable to capture the area's public enemy number one. Romano was catching a load of political heat, and, as any cop can tell you, shit always flows downhill.

"What have you got?" the sheriff snapped without preliminaries. Romano was a burly man with thick, wavy black hair and the weathered complexion of someone who has spent a lot of time in the tropical sun. There was always high color along his cheekbones, and some blue and broken veins were beginning to show on the sides of his nose, a pretty good indication of the love affair he carried on openly with imported, high-priced gin. He was never without a fine Jamaican cigar, although he couldn't light up inside the smoke-free office complex, so he wound up holding it in his thick right hand or sucking on it. The departmental joke was that he gummed to death three or four of the things each day.

Britton filled him in on the latest killing.

"Don't tell me there was nothing at the scene to help us," Romano said, waving his unlit Jamaican in the air.

"Okay, I won't tell you that," Britton replied. "I found a small spill of a fluid that smelled like bourbon. Once it's analyzed, we'll know the killer's brand. It's information that could be useful. I'm hoping Jerry can come up with something new. This is the first victim he didn't strangle. Maybe that will be a help, although I haven't had any brainstorms yet. My brain seems to have turned to clay."

"When's the team meeting?"

"First thing in the morning. Seven-thirty."

"I want you to know something, Ben," Romano said. "Every county commissioner, the county administrator, and the mayor of Tampa have had me on the phone tonight. They aren't satisfied we're doing all we can."

"They know better."

"They're taking a lot of flak. People are scared to death, and they expect their public officials to do something. These commissioners, these mayors, they don't have principal responsibility, so they lay the flak off on me, and . . ."

"In turn, you lay it off on me," Britton said, finishing the thought.

"I'm trying not to do that," Romano protested. "But the situation is real serious. A couple more women die, you still got your job. But the voters will can me. And I don't want to get canned. I need the money. Understand?"

Britton nodded.

"I don't want to sound callous," Romano continued. "I care very much about catching this asshole and putting a stop to the slaughter. But I care very much about my job, too, and I don't apologize for it. I don't care what it takes. I want this guy off the streets before he kills again."

Romano turned and walked away, muttering to himself around the unlit cigar stuck in a corner of his mouth.

Britton went to his office and had Andy Christopher brought in. Britton thought he would meet a devastated man, as Dr. Winfield suggested. Instead, he met a man ready to punch his lights out. Christopher refused to shake hands, and when Britton offered him a seat, he picked up the chair and flung it against the wall. Britton didn't blame him, really.

"Goddamn you people to hell!" Christopher shouted. "You've got what, dozens of cops tracking down one single killer, and you can't get your hands on him before he kills somebody like Marilyn? That's crazy! That's insane! Why the hell should anybody in this lousy backwater of a town pay a dime in taxes for police protection? There is no protection! It's a joke, a great goddamned farce. Did you even try to get him when he was killing prostitutes, or did you let him go on then because he was doing more to clean up the city's streets than you were? Is that it, you didn't get serious about him until he killed some young teacher from Brandon? And then you couldn't catch up with him before he killed Marilyn? You bastards! You lousy, stinking, incompetent bastards!"

Britton let Christopher yell himself out. There was nothing else to do, no way to answer his questions, no way to offer condolences or assurances.

Britton's own questions had to wait nearly half an hour until Christopher, his chest heaving and his eyes brimmed with tears, finally spent himself and agreed to sit down. And then the questions didn't yield much information. No, he said, Marilyn Erlich had no enemies that he was aware of. No, she had not told him she was being followed by a man she didn't know, or any other man, for that matter. No, she had not recently expressed apprehension about her personal safety. In fact, she'd never expressed concern for her personal safety that he could recall.

"Didn't it concern you that she was down there alone in the office at night?" Britton asked.

Christopher nodded. "But she said she needed a quiet place to study, and it's a decent neighborhood, so I respected her wishes. Obviously, now, I wish I hadn't."

Britton's phone rang. It was Estevez. "Jerry called," the detective said. "He's got the body at the morgue ready for an ID. Dr. Winfield crapped out. Is Christopher up to it?"

"I think so," Britton said. "Send a car around."

Having gleaned nothing at all from his talk with Christopher but a headache, Britton sent him off on the grim chore of viewing his fiancée. Jerry Lowensdorf would make it as easy as possible. He would have cleaned up her face, and the rest of her body would be covered so Christopher couldn't see the damage. Still, it would not be easy.

Britton closed and locked his office and headed for his car, stopping on the way at the room that served as headquarters for the MAIT squad—the Multi-Agency Investigative Team comprised of police and other investigative components from all jurisdictions in which the serial killer had struck. All the lights in the room were off but one, the spot illuminating a board with the list of the names of the first six victims and small photographs of each.

Mabel Brown, 23, prostitute, Ruskin, 2/27. She had been driven to a remote area called Fort Lonesome, bound hand and foot with nylon rope, cut on the belly and thighs with a knife, raped, and strangled. Her heart was punctured once by a knife plunged through her chest wall after she was dead.

Christina Samprezze, 24, prostitute, Ruskin, 4/2. Her body was found along Bullfrog Creek, east of Apollo Beach. She, too, had been bound and gagged, like Brown, tortured with knife cuts to her belly and thighs, then raped and strangled. Her heart was punctured once through her chest wall after she died.

Lucy Isabel, 19, homeless, Ybor City, 5/14. She had been dragged into an alley on a Saturday night. Ybor City is very busy on Saturday nights, so the killer didn't have as much security or time as he did in Ruskin. He didn't tie up Isabel or gag her. He knocked her unconscious and attempted to rape her, although most of his semen was discharged on her thighs. Then he strangled her. There was no evidence of torture while she was alive, but she was stabbed in the heart at least twice after she died.

Linda Serruto, 20, prostitute, Seffner, 5/22. She apparently was driven from the rural east-county community to the Banana Docks at the Port of Tampa, where she was found with her legs spread wide apart and her hands bound to a rusting bollard on one of the docks. She had been cut on the thighs, belly and breasts, raped, and strangled with one of her own stockings. After she was dead, the killer cut open her chest at the sternum and stabbed her heart four times. Experts assisting the police speculated the attack on Serruto followed the Isabel murder so closely and showed such a marked increase in violence because of the killer's frustration at botching his previous assault. Word leaked to the media of the killer's penchant for brutalizing his victims' hearts, and he was dubbed the Heartbreak Killer.

Marian Cipriano, 21, prostitute, College Hill, 6/20. In that less-than-savory area of Tampa, Cipriano had been an easy mark. She was found bound and gagged at the Florida State Fairgrounds, tortured, killed, and mutilated in a fashion almost identical to Linda Serruto.

Constance Evans, 22, kindergarten teacher, Brandon, 7/17. The pattern changed with Evans. She was neither homeless nor a prostitute. Why did the killer change? Was it a mistake? The killer trapped her in a workshop on the ground floor of her apartment building. He knocked her out, bound and gagged her, sliced up her belly and breasts, raped and strangled her. And he hadn't been satisfied with simply stabbing her heart. He literally shredded it.

Britton walked over to the board and picked up a black marker pen. In a very precise hand, he lettered at the bottom of the list:

Marilyn Erlich, 32, physician, Carrollwood Village, 8/16.

Now there were seven. By morning, there would be a small picture of Dr. Erlich taped beside her name, just like the others.

As he switched off the light, he noted grimly that space on the board was running out.

3

It was 11:30 when Britton let himself into his house. Laura had left a living room light on for him when she went to bed. He thought he'd find her asleep, but she was propped up on three pillows watching a local news special on the serial killings. He leaned over and kissed her forehead, with one eye on the screen.

"Hard to believe they could put together enough to fill thirty minutes based on the information we released," he said.

"They opened with the new killing, and now they're rehashing the first six," Laura told him. "They say positively tonight's victim is number seven."

"That's more than we've done, officially, although it's probably right," he said. "I bet they're quoting 'informed sources.' "

"They always say they have sources close to the investigation."

"Uh-huh. Same thing."

"They didn't have much to add to what was already on the eleven o'clock news." She reached out and took his hand. "Want me to turn it off? They're going to talk to a shrink and a criminologist later in the show. I know how you love that."

He smiled. "No doubt they will break the case right before your eyes."

She squeezed his fingers. "No," she said. "You're going to do it. Very soon."

He withdrew his hand gently and patted hers. "Leave it on," he said.

Britton went into the kitchen and pulled a bottle of Dewars out of the cabinet by the refrigerator. He poured himself a stiff drink, close to three fingers, neat. He carried it to the bedroom in time to see the special resume.

He held the drink toward Laura. "Want one?" he asked. "I should have asked."

She shook her head.

"Already brushed," she said.

"You could brush again. It wouldn't kill you."

He undressed and showered and returned to the bedroom in time for the start of the scholarly discussion. Cynthia Diamond, anchor woman for channel seven, WFSC-TV, the Eye on the Florida Sun Coast, sat with two serious-looking men. The gemstones on her dress caught the stage lighting and flashed in the camera lens. Britton found it an annoying distraction.

"We're back now to try to learn what we can about the personality of the killer terrorizing Tampa Bay," Cynthia said. "Joining me are two guests we've had before on this subject, members of the staff of the University of South Florida, Dr. George Buchofski, a psychologist who has studied the minds of famous serial killers, and Dr. Frank Columbine, a professor of criminology. Welcome back, gentlemen. I'd like to say it's nice to see you again, but circumstances preclude it. We all appreciate you staying up so late to help us inform our viewers."

"Happy to be of service," Buchofski said solemnly, and Columbine nodded his agreement.

Britton sipped his drink. "Humf," he snorted. "They probably stayed up to collect nice fees for their expertise." He slipped into bed. He had no interest in the discussion. He had a psychiatrist assigned to the investigation who was better than both these guys together. But Laura was fascinated by the case. Occasionally he discussed it with her, but he wasn't supposed to. So he indulged her desire to read everything about it in the newspapers and watch everything about it on television so she wouldn't keep trying to pry information from him.

"Let's start at the beginning," Cynthia Diamond said. "Dr. Columbine, what can you tell us about the victims?"

Britton shut out the sound and tried to figure out why a woman smart enough to become a successful obstetrician wasn't smart enough to lock her windows and bar them. And how had a pretty, thirty-two-year-old internist who was about to get married, start a family, and become a surgeon to boot, so offended the gods they decreed her life end early and hideously? He set the drink on the nightstand, worked his way under the covers, and turned his face to the air-conditioned breeze generated by the ceiling fan. The questions had no answers. Britton was depressed and suddenly very, very tired.

When he opened his eyes, the room was dark. He was still lying on his back. He turned his head and looked at the clock. It was 12:52. The program must have ended, and Laura turned the lights off. He had slept right through it.

His mind, fooled into thinking it was rested by a forty-five-minute nap, clicked into gear. There would be precious little additional sleep this night.

Next to him, Laura could see by the light from the street filtering through a gap in the bedroom drapes that he had awakened. His eyes were fixed on the ceiling. She turned toward him and felt for his hand under the covers. When she found it, he squeezed hard, as though holding on for his life, or his sanity.

"It was incredible," he said without prologue. "I've never seen so much damage inflicted by one human being on another for no purpose other than to generate terror and pain. She suffered unspeakably, and for a long time."

"Like before, no clues?" she asked.

"Actually, for whatever it's worth, I found some bourbon spilled in an office corridor," he said. "We can eliminate all the Scotch and martini drinkers in the county."

"Could it help?"

"Yeah, it could, as corroborating evidence more than anything. If we identify the brand, and if we ever get a suspect and find out it's what he drinks . . . well, it's one more piece of the puzzle."

Once more, Britton was telling Laura more than he should, more than she had a right or a need to know. But he desperately needed somebody who would hear and understand his frustration. He couldn't vent at the office because he was in charge, and a display of angst from him would damage the morale of the staff. So he talked to Laura.

"Any chance it wasn't his bourbon?" she asked.

"Probably not," he replied. "There wouldn't be any reason for the doctors to keep whiskey in the office. I don't think they sterilize bullet wounds that way anymore. It also fits the serial-killer profile. Most of them are high on booze or drugs or both when they kill. This one probably brought his bottle along and took a time out at some point to reinforce his courage."

"And now you can't sleep."

He rolled on his side to face her and caressed her cheek with his hand. "No," he said. "I can't sleep. I can't get my mental snapshot of the late Marilyn Erlich to stay in a lockbox. I keep trying to figure what we're missing."

"That's work for the team to do in the morning."

He snorted. "I wish I could turn it off like that: Item A will not be considered before seven-thirty in the morning. Item B cannot come to mind before noon. Nothing can interfere with the normal conduct of family life between eight P.M. and six A.M."

"Sounds about right."

He sighed. "But it doesn't happen like that. I can't make it happen like that. It's not only this case; it's the whole damned job. It never ends. I feel like I'm missing the kids' childhoods, our marriage, our life together as a family. I don't want to miss those things. I don't think you agreed to marry me with the idea I was going to miss them, that you were going to keep our home and raise our sons alone."

She rubbed her hand along his outstretched arm. "I knew I was marrying a cop, and I understood everything it meant," she said. "It might have escaped your attention, but it was no naive young thing you led away from the altar eight years ago."

"You were only twenty-two years old!"

"Almost twenty-three. Out of college two years. Working. And clued into the world pretty good, sonny boy."

He didn't respond to her kidding, and she thought for a moment he might have fallen asleep. But he was steadying himself to break some news to her.

"I'm thinking of retiring from the force," he said, finally.

She propped herself up on one elbow. "Really?" She sounded surprised, although she wasn't totally shocked by the news. She'd watched the last eighteen months take their toll on him. As the sheriff's lead homicide investigator, he rolled on every murder in county jurisdiction, and lately, it seemed, the numbers of killings and their particularly random and brutal nature had become mind-numbing.

He had been particularly devastated by the shooting deaths of two brothers, ages five and four, who'd responded with little-boy curiosity to the sounds of an argument in a school yard behind their home and got caught in the cross fire of a gun battle between a sixteen-year-old drug dealer and his thirteen-year-old disgruntled client. And then there'd been the seven-year-old girl driven nearly mad by the sexual abuses of her stepfather. One night after he fell asleep in a drunken stupor on the sofa, she fished his .38 from a kitchen cabinet and shot him at point-blank range in the genitals. She didn't even know what to call those body parts, but she was able to explain to detectives that those were the parts he used to hurt her. He wouldn't be hurting her anymore. He bled to death in sotted agony on his living room floor.

Most of the killings, of course, were adult-on-adult, for such supreme offenses as cutting too closely into traffic, for being an unwary foreign tourist, for being of the wrong skin color or nationality or lifestyle or sexual orientation. And on top of it all came the serial killer. The deaths were so senseless, so wasteful, so unpredictable, the cases simply wore down those whose charge it was to solve them, as Laura

Britton watched them wear down her husband. So while she was a bit apprehensive about the future of their family if her husband left the Sheriff's Office, she was actually relieved for his sake that he was considering it.

"I certainly wouldn't object to you leaving the force if you had something else in mind to do, some other job to go to," she said. "I didn't marry you to have to fix your lunch every day, at least not until you're sixty-five."

He smiled. "Oh, I wouldn't hang around under foot," he said. "I've got a couple of things I'm looking at. And I've got fifteen years on the force—can you believe it? Fifteen years already. Joined right out of college when I was twenty-one, turn around and suddenly I'm a thirty-six-year-old veteran of fifteen years. The pension wouldn't be as good as if I stayed twenty years, but it would be a very nice supplement to what I earn in my new endeavor, whatever the endeavor might turn out to be."

She leaned into him and kissed his forehead. "Whatever you want will be fine with us," she told him. "It truly would be nice having you around more and not so strung out all the time. I might even be willing to fix your lunch on alternate Wednesdays if you're a good boy and mind your manners."

He chuckled and worked his shoulder under her, so when she laid back, her head was resting there with his arm curled around her shoulders. "Well, ma'am, I'd certainly be much obliged," he said in his best imitation of a Western drawl. "I'd be happy to return the favor, perhaps mend some fences for you, do other chores around the spread."

"Like what?" she asked.

"Well, I slop hogs pretty good."

She chuckled. "We don't have any hogs, except perhaps for your two sons, and they only eat that way."

"That's what you think. I've seen their rooms."

"You could clean out the garage," she suggested.

"Well, that takes care of one day."

She ran her fingers seductively across his bare chest. "You could, well, shall we say, service the needs of the lady of the house."

"Okay, there's two days," he deadpanned, and squeaked when she pinched him.

She leaned over and kissed him, then snuggled into him. They remained that way, holding each other, for a long time.

4

Hours earlier, as Ben Britton was getting his first look at the body of Marilyn Erlich, Eugene Rickey let himself into his house through the carport access door and turned on the lights in the living room with a voice command, "Lights, L-R." It was a system he'd designed and built himself during one of the times he wasn't paying slavish attention to his secret life.

Rickey was one of those individuals blessed with the capacity to visualize the design and means of construction of almost anything within imagining in home and office improvements. If the materials were available, Eugene Rickey could make it happen. He had the added advantages of an honest nature, a sense of obligation, and a thrifty streak. These virtues combined to make him a reliable, dependable workman who never gouged customers or inflated his prices and always did exemplary work.

If he had a failing, and few would have called it such except perhaps for the state of Florida, it was that Eugene Rickey never bothered to obtain licenses for the carpentry, plumbing, painting, masonry, or electrical work that were part of his repertoire. His customers understood they could lose their property owners' insurance if their carriers discovered recent improvements were done by a person subject to no official oversight. But if the knowledge adversely affected Rickey's business, it wasn't apparent from the work orders he had backed up on the little oak desk he'd built into a corner of his kitchen. Rickey himself felt no compunction about working licenseless. Damn pieces of paper weren't any good anyhow. Three months earlier, he'd done a job in a tony neighborhood in Brandon, in a house where all the original construction was done by fully licensed crews and then officially inspected. When he got inside the electrical system, he discovered that the original contractor had used undersized wire everywhere. It was a wonder the whole house hadn't burned down. Rickey not only did the job he contracted for, he wound up rewiring nearly everything to undo the errors of the licensed electricians. And except for materials, he hadn't charged an extra nickel for putting the wiring straight, either. Nope, those damn licenses weren't worth the paper they were printed on. They ensured neither honesty nor competence.

That he hadn't charged for his labor to make the posh home safe from its creators bought him a fortune in goodwill from the owners. He figured he'd probably get a half dozen new jobs from their word to friends and neighbors. He already had one: a big kitchen remodeling job in Culbreath Isles, one of the very best neighborhoods in all of Tampa. That's how Rickey built his private business; he'd yet to use a single dollar for advertising.

His own house was a wonder of gadgets and gizmos. He never put an innovation into somebody else's home until he'd tried it in his own—at his own expense, of course. Yet his house wasn't grand in any regard. It was a thirty-two-year-old, twelve-hundred-square-foot, peach-colored stucco box with two bedrooms and one bath on Delany Creek in Clair Mel, a modest suburb in an unincorporated area east of Tampa, separated from the city by Hillsborough Bay. Because of Rickey's skills, his house was in better shape, and looked it, than any other house on his block, except for the yard. He'd no sooner hack back the plants passing for landscaping than they'd overgrow again. And the lawn? Well, there wasn't any accounting for the lawn. Between the tropical sun and the chinch bugs and mole crickets, it was a battle he couldn't win.

Rickey considered asking his neighbor across the street, who had a lawn service, to swap out; the yardman would look out for Rickey's lawn and landscaping, and Rickey would take care of the workings of the yardman's house. But he couldn't make the math come out right. The yardman's house was more than thirty years old, too, and potentially could cost a lot more to fix up than Rickey's yard. So he did the best he could with the flora by himself and left it at that.

Rickey glanced at his answering machine. The red light was blinking, but he was in no mood to listen to messages, even if they offered the promise of future employment. He was sinking into a deepening depression. Whatever he hoped to gain from this night had eluded him, just as it eluded him all the previous nights. And that confused him. What must he do to satisfy Opal, finally, and forever to win her approval?

He drew his blinds, muted the lighting, and pulled a pair of blood-stained surgical gloves from the left pocket of his blue jeans. When he left the doctors' offices, he took them off and turned them inside out, one inside the other, like a pair of dirty socks. Now he looked at them in disgust and threw them in the trash can under the kitchen sink.

In the living room, he found a new bottle of bourbon in a cabinet next to the stereo. He had finished the other bottle during the drive back from Carrollwood Village. He cracked the seal and took two long pulls, then reached inside his shirt and extracted the framed photograph from its place against his skin, glass side out so it didn't get smudged. It was a picture of a lovely young woman standing beside a man Rickey pretended not to see on the deck of a huge sailboat. Rickey set the frame on his coffee table, stared at it a moment, then went to his bedroom. He emptied his pockets, gently placing Opal on his nightstand, peeled off his blood-soaked sport shirt and blue jeans, and examined his shoes. Everything was ruined, even his underwear and socks. It was a good thing he hadn't been stopped by the cops on the way home. He looked like he'd been to a slaughterhouse, which wasn't far from the truth.

There was no sense trying to wash the blood from the clothes. Some stain would linger, and it might rouse someone's curiosity someday. It wasn't worth the risk. He took off the underwear and socks and stuffed them into his shoes, which he wrapped in the jeans and shirt, and set the gory pile in the bathroom sink. Then he showered and dressed in clean clothes. He dumped the bloody wad of clothing on top of the surgical gloves under the kitchen sink, wrapped a plastic tie securely around the top of the trash bag, dropped it into a heavy plastic garbage container outside the back door, and rolled the container to the curb for the trash haulers, who would be by before dawn the next morning. By midday, the evidence would be burning in an incinerator or buried in the landfill with empty tuna and soup cans.

Then Rickey retrieved Opal and took the knife into the kitchen for its ritualistic cleaning. It wasn't until he had a sink full of soapy water, with a bottle of rubbing alcohol and some cotton swabs standing by for the detail work, that he took a close look at his blood-caked tool of human sacrifice. First his eyes widened, then his face flushed with rage.

"Goddamn it to hell!" he yelled, loudly enough that if he'd had close neighbors, they might have heard. Deliberately, he rubbed his right thumb across a fresh chip in the multihued, iridescent handle. Folded inside the handle was a finely honed six-inch, stainless steel blade polished to a mirror finish. In other circumstances, the knife would have been called a thing of beauty, even with the chip, which wasn't large, a tenth of an inch across at most. But it was Opal's first blemish after so many years, and Rickey couldn't recall how it happened.

"I didn't mean to hurt you, Opal," he wailed, genuinely grief-stricken. "I'll clean you up and make you feel better. Someday maybe we can find somebody who can make you whole and perfect again. I'm so sorry."

He took great care, first washing the knife clean in the sink and then tending to the tiny crevices with the alcohol and cotton swabs. When he finished, he dried it carefully, folded it up, and looked once more at the chip. A sob constricted his throat. Gingerly, he slipped Opal into the pocket of his pants.

Back in the living room, Rickey leaned back in his sofa and propped his feet up beside the photograph of Marilyn Erlich and Andy Christopher. He took two more deep swallows from the bourbon bottle and set it on the floor.

He stared at the picture, and his eyes glazed. He remembered the first time he saw her, stopped at a traffic light on Dale Mabry. She was driving a Mustang convertible with the top down, and the sun shone on her hair, the same color Opal's hair had been when she was young.

Something had flashed in his eyes at that moment, and all his senses went on alert. He could feel the tension bunch the muscles across his shoulders. Dark spots danced in his vision for a few seconds, and when they cleared he saw that the glint had come from one of those goddamned rainbow crystals. It was hanging from the Mustang's rearview mirror by a loop of fishing line, just like Opal always hung crystals from her rearview mirror.

Watching the crystal swing for what seemed a half hour, but was only about ten seconds, Rickey felt the anger and the demand surge inside him. Whatever errand brought him to the traffic light on Dale Mabry that day was forgotten. When it changed, he let the Mustang slip ahead of him and dropped in behind it. For the next eleven days he stalked her. And then, when Opal said it was time, he struck.

Rickey let his head fall back against the wall and closed his eyes. He unzipped his pants, reached inside, and began masturbating. It never occurred to him to wonder where the chip from his knife handle had come to rest. He had other matters to contemplate.

In Eugene Rickey's tangled mind, Dr. Marilyn Erlich was dying again.

RICKEY unzipped his fly at almost the same moment Jerry Lowensdorf, the Hillsborough County medical examiner, finished his preliminary check of the night's worst crime scene. Twenty minutes later, at about the same moment Ben Britton and Nick Estevez followed Nadine Winfield into Dr. Erlich's office, Rickey swore softly, withdrew his hand from his fly, and zipped up. It was no use. He was getting no satisfaction from his memories. He decided his mind's wonderful video of Dr. Erlich struggling on her examining table was being short-circuited by the photograph of her with the man on the sailboat. The man was getting in the way of Rickey's fantasy. He should have taken the medical school diploma.

Rickey was thirsty. He got up and walked into the small kitchen he'd renovated from a greasy, grime-layered mess to a minor showplace and snatched a cold can of Busch from the refrigerator. He downed it quickly and opened another. Maybe he could revive his buzz by dumping a few quick brews on top of the bourbon. If not, he'd go back to straight whiskey.

Beer on whiskey, mighty risky.

Well, fuck it, he thought. He finished the second beer and took a third out to his front porch.

"Porch light on," he ordered gruffly as he sat down on the steps and sipped the brew. Two mustard-yellow lanterns mounted on either side of the front door winked to life. The color was supposed to repel insects, though Rickey had never been able to tell it did much good.

The Busch began working malt miracles on his brain, although his mood remained mired in bleakness. A Chevrolet pickup stopped under a street lamp in front of the yardman's house, and the yardman's daughter got out with her boyfriend. It was the same young man and the same Chevy pickup that'd been around since spring. Must be serious love involved. Too bad there would never be the same sort of relationship for him.

The thought pounded Rickey's mood down another notch.

The young woman spotted him sitting under his porch lights and waved cheerily. Cheery was the last thing Rickey felt at the moment. Nor did he want conversation, but he knew it was important that everything about his life appear normal. He returned the wave. It would have been out of character not to.

"How ya doin', Mr. Rickey?" the young woman called across the unkempt expanse of Rickey's front lawn.

"Pretty good, Julie," he replied. "How's yourself?"

"Wo-o-o-nderful!" Julie bubbled. "Shawn and I are getting married. He just proposed, and I accepted. Mom and Daddy don't even know yet."

"Best wishes to you both," Rickey said, nodding toward the beaming young man who must have been Shawn. "When's the big day?"

"Probly in March, or maybe April," Julie said. "It's so-o-o pretty around here that time of year. Well, you take care now, Mr. Rickey. Hope business is good."

"Can't complain," he replied. "Y'all have a good evenin'."

They walked toward the neighbor's house to break the marriage news to the yardman and his wife. Rickey watched Julie's round behind move enthusiastically inside her tight shorts as she bounded up the front sidewalk, caught in the illuminating arc of the street lamp. He had vivid memories of his mother's behind moving like that before she fell into a bottle of rye and began bloating and drowning in the stuff. He thought Julie might have fit right into his fantasies someday had she lived somewhere else, but he never trolled in his own neighborhood. He had made that pact with whatever devil possessed his soul, and he never violated it.

He wondered what the yardman would do if he found out his neighbor across the street was entertaining such thoughts about Julie, even in the negative.

Probably castrate him with a Weed Whacker.

Rickey slapped at a mosquito, one of many with designs on him as a next meal. It had been a rainy summer, and the bugs were about as bad as he ever remembered, and they were always pretty bad around Delany Creek. He glanced at his watch. It was nearly ten. The bugs would have to find sustenance somewhere else. He was going to take his black mood back inside and catch the early news on channels thirteen and forty-four. Maybe it would help rekindle the excitement of his latest kill. Or maybe he'd have to get into the purloined frame and rip the photograph lengthwise down the middle, to get rid of the man.

He swallowed the last half-ounce of Busch, now nearly warm, and went into the house, dousing the porch light with another verbal command. He pulled a fourth beer from the refrigerator and put it back. He wanted bourbon and lots of it. He set his twenty-seven-inch television to alternate between the two channels and fished in his pants pocket for his knife.

"Come on, Opal," he said, swinging the blade out from inside the handle. He inspected it closely to be certain he'd cleaned and dried it completely, and his heart ached again when he saw the chip in the handle. He rubbed the cool shell against his cheek, almost sensually. "Be still now, Opal. You and me gotta watch the results of our work on the tee-vee."

He and Opal and the bourbon bottle were settled in comfortably as the first images from the dead doctor's office blazed onto the big screen. Rickey kept glancing from the television to the photograph on his coffee table and back again. But it wasn't working. As hard as he tried, he couldn't get the same old feeling again.

HE was still trying at eleven, when the news shows came on other channels. Although he'd read someplace that channel seven, WFSC-TV, had only the second-highest news ratings among local stations, he always liked it best because he liked the anchor, Cynthia Diamond. She was pretty, and she spoke with an air of authority that said she was one of those rare women who could be trusted. He liked her despite the fact that all her clothes were studded with sparkles that caught the stage lights and flashed at the camera. (He knew they were supposed to be diamonds—diamonds for Diamond, get it?) At least the flashes didn't make rainbows, so he endured them and allowed Cynthia Diamond to sparkle for him every night.

Several minutes into the broadcast, beyond the initial report from the scene by a pasty-faced reporter named Luke Galant, beyond a statement saying nothing from sheriff's spokesman Pete Sisko and halfway through a recap of past murders attributed to this serial killer, Rickey felt himself getting excited. He glanced around the room to be sure his blinds were still drawn, skooched down in the sofa some, laid Opal on the cushion beside him, and opened his pants again.

Rickey climaxed as Cynthia announced a thirty-minute special on the serial killings to air at 11:30, immediately following the news. He had no idea what caused the sudden and altogether satisfying arousal. But he didn't have time to dwell on it. The special was starting.

The first part of the hastily prepared program covered the same things the news had in the previous half hour, although at greater length. What Rickey awaited with mounting anxiety was the promised segment with a shrink and a criminologist who, it was said, would offer the viewers a profile of the killer terrorizing Hillsborough County.

"Bullshit," Rickey spat at the television. "Ain't nobody knows the Handyman."

But they did, in theory at least. Rickey listened in rapt fury as Drs. George Buchofski and Frank Columbine dissected his conquests and his mind.

"The victims are an unusual group, being so diverse in their, uh, economic profiles," said Columbine, the criminologist. "Yet as diverse as the victims, the Heartbreak Killer's methodology appears consistent. The police haven't released many details of the latest death, but they've said the first six victims were raped and strangled, and we know from other sources of the killer's pattern of torture and mutilation. It remains to be seen if the pattern was followed again tonight."

"Assuming it was, does this suggest anything to you, Dr. Buchofski?" Cynthia asked.

"It would be consistent with one common type of serial-killer personality," the psychologist said. "The Heartbreak Killer always takes time to bind and gag the victims and always takes time for torture. That suggests he's confident that he's in full control of the situation and likely to remain so for as long as he wants. It's definitely a part of his fantasies to control and dominate the women totally. Stabbing the dead bodies would be the ultimate act of contempt."

Rickey was leaning forward on his sofa, toward the television screen. His expression was dark. "You asshole, I dominated the *fuck* outta them! Every one of 'em!" he cursed harshly.

"Can you surmise anything else about him?" Cynthia asked. "How old is he?"

Buchofski nodded. "My opinion on that hasn't varied. Young serial killers tend to be skittish, nervous, sloppy even. So this killer is probably older, his early to midthirties, but probably not much more. Serial-killer personalities don't tend to develop in men much past that age. Or, put a better way, if the serial-killer personality hasn't fully developed and presented itself by age thirty-five, chances are good it isn't going to. There have been a few rare exceptions."

"Lucky stinkin' guess, you fuckhead!" Rickey replied.

"Why such a horrendous level of violence?" Cynthia asked. "Why the torture, the mutilation of the hearts?"

"It suggests a high degree of frustration, of tremendous anxiety," Buchofski said.

Rickey jumped up and began pacing back and forth in front of his set. His hands beat a nervous rhythm on his thighs and his head swiveled sharply so he never lost sight of the screen. "Fucking thieves! Fucking brain thieves!" he shouted. "Stay outta my head!"

"Why, Doctor?" Cynthia asked. "Why the frustration and the anxiety?"

"Not always, but typically, a serial killer was abused as a child, physically and psychologically, often sexually. He has a history of difficulty getting along with other children, trouble in school, trouble on the streets. He tends to have brain damage, the result of an accident or the abuse I spoke of, or birth defects or illness, such as epilepsy. Typically the damage tends to be in areas of the brain controlling primal emotions—fear, lust, love, hate. He is unprepared or unable to deal in a rational manner with those primal emotions, so the physically and psychologically damaged child grows up to be an emotionally dysfunctional adult. He abuses drugs and/or alcohol. He might abuse animals. Furthermore, the abuse he suffered as a child generally leaves him with no sense of self-worth to speak of, but with a lot of residual anger and the sense his life isn't worth much. He's also likely to think the world is against him. You pack layer upon layer of negative feelings, negative memories, negative outlooks one on top of another, add to it the brain damage that leaves this individual without the capacity to control his outrage or his tendencies toward violence, throw in substance abuse that strips the last vestiges of control, and you've built the model for a serial killer."

"Go to hell!" Rickey swore.

Buchofski continued. "Chances are this man's violence is triggered by the sight of an individual who reminds him of some aspect of his violent, negative childhood, and he erupts. It might be that his abuse came at the hands of his mother or his grandmother, or some other woman who dominated his young life, even a teacher. So he directs his adult violence at women whose looks, whose voices, whose gestures, or makeup—or something else real or imagined—remind him of the woman who abused him. He can't control what he does any more than you can control your heart rate. He becomes possessed and obsessed by whatever demon is living in his head. And he knows— believe me, he thinks he *knows*—that only by hurting and destroying the individual who triggered the awakening of the demon can he exorcise the obsession. He might be escalating his violence because he thinks at some point, if he can get violent enough, he will satisfy his demon, and it will go away forever. Each time, he's fallen short of his goal, so he kills again, again trying for permanent relief."

"Is there a chance he might achieve it?" Cynthia asked. "And if he does, what will happen to him? How will he react?"

"Occasionally, one of these men does achieve a permanent release, but it often comes at a terrible price. One case I know very well involved a man who tortured and murdered young boys. He experienced the permanent destruction of his fantasy at the moment he killed his own son. He became suicidal."

"Dear God," Cynthia gasped, genuinely shocked. "This is a digression, I know, but why did that killer pick young boys?"

"Whyn't you shut up, bitch!" Rickey hissed. "Whyn't you just shut *up!*"

"He was seriously abused as a child by two older brothers, who were about the same ages as the boys he killed as an adult," Buchofski said.

"Incredible," Cynthia replied, shaking her head. "We have just a moment left. Is there anything else?"

Columbine began, "I suspect the victims didn't know their killer. When the women found themselves in isolated places with this man, they began to suspect his motives and struggled. He responded with violence. In no case was it simple sex that went too far."

Buchofski picked up. "My bet is this guy's local. A drifter would have packed up and moved on by now, I think, trying to run away from his crimes. Of course, moving wouldn't stop the killings for any more than a few months, a year at most. After a time, the old compulsions would take control again. But our problem isn't going to move out of state. I'm certain this is where he was born, in all likelihood, and where he was raised. This area is his comfort zone, or his cell in hell. And I would guess it's his only killing field."

"Shut up!" Rickey shouted. "Shut up! Shut up! Shut *UP!* Leave me the fuck alone!"

By the time Cynthia signed off, Rickey was standing in front of his television, bouncing on the balls of his feet, intensely agitated. He ran both hands through his thick brown hair and grabbed two fists full, yanking as though he wanted to tear it out.

"Bitch! Bitch!" he kept repeating. "Why are you hammerin' at me all the damned time? I trusted you, and you betrayed me. You're just like Opal, all the damned time on my case. Them stones in your clothes, they *are* crystals, ain't they? Them same damned crystals."

His voice was sad.

"I shudda known it. Shudda known . . . Damn you, anyway."

He began rocking back and forth, from his toes to his heels, making a shrill keening sound, a high-pitched tone meant to block out all other sounds in the world.

Then he collapsed, sweating and crying, onto the sofa. He grabbed the bourbon bottle, now less than half full, and took several more swallows. Then he stretched out.

Rickey closed his eyes, sobbed, and let the Cynthia fantasy come.

And with it, new arousal.

"My God, when's it going to stop?" David Janacek asked rhetorically as he set his snifter of brandy on the table beside the sofa without taking his eyes off the television. He and his wife, Kirin, were in the family room of their home in Culbreath Isles. Their eleven-month-old son, Kevin, who early in his life acquired the nickname Casey, was in the nursery in the next room. The baby finally was asleep after a fussy flight back to Tampa from New York City earlier in the evening. When they finally got him down, David and Kirin switched on the television to watch the *Tonight Show* and unwind for a few minutes before going to bed themselves. But instead of Jay Leno, they got a special on what the broadcasters were saying was the seventh in a series of serial killings in Hillsborough County. The special was the first they'd heard of the latest ritual murder.

"You know her, don't you?" David asked, nodding toward the televised image of Cynthia Diamond. "She interviewed you once, I think."

"Twice, actually," Kirin replied. "About the Water Street project. I like her. She's very professional and does her homework."

Kirin Cox Janacek nestled close to her husband. She was as exhausted as he from the trip, but unable to divert her attention from the story. The woman killed this night had been a doctor, attacked in her own office in a very decent neighborhood. The previous victim had been a teacher from a nice area of Brandon. No place could be considered safe anymore, she thought, and involuntarily, she shivered.

"Why are they having so much trouble catching this guy?" Kirin asked. "Don't they catch most serial killers before they kill this many people?"

"Not necessarily," David replied. "There've been cases where the killers claimed dozens and dozens of victims. You never know."

She took her head off his shoulder and looked up into his face. "Could you ever defend a man like that?" she asked earnestly. "Could you actually walk into a courtroom and sit next to him and try to convince a jury he should go free?"

He smiled down at her. "What if I believed he was innocent?"

"No," she said. "You know he's not. But you're trying to get him off."

He stroked his wife's hair absently. "Not to worry," he said. "It wouldn't ever come to that. Serial killers are mentally and emotionally ill. I doubt the prosecution could get this guy certified to stand trial."

"A lot of people are emotionally ill, but they don't all become serial killers."

David bent his head and kissed his wife on the forehead. "That's true. Look at your Aunt Louise. She's emotionally ill, but so far as I know, she's never committed murder. She could induce someone else to commit that crime, however."

Kirin sat up and clicked off the television.

The newscast was beyond anything she cared to watch, and Aunt Louise was a topic she had expected him to bring up sometime during the flight back from New York. When he didn't mention the old biddy all the way home, Kirin began to hope the expected confrontation at the Cox family reunion hadn't happened. But she wasn't surprised to find out otherwise, and she could feel the anger with her spinster aunt begin to boil to the surface even before her husband told her what had passed between them.

"Let's hear it," she said.

"Oh, it was the same old crap," he told her. "She looks down her patrician nose and over those half-glasses at me for about two hours, then she walks over and says, 'Tell me again, young man, you're from Michigan aren't you?' And I tell her, 'No. Kirin and I and Master Kevin Cox Janacek live in Tampa, Florida.' 'But,' she says, 'you're *from* Michigan, aren't you? Your family makes those Chev-row-lays.' She draws the word out real long like that. I explain, 'No, my father and two of my brothers work on a Buick assembly line,' and she says, 'Buick, Schmuick, Chev-row-lay, what's the difference?' "

Kirin dropped her face and shook her head. "Oh, God, David, I'm so sorry."

"Ah," he said. "There's more. She asks me, 'What kind of name is Janacek, anyway?' 'Slavic,' I tell her. And she mutters, 'Well, I don't believe we've ever had one of *you people* in the family before,' then flounces off." He sighed deeply. "Kiri, I went to this reunion with you because so many of your relatives hadn't met Casey yet, and I wanted to be there for the introductions. But God help me, don't ever ask me to go back to New York."

She was running her hand over the slacks along his thigh soothingly. "I'm really sorry," she said. "Aunt Louise is old and stupid. She doesn't mean to hurt anybody."

"Sure she does," he objected. "She knows *exactly* what she's doing, and she's counting on people letting her get away with it because she *is* old. And she's not so stupid, either, because people *do* let her get away with it."

"Ignorant, then."

"I'll accept ignorant. And mean. Flat mean. She's been on this kick with me since the first time I met her before we were married. And, lest you've forgotten, she wouldn't even walk through our reception line because she disapproved of me and my family so deeply. That's more than nine years ago!"

"Honey, she's my father's only surviving sister. Could you be nice to her for his sake?"

"I am nice to her. It's she who isn't nice to me. I'd like just once to treat her the same way, to give some back, to tell her she's a mean-spirited, aristocratic old bitch with too much money for her own good. She's the only one I've met in your whole family who's that way. Where does she get it? Your parents aren't like that. Hey, when they want to come down here to visit us, fine. Great. But I'm not ever again going to put myself within hearing distance of Aunt Louise. Not even for you."

"Is once a year so bad?"

"Once a decade is so bad. Once a century would be barely tolerable."

She laughed lightly but said nothing. The disparity in their backgrounds had stalked the fringes of their relationship since they first realized they were falling in love. By chance, she had been born into the Episcopalian aristocracy of opulent Port Washington, Long Island. Her father was a venture capitalist; her mother a member of the boards of directors of the Metropolitan Opera and the Metropolitan Museum of Art in the city. They had a summer home in The Hamptons and a six-bedroom ski chalet on the slopes at Steamboat Springs, Colorado. She and a sister and brother went to the finest private prep schools and Ivy League universities. She became a commercial architect and built a national reputation three years out of college. Her older sister was the editor-in-chief of *Vanity Fair;* their younger brother was a Wall Street stock analyst.

David, on the other hand, grew up in blue-collar Flint, Michigan, the son of a family of Roman Catholic autoworkers. He graduated from public schools, put himself through Bowling Green State University in Ohio, and won a fellowship to law school at Florida State University. His reputation was slower to grow, but a series of high-profile murder defenses to which he brought Perry Mason courtroom twists thrust him into focus at Tennyson, Girrard, Lorenzo and Hoffman of Tampa, one of the best-known criminal law firms in the southeastern United States. When Hoffman left, the firm became Tennyson, Girrard, Lorenzo and Janacek, although David had been there only four years. It was quite a coup.

Kirin and David both had high six-figure incomes, a financial comfort level to which she had been born and enjoyed, but to which he had never aspired. Kirin knew David would have been as happy as a $60,000-a-year civil lawyer with a modest home and maybe an eighteen-foot bass boat. But his parents had instilled in all their children the notion that it was a sin not to develop the talents God gave them to the very fullest. For David, it meant taking more and more challenging cases, and the more he won, the more his reputation, and his bank balance, grew. It also meant he was increasingly in demand at civic functions and society parties, and one couldn't very well entertain people who ran in those circles at a three-bedroom bungalow in Temple Terrace. His success, and Kirin's, required them to live in a home commensurate with their community standing. Kirin was comfortable with it for herself; David wasn't, and it troubled her. Truth be told, it also annoyed her. Why shouldn't they live as their success enabled? She didn't dismiss his concerns, but she had no idea how to resolve them, either.

She decided he was having some of the same thoughts when she saw him take a sip of his brandy and look at his surroundings with a hint of a frown on his face. They were sitting in an enormous family room, twenty-two-by-twenty-eight feet as she recalled it from the plans, and it had something called a volume ceiling and an off-white ceramic tile floor that together only served to make the room appear larger. The whole house—five bedrooms, four and a half baths, living room, dining room, family room, den, library, huge eat-in kitchen— was more than five thousand square feet, not counting the three-car garage or the deck off the family room. The wall beside the sofa where they sat was an expanse of four sliding glass doors opening to the lanai, which was caged in white screening. Inside the cage was a pool, big for a private home, a spa, and an outdoor kitchen. By the light of the security lamps, Kirin could see beyond the cage, where the green blades of their St. Augustine lawn sloped to the seawall holding off the water of Old Tampa Bay. Far across the water she could make out the lights of Pinellas County. She dropped her head back onto her husband's shoulder and watched in silence.

Kirin knew the confrontation with Aunt Louise would have reminded David about his roots, which in turn would remind him of his uneasiness with their lifestyle. What, after all, did two adults and a baby need with five-thousand square feet of living space? He'd once asked her that, and she didn't have an adequate response. He'd grown up in a house holding six people and never fewer than two dogs comfortably, and it was less than two-thousand square feet. She could feel his discomfort grow when his parents or his brothers and their families visited. All of them were comfortable, but none of them was wealthy. If they resented his means, they never let on, but he never failed to project embarrassment at the display of materialism.

Now, of all things, Kirin thought with a twinge of guilt, she had decided she couldn't live without an expansion of the morning room section of the kitchen that would give her a pantry large enough to stock food for the entire population of Switzerland for a year. When he'd first seen the plans, he'd shaken his head. She knew he would never tell her no, that he would learn to accept it. But she also knew he thought it was a huge waste of money, and sometimes, like now, she felt selfish for insisting on something that would make her feel good but added to his discomfort.

She closed her eyes and rubbed her cheek against the warmth of his shoulder. If he could accept the trappings of his own success, she thought, life would be near perfect.

"What say we go to bed," he suggested. "I have to be in court at eight in the morning."

The pressure of her hand on his arm stopped him from getting up. "I really *am* sorry about Aunt Louise," she said. "I hope you know she doesn't speak for anybody else in the family. Everybody else thinks you're terrific. Including me."

"Yeah, but you have to like me. It's in the small print in your contract."

"What contract?"

"The one you signed when I proposed. The one that says you would always make me think I'm the luckiest man in the world."

She smiled. "Is that what you think?"

"Every single day. Except maybe those days you hang your wet hose over the shower door so they hit me in the face."

She chuckled and got up. "You're such an incorrigible romantic. You get the lights, and I'll check the baby," she said.

He pulled her to him. "After you check the little baby, come on in and check the big baby," he said coyly.

She leaned against his chest and put her hand against the zipper in his slacks. "Hmmm, baby's growing up fast," she said with a grin.

"He's going to grow faster if you leave your hand there."

"I thought you had to be in court at eight. You need your beauty rest."

"I'd rather be contented than pretty," he said.

5

Jerry Lowensdorf stood at the front of the meeting room in the Hillsborough Sheriff's Office headquarters, ready to make his report. He held an enormous Circle K coffee cup, something near thirty ounces. He had filled it up at the convenience store, added five creams and six sugars, and gulped it as fast as the heat of the liquid would allow. When he got to the Sheriff's Office, he filled it again, drank about a third of it, and topped it off before entering the squad room. He was wired. He had been up all night, sustained by caffeine and adrenaline, and he looked it.

His beard stubble was more grizzled than his hair, and dark shadows outlined his gray eyes. His idle hand was shoved deep into a pocket of his pants, as though to take weight off his shoulders, which slumped inside a sea-foam green, V-necked surgical smock. Lowensdorf had worn a heavy apron while doing the autopsy, but there was a reddish brown smudge on the left hem of the smock that certainly looked like blood.

Beside Lowensdorf was a huge corkboard on an easel. Two dozen color photographs were pinned to the board, each showing a different view of the torn body of Dr. Marilyn Erlich. There were close-ups and long shots, crime-scene shots and autopsy shots. Ben Britton studiously kept his eyes averted. Lowensdorf would cover each one in detail, and Britton would have to look at them then. Why rush it?

Nick Estevez sat down next to Britton. The captain turned and nodded, started to say something, then stopped. He saw Estevez's eyes fix on the board and a look of abject horror commandeer his face. "Jesus," the detective whispered. "Jesus." Britton began toying with the idea of never looking at the photos. He was sure he'd seen more bloodshed than anyone should have to look at in a single lifetime.

It was 7:40 in the morning on the day after serial murder number seven. Members of the MAIT team assembled, as they had with sickening regularity all year, at the Hillsborough Sheriff's Ybor City headquarters. It was as convenient as anyplace else, between Interstate 4 and the Crosstown Expressway, just a short hop from Interstate 275. The roads led, one way or another, to anywhere anybody would want or need to go in Hillsborough County.

Hillsborough Sheriff Armand Romano headed the investigative team because the string of murders attributed to the Heartbreak Killer began in his jurisdiction. Also attending the meeting were Powell Reemer, chief of the Tampa Police Department, because three of the seven killings occurred in his jurisdiction, FBI Special Agent Charlene Bradford, a forensic psychiatrist who was trying to get into the mind of the murderer based on evidence at crime scenes and her extensive knowledge of the mentality of serial killers, Hillsborough State Attorney Joseph "Jock" Salerno, who would have first shot at prosecuting the killer if he was ever caught, and Pete Sisko, the chief spokesman for the Hillsborough sheriff, who also served as the spokesman for MAIT, a job consisting mostly of saying, "No comment."

At a table, surrounded by stacks of binders and computer printouts, Detective Lieutenant Ditmer O'Brien, of the Tampa PD, served as case review coordinator, the one person through whom every scrap of investigative information flowed. O'Brien analyzed the most trivial information on suspects, assuming there were any, which in this case there weren't, on victims and witnesses, on physical evidence, and on investigators' reports. He organized it, kept the computerized files cross-referenced and updated, and made certain everybody with a need to know knew what he or she needed. The job couldn't have been done without computers, and Dits was tapped for it because he was, in his words, the best damned electronic file clerk alive. While file clerking wasn't a dream job on a police force, it earned Dits his gold shield. He had a national reputation and lectured at the FBI Academy on his cross-referencing techniques.

More than a dozen other detectives and investigators slumped in scattered chairs. All of their faces were lined and gray with sorrow, fatigue, and frustration.

"Gentlemen," Romano said by way of opening the meeting, failing in his Latin chauvinism to recognize the presence of Charlene Bradford. Under different circumstances, she might have mentioned the slight. "By now all of you know we're looking at a seventh victim. I'm going to turn this briefing over to Captain Britton, who was at the scene last night and pretty much knows what there is to know. Then we'll hear from Jerry Lowensdorf about the physical evidence and from Dr. Bradford. Ben."

Britton stood, appalled to realize how little new information he possessed. He mentioned the splash of liquid found on the floor outside the examining room where Dr. Erlich was killed. A sample was in the hands of TPD crime lab technicians. He described the photograph that appeared to be the only item missing from Dr. Erlich's office, most probably the killer's newest totem. And he dwelled a moment on the developing trend by the killer to move away from more vulnerable women to targets of greater and greater challenge, both in degree of education and age. He professed not to know the significance of the change and suggested Charlene Bradford might have something to contribute.

Then he turned the meeting over to Lowensdorf, who soured everyone's breakfast with an anatomically correct description of the killer's escalation of torture and his growing obsession with his dead victims' hearts. He made extensive use of the photographs of Dr. Erlich's body. Britton barely glanced at them.

"In the first three cases, our man was content to conduct his mutilation through the closed chest wall," Lowensdorf said. "It was sloppy but effective. With the Serruto killing, however, he began opening the chest, presumably coming in direct contact with the heart, possibly while it was still in spasm after the victim died. He was consistent in that regard with number five, and even more aggressive against number six. Last night, in addition to opening the chest, he removed the heart and left it beside the victim's head." His pointer slapped the pertinent photograph. Britton studied his cuticles.

"Does it mean at some point in time he might actually start taking the hearts away with him?" asked TPD Chief Reemer.

"That sort of speculation is out of my league," Lowensdorf said quickly. "I'd have to defer to Charlene. Let me move away from discussing hearts and fill you in on some other matters." He pointed to another group of autopsy photos. "This is the first victim to die by means other than strangulation. The perpetrator punctured her carotids and let her life pulse out of her with each beat of her heart. But virtually everything else is consistent with the previous killings. He took particular care to be sure this one suffered before she died, far more than the others, and he took his time about administering the pain. But even though the level of torture is greater, the nature of it is dead on what I expected to see, including the escalation of the cruelty. There are a number of other points of similarity between this killing and the first six: There was a rape, and I think it occurred before the victim died because the semen was mixed with her blood."

"You *think?*" asked Jock Salerno, the Hillsborough state's attorney. Uncertainty in a potential expert witness was a prosecutorial nightmare.

Lowensdorf nodded. "I can't be absolutely certain, because during the torture phase the perpetrator used his knife to cut the victim's genitals three times, once each on the clitoris and the labia minora, left and right." The medical examiner paused as several of his audience groaned and squirmed uncomfortably. He pointed to a photograph at the lower right corner of the board. Britton put his elbows on his knees and intently studied the floor between his shoes. "It's at least possible the victim was dead at the time of the rape, and the blood found in the vagina was from the cuts within the vulva, carried inside the victim on the killer's penis."

"But she was alive when she was cut?" Salerno asked.

"Absolutely, or she wouldn't have bled like she did," Lowensdorf said. "And she did bleed. Profusely. I also found severe bruising within the vagina, but it isn't consistent with what I expect to see after a rape. It's more random and more severe. It's more likely he did it with his fingers, or perhaps with a blunt instrument. But the victim was definitely alive when the activity occurred that created the bruising."

Romano spoke up. "So we've got a different cause of death, the heart was damaged differently, and you can't say for sure the rape occurred prior to death. Is there any chance this was *not* the same man?"

"Don't misunderstand me," Lowensdorf said. "The preponderance of evidence says it *was* the same man. I typed his blood from the semen. A-positive, like the others."

"DNA?" Romano asked.

"A semen sample and a hair are on their way to the lab in Jacksonville," Lowensdorf said. "It'll be several weeks before we get the results, but if I had to guess, I'd bet money we'll get a match with samples from previous killings."

"Why are you so sure this was the same killer when there are at least three major areas of departure in his routine?" Romano persisted.

"I'll be honest with you, Sheriff," Lowensdorf said. "I don't think those departures are all that important. It's happened in other serial-killer cases. They don't do precisely the same thing each and every time. Cutting the vulva was an escalation in the violence, and it's been escalating all along. Puncturing the arteries instead of resorting to strangulation, and cutting out the heart instead of being satisfied with mutilating it inside the chest cavity, maybe he did those things as sick anatomical jokes on a doctor. They're not necessarily significant changes."

Britton was enraged. He gritted his teeth so tightly his jaw ached, and his fingernails clawed his palms inside clenched fists. He'd seen the body himself, shortly after the killing, and he could see from the blood patterns it had been bad. But his mind hadn't been able to grasp how bad until he heard the medical examiner's report. He'd read dozens of serial-killer case histories and couldn't recall any this sadistic, unless it was the man who forced his victims to watch as he sawed off their fingers and toes. Or the ones who preyed on children. They probably were the worst. But this one was right up there. The details of what Marilyn Erlich suffered made him nauseated.

When Lowensdorf paused for a breath, Britton stood up so forcefully he knocked his folding chair backward into Powell Reemer's knees. He didn't turn to apologize, and in the tense emotion of the moment, Reemer assumed Britton probably didn't realize what he'd done.

"Damn him to hell!" Britton cursed as he strode to the front of the room. "I need ideas, people," he told the group. "I want this asshole off the streets, by noon today if possible. What are we missing? What signs is he leaving for us we aren't seeing? Come *on!*"

"Well, actually, Ben, I have something more for you," Lowensdorf said. "It's a real, honest clue. I don't know that it will finger our man by noon, but it could help."

All eyes fixed on Lowensdorf. He reached into his right pocket and extracted a small manila envelope. He opened the flap and upended it over his right palm. Britton saw something small and dark slide out, but he had no idea what it was.

"Found this when I suctioned the chest cavity," Lowensdorf said. "It's small enough, I should have missed it, but I guess we can't be unlucky all the time."

"What is it?" Britton demanded.

"I didn't have the foggiest idea," the medical examiner said. "But one of my assistants is particularly fond of this stuff made into jewelry. She recognized it as a sliver from an abalone shell. It's not something naturally occurring inside human chest cavities, that's for sure."

"Can you put it on the overhead?" Romano asked.

"I can try," Lowensdorf said. "I'm not sure it will work."

He placed the tiny shell fragment on the glass plate and brought its image into focus on the opposite wall. Pete Sisko jumped up and turned off the room lights.

"Hmmm," Lowensdorf mused, reflecting on what appeared to be little more than a dark spot against the ivory wall paint. "Doesn't show up very well on this thing, so let me describe it for you. I guess you all know what mother-of-pearl is. It's the inside of—what?—the oyster shell, I think. Well, this is the same thing, but from an abalone. It looks like tiny platelets of green and gold and various hues of blue and aqua with a blush of pink. It's made into earrings and brooches and watch dials. Very popular with women. What we have here is a chip from something made of abalone shell. I took pictures. They'll be available by this afternoon."

"Our guy was wearing women's jewelry?" Dits O'Brien asked.

"Not likely," said Lowensdorf. "I don't think this came from jewelry. If he was wearing a watch with an abalone dial, he would've had to lose the glass face before he could've chipped the shell, and I would've found the glass in the victim's chest. I didn't."

"Maybe he broke the face earlier and chipped the dial during the assault," Estevez suggested.

"That's possible, yes," Lowensdorf conceded. "But I'd expect someone who could afford a watch with a genuine abalone dial to take better care of it."

"An abalone ring?" Estevez asked.

"Doubt it," the medical examiner said. "Remember, he was wearing surgical gloves. Given how hard it is to pull those gloves over a ring, particularly a large man's ring, I think it's unlikely he was wearing one. And how would the chip have fallen out unless he ripped the glove open somehow? That's too many improbabilities."

"Could it have come from jewelry the victim was wearing?" Britton asked.

"She wasn't wearing anything even faintly resembling abalone. What little she had on was gold and very simple. And it didn't appear any items were missing."

"Then what?" Britton asked.

"What if it came off the knife, itself?" Lowensdorf guessed. "What if it got chipped while he was hacking around in the chest? Maybe there was some decorative abalone on the handle. That's not far-fetched. It's done with mother-of-pearl. Maybe he banged it against a rib or the sternum. That seems more likely than a watch without a crystal or a ring under a surgical glove." He plucked the tiny piece of evidence from the projector and slid it back into its envelope. "You find who owns the rest of this shell, and you've got your killer. That's all I have."

Britton shook his head. They had so much, and it added up to so little: a blood type, hair color, DNA, whiskey sample, and now a fleck of seashell. And it led nowhere.

He turned to Charlene Bradford. "What about you?" he asked. "Does any of this help?"

Charlene Bradford was stunningly beautiful, a tall, slim African-American. Britton thought she could have been a model, but her vocational choice was one of mind over body. She was a forensic psychiatrist, specializing in profiling criminal personalities. She was one of the best the FBI had to offer. Fortunately for this MAIT group, she also lived in Tampa Palms, one of the city's northern, tonier suburbs.

"Actually, abalone isn't my area of expertise, although I do admire it in jewelry," Bradford said. "And what the killer did to this victim's heart really adds little to what we already know. It's probably a way of taunting the authorities, getting grosser and grosser, as my thirteen-year-old daughter would say, in an attempt to make us ever more desperate to catch him. I can see it's working. Quite frankly, I'm more interested in this turn he's taken in the nature of his victims. It's obvious to me he's moving uptown and upscale."

"Why?" Britton asked.

She shrugged. "Speculation?"

"We'll take anything at this point," Britton replied.

"Ever greater challenges," she said. "This is somebody with something to prove. After he proved it five times on vulnerable women, he picked someone less vulnerable for number six, then someone less vulnerable still for number seven. Number seven was a quantum leap. And, he's also taking greater risks of being caught. A woman like Constance Evans, and the doctor killed last night, are more likely to notice someone watching them, following them. They're more likely to see a face in a crowd and recognize it as somebody they've seen somewhere else. They're more likely to tell friends if they're frightened, or to call the police and provide a description of the man they're frightened of."

Dits O'Brien was shaking his head. "I checked on Dr. Erlich and rechecked the Evans women," he said. "Nothing. Neither of them ever called in a complaint to any jurisdiction in Hillsborough, Pinellas, Polk, Pasco, or Manatee Counties. If they were aware of this guy, he didn't scare 'em bad enough to report it."

"Dr. Erlich's fiancé said she hadn't expressed concerns about her safety," Britton recalled.

"That's a shame," Bradford said. "I would strongly suggest we tell the public about this, tell women to be aware of those around them and to report unexplained, repetitive encounters with men they don't know and whose presence they can't explain."

"I'll take care of it," said Pete Sisko, the team spokesman. He sounded almost relieved to have something real to feed the media.

"How about the profile?" Britton asked. "Does last night flesh it out at all?"

"Not really," she said. "Have we notified VICAP?"

The Violent Criminal Apprehension Program run by the U.S. Justice Department had the capacity to compare local murders with homicides everywhere else in the country. But so far, VICAP had turned up no match to the Tampa Bay killer's method of operation. Dits O'Brien had been the liaison officer.

"I talked to Washington first thing this morning," he said. "The vulva cuts added a new element, and a preliminary computer run turned a couple of possibles, but nothing in this part of the world. I'll get a more complete report from VICAP later in the day. And I'll tell them about the abalone shell. If they turn anything, y'all'll be the first to know."

"Anything else you can add, Doctor?" Britton asked.

"That's about it," she said.

Britton sighed in dismay. "Anybody else have anything?" he asked.

Lowensdorf waved his hand casually, the way a very tired man tries to catch someone's eye. "One thing I mentioned about previous cases, but it bears repeating. The killer's knife is very sharp and evenly honed. The cuts are very clean. No tears or ragged edg—" He interrupted himself and paused. "Now, that might be something," he resumed, speaking softly, like a man talking himself through an idea. "It's a bit of a wild hare, but . . ."

"What?" Britton demanded.

"You carry a pocketknife, Captain?" the medical examiner asked.

"Sometimes," Britton replied.

Lowensdorf turned to his left. "Dits, how about you?"

"Uh, no. Sorry," the detective said.

Lowensdorf turned back to the room. "Sheriff, you?" he asked Romano.

A nod. "It means a lot to me," he said. "Belonged to my granddad."

"Chief Reemer?"

"Yes, my father's."

"You keep your knife sharp?" Lowensdorf asked.

"Yes," the Tampa police chief replied. "Rather religiously so, in fact. My father taught me, you take care of your tools, and they'll take care of you."

"You keep your kitchen utility knives sharp, too?"

Reemer snorted. "Not to hear my wife tell it." There was a smattering of laughter around the room. "She takes the kitchen knives out somewhere when they get too dull to cut an apple, but she's got the time to mess with them. It would be too much of a hassle for me, working the hours I do. Now, the pocketknife is a quick job. I can have it sharpened anywhere in a matter of a few minutes. And I'm good about remembering to do it."

"Yeah," Romano added, "me, too. My wife bought one of those electric gizmos for the kitchen knives, but I don't trust my pocketknife to it. I have it done professionally."

There were scattered nods and murmurs of agreement from others.

"So what if our killer is the same way?" Lowensdorf asked.

"Walk us through it, Jerry," Britton urged.

"This guy's used his knife to saw through cartilage a couple of times," the ME said. "That'll dull a blade in real short order. But as I said, every flesh cut he's made has been clean as a whistle. And I've examined them closely under high magnification. The blade doesn't show any sign of getting dull or rough or chipped up. Ergo, he must take care of it the way all of us take care of pocketknives we prize."

"But I thought you said the murder weapon is bigger than a pocket-knife," Britton said.

"Almost certainly bigger than an ordinary pocketknife, but not necessarily so big it wouldn't fit into a pocket," Lowensdorf said. "Maybe he doesn't carry it all the time. Maybe he keeps it in a bureau drawer, or in his glove compartment. That's not important. What is important is it's always uniformly smooth and sharp, which means he either sharpens it himself, or somebody else does it for him on a more or less regular basis."

"Is it possible he uses a different knife, a new knife, each time?" Britton asked.

"Oh, I'd bet a month's salary against it," Lowensdorf said, "especially if the fragment of abalone came from his weapon. An abalone-decorated knife would be something special, perhaps even part of the killer's ritual. Another part of the ritual is keeping it sharp."

"Possibly having it sharpened after each killing," Britton suggested.

"Probably," Lowensdorf said.

"Find the sharpener and find the knife, is that what you're saying?" Bradford asked.

"Exactamundo, lovely lady," Lowensdorf replied.

"Checking every merchant in the county who sharpens knives could take us well into next year," Estevez said.

"Then you'd better get started," said Britton.

"What are we looking for?" Estevez asked.

Lowensdorf answered. "A man in his thirties with brown hair who brings in the same knife to be sharpened with a fair amount of regularity," he said. "The knife possibly has abalone on it somewhere. It could be a pocketknife, but it wouldn't be a small one. It has to have a fairly long blade to reach behind the victims' sternums to their hearts—five, six inches, anyway. And I'd say the blade is approximately a half-inch across."

"And if it's a special knife, it's probably the only one he takes in to be sharpened," Bradford added. "He'd want the honer's full attention focused on it, not diffused by a stack of kitchen knives waiting to be worked on."

"And if he does the sharpening himself?" Britton asked.

"We're fucked," Lowensdorf said flatly.

"Let's hope it isn't so," Bradford added. "I don't think we have any time to waste."

"What do you mean?" Britton asked.

"The escalation in violence is a clear signal he's increasingly frustrated at his inability to exorcise whatever it is that's haunting him. Each time he kills, each time he relives the kills, he is hoping for erasure, to be free of torment. When it doesn't happen, the cycle starts again. By moving from homeless women and prostitutes to more educated and older women—Dr. Erlich, by the way, was the first victim over thirty—the killer is hoping the greater challenge, the greater danger, will give him greater relief. As each murder fails to do so, he'll continue trying for more and more challenge, and at the same time, I suspect he will escalate the level of torture as well.

"As much as I know you don't want to hear this, gentlemen, I fear if we don't catch him first, he might try to cut the heart from his next victim while she's still alive."

6

Ben Britton, Nick Estevez, and three of the detectives assigned to the MAIT task force divided up the alphabet and placed calls to shops and stores all over Hillsborough County that qualified as outlets for knives. As second-in-command of the task force, Britton normally wouldn't have participated in the drudge work. But his sole job for the Sheriff's Office at the moment was supervising the hunt for the serial killer, and sitting at his desk, reviewing files, and waiting for others to come up with answers was too difficult; it gave him too much time to fret about mysteries without solutions, too much time to let the stomach acid build toward an inevitable ulcer. So to keep busy, he added his brain and his eyes to the front lines of the war, although when he and the detectives started making a master list of stores, and he saw the daunting task ahead of them, he began to regret his decision.

They listed gun dealers, knife dealers, gun-and-knife dealers, sporting goods stores, bait-and-tackle shacks, hunting outfitters, cutlery outlets, and hardware stores. With each call they asked for the names of other businesses and individuals who might do custom knife sharpening. The list seemed to grow rather than shrink.

They were into their second hour of fruitless calls when a few miles to the south, on Gandy Boulevard, just before it becomes a bridge westbound over Tampa Bay to Pinellas County, Cynthia Diamond pulled into her reserved parking space at the studios and offices of WFSC-TV, channel seven. In the trunk of her dark green Lexus coupe were fourteen brand new outfits she had gathered up at Burdines and Dillards department stores and a specialty dress shop she liked in South Tampa. All the clothes were out on approval, something stores didn't do much for the average customer, but television news anchors weren't average, and if she kept any of the clothes, their company name would appear on screen at the end of the newscasts. You couldn't buy advertising like that.

Still, Cynthia didn't feel special or pampered. What was in store for her today was the part of her job she loathed. It was modeling day at the office.

She pushed through the front door of the studio building.

"Morning, Miss Diamond," the receptionist said.

"Good morning, Susan," she replied, tossing her car keys on the desk. "Would you have Robert bring in the clothes from my trunk and hang them in my office, please? There are quite a few, so he'll need a dolly."

"Sure," Susan replied. "Miss McCormick brought in some things to show Mr. Townsend, too. She didn't look any happier about it than you do."

"I'm certain not," Cynthia replied. "She's been doing it a lot longer than I have, and I don't imagine it gets any easier."

"What do you do with all those neat clothes when you're through with them?"

"We're allowed to buy any of them we want from the station. No big discount, either, I might add. I don't know what Peter Prick does with the rest. Maybe he takes them home and wears them himself."

Susan grinned as Cynthia disappeared into an elevator to the third floor. Most of the news staff despised the news director, but they didn't often use his secret nickname in front of her.

Cynthia walked briskly down the dark hallway toward her office. She didn't notice Liz McCormick's office door was open until she heard the muffled crying coming from within. She let herself into her small quarters, stashed her purse in a desk drawer, and recrossed the hallway to check on the veteran who now anchored the morning and noon newscasts.

"Liz, you okay?" she asked, knocking softly on the door frame.

She could see clearly that Liz wasn't. Her eyes were red and puffy and her face was wet.

Cynthia entered the room unbidden and sat down next to Liz's desk. "What in the world brought this on? Can I do anything?"

Liz stared at the tissue she held crumpled in her lap. She was silent for several seconds, then took a deep breath and exhaled it slowly, calming herself.

"Lee told me I had to lose seven pounds and have my hair restyled or I could kiss my job good-bye," she said sadly.

Cynthia studied her colleague. Liz looked no leaner or heavier than she'd ever been, and her light brown hair was done in a neat, simple bob.

"Did he say why?" she asked.

Liz shook her head, not looking up from her lap. "He never says why he demands things. He just does."

"Well, he can't yank you off the air," Cynthia insisted. "You have a contract."

"He can give my job to somebody else and move me to overnight duty," Liz said. "He can continue to pay me and have everybody ignore me, or he can buy me out and confiscate my office key. He can do anything he wants to, when you get right down to it. If I don't do what Lee Townsend demands, I'm history at this station, and maybe in the whole market."

"Tell me what happened," Cynthia said.

Liz looked up at her, sniffed, and blotted her nose. For the time being, the tears had stopped.

"This morning, after the last cut-in on the *Today* show, I modeled some new clothes for him," she began. "He hated the first two outfits I tried on, said if I didn't have any more taste than that he'd get somebody to start picking my clothes for me, that a studio soundman could do a better job than I did. He said the third outfit made me look fat. Then he got up and grabbed me and pinched my waist and said, well, maybe I was fat. That's when he told me to lose seven pounds. Seven pounds! And he started in about my hair. He said it made me look too old. He made me stand and listen while he called a stylist over in the West Shore area and made an appointment for me to get it cut short and combed forward, oh, and blonded up a bit, as he put it. It was humiliating. When I objected, he told me the only way my protest would mean anything was if I uttered it as I walked out the front door for the last time. Then he laughed and said he should have expected my bad reaction, that I was probably getting menopausal."

Cynthia thought she could feel her blood pressure jump. "He always makes infantile remarks on modeling day, but I've never heard him say anything that stupid," she told her colleague angrily. "That's sexual harassment. It's illegal."

Liz laughed. "So who's gonna sue him?" she asked. "Besides, I think he was just showing off for Chris."

"Chris Pappas? He was there?"

Liz nodded. "He says he's going to sit in more and more, doing his duty as the station manager. And besides, he doesn't like the idea of Lee having all the fun."

"He actually said that?"

Liz nodded.

"The bastard!" Cynthia felt sick for Liz McCormick, but she knew she would be put through the same thing later in the day. It would be nice if she could summon the nerve to leave, to slap the shit out of Lee, leave his office, and keep right on walking to the newspapers or the Equal Employment Opportunity Commission, or both. But she couldn't do that any more than Liz. The truth was, she, too, probably would submit to the abuse in silent fury.

Simply put, she couldn't afford to lose the income. Since she and her now ex-husband had no children, and since she made enough money to support herself well, she got nothing but the Davis Islands house out of their divorce. And she only got that because she had bought it herself, with her own money, before the marriage. Even if she found a job with a station outside the Tampa Bay area, there was no guarantee the situation would be any better. Disdain for women was a long-standing part of the culture of local news operations. And there was no guarantee she could find another job. She was thirty-five now, closing in on the age where news directors start thinking about putting female anchors in less-prestigious morning and noon news slots or, heaven forfend, giving them the weekend assignments where rookies break in and enfeebled former stars work out their days locked into horrible schedules.

She looked closely at Liz, who was forty-two. She'd been moved to the morning/noon assignment two years earlier. Even giving her some latitude for the temporary damage the weeping had done to her features, the tiny lines of middle age were beginning to crease her otherwise telegenic face. How much longer, Cynthia wondered, until they began showing up on her own?

"What's wrong with you girls? The looks on your faces could sour a quart of milk."

Cynthia and Liz looked up simultaneously when they recognized the resonating voice of Cynthia's co-anchor. Max Clevenger's six-foot-four frame filled the doorway. He wore jogging shorts and a tank top soaked through with sweat, and rivulets were running down his body. A big blue towel that might have helped hung uselessly around his neck.

"Oh, I know," Max said. "You're upset about the serial murder last night, aren't you?" He shook his head solemnly, as though he were performing for a television camera. "These are very, very upsetting times."

"For chrissake, Max, save the dramatics for the studio," Cynthia snapped. "You're dripping on the carpet. You smell like a gym that hasn't been aired out since last year. Hit the showers and leave us alone."

He dragged the towel off his neck and began blotting himself. "Come on, girls," he urged. "This is me, Max. Talk to me."

"Goddamn it, we're not your *girls,* and I didn't hear anybody invite you to join this conversation!" Cynthia exploded, venting her irritation at a target who had neither the brainpower nor the compassion to understand. For Max Clevenger, stumbling in on the two women was nothing more than an exercise in voyeurism. "Take a hike, Max," Cynthia insisted.

Clevenger pushed himself off the door frame and backed out of the room, disappearing with a child's look of bewilderment set on his face.

"He doesn't have a clue." Cynthia said. "Big voice, great face, fair body, empty head." She chuckled. "You ever hear the story about the day one of his female fans asked him if he deserved his reputation as a man who could seduce any woman he wanted? He put on his best on-air voice and said, 'Yes. Sometimes, I only have to talk to them.' "

Liz smiled thinly but didn't respond right away.

"How old is he?" she asked after a time.

Cynthia shrugged. "Not sure, exactly. Mid, late forties. Forty-seven, I think."

"How come he doesn't get bounced to the weekend?"

"What? And upset all his femme fans around the Bay area?"

"Then why do they do it to *us?*"

Cynthia sighed, thinking Liz terribly naive. "You thought when you trained for this job you were going into journalism, didn't you?" she asked facetiously. "Well, you weren't. You were training to be a porn star, a sex object in a half-million male fantasies. It's all in the Q-ratings. The way it works for Max is, young women dig sexy older men, and middle-aged women love a guy who's middle-aged and doesn't look it because it reinforces their own hopes that they don't look it, either. So the older Max gets, the more popular he is among women. But with male viewers, it's just the opposite. They dig the young babes. When we show up in all those living rooms, we're telling every male viewer we're there for him. It makes the guys from middle age on up feel good about themselves, that they could attract sexy young things like us, or at least like we used to be. When the managers think we don't project that sexy aura anymore, they stash us in time slots where ratings aren't as important."

Liz was scowling in disbelief. "That's the most ridiculous thing I've ever heard," she said.

"Not ridiculous at all, and stop frowning or you'll get wrinkles and lines before your time," Cynthia insisted.

"There are a lot of men who aren't like that," Liz insisted, still frowning.

Cynthia nodded. "True," she agreed, "but television news directors all over the country buy into the fantasy. Nobody escapes unless you make it to big-time network status, and sometimes the formula stays in play there, too. Face it, kid, we'd better start looking at backup careers, cause we'll both be on the streets by the time we're forty-five."

A DARK gray cloud of self-pity, or perhaps it was self-loathing, parked itself over Cynthia Diamond's mood right through the morning and into the time she was scheduled to have her own new clothes session with Lee Townsend. This was not the life she envisioned when she left Ocala, where her father was the chief trainer on one of the big thoroughbred racehorse farms, and enrolled at the University of Florida in Gainesville. Nor was it what she expected on the life-changing pivotal day at the beginning of her junior year when she was "discovered" by a revered professor of broadcast journalism.

To be honest, she and the professor discovered each other. He was a former network news anchor who wrote novels about a rugged television investigative reporter who had an uncanny knack for uncovering diabolical international plots to destroy the United States. The novels made him fabulously wealthy and even more famous than he'd been behind an anchor desk. So he threw over his television career for a tenured, ivory-tower position on the beautiful central-Florida campus, where he had all the time he wanted to perfect his fiction and his romantic techniques with women under twenty-five. When they met, Cynthia was a student of serious journalism, with aspirations to *The New York Times* or *Harper's*. He invited her for a cup of coffee at the student union, to talk to her, he said, about changing her focus to television news. She was aware both of her good looks and his reputation with women and prepared herself not to be swept away, but he swept her away anyhow.

The torrid portion of their affair lasted through her junior year and the first semester of her senior year. Then it cooled a bit as both realized the expanse of their love was bordered inevitably by her graduation and departure from Gainesville. Still, he helped her get her first on-camera job in Jacksonville and visited her there occasionally. She had stopped in Gainesville to see him a number of years later on her way to take a new and better assignment at WFSC-TV in the big Tampa Bay television market. But he had departed by then for some remote Pacific island to live on his millions and write "serious" books. She never heard from or of him again.

He had been the only man she ever loved until four years later when she met Connor Buckley, a pediatrician who gained worldwide fame for his high-risk expeditions into drought-stricken East Africa to save thousands of children starving there. She was on the tarmac at Tampa International Airport to interview Buckley on the day he returned to the United States from one Africa trip during which he'd not only seen to the care of untold numbers of children, but had single-handedly tracked down and rescued two members of his entourage who'd been kidnapped by a freelance band of rebel terrorists. It was love at first sight and marriage three months later.

To all appearances, Connor Buckley was a saint, a man totally committed to improving the lot of the world's less fortunate, sparing no expense or danger to himself. Two years into their marriage, however, the impromptu weekend trips to Paris, the luxury cruises, the weeks on the beach at his seaside mansion in Jamaica, began to pale under the waves of abuse he heaped on her.

It wasn't physical; Buckley never hit her. But he belittled her constantly about the nature of her work and, in his warped view, its total lack of relevance in the larger scheme of things. He heaped scorn on her for her expressed desire to have children, forcing her to listen to his pretentious and wholly irrelevant diatribes about how there were too many children in the world already. When she suggested adopting, he became enraged, demanding to know why he should be responsible for the life and conduct of offspring not derived from his superior genetic pool. He let it be known he expected to be regarded as Zeus might have been, had the mythical god ever walked the earth among mere mortals.

And he had no end of other women, all younger, prettier, more doting and reverential than she could bring herself to be. When she couldn't get away because of a conflict at work, he would take one or more of his admirers to Jamaica, instead. His stays there stretched over longer and longer periods of time. Finally, he stopped coming back to Tampa at all.

His lawyer called her one day out of the blue and suggested she file for divorce. Dr. Buckley would not contest the action, the lawyer said, and if she wouldn't try to raid his fortune, he would be willing to make a substantial, one-time, off-the-books settlement payment to help her get back on her feet. She had done as he asked, almost relieved to be rid of him, although she hardly considered his settlement payment of $150,000 to be substantial. It did allow her to refinance her house, greatly increasing her equity and lowering her monthly payments and leaving her more disposable income for investment each month. She would never be rich, but she was comfortable and free of the torment he dispensed.

Or had she simply replaced the misery meted out by Connor Buckley for the grief administered by Lee Townsend?

Cynthia smiled mournfully at the thought as she picked apart the carryout Caesar salad sitting, half-wilted, in its plastic plate on her desk. She kicked a crouton around with her fork. The last she had heard from Connor was five years ago, and she had been serious about no one since. Her woeful experience with men did not inspire confidence that her next encounter, should there ever be one, would have a better outcome. She had to learn to live with the likelihood she would never be nominated as the happy-marriage poster child.

ROBERT, the gofer who had more years at the station than any of the people who gave him orders, knocked softly on Cynthia Diamond's door. He had come to retrieve the outfits he'd hung in her office earlier and take them up a floor to Townsend's suite. Cynthia waved him in, saying nothing, and continued picking at the Parmesan-flaked greens in front of her. Robert nodded and went about his work quietly, recognizing her melancholy as typical of the mood at the office on modeling day. Robert knew what went on during these sessions, and he wondered why the women put up with it. He might be an errand boy, but nobody at the station had stolen his pride, and nobody ever would.

He glanced at Townsend when he entered his office. The news director had his back to the door, his feet propped up on the credenza behind his desk, and his temper in high gear. He was having a telephone conversation with someone about the latest in the string of serial murders. Near as Robert could make out, Townsend was pissed off because nobody had yet succeeded in getting an on-camera interview with the latest victim's fiancé.

Of course it never would have occurred to Lee Townsend to leave the poor guy alone for a few days. It would have taken a measure of humanity to reach the conclusion that a man who had just lost the woman he loved to a vicious killer needed some time to mend. In the cutthroat television news business, at least the way Lee Townsend practiced it, there wasn't any room in the day for humanity.

Moments later, Robert passed Cynthia Diamond in the hall as she glumly approached Townsend's office.

"Everything's right there for you, Miss Diamond," he said.

"Thanks very much," she replied. "When we're done, would you mind very much putting it all back in my car?"

"Same as always, yes, Miss," Robert said. "Just ring me up."

CYNTHIA presented herself to Townsend's secretary, Nancy Brewster.

"He's on the phone," the secretary said. "You can go on in and get started changing. Mr. Pappas is coming in for a meeting, but they said you wouldn't disturb them; you could model your clothes while they're talking."

Cynthia's shoulders sagged. "It's enough of an ordeal doing this for Lee. I don't need Chris here, too," she said. "Can we reschedule?"

"I don't think so, dear," Nancy replied pejoratively. "I think Mr. Pappas wanted to be here for your session. After all, the station pays for your clothes. The station manager has a right to help decide what the money goes for."

I am not going to take a lot of crap from these men, Cynthia thought as she buttoned up the front of the kelly green dress, one of her favorites among all the clothes she had chosen this month. She was in the large private bathroom off Townsend's office. A former news director who designed it meant it only for his use—he liked to run in the morning on his way to work and shower when he got there, then play handball at lunch and shower again. It was Chris Pappas, when he was the news director before being promoted to station manager, who began using it as a dressing room where the women news anchors could change into their new on-air clothes for his approval. It was sick sport.

Cynthia checked her appearance in the full-length mirror, fixed her hair, and opened the door. Townsend was sitting behind his desk, and Chris Pappas was in an oversize blue-and-green armchair against the wall opposite the bathroom.

"Now that's a green dress," Pappas exclaimed when he saw her. "We'll have to put color filters on the cameras or you'll burn 'em out, dear."

Cynthia ignored him and faced Townsend. He made a circling motion with his finger, which meant she was to turn around, a demeaning command and unnecessary, since her viewing audience saw her only frontally, from the waist up. But she gritted her teeth and obliged, prompting another comment from Pappas.

"You still have the sweetest ass in the industry, babe," he said, leering openly at her backside over his half-glasses.

That was it. Cynthia stopped in midturn. "Mr. Pappas, there's absolutely no need for that sort of remark here," she said. "It's entirely inappropriate. It probably qualifies as sexual harassment, and that's illegal."

"She's right, Chris," Townsend said. "Besides, her tits are her best attribute."

The two men howled at their joke. Cynthia glared at them and considered walking out, but it would have been too awkward. She was in a dress she didn't own, with her own clothes hanging in Lee Townsend's bathroom. To leave in anger now would only mean returning meekly in a few minutes to retrieve her belongings. Not exactly her idea of a grand exit. So she sighed deeply and tried to ignore their merriment at her expense.

"You wearing one of those underwire bras?" Townsend asked.

"That's none of your business," Cynthia snapped.

"I think the dress would look better if you had a little help with lift," he said. "You're not getting any younger, you know."

"I don't need a little help with lift, Mr. Townsend," she insisted with anger shaking in her voice. "My natural lift is fine, thank you."

His eyebrows shot up. "Really? You want the dress or don't you?"

"Yes," she replied.

"Then get the right bra," he ordered roughly. "Don't you ever forget where the money comes from to outfit you in the style to which you've become accustomed. If we pay, we get to decide what you wear and how you wear it. No exceptions. Got it?"

And so it went through the entire wardrobe session, which took nearly ninety minutes. When it was over, Townsend and Pappas had approved six outfits and rejected eight. Among the rejects were her two favorites. She pleaded a case for them, but they refused to reconsider. She suspected they turned them down precisely because they knew how much she liked them.

"Okay," Townsend said. "Take the losers back where they came from and get the others to your rhinestone place. I don't want to see you wearing any of the new clothes until they've got the stones on 'em."

"Not all of them," Cynthia challenged. "I want to keep a couple plain. I don't think rhinestones will look good on the red one."

"All of them," Townsend repeated. "Each and every one. They're your trademark, Cynthia. Your name and your trademark. Not some nights. All nights. The male viewers tune in for it, and I want to keep them happy."

"Gee, I thought they tuned in for the news," she replied sarcastically.

"I think there might be one really old guy up in Port Richey who tunes you in for the news," Pappas said. "Or maybe he died. I'm not sure."

She turned her back on the renewed laughter and sought the sanctuary of the bathroom, cursing both of them.

"They probably gather in here and compare the sizes of their penises," she muttered to no one in particular as she shrugged out of dress number fourteen and hung it up. "And they're probably disappointed, too."

7

Cynthia Diamond was getting into dress number eleven when Ben Britton and Nick Estevez pulled up in front of Sampson's Live Bait Shop on Twenty-second Street, just north of the Twenty-second Street Causeway. In the third hour of phone calling, Estevez finally turned up this one business that offered knife-sharpening services and a customer who came in occasionally to have one decorative knife honed, always the same knife. While the other detectives finished the call list, Britton and Estevez hit the streets.

This was one of the oldest parts of Tampa, a place of tough bars and crab shacks and old, fading houses. But the strong fragrance of salt and sea hung in the air, and the neighborhood smelled fresh. Britton knew the area well, since he and Laura spent many a winter weekend day nearby, at McKay Bay, one of the most important seabird sanctuaries in the Southeast. It was a tidal basin as much as anything. When the tide came in, the saltwater carried all manner of marine life, which, in turn, attracted the birds: snowy egrets, great blue heron, white ibis, and roseate spoonbills, as well as the smaller plovers, willets, sandpipers, ruddy turnstones, and dunlin. When the tide ebbed, it left upper McKay Bay a prairie of mudflats, and the marine life trapped on the surface or burrowed beneath it became easy prey for the birds. It was a marvel the sanctuary thrived since the lower end of the bay was part of the Tampa's port system, with its share of fuel leaks, oil spills, and assorted flotsam.

Sampson's Live Bait Shop was one of those weather-beaten buildings that had seen better days fifty years earlier. The clapboard was gray with grime and mildew, and large patches of roof lay exposed, stripped of shingles. The rickety wooden front door was standing open, and the screen door that served as the last defense against insects was missing a hinge. It was held in place by a piece of wire coat hanger. Britton swung it out for Estevez and followed him in, letting the door smack shut behind him. He moved swiftly so it wouldn't catch him in the rear. Having a screen door assault you was not the most dignified way to begin questioning a witness.

There wasn't much to see inside, but what was there had been around awhile. An old Coca-Cola chest squatted to the left of the door, its red paint chipped and cracked. Britton slid back one of the three top panels. As he'd expected. It was full of crushed ice imbedded with soft drinks in sixteen-ounce glass bottles. Britton smiled. He hadn't seen a cooler like that in years. They made soft drinks much more appealing—and kept them much colder—than tall vending things that sucked in your dollar bills and spit back twelve-ounce cans and change. He bet himself if he dug deep enough in the ice, he'd find a grape Nehi.

On the left wall, an old Kelvinator with a bottom-hinged, pull-back handle hummed softly. Britton assumed it was full of bait: shrimp, chunks of mullet, and maybe a few white plastic containers holding moss and night crawlers. The right side of the shack was taken up with fishing gear, much of it previously owned. Most of the rigs were for saltwater flats and deep-sea use. The glass counter held an assortment of fishing line, reels, stringers, landing nets, scaling knives, and a few dozen lures.

Behind it sat one of the biggest humans Britton had ever seen.

"Afternoon," the huge human said.

The detectives pulled their badges and flashed them. "Afternoon," Britton replied. "I'm looking for the owner."

"I'm Sampson," he said. "You the cop I talked to on the phone awhile ago?"

"No, I am," Estevez replied, introducing himself and Britton.

"You're a little outta your territory, aincha?" the big man asked. "This here property's in the City of Tampa."

Estevez nodded. "Got special dispensation from the mayor," he said.

Sampson flashed a broad grin. "In that case, since I got a good relationship with the mayor, it's good to meetcha."

He rose off his stool to stand at least six feet seven. He was pretty much that wide, too.

I could take him, Britton thought. *To lunch, maybe.* He pulled a small leather notebook from his side pocket. It had a Bic pen clipped to it.

"You said on the phone you have a customer who comes in once in a while to have one knife sharpened," Britton said, flipping the notebook open. "Always the same knife."

"True," Sampson replied. "Purty knife, too."

"Can you tell me about it?" the detective asked.

"Yeah. It's a typical Schrade. Maybe a six-inch blade, seven-inch haft. Something like that."

"What's a Schrade?"

"The manufacturer."

"Fishing knife?"

"Well, a lotta fishermen use 'em," Sampson said. "They're sold in tackle shops all over. But small-game hunters might be able to use 'em, too, although the blade's not real wide."

"How wide?" Estevez asked.

" 'Bout a half-inch. It's a real good balanced knife. It might have lotsa different uses for different people."

"But there's something special about this one?"

"Yeah. Mosta the Schrades I've seen have wood hafts with a metal release bar down the spine. And . . ."

"Wait. A release bar?"

"Yeah. The blade stores in the haft, like with a penknife. You swing the blade out, and it locks in place." Sampson demonstrated with his hands while he talked. "With a penknife, you push the blade back in when you're done with it, but with this Schrade, you have to press on the metal bar running down the top side of the haft, and it releases the blade so you can swing it in."

"All right," Britton said. "You were about to tell me why this Schrade is so special."

"Yeah. There's real purty shell set in all along the handle, the whole length on both sides. I thought it was abalone, but this guy says it's mother-of-pearl." Sampson shrugged. "He can call it what he wants. It's his knife."

"Mother-of-pearl, huh? Is it cream-colored and sort of iridescent?"

"No, that's why I thought it was abalone. It's a bunch of different colors. Blue and green, mostly. Real purty. I was sure it was abalone."

"I think you're probably right," Britton said.

"Good," Sampson replied. "I was real sure, you know? I know my sea life."

"I thought abalone was a Pacific shellfish," Estevez said.

"Not all of it's from the Pacific," Sampson replied. "Ain't none that's local, but that don't mean I don't know about it."

"I guess you do," Britton said. "Anything else about the knife?"

"Nope. 'Cept he brings it in every so often to have me sharpen it."

"Why you?"

"Dunno. He says I'm convenient. I don't know if he means to his home or his work."

"Well, it could be helpful to know which," Britton said. "You see him around here other than when he brings in his knife?"

"Never."

Not so helpful, after all. "Did you ever see any blood on the knife?"

"Like he'd been guttin' fish? No. Never. The knife is always spotless."

"So tell us about him."

"Why you askin' all these questions?"

"It's part of an investigation, Mr. Sampson. That's all I can say at the moment."

"It's Sampson. No mister. Just Sampson. That's my first name."

Britton looked up from his notebook and smiled. "It fits," he said.

"Yeah."

"So. The guy who brings the knife in, you know his name?"

"No. Sorry."

"You don't know his name?"

"Nope. Never told me." Sampson rubbed his chin.

"Doesn't he leave his name when he leaves the knife?"

"He don't leave the knife. Waits for it. I asked him one time if he wanted to leave it and pick it up later. It was a day I was sort of busy. He said, no, he'd wait. And he did."

"How does he pay you?"

"Cash. Everytime cash."

"No checks? Credit cards?"

"Cash. Hey, it's only three bucks."

"Describe him."

"Wiry. Hard. Tanned real good. Like he works outside a lot."

"White? Black? Hispanic?"

"White."

"Height?"

"Oh, five eight, five nine, somethin' in there. Short, ya know?" Sampson laughed heartily. "Hey, everybody looks short to me. How tall are you?"

"Six feet."

"Yeah, you're short, too." He laughed again.

"Hair?"

"Huh?"

"The guy's hair. What color is it?"

"Um, medium brown."

"Eyes?"

"Couldn't say."

"Any distinguishing marks or scars?"

Sampson chuckled. "You guys really ask that?"

"Ask what?"

" 'Any distinguishing marks or scars?' I heard 'em say those things in cop shows on TV, but I didn't know real cops said 'em."

"We do. How about it?"

"Don't think so, no."

"Tattoos?"

"Not that I remember."

"How many times has he been in here?"

"Four. Five, maybe. Maybe six. More than four."

"Which is it?"

"Five or six."

"And you never noticed his eyes?"

"He's not my type."

"Wonderful," Britton said. "How old is he?"

"Can't say for sure. Thirties, I guess. Early to middle. Closer to middle."

"How does he dress?"

"Blue jeans sometimes. Or them shorts with the big, deep front pockets."

"Cargo shorts."

"Whatever. And T-shirts. Some of 'em got writin' on 'em, like Budweiser and Harley, you know? And some are plain colors with pockets. No writin'. Never noticed his shoes." Sampson paused. " 'Cept once. He was wearin' them shorts I mentioned, but he had on work boots, them lace-up work boots with the big bulgy toes. Tan. I remember 'em 'cause they looked so heavy with his lightweight clothes an' all. That day, I think, he was wearin' one of his Harley T-shirts. I remember 'cause I asked him if he was a biker."

"Was he?"

"He said not."

"You keep a record of the dates he came in?"

"Hell, no. It's not like a doctor's office here, ya know. I keep register receipts, in case I ever hafta prove to the state or the feds I paid all the taxes I owed. Beyond that, I don't bother with records. They just clutter up the place."

"What does he talk about while he's here?"

"Nothin'."

"Nothing?"

"Nope. He comes in, hands me the knife. I go in the back, sharpen it, bring it back to him. He hands me three dollars. He checks the knife, inspects my work, and sort of pets it, ya know, puts it in his pocket and leaves. Oh, he says thanks sometimes. But he's not a conversation person, that's for sure. Strange how he'll stand right where you're standin' and fondle the knife, like he's in love with it or somethin'. It's real strange. Funny, I never thought about it till right now. Don't you think that's strange?"

Britton shrugged. "And he never talks about himself, or how he uses the knife?"

"Not a word."

"And he always comes during regular business hours?"

"Yeah, I think so. Don't ever remember him comin' to my house to fetch me."

"How does he come and go?"

"Walks in like you did, and walks out same as I 'spect you will."

Britton laughed. "I mean his transportation, his car," the detective said.

"Oh, yeah," Sampson replied. "Lemme think. I know I seen it cause once or twice he parked right outside the door, where you did. It's not a car. It's a pickup. Not real new but not old, either, and in purty good shape. Windows are tinted dark."

"What color was it?"

"Huh?"

"The truck. What color was it?"

"Oh, gosh, lemme think. Light. It was a light color. White, maybe. Light gray. Light blue. I'm not real sure. But it was light. Most people in Florida who have any sense buy light-colored wheels. Reflect the heat better, ya know?"

"I know. Did you notice the nameplate?"

"The what?"

"The nameplate. Who made the truck? Ford? Chevy?"

"Don't think so."

"Was there anything unusual about the truck?"

"Don't recall. Had one of them toolboxes in the back, you know, the kind sits up right tight behind the cab and hangs on the sides of the bed? The top covers flip up and open back toward the center. It was black, I think. Sort of blended in good with the dark windows. And he had an aluminum stepladder in the bed, too. Them things and the boots, I guess, is what made me think he's probably some sort of construction worker."

"Or an electrician, or a plumber, or a carpenter."

"Yeah," Sampson said.

"Or a CPA who likes to go home and get out of his suit and tie and do work around the house in his spare time."

"Yeah. But usually those folks keep their tools in the garage."

Britton nodded. "Point taken," he said. "How come you remember so much about the toolbox and the ladder and the windows, but you can't remember what color the truck was?"

"Dunno. I mighta noticed then. But I don't recollect now. It's been awhile since he was in, and he doesn't always park right in front where I can get a view of the truck. All I'm sure of is it was a light color. And I *am* sure of that."

"What about the truck cab? Regular? Extended?"

"Regular," Sampson said. "A plain old regular pickup."

"Was there any sign or writing on the side of the cab, like a commercial vehicle?"

"I don't recollect seeing any, no."

"How about pin-striping or tape designs? A light-colored truck's usually a candidate for some dolling up, factory-equipped or aftermarket."

Sampson thought a moment and shook his head. "I don't think so. At least, I don't recall any right offhand. I think it was a plain old truck."

"Can you think of anything else you haven't told us about him?"

Sampson frowned and continued to shake his head. "Nope, I don't think so." Then he brightened. "It was a Toyota pickup," he said. "I remember now one time he made a U-turn in the street out there, and I saw the word Toyota on his tailgate."

"So it had a factory-installed tailgate, instead of one of those mesh closures?"

"Sure, otherwise I couldn'ta seen where it said Toyota on it, now could I?" Sampson said with a tone of impatience."

Britton looked up from his notebook. "You don't happen to recall . . ."

"Not a chance. The license numbers, you mean?"

Britton nodded.

"Nope," Sampson repeated. "Not a chance. Didn't pay any attention to 'em."

Estevez jumped into the conversation. "You remember which Florida plate it was?" he asked.

"Huh?"

"You know what I mean. This state's got twenty different license plates. At least. One with the silhouette of the state in green and the numbers in red. One with the state in orange and the numbers in green. You got the manatee plate and the panther plate and the Super Bowl Twenty-five plate. One for each university, one for the shuttle disaster, one for World War Two vets, one for guys who got Purple Hearts, one for ex-POWs . . ."

"Yeah, yeah, I guess I knew that," Sampson interrupted. "Must make cop work tougher, tryin' to identify all them plates, not that I mind when I'm speedin' on the interstate." He guffawed. "Nope. Sorry. I don't know what plate he had. Don't think I ever looked at it. Wouldn'ta had any reason to."

Estevez sighed in disappointment. "When he made the U-turn, which way was he headed?" the detective asked.

"North."

"Okay, Sampson, I've got one more question, and you need to consider it carefully," Britton said, and the big proprietor nodded. "You said this guy hadn't been here in a while. When was the last time you saw him?"

Sampson rubbed a big ham hand up and down the beard stubble on the right side of his face and frowned. "Lessee," he said absently. "I can't say certain. It's not real recent. Three, maybe four weeks."

"He hasn't been in today?"

"Oh, no. Don't you think I'd remember if he had?"

"And you're pretty sure the last time was three to four weeks ago? I need you to be as certain as you can be about it."

"Yeah, I'm purty sure." Sampson brightened. "Hey, you could maybe check it, after all. He was in here the morning after the big fire on the ship over there." He hooked a thumb back over his shoulder, toward the harbor. "That was really somethin', that fire. I watched it out my bedroom window, flames shootin' up a hunnert feet at night. It was really somethin'. I was still excited about it the next day. An' here comes the guy, walkin' in the door, and I remember I asked him if he seen the fire, and he looks at me like he don't know what I'm talkin' about. So I tell him about the fire—I don't know how he missed seein' it on the news—an' he just shakes his head. I don't know how he

missed seeing it. I truly don't. But he did. Anyhow, that's the last time
I saw him, the morning after the ship fire."

"And he brought in the knife to be sharpened that day?" Britton
asked with a sudden, urgent edge in his voice.

"Yep. That's the only reason he ever comes in."

"Okay," Britton said, suppressing a smile. Like Sampson, he remembered the harbor fire vividly. It had occurred in a dry dock at the
northern tip of the Port of Tampa on July 17, the same night Constance Evans had been killed. Britton was trying to get back to headquarters from the apartment complex in Brandon where the murder
happened, and he got snarled in traffic on the Crosstown Expressway
and on Adamo Drive, both of which snake past the fire scene. The
roads were jammed with emergency fire and rescue equipment and
police units. And the mystery man had appeared at Sampson's the
next day to have his knife with the abalone handle sharpened. The
possibility of progress on this case ratcheted Britton's hopes sky high.
He forced himself to turn his attention back to Sampson.

"Can I get your full name?"

"Jones. Sampson C. Jones."

Britton looked at the big man skeptically. "Is that for real?" he
asked.

"That's what it says on my birth certificate."

"And what's your home phone?"

"Same as the number you got for me here. I live in the house out
back." Sampson jerked his head back toward a small, run-down structure behind the bait shop. It, too, had seen better days. "Ain't much
for looks, but it's paid for," he said. "The phone rings both places."

"What time do you close here?"

"When I feel like it, mostly. Usually around four-thirty."

"I'd like to send a car to pick you up and bring you down to headquarters to meet with a police artist, to see if you can come up with
enough of a description of this customer to create a decent likeness of
him. You available?"

"Sure, but I got a car. I can drive."

Britton shook his head. "This way you'll have a guide to take you
right where you need to go. He'll bring you back when you're finished."

"And it's your way of makin' certain I show up."

Britton smiled. "Something like that," he admitted.

"Okay, that's cool," Sampson said. "This is about the Heartbreak
Killer case, isn't it?"

"Yes," Britton acknowledged, "it is. This will be our first chance to
distribute a picture that might look something like him."

"Is anybody gonna know who gave you the description?"

"Not before he's captured. You have my word on it."

"Later? At his trial?"

"I imagine you'd be called as a witness, but that's the state attorney's decision."

"Be good for business," Sampson said. "I'd be a celebrity. Interview on television."

"I don't doubt it," Britton replied. He took a business card from his pocket and handed it across the counter. "Meanwhile, my name and number are there. If you remember anything else, I'd appreciate it if you'd give me a call."

"Yeah," Sampson said. "Count on it. Any friend of the mayor's is a friend of mine."

Outside, Britton and Estevez exchanged knowing looks.

"Closer," Britton said. "Inch by inch, we're getting closer."

"You want me to get somebody to baby-sit this place?" Estevez asked.

"I think you know the answer to that," Britton replied. "Put Dutch and Bobby on it as primaries, plainclothes, unmarked cars. And assign at least two backup units nearby but out of sight. I don't want anybody to have to wait for help if the suspect shows."

"You want them here round-the-clock or just for store hours?"

"I think store hours are probably enough," Britton said. Then he frowned and ran his fingers through his hair. "On the other hand, what if the guy should want special attention, say he pops in for an after-hours hone?"

"Sampson said he's never done it before," Estevez said.

"No, but I don't think I want to chance missing him to save a couple bucks on overtime. Let's sit the place round-the-clock, for a few days anyway, then we'll reassess. Tell Dutch we'll wait here till he and Bobby relieve us, but I want 'em to step on it."

Estevez made the arrangements on a tactical radio channel, secure from monitoring, and the relief car showed up sixteen minutes later.

They needn't have bothered.

Eugene Rickey had already been there and gone.

While the detectives were still in the bait shop, Rickey had crossed the Twenty-second Street Causeway from Clair Mel with Opal. They were headed for Sampson's. He braked his truck abruptly when he saw the plain white car with the canary-yellow county license tag on its rear bumper sitting in front of the bait shop. The star denoting a sheriff's unit was clearly visible on the plate. It might be a coincidence, Rickey thought, or it might not. He wouldn't take a chance. He steered a U-turn over the curb and headed back south. He knew of a good knife shop in a rural part of Brandon that could take care of Opal for him.

And from now on, he vowed, it would be a different shop each time.

AT six P.M., sharp, Eugene Rickey was at home, sitting deep in his sofa and sucking on a bottle of bourbon from his stash. Marilyn Erlich was virtually forgotten. Rickey had thoughts only for Cynthia Diamond.

And then there she was, right there on the television with those damned crystals flashing in the studio lights. How had he failed to realize all this time that she wasn't wearing real jewels? How could he have trusted her?

His face gnarled into a mask of anger as he listened to her reading the top story about the ongoing police search for the Heartbreak Killer. He didn't want her to talk about that. He found it depressing. He wanted her to talk about things he didn't have to pay attention to, things that wouldn't distract him from the new terror-and-torture fantasy he was creating around her and the damned crystals that reminded him so much of his mother.

Opal had loved bright things, jewelry mostly, though she couldn't afford much of it, especially when she was boozing heavily. When she had a yen for a new sparkly thing and couldn't afford a fake diamond, she'd buy a crystal and hang it on fish line from a nail pounded into the frame of a window of their rented mobile home. When the sun cascaded through it, it would make rainbows all over the walls and floors and ceilings. Over the years, she must have accumulated two hundred crystals, from tiny ones to two or three the size of baseballs. She had dozens hanging at various heights in every window, even in his bedroom. She set the big ones on window ledges to catch the sunlight. She'd hang 'em from the rearview mirror of whatever vehicle she was driving at the time, like the bitch doctor did. Opal had a lot more crystals than fake diamonds, for sure. And he'd come to despise them as symbols of all her wretched excesses.

From the time he was eight or nine, he tried to distance himself from her, hanging out and earning a little pocket money doing odd jobs for a local Mr. Fixit, name of Bud Westerly. When Eugene started work, his assignment was to clean up around Mr. Westerly's shop. But he studied everything the man did and asked a lot of questions. When he got older, Mr. Westerly would let him do some of the locksmith work and appliance fix-ups himself, watching all the time over his shoulder to make sure he got it right. When Eugene learned the electrical side of the business, he began to go out on carpentry and plumbing jobs with his boss, and by the time Eugene was sixteen, he was almost a partner in the business. But he was a partner with a dirty little secret.

During the years he worked for Westerly, he stole tools, one at a time, every so often. Nothing big, and not too much at once. He wanted his boss to think the items had been misplaced, not to suspect he was the victim of organized, selective thieving. He copped a couple of hammers, screwdrivers, wrenches, that sort of thing. He'd been able to snatch whole sets of tension bars and lock picks by taking them a piece at a time. It was legal to own them if you were bonded, but Eugene wasn't. That made him guilty of possession of burglary tools, assuming the cops found out, which they didn't. Not that he cared. Amassing tools gave him a feeling of power and authority. A man who had tools and knew how to use them was a man who could get things done.

When he turned sixteen, he was expelled from school for chronic truancy. It didn't matter to him. When he was in school, he was constantly in trouble for fighting with classmates. He never tried to return. Instead, he moved east, to Polk County, where he lived in a beat-up trailer with a couple of laborers and picked up whatever odd jobs he could. They were a hard-drinking pair, and Rickey suspected they could be dangerous. But anything was better than the situation he left behind. He was certain his mother hated him and just as certain he hated her. He had fantasies about sneaking up on her when she was in one of her drunken stupors and strangling the life from her with his hands.

He was seventeen when he had his first sexual encounter. She had been a prostitute working out of a seedy bar in Bartow, a phosphate-mining town in central Florida. He picked her because he heard she didn't mind rough sex. And he meant to be rough. He paid for a room in a rent-by-the-hour motel and told the hooker he wanted to pretend to rape her. The woman consented. Rickey ripped her clothes off, answering her protests by promising to pay for the damage. After that, the woman threw herself into the role of submissive victim. She enticed Rickey into spanking her breasts and her behind, into taking a few swings at her ass with his belt. It was sheer luck that she hit on exactly the fantasy he wanted from her.

"Who am I?" she asked him as he swatted her. "Who do you see here?"

"Opal," he replied, his face pinched in hatred, his belt landing harder than before. "You're Opal. My mother. A whore and a bitch."

When Rickey got around to taking the prostitute, she blubbered in imaginary pain and pleaded with him not to hurt her anymore.

It was the most glorious experience of Rickey's life. It made him feel manly, and the feeling lasted almost a week. When it began to dissipate, he found the hooker and took her again.

Over the years, his fantasy took on dozens of different variations and levels of violence. Once, in the throes of his ecstasy, he had nearly strangled a prostitute. He escaped being charged with manslaughter only because she had the presence of mind to belt him in the face and break his reverie. Afterward, she took every dollar he had as repayment for his abuse. For months, he kept a tighter rein on himself, purposefully toning down the violence of his sexual encounters.

But somehow, his fantasy of brutalizing his mother was never as vivid as it was on the night of the near strangulation. At least not until he began to kill.

OPAL was dead nearly a year now. Rickey learned of her death only by chance, when he read an article in a local weekly newspaper that his mother's body had been cremated at a local funeral home, and she was about to be buried in a pauper's field. He retrieved her remains, took her ashes back to her mobile home, and scattered them around her trailer. He used his stolen lock picks to let himself inside and took her few possessions, which he figured had rightfully passed to him since she never had anything like a formal will, and he was her only living relative. His acquisitions included the pickup parked outside. He also took all the crystals he had come to hate so much, put them in an old booze carton for a planned burial in a muddy field near Wimauma. That's when he found the knife with the abalone-inlaid handle.

Rickey hadn't thought of the knife in years, not since the carney guy she was living with at the time gave it to her. He was just a kid, then. He remembered how she loved the way the handle shone in bright light.

For a moment, he thought about throwing the knife in the box with the crystals and burying the whole lot. But the knife fit into his new fantasies. It fit beautifully. And there was a cruel irony in his desire to use an object Opal had loved to commit acts of unspeakable violence.

HE fondled the weapon now as he stared at Cynthia Diamond's image on the television screen. Rickey never took his eyes from her; he barely blinked. He cursed when the station cut to commercials, or to reporters in the street, or to weather and sports segments. But she always came back to him, sparkling bright as ever, until the program ended at 6:30.

He was deeply dissatisfied.

A television set was no way to watch her. He had to get closer, to see her in person, to find out where she went and when, who she saw and exactly where she lived, and what her habits were. Because the time would come . . .

Rickey heaved himself up from the sofa, belching bourbon loudly, and retrieved a four-inch portable color television from his bedroom. He rummaged in a drawer in his kitchen until he found enough C-cell batteries to operate it. Then he remembered he had a special plug so he could run the little set from his truck's cigarette lighter. It took ten minutes of rummaging in his tool room to find it. He decided he would take the batteries, too, in case he found himself in a situation where he had to shut off his engine to avoid detection.

He capped his bourbon bottle, still two-thirds full, locked up his house, and headed for his pickup. He was humming his song.

When Cynthia Diamond appeared for the eleven P.M. news, Rickey was watching from his truck in the parking lot of the station. When she emerged from the station at midnight, he was watching again, and scowling. He held the seven-inch Schrade in his right hand and burnished its chipped handle against his erection under the soft cotton of his old blue jeans. The bourbon bottle was in his left hand, now less than half full.

He saw Cynthia glance toward him, but if she noticed a truck parked in the station lot that had never been there before, she gave no indication.

When she pulled her Lexus coupe onto Gandy Boulevard and headed east, Rickey's truck was behind her. He followed her across the South Tampa peninsula, over to Bayshore Boulevard, where she turned north for several miles to the Davis Islands exit. He watched to see if she glanced in her rearview mirror, but it was hard to tell through the dark tint laminated on her car's back window. The short bridge across the water provided the only land access to and from Davis Islands, and he followed her, past Tampa General Hospital, to an impressive home on Riviera Drive facing Hillsborough Bay.

He parked across the street at the curb and killed his engine and headlights. He watched as various lights went on and off inside the house, and he tried to imagine what room she was in and what she was doing. As he fantasized, he continued to let Opal massage his erection.

About fifteen minutes after Cynthia went in through the garage, she came out the front door, dressed casually now in shorts, sandals, and a golf shirt. The shorts were very short, Rickey thought. She was displaying herself for him, the filthy slut.

She did not lock the door behind her, a fact Rickey didn't fail to notice. She was being led by two long-haired dachshunds. They took care of business quickly, obviously in need of the outing, then danced around their mistress seeking praise and edible rewards for their patience and obedience. She was lavish with the praise and head-scratching.

When Cynthia stood up, Rickey saw, she noticed his truck. She stared at it for perhaps five seconds, a look of curiosity on her face. Did it look familiar to her? Or did she think it belonged to someone visiting one of her neighbors? It didn't matter, as long as she saw it. And remembered it.

Then she turned her back and walked up the sidewalk to the front door.

It was the last Rickey saw of Cynthia Diamond that night. But he would return each night from now on, until Opal told him it was time.

It was a perfect beginning.

8

"How the hell many, did you say?" Ben Britton's eyebrows were pinched at the top of his nose, a sign of the stress he was feeling. It didn't help matters that they'd been baby-sitting the bait shop on Twenty-second for a full day without so much as a nibble or, now, that the Hillsborough County Clerk's office had run a computer check on automobile registrations looking for Toyota pickup trucks, any model, any year, as long as they were light-colored or white.

"Two-hundred thirty-nine," Dits O'Brien repeated.

Britton groaned.

"That's not all the bad news, Cap'n," Nick Estevez said as he walked into the room. "The Schrade people got back to us. They have fifty-nine customers in Hillsborough, large and small. Most all of them carry a knife of a size fitting Sampson Jones's description, but the company doesn't make one with an inlaid abalone handle. Never has. So it has to be a custom job. Maybe somebody buys a few knives retail, customizes 'em and sells 'em privately for a jack-up, which means we have to check every outlet for repeat customers. But there might not be a record if he pays cash or comes in so irregularly nobody remembers he's been there before. It's also possible our man only bought the one knife for one custom job. Then we may never find out who he is. Of course, maybe he did lots of knives and there's a retailer out there who knows all about him. We could get lucky that way."

"Or be shit out of it," Britton groaned, rubbing his eyes. "I needed this." He'd been working eighteen-hour days, as had most members of the team. They were haunted by Charlene Bradford's speculation on the brutal turn their killer might take next. And the political pressure, as always in these cases, was becoming unbearable. The mayors of Hillsborough's three incorporated cities, Tampa, Temple Terrace, and Plant City, held a joint news conference and virtually promised the killer would be caught before he could strike again. The County Commission was leaning heavily and publicly on Sheriff Romano, who answered only to the voters, but it was the voters who were leaning on the county commissioners. Even the Florida Highway Patrol was catching crap. The Tampa Bay area was as close to panic as Britton could ever remember.

"Dits, have the clerk's office supply us with a list of truck registrations," Britton ordered.

"It's on its way over now," O'Brien replied.

"When it gets here, feed the data to your computers and generate a map of the addresses where the trucks are registered."

"Will do. Are we gonna check them all?"

"Well, Sampson Jones told us the guy used him because his location was convenient . . ."

"So we're using Sampson's as ground zero and working our way out," Estevez finished.

"That's it," Britton said. "Take every street leading to Twenty-second—there aren't that many—and figure out how many blocks or miles you could go out each one and still think of Sampson's as convenient. That'll give us a perimeter. Every truck inside that perimeter is fair game. If we don't turn something, we'll widen the perimeter."

"You're talking about a whole lot of manpower," O'Brien said.

"It might not be as horrendous a job as it sounds," Britton said. "First off, Jones said the truck didn't have commercial lettering or tape striping on it, so we'll be able to eliminate a lot by simple visual inspection."

"That's still one hell of a lot of trucks," O'Brien added.

"I'm open to suggestions if you have any better ones," Britton said, a bit testily.

O'Brien shook his head.

"I saw a *National Geographic* nature show years ago about salmon in the Northwest," Estevez said. "They jump up fish ladders built into waterfalls to get upstream to spawn. Half of 'em beat themselves to death making the effort. I'm beginning to feel like one of those salmon, beating myself to death. And I haven't had the strength to spawn in weeks."

"Well, we're not going to get up the ladder sitting around beating our jaws about it," Britton said with a yawn. "We've got fifty-nine Schrade knife outlets to check on, and when the truck map is ready, you and I are going to shift gears and focus on it."

"I'll set up a phone crew to start looking for the Schrades," Estevez said, heaving himself out of his chair. "Maybe we'll have made some progress by the time Dits has the map."

He needn't have hurried. The Toyota pickup they were hunting was registered in the name of Calvin Hathaway, the third and last common-law husband to Eugene Rickey's mother. Hathaway, who had a small auto shop in a rural southeast crossroads of Hillsborough County called Fort Lonesome, paid cash for the truck five weeks before he met and took up with Opal. He registered the truck to his garage for the tax benefit. He died a year after he moved into Opal's rented trailer in Gibsonton. She took the truck as her own, and when she died, Eugene took it.

He had no idea where the title was, so he forged a post office document directing that Hathaway's mail be forwarded to Rickey's general delivery address. He renewed the forwarding request every year. In this way he was able, every year, on time, to pay for an emissions test, new tag stickers, and bare-bones insurance for a vehicle that wasn't his.

To the detriment of current police work, the light gray Toyota pickup traveled the roads in the name of an abandoned and rotting auto shop owned by a dead man from Fort Lonesome who had nothing whatsoever to do with the ongoing hunt for a serial killer.

ESTEVEZ rubbed his eyes and got himself another cup of coffee. His stomach was awash in acid. He figured this was maybe his tenth cup of the day, and it was just past two o'clock. He was through half of his share of the list of Schrade dealers in Hillsborough without success. He found none who recalled having a customer who bought seveninchers by the dozen and none who ever heard of anybody customizing the knives. Of course, at eleven stores there was nobody to talk to but clerks who were new to their jobs and knew nothing. Each promised to give his boss a message to call Estevez as soon as possible.

Estevez concentrated first on the outlets closest to Sampson's Bait Shop and worked his way out. When he had no luck around the Port of Tampa, he began going north, toward Carrollwood and Temple Terrace, because Sampson said the one time he noticed, the knife customer drove away from his store headed north. Maybe, Estevez thought, it would change his luck if he went south for awhile, toward Ruskin and Gibsonton and Sun City.

He struck paydirt when he called Henry Haney's Knife and Gun Outlet in Gibsonton.

"Lived here all my life," Haney said over the phone. "Seventy-two years. Had this store through good times and bad forty-nine of those years come December. Fiftieth anniversary next year. Hafta do somethin' special. Maybe a big sale with cake and ice cream and strawberry punch. Got some fresh berries froze I could put in for extra color. Heck, that time of the year, might even be some of the new crop comin' in."

"Mr. Haney," Estevez interrupted, "you said you have a customer who bought a number of seven-inch Schrade knives."

"Said I used to," Haney corrected him. "Never forget a customer. Never. Remember every one for the whole forty-nine years. This fella I'm thinkin' of was with the carney. Seasonal resident here. Customizing knives was his hobby. It's what kept him busy during the winter months. Said he didn't have time to work on knives when the carney was travelin', so he'd store up all his creativity for when the carney closed up and he come home to Gibsonton. Never bought no knives from nobody but me. No, sir."

"A name, Mr. Haney," Estevez said. "I need a name."

"Well, I'm thinkin'," the store owner replied. "That's why I'm ramblin' on like I am, tryin' to recollect a name while I'm talkin'. First name was Edgar. Edgar, ah, Best! Edgar Best."

"Do you know if he's still around?"

"Think he is," Haney said. "Retired now, I believe. Had to quit the carney cause the arthritis stove up his hands too bad to work. Left hand especially. It got swole up somethin' awful when the weather got cold and wet. Had to give up workin' on knives for the same reason."

"You know where I could find him?"

"The phone book, I suppose, son. Ain't nobody in this town got any reason to have an unlisted number. He used to live over on Estelle Avenue. Wouldn't live there myself."

"Why not?" the detective asked.

"Too close to the Alafia River," Haney replied. "Git flooded out twice a year. Ain't worth it."

Estevez thanked the shopkeeper for his help. He checked his East Hillsborough phone directory and found Edgar Best right where Henry Haney said he would be.

Then he checked the list of county registrations of Toyota pickup trucks. There was no Edgar Best on it. Not surprising. A man so crippled with arthritis and as old as Edgar Best wasn't a good candidate to be a serial killer. But he might lead them to one.

Estevez gave the rest of his call list to another detective and told Britton they should run down to Gibsonton.

"This guy customized knives that fit Jerry's supposition about the murder weapon," Estevez said. "I think we should ask him if he ever did one with abalone."

"Are Dutch and Bobby still baby-sitting Sampson's?" Britton asked.

"Don't think so," Estevez replied. "I think they farmed it out to somebody else."

"Then let's take them as backup," Britton said. "This guy Best doesn't fit the profile, but you never know who might be living with him."

EDGAR Best lived on Estelle Avenue east of Route 41 about a quarter-mile south of the Alafia River. He was indeed in danger of some flooding, especially in a storm with high winds out of the west, so the river water got jammed up in its channel and couldn't escape into Hillsborough Bay. That and heavy rain could bring the water level up to flood stage in no more than a few hours. Britton helped evacuate people from the area during the big no-name storm of March 1993. It had been a frightening experience. But the area had recovered fully, and the detectives found Best's modest home without a problem.

Britton pulled up onto the twin ruts of sand that passed for a drive-way and led to nowhere because the house had no garage, not even a carport. No Toyota pickup, either, he noticed. Just a rusting green Dodge Caravan a decade or more old. If the killer was living here, he wasn't around at the moment.

Hale pulled in behind him. By prearrangement, Hale and Brown went around to the back of the house to cut off a possible escape attempt.

Britton walked up the three stained cast-concrete steps of the stoop and knocked on the front door. Estévez stood at the bottom of the steps, ready to back up his partner should it be necessary. Best came to the door on the second knock. He was a man of medium height, and his build could have been described as medium, as well, were it not for the enormous gut hanging over his belt. His eyes were a rheumy brown. His hair was longish and very gray. He appeared not to have shaved for several days.

"Afternoon," he said. "Hep you?"

"Afternoon," Britton replied, flashing his badge. "Are you Edgar Best?"

"I am, sir, but I don't think there's anything you'd be wanting with me. I'm not capable of doin' crime. Been crippled for years." He held out his hands, palms down, for the detective to see. His knuckles were horribly swollen and his fingers extended at odd angles, mangled by the ravages of his arthritis.

"Nobody's accusing you of anything, Mr. Best," Britton said quickly, acknowledging to himself that this man appeared incapable of physically dominating another human being. "Do you live here alone?"

"Yep. Always have."

"We need to talk to you. May we come in?"

"You can. But the place is kind of a mess. Hope you don't mind."

"No, sir," Britton replied, following Best inside.

And a mess it was. The front room, which was as far as the detectives got, contained an old sofa covered in a sea-foam green fabric split at several seams. Padding showed through the holes. A similarly worn brown armchair sat in the center of the room facing a television set tuned to a soap opera but muted. Best made no move to turn it off. A floor lamp stood behind the chair, its cord and the TV's snaking across the floor to the nearest wall outlet. A folding table was pushed up against the wall opposite the television. The surface was covered with old newspapers and dirty dishes. A droplight hung over the table. It had four stalks meant to look like candles with lightbulbs meant to look like candle flames, although one of the stalks was empty. That and the floor lamp were the only lights in the room. The floor was the bare concrete pad on which the house was built, although a small oval rug woven in many colors was laid out in front of the brown chair.

Several items of clothing—a ratty cardigan sweater, an undershirt, a pair of pants, and what appeared to be a pair of rubber wading boots—were scattered around the floor. An old window air conditioner struggled valiantly against the heat and humidity, but was only able to keep the room's atmosphere barely tolerable.

From the front stoop, Estevez contacted Hale and Brown by radio and advised them there appeared to be no danger. Hale said they would wait in the car. The gnats were swarming and driving them crazy. Estevez followed Britton in and closed the front door.

"Why don't you gents sit?" Best suggested, waving toward the sofa. They complied, although somewhat gingerly, unsure whether their combined weight might further split the fabric seams. It didn't.

Best pushed the brown chair around so it faced the sofa. He used his knees, mostly, sparing the stress on his gnarled hands. Britton considered getting up to help, but decided such an offer might be construed as condescending and hurt the old man's pride.

"Mr. Best, I understand you used to do some real nice work customizing knife handles," Britton began.

The old man's face brightened. He was pleased his work was remembered. "Yep, sure did," Best replied. "Mostly Schrades. They weren't so expensive that after I finished workin' on 'em I had to charge an arm and a leg to get back my investment. Good knife, though. Real good knife. Good balance. Good steel."

"Sold a lot of them, did you?"

"Maybe sixty, seventy, over the years. Why?"

"It's a police investigation, sir. I can't really say any more."

"Okay. Say seventy." Best paused and furrowed his brow. "Say, the Schrade people ain't complainin' to the police about me, are they?"

Britton chuckled. "No, sir, not at all. Can you tell me what you did to the knives?"

Best snorted. "Sure I can tell ya. Ain't no state secret," he said. "I did lotsa different things. I'd inlay 'em with pretty stones and shells, and some with wood carvings. I'd do the carvings on thin veneer, lay 'em over the wood handles, and cement 'em down. I was so good you couldn't tell where the handles stopped and my carvings started. It was real fine work. I did ducks and dolphins and bass and whales and sharks and snakes, all sorts of wildlife. Took a lot of time, I'm here to tell you."

"I'll bet it did. Ever do one with abalone?"

Best smiled again, the expression spreading over his face slowly, like a warm memory pulled from the recesses of his mind.

"Only one," he said. "It was for somebody very special to me back then, back before I got older and a hell of a lot wiser."

"Who?"

"Her name was Opal Godfrey back then," Best said. "That was . . .

gosh . . . twenty, no, twenty-five years ago. Hard to believe it's been so long. It was the prettiest shell I ever saw. All green and aqua and blue, and it had gold flecks all through it. I gave her the knife for her birthday. I didn't have any money to do more, but she appreciated it. Said she didn't know how she was gonna use it cause she didn't fish or nothin', but she said if she didn't do anything but look at the pretty handle, it would still give her pleasure. Made me feel good. Opal liked pretty things. She used to keep a lot of glass around her house, the kind makes rainbow patterns on everything when the sun shines through it."

"Crystals?" Britton suggested.

"That's it," said Best. "That's it." He chuckled. "Boy, she had 'em everywhere."

"Do you know where she is now?"

"She's been dead maybe a year now. Drank herself to death I suppose, poor soul."

"Drank herself to death." Britton repeated, taking notes.

"Uh-huh. She was a drunk most all her life. Oh, she could function during the day all right, doin' her waitressing. But come late afternoon, she'd have the bottle out and the bourbon flowing. Her and me together used to get rid of a quart, sometimes a quart-and-a-half of an evening, then hop in the hay. Don't quite know how we ever got around to screwing in that condition, but we did. I can't do it these days—the hard drinking, I mean. Too hard on the system. For that matter, I guess I don't know if I could screw anymore, either."

"Where did she work?"

"Downtown, at the Three-Ring Cafe. You might imagine from the name it was a place that catered to the circus and carney folk who spent the winter here. Opal told me business and tips was good in the winter when the town was full. But when the circus and the carneys went back on the road in the spring, times got hard. That's why she never had much money. She would save what she could during the winter to tide her over during the down times, but it never seemed to be enough, especially when she was drinking her way through a small fortune each week."

"What happened to the knife?" Britton asked.

Best considered the question, then shook his head. "Don't know for certain," he answered. "I guess her son got it, along with her other belongings. Or maybe somebody stole it. Who knows? I never heard nothin' more about it."

Britton felt his heart rate jump. "She had a son?"

"Yep. Pathetic thing, he was, the way she'd ride him all the time."

"What was his name, do you recall?"

Best shook his head. "Nah," he said. "That was twenty-five years ago. And the kid wasn't home much, not that I blame him. I'm sure he didn't want to spend any more time than he had to around his mama."

"Think, Mr. Best," Britton implored. "It's very important. We have to know his name."

The old man shook his head. "I just don't . . . well . . . I guess I do remember she called him Short Stuff, or Shorty. I think she used both at one time or another. They were nicknames, mean nicknames, meant to put him down. I don't think she ever called him by his legal first name, if he even had one, at least not in front of me."

"But the boy's last name was Godfrey?" Britton repeated.

"No," Best said. "She told me she gave him the last name of the man who fathered him. I don't know what the name was. But I know it wasn't Godfrey. For that matter, Opal's last name wasn't Godfrey anymore when she died."

"How so?" Britton asked tightly. He could feel frustration returning.

"Well, let's see if I can put this together. It's been a long time," Best said, scratching thoughtfully at his beard stubble. He held up a badly bent index finger. "There was the first husband, a common-law thing. He was the boy's daddy, and the boy got his name. Like I said, I don't recollect what the name was, if I ever knew." Another gnarled finger popped up. "Fella named Godfrey was her second husband, also common law. It didn't last long. Then I came along." A third finger rose. "Never would let Opal call us man and wife, though. Had a lot to do with why we broke it off. She wanted my name, and I wouldn't give it to her. Didn't want no legal ties during them long summers on the road, if you get my meaning. After me came live-in number four, who consented to be husband number three."

"Was there a wedding with the last guy?" Britton asked hopefully. "Something likely to leave a paper trail?"

"Dunno, but I'd bet not," Best said. "Opal never was much for legal stuff. Or maybe she was never sober enough to care."

"Wonderful," Britton said sarcastically. "I don't suppose you know where we could find husband number three?"

"No clue," Best said. "Got no idea who he was. For that matter, I don't even know for sure he was the last. She mighta had two, three more after him. She went through men 'bout as fast as she went through cases of hooch. I lost touch after her and me broke it off. Dunno what happened to the boy, the poor kid. He could be dead now, too, for all I know."

"You keep referring to him like there was something wrong with him."

"Well, he was an accident, you know? He was a burden and expense she had no use for. She hardly never had no money. She resented having to support him and told him so. I heard her say a coupla times that he was a mistake, and the only reason he was walkin' the earth is she couldn't afford no abortion. She said it right in front of the kid. And she was always puttin' him down because his thing was too small, or at least she claimed it was. She was real nasty about it. Got real profane about it. But then, Opal was always profane when she was drunk. I used to think it was funny and kinda sexy."

"His 'thing'?" Britton asked, not doubting for a moment that he understood the reference.

"His cock, yeah. She'd make him unzip and show himself to people, and then she'd call him Short Stuff or Shorty, and she'd laugh at him and comment on how small he was and how he'd never be successful with women. One time she told him he wasn't even gonna be able to reach a woman with that little thing, let alone fuck anybody with it. She said, "How you gonna capture a woman's heart when you can't even get into her pussy?' Real mean, like. There was one night she told me to unzip and show the kid how a real man is hung. I'm kinda bigger than average, too, so it really made the kid feel humiliated. I wouldn't'a done it if I wasn't drunk at the time. I felt sorry for him."

"Did he ever talk back to her?"

"Oh, yeah, but then she'd whip him, make him drop his pants—briefs, too—and thrash him with his own belt, crisscross his butt with welts. She'd hit him over and over until he pleaded with her to stop, then she'd give him one more big wallop and make him stand up and turn around so I could see his cock. Then she'd make remarks and laugh some more. And if the boy started cryin', she make him bend over and take two more lashes."

"Was he old enough, big enough, to put up a fight?"

"Probly. But he never did, and she said he never would, because he pushed her one night in front of Godfrey, the second husband, the man who lived there right before me. Godfrey apparently pitched a fit, smacked the kid upside the head. When the kid started to cry, Godfrey smacked him again, harder. Opal said she screamed at Godfrey to stop the beating, but she was afraid if she intervened physically, he'd beat the crap outta her, too, cuz they was both too drunk to know what they were doin'. One smack was so hard the kid went flying across the room. Opal said he fell into a table, hit his head on the corner, and blacked out. When the boy came round, Godfrey hauled him to his feet and started smackin' on him some more. To hear Opal tell it, the boy complained about being dizzy for months after that. Then he started gettin' in trouble in school, out on the streets, everywhere. Couldn't control his temper. Flew into a rage at the drop of a hat. Screamed at people. Hit people. Those licks on the head screwed up something in his brain, I guess. Least that's what Opal thought."

"How old was the boy when this was going on?" Britton asked.

"Oh, ten, maybe. I was with Opal in seventy and seventy-one. If the kid is still alive, I'd say he's thirty-four, thirty-five now."

Britton nodded. "And you don't know where he is now?"

"Nope. Don't know anything that happened to him after I split."

"And you never heard her use his given name?"

"Not that I recall."

Britton and Estevez stood, and Britton held out a business card. "I'd appreciate it if you'd think about the kid's name real hard and keep this handy so if you remember anything else, you can call me," he said.

Best took the card by clamping it between the first and middle finger of his right hand. "I don't think there's much more to tell," he said. "But I'll think on it."

When they left the house, Estevez went back to their car while Britton walked to Dutch Hale's. The detective rolled down the driver's-side window.

"Dr. Bradford's gonna have a ball with this one," Britton said, briefly hitting the highlights of the interview with Edgar Best.

"So, we have a sexually and emotionally abused kid who grew up in Gibsonton, no first or last name known, who might have a pretty knife he likes to keep sharp, and his horrible childhood might—or might not—generate a serial-killer personality in later life," Hale summarized. "I guess that's progress over where we were yesterday."

"Damned little," Britton said. "You and Bobby can go back downtown. I'll do a report later. Nick and I are going to see if we can find the trailer park south of town where Opal Godfrey lived and the restaurant where she worked. We're going to talk to everybody in this little burg until we come up with somebody who remembers Opal's kid's name. *Then* we'll be ahead of where we were yesterday."

"I SURELY wouldn't know," the trailer park owner said. "You're talkin' twenty years ago, or more, and I didn't live here then. I bought the place a few months before Opal died. By the way, it was Opal Siefert by then. I'm certain she's gotta be the one you're referrin' to when you ask about Opal Godfrey."

"Siefert?" Britton repeated. "That the name of her last husband?"

"Haw! She never had no real husbands from what I heard," the park owner said. "Just a steady stream of different men she shacked up with. Some of 'em let her take their last names, some didn't. I didn't know any of 'em personally. Last one flew the coop before I got here. But none of 'em was named Siefert, I know that. She told me once she was fed up with men, all men, so she took back her maiden name to get even with all of 'em. That was Siefert. That was the name she was born with, and that's the name she took to her grave."

"You talk to her much?"

"No more than I had to to tell the truth."

"How so?"

"We'd pass a few words when she brought over the rent money. Not much beyond that. She was pretty unpleasant, the way she was drunk all the time. Hardly ever bathed. Had to fumigate the trailer 'fore I could rent it again. To be honest, I didn't even know right away she died. One of the neighbors told me a few weeks after the fact. Said her kid came and sprinkled her ashes around the place and cleaned out her trailer, but I didn't see him. Best for him I didn't. Wouldn't have let him sprinkle nobody's ashes around here without a Health Department permit, and maybe not even then. Gives me the willies when I walk around the place now, like I'm steppin' on somebody."

"So you don't know the son?"

"Wouldn't know him if he walked up and introduced himself. Might check with the neighbor who saw him, though."

Britton started to turn away and stopped.

"What's the address of Opal Siefert's trailer, the address the post office would use?" he asked on a hunch.

"Five twenty-four Barnum Circle," the park owner replied.

"Thanks," Britton said.

He and Estevez split up to interview the new tenant and the neighbors. The tenant was a retiree from Ringling, who planned on living the rest of his years among friends.

"Circus and carney people are different from everybody else, you know?" he told Britton. "Carney people got their own language, and if you don't know it, they could be talkin' 'bout you, and you'd never realize. It's their way of bein' to theirselves. And part of bein' to theirselves is lookin' out for one another. Way crime is today, I figured it would be best to live out my days among people who'd look out for me, who wouldn't turn their backs if somebody was to try to break into my place. We're a close-knit community, but we tend not to trust outsiders, like yourself. Still, I'd probably help you if I could."

"Did you know or ever hear anything about the son of the woman who lived here before you?" Britton asked.

"Nope. I don't know nothin' 'bout no son. Don't know much about the woman, now you mention it, 'cept she was supposed to be a lush, according to the neighbors."

Britton had no better luck with the neighbor lady on the right.

"I remember a younger man bein' here after the old woman died," she said. "Couldn't tell you nothin' 'bout him, though. He loaded her stuff in a pickup an' took off with it. There was clothes, and boxes of stuff, but I couldn't tell you what any of it was. Didn't even know it was her son till sometime later when somebody mentioned it. He got in without bustin' the door down, so I figured it was okay, him bein' there."

"Who mentioned it to you, that he was her son?" Britton asked.

"Old Miz Patrick, who lived in the trailer back yonder," she replied, pointing to a blue double-wide a half block down the road. "Poor ol' soul, passed on 'bout two months ago."

"Damn!" Britton barely breathed the word, but his head and his gut were in a tumult. Each time he got an inkling of a lead, he turned around and it evaporated into a graveyard. He couldn't remember ever being so frustrated.

"Did Miss Patrick ever mention the son's name, by chance?" he asked.

"Uh, no, don't guess I remember her ever calling him by name."

"Could you describe him, or the truck?"

"Truck was gray I think . . . or maybe it was silver, but I don't know the make," said the neighbor. "Actually, it looked a lot like the one she drove herself 'fore she took sick. But maybe not, cause I thought her truck was white. But hey, all them trucks look alike to me. And him? No. Nothin' sticks in my mind particularly. He was dark, like well-tanned, you know? Brown hair maybe, maybe dark blond. Can't be sure. Sorry."

"Did the truck look like it was privately owned or commercial?"

"Don't follow you."

"Did it have signs or logos for a business on it?"

"I don't think so . . . no, at least I don't remember any. But like I said, I really wasn't paying all that close attention."

"I thought you folks looked out for one another down here," Britton chided. "But you say you saw a strange man at a dead neighbor's trailer and didn't notice much?"

"Well, she *was* dead, and somebody had to clean out the place, so I figured he was the one doin' it," she replied defensively. "He wasn't actin' suspicious, skulking around and the like. So I didn't hang around to watch. Wasn't my business." ·

"Do you know anybody who's been in this trailer park for twenty years or more, ma'am, anybody still alive, I mean, who might remember the boy when he lived here?" Britton asked.

"Hmmm, well, old Henry Dash over there might go back that far," she said, pointing to a trailer across the road. "He's in his nineties now, I think, and he's been here a long time."

Britton thanked her and walked toward the trailer she'd indicated. He spotted Estevez, who was working homes farther down the street. They made eye contact, and Britton spread his hands in a silent question. He saw Estevez shake his head and give him a thumbs-down sign. So the grass wasn't greener in the next pasture, after all.

Britton knocked at the front door. There was no response, and he knocked again. He was reasonably certain the old man was home. There was a beat-up tan-and-rust Ford Fairmont from the seventies parked in the carport, and a man in his nineties didn't go very far without wheels.

"Yeah, who is it?" came an angry voice from inside after Britton knocked four times.

"Hillsborough County Sheriff's Office, Mr. Dash," he responded. "I'd like to ask you a couple of questions."

"Well, I ain't got no answers," said the voice from within.

"I think maybe you do, sir. Now open up, Mr. Dash."

"How's I supposed to know you ain't a crook come to kill me?"

"Look through your peephole. I'll hold up my ID."

"Anybody can fake ID."

Britton's exasperation was straining his civility. "It's not fake, Mr. Dash. It comes with a gold shield. Look through your peephole. I'm holding them up for you to see. Now look at 'em, sir, or I'll kick your door in and slap your face with 'em."

"Can't see through the peephole. Eyes ain't as good as they used to be."

Britton dropped his arm and heaved a huge sigh. Beside the stoop, there was a window. "Go to your front window and look out," he said tightly. "I'll stand there holding my identification so you can see it. You understand, sir?"

There was no answer, and Britton hoped the reclusive Henry Dash might be moving toward the window. An old, creased face topped by a shock of white hair appeared inside. Britton held his ID and badge to the window glass so Dash could get a good look. The old man

peered at them intently then turned and left the window. He appeared
to be returning to the door, so Britton did the same.

Moments later, the door opened a crack. Britton could see it was
still secured by a chain lock.

"May I come in, Mr. Dash, or will you come out?" the detective
asked.

"Neither," the old man said. "You want to talk to me, we'll talk like
this."

Britton wondered what the world was coming to when people kept
their doors locked against the police. "How long have you lived in this
trailer park, Mr. Dash?" the detective asked.

There was a pause. "Twenty-seven years, I think," the old man
said, finally. "Don't remember things too good anymore. Moved here
in nineteen sixty-eight or nine, when I retired from the Kothos Carney.
You know it?"

"Can't say I do," Britton replied. "You remember a neighbor name
of Opal Godfrey, or Opal Siefert? She lived across the road."

"I was a traditional old carney barker, I was, for more than forty
years," Dash persisted. "Worked the games before that, for eleven
years. Before that, took care of the animals. Good job, the carney. Better than school. Left school after the fourth grade to run away with
the circus. Ran away with a carney instead. Good thing, for me, too.
Carney took good care of me."

"How old are you, Mr. Dash?"

"Lemme see. Either ninety-two or ninety-three."

"Then you were still a pretty young man when this Opal Godfrey,
or Opal Siefert, was living here with her son," Britton said. "You recall either of them?"

"Both," Dash replied.

"Good," Britton said. "What was the boy's name?"

"Hell, I don't remember!" Dash said. "Too long ago. Wimpy little
kid, anyhow. Never woulda made it in the carney biz. His mother
asked me to day-sit with him for a few weeks while her regular sitter
went outta town, but I wouldn't have nothin' to do with the little shit."

"And who would the regular sitter have been?"

"Virginia Calladay. Lived in the trailer right behind Opal. She'd
probly know the boy's name, but she's dead seven, eight years now."

"That figures," Britton growled. "The child had a couple of nicknames, Short Stuff and Shorty," he said, hoping a prompt would help.

"Well, hell, boy, if you know his name, whatcha askin' me for?"

"I know his *nickname*, Mr. Dash. Do you remember his real name?"

"If his mama was Opal Godfrey, I imagine he was a Godfrey," Dash said. "If his mama was Opal Siefert, he was a Siefert. Would make sense to me."

"His name wasn't Siefert," Britton said. "That was the mother's maiden name. His name wasn't Godfrey, either. Godfrey was the mother's second husband. The first husband was the boy's father. That's the name he was given."

"Hell, from what I've heard, she had so many men in and out of there, wonder if she knew who the father was," Dash said.

Britton stuck his card through the crack in the door. "If you remember anything else, would you call me, Mr. Dash?" he asked.

"I won't remember nothin' else cause I'm not goin' to try," Dash replied. "Now go away and leave me be. I don't want no more questions."

He slammed the door, and Britton heard the sound of two dead bolts sliding into place.

Britton and Estevez walked the streets of Gibsonton for hours, searching for anybody who recalled Opal Godfrey's little boy. They found only one man who did, the owner of the Three-Ring Cafe, the restaurant where Opal waitressed for so many years.

"She took some time off to have the kid, but my recollection is she was back a week later," he said. "I never saw the child myself. She left him with somebody during the day while she worked. Never said much about him, either, though I think I remember hearin' from somebody that he got himself into some mischief growing up. Nothing real serious, mind you, but enough it got him a reputation as a troublemaker. Now I think of it, he was doin' odd jobs for Bud Westerly over at the Fix-It-Up shop. Stayed with him a fair number of years, then disappeared. Old Bud, poor soul, never married and didn't haven't any kids of his own. I think he kept hopin' Opal's boy would come back and take over the business and keep it going. But the kid never came back. I never heard anything about him, either, after he left town."

"And I suppose Bud Westerly's dead," Britton said sourly.

"Might as well be. He's over to a nursing home, Happy Trails, I think it's called, in Apollo Beach. Alzheimer's got him bad."

It was nearly midnight, with most of the town asleep, when the two detectives climbed in their car and headed north for Tampa empty-handed. But they would be in Apollo Beach first thing the next morning.

* * *

BRITTON and Estevez were leaving the Gibsonton restaurant as Cynthia Diamond left the WFSC studios at 11:52.

Eugene Rickey had parked his truck in a dark place on the station lot and had worn dark clothes to make himself all but invisible behind his tinted windows. It turned out to be a good decision, because the truck caught Cynthia's eye, as he hoped it would, and her glance lingered a few seconds. Did she remember it from the night before?

He let her get well out on the road before following. This time he was sure he saw her peer several times at her rearview mirror as they crossed Gandy Boulevard. So he dropped back and let several cars come between them on Bayshore and let her go when she made the turn to her house.

Riviera Drive was shaped like a flat oval. Cynthia lived on the western stretch overlooking the water. He parked on the eastern stretch, doused his lights and engine, and cut quickly through the yards of two darkened houses to get to a vantage point across the street from hers.

He waited only a few minutes before she emerged with her dogs. He saw her take a long look around, up and down the street, before she left the safety of her portico. Apparently satisfied no pickup truck or other unwelcome visitor was lurking about, she let her animals tug her away from the house.

Once again, Rickey noticed, she left the door unlocked.

He stayed in the shadows for another hour, fantasizing about her movement through the house and her activities in each room as lights went on and off. He fantasized being inside with her, of strapping her down to her bed, stripping her . . .

Then the last light died, and he knew she had gone to bed.

He turned to leave.

He had been rubbing Opal in the pocket of his blue jeans and it, in turn, had been rubbing through the denim against his penis. Rickey realized he was breathing very hard. A raging erection was straining against the zipper of his fly, and he knew it would not go away without help.

He jacked off in a stand of pampas grass, taking his time, pretending he was inside Cynthia, hurting her terribly.

The evil in his mind curled his upper lip into a snarl.

And around him, he thought he felt the night air chill.

9

Britton and Estevez were at the Happy Trails Nursing Care Center in Apollo Beach early the next day, too early, in fact, for the patients to be ready for visitors. The director was a stout woman with a graying bun sitting just above the back of her neck—a style Britton hadn't seen since he was in grade school. She invited the detectives into her office for coffee. Her name was Ethel Gleason, and she was powerfully curious.

"My, my, but we're out and about early this morning, aren't we, gentlemen?" Mrs. Gleason said as she settled her bulk into her office chair. "If you'd called ahead, I would have told you not to come before ten. Now, what is it we may do for you?"

"We'd like a chance to talk privately with one of your patients, an Alzheimer's victim, a Mr. Bud Westerly," Britton said.

Mrs. Gleason turned to the computer terminal behind her, called up a file, and put it in a search mode for patients' names. "Westerly. Hmmm. Westerly. No, no Bud is staying here. We have a Harold, however."

"I believe that's his real name," Britton said. "Bud is a nickname."

"Do you have his family's permission?" she asked.

"I was informed he had no family."

"Still, it seems you should have someone's permission. Perhaps if you told me what you wish to see him about . . ."

"We want to know if he remembers the name of a young man who used to work for him a number of years ago."

"And what's this for?"

"It's a police matter," was all Britton would reply. "We can't discuss it, but we won't do anything to upset him."

"Well, if that's all it is, I suppose . . ." Mrs. Gleason began and paused and began again. "But I'll have to be with you."

"No, ma'am, I'm afraid that's not possible. This is official Sheriff's Office business, and it's highly confidential." He added as an afterthought, hoping to shut off discussion, "I can get a court order if I have to."

"It wouldn't be about those awful serial killings, would it?" she pressed, apparently oblivious to Britton's threat. "Mr. Westerly couldn't have had anything to do with those. He never leaves this building unless he goes into the garden for some fresh air, and then a nurse is with him at all times, to prevent him wandering off. Alzheimer's patients do that sometimes."

"I can't discuss what we're here to talk about," Britton maintained. "But if it's any balm to your curiosity, I would tend to agree with you. Mr. Westerly is very probably not a candidate to be a serial killer. In fact, I'd bet a week's salary on it."

After a cup of coffee and small talk, during which Mrs. Gleason tried and failed no fewer than a half-dozen additional times to determine what the detectives wanted with Harold Westerly, a prim woman in a starched white uniform looked in and announced the patient was ready to see visitors but was not very responsive this morning.

Britton and Estevez found Westerly in his room, sitting in an armchair, staring at absolutely nothing. Britton nodded pointedly at Mrs. Gleason to stand aside as he walked in and firmly closed the door. The last look he caught on her face was a deep pout.

Britton sat on the edge of the bed, facing Westerly. Estevez stood by the door.

"Mr. Westerly, my name is Benjamin Britton," the detective said softly. "I'm from the County Sheriff's Office. Can you hear me?"

The old man nodded.

"May I call you, Bud?"

The old man nodded again.

"Well, Bud, I heard you used to be the best fixer-upper in Gibsonton. Is that true?"

There was no response. Britton spoke slowly and carefully.

"Do you remember your repair shop, Bud?"

No response.

"Your shop, Bud. And the young man who used to work for you there?"

Westerly shook his head slightly and frowned.

"Your store, Bud. You used to fix things there, and you'd go out to people's homes and do carpentry and other work."

No response.

"It's how you earned your living. You were in the business for many years. You had a reputation for excellent workmanship."

Westerly nodded slightly.

Britton thought it time to take the plunge. "Bud, do you remember a young man with the nickname Shorty? Or maybe Short Stuff? He went by both names."

For the first time Westerly appeared to focus on Britton, and the detective thought he saw a glimmer of recognition on his face. But as quickly as it came, it was gone.

"Shorty. Do you remember him, Bud?"

Westerly hesitated, then repeated the name, the first word he'd uttered since the detectives arrived. "Shorty," he said softly. "I think I knew a Shorty . . . once. He didn't like people to call him by that name, though." He fell silent again.

Britton, encouraged, tried to prod him gently. "What did he want people to call him, Bud? Do you remember his real name?"

Westerly frowned deeply, and Britton's heart sank when the old man shook his head weakly. But he tried again.

"Who was Shorty, Bud?"

The frown returned, and Bud Westerly sat there in his armchair that way, frowning, his eyes unfocused, saying nothing.

Britton tried once more. His tone was gentle, belying the desperation in his heart and the frustration in his head. "Who's Shorty?"

A frown. Nothing more.

"I don't think he even hears you," Estevez said from the corner.

"He heard me a minute ago," Britton said.

"Looks to me like he's slipped away again," said the detective. "Awful goddamned disease, Alzheimer's. If I get it, I hope my wife has me put to sleep."

Britton looked at Estevez without amusement. "I don't think we do that in this society," he said. "Except to condemned murderers. Sometimes."

"Then I'll find one of those death doctors who'll hook me up to a suicide machine."

"If you get Alzheimer's, you won't be able to remember wanting to do that."

"That's what I said. Awful damned disease." Estevez pointed at Bud Westerly. "If you don't agree with me, look at this poor bastard."

Westerly continued to stare into empty space, the frown now fixed on his face.

Britton watched him for a few seconds and allowed his shoulders to slump. "Damn," he said softly. "Damn." But he tried once more, drawing the words out slowly. "Bud. What was Shorty's real name? . . . Can you tell me Shorty's real name? . . . Please, try to remember . . . Shorty's real name. What was it?"

Nothing.

The detective took a last look at the old man, rose from the bed, and opened the door. Mrs. Gleason was waiting outside.

"Done already?" she asked.

"Done already," Britton said.

"Get what you needed?" she pried.

"Mrs. Gleason, please," Britton said with an edge of impatience. "It's a police matter. And we might be back."

"Well, I'll show you out, then," she replied, bustling off down the hall in a huff.

Back in Bud Westerly's room, the old man continued for several minutes to frown and stare at something only he could see. He leaned forward slightly. Then his lips began to move. "Shorty," he whispered. "His mama called him that. I wouldn't ever call him that. He hated that name. He was Eugene. Gene." A trace of a smile trembled on his lips, and his eyes became dreamy. He repeated the name. "Gene Ri . . . Ri . . . Rickey."

But those who so desperately wanted to hear him were no longer in the building.

DAVID Janacek had the local newspapers spread out around his breakfast in the morning room of the house in Culbreath Isles. He'd made pretty fair progress at reading them, despite Casey's determined efforts to distract him. Fortunately, the eleven-month-old was locked firmly in his high chair. Immobilizing him at mealtime was an exercise in damage control.

"He'll hate us when he grows up," Kirin said, drawing David's attention from his sports pages. "He'll think we called him Casey because we wanted him to be a baseball player or a railroad engineer."

"If he becomes a baseball player, we'll be able to retire. At today's salaries, he'll be able to afford to keep us in the manner to which we've become accustomed," her husband suggested. "Sounds good to me."

"What if he became an engineer?"

"Fine with me," he said. "Nothing wrong with good, honest labor. Don't think your Aunt Louise would approve, however."

"Fuck Aunt Louise," she said with a giggle.

"Thank you, no," he replied. "You're much more my type. And you shouldn't be using those words in front of the baby."

"He probably knows them all already, and he's exercising great self-control not saying them in front of us," Kirin suggested. She brightened. "Hey, he could grow up to be president of the United States."

"Heaven forfend," David replied in mock horror. "Why did you want to have this baby if you're going to exile him into a life of servitude and ridicule? He should do something far more worthwhile than that."

"Being president is worthwhile."

"I hadn't noticed."

At the moment, Casey was transfixed by the discovery that if he hit his oatmeal hard enough with the bowl of his spoon, he could splatter the gooey cereal, and by changing the angle of the spoon, he could change the direction of his salvos.

Kirin reached for her son's weapon. "Down the throat, not on the walls," she said, lifting some cereal on the utensil and shoveling it into the baby's mouth. Casey ate willingly, but clearly he preferred playing.

"Don't you think you're stifling his creativity?" David asked his wife. "Where would Picasso be, where would Salvador Dali be, if their mothers had stopped them the first time they splattered paint on a canvas?"

"Trust me on this: Oatmeal is not a recognized art medium," she replied. "And the kitchen floor is not a canvas."

"Perhaps Casey's finding his own style," he suggested.

"Uh-huh," she said, pushing more cereal into the budding artist's mouth. "I'm sure."

"Well, if you put croutons on the oatmeal, you could say he's entering his cubist phase. Put Smurfs in the bowl, and he'd be in his blue phase. Let him smear it on the shelf of his high chair, well, that's his abstract phase. Or let him find new ways to shoot oatmeal around the room and call it his postmodernist phase."

"You're enjoying yourself this morning, aren't you?" she asked.

"I'm trying to keep you from blocking my son's inner discovery, his search for self, for purpose, for an answer to the question: What is the meaning of life?"

"And you think the meaning of life is *oatmeal?*"

"I don't know," he said with a shrug. "You don't know. I don't want Casey to grow up not knowing, condemned by his mother to eternal ignorance at the age of eleven months. Or worse, growing up and thinking the meaning of life is Cocoa Puffs."

Her cascade of laughter erupted, and he smiled to see it. "I think you've entered your goofy phase," she said.

Her laughter was contagious. No sooner had Kirin started than the baby started, taking his parents' mirth as a signal to pick up the spoon abandoned by Mom and slap once more at the oatmeal. His first volley landed in the middle of his father's English muffin, and Casey shrieked with delight. Kirin chuckled with him.

"You're going to be some handful when you start walking, buddy boy," she whispered.

"That shouldn't be long," David suggested. "I've seen him pull himself up a couple of times lately, on the coffee table, the sofa, in his playpen."

Kirin nodded. "He's actually trying to take steps," she said. "But as soon as he gets out of reach of the furniture, he goes down on his butt. Then he laughs and crawls back to the furniture and tries again. He's stubborn."

"All infants are stubborn," David said. "That's the first rule they learn in womb school."

The shock wave of emotion that slammed into Kirin at that instant made her dizzy, and it was all the more powerful because it was so unexpected. She gasped as though she'd been punched in the stomach.

It wasn't that she'd been able to forget Amy. In point of fact, she thought of the little girl several times every day. Probably she always would. But the wave of grief washing over her at the kitchen table was as coldly intense as the moment she learned her firstborn had died, barely a week old, doomed by a series of birth defects so severe they should have caused a miscarriage early in the pregnancy. Not only had they failed to trigger a miscarriage, they defied medical detection until the fetus was in its seventh month, and by then, Kirin and David wouldn't consider terminating the pregnancy. Whatever life brought them, they decided, they would deal with it, something often easier said than done.

Neither was prepared for the sight of the newborn girl, who looked perfectly healthy to all outward signs, but was so profoundly flawed beneath her pale skin that no amount of surgical skill could have corrected her problems and saved her life. For seven days, Amy held on tenaciously in infant intensive care, so beautiful but so frail, her body pitiably wrapped in tubes and dwarfed by cribside monitors. Although they knew the inevitable outcome, Kirin and David lost their hearts to her, and their hearts were broken, almost irretrievably, when their child lost her fight to stay alive.

For a time, Kirin was helpless in her grief, rarely leaving her bed, and David was incapable of comforting her for he was inconsolable himself. They actually questioned whether they would ever again attempt to have a child.

A month passed before Kirin could return to her work. And even then, she couldn't completely shut out the horror of losing Amy. It would hit her at odd hours, in the middle of business conferences, while she was alone with her designs, when she was on the phone. Her partners, employees, and clients accepted these moments as inevitable, giving her the space and time she needed to heal.

Finally, she was able to force her torment into the background, replacing it with an obsession to complete the plans for her greatest architectural achievement, Water Street Plaza, a state-of-the-art office complex harborside in downtown Tampa. The twin ice-blue-and-marble towers were the most expensive commercial space in the city, yet businesses were falling all over themselves to lease offices there even before the plans were finished. The view alone was worth an extra twenty to forty dollars a square foot.

Offices on the north side of the buildings had an exquisite panorama of the modern Tampa skyline, bristling with high-rises. Yet those were the cheap seats. The best view was to the south, across Garrison Channel to Harbor Island, an exclusive development of private homes and condominiums, and beyond, to the briny waters of Tampa Bay and the Gulf of Mexico.

A little to the west, across Seddon Channel from Harbor Island, was Davis Islands, another expensive residential enclave boasting Tampa General Hospital at its northern tip and a small airport and seaplane basin at the south end. Farther to the west was the South Tampa peninsula and MacDill Air Force Base. The view to the east was the bustling Port of Tampa, with its beautiful new aquarium, the assorted tankers and freighters coming and going every day, along with massive white cruise ships whose very appearances promised the most elegant of vacations.

When ground was broken eighteen months after planning began, and the twin towers began to rise from sand, Kirin couldn't stay off the site. She often beat the first construction workers there in the morning and sometimes stayed after the last of them had gone home at night. She was acting as her own general contractor and oversaw every aspect of the project, including many in which architects rarely get involved.

Water Street Plaza was Kirin Janacek's new baby, and she was adamant that this one would be born perfect and thrive.

But ironically, as work on the west tower neared completion, a confounding problem developed. It wasn't fatal, but it was disturbing because there was no obvious explanation for it. The large, ice-blue plate glass windows on the building's south side developed a tendency to explode from their mountings and fall in shards to the ground. Miraculously, no one had been hurt, but neither had anyone been able to figure out how to resolve the situation.

This morning, the mention of Casey's tenacity triggered a thought about the persistent problems at WestWater and then a memory of a stubborn baby losing her fight for life. That thought dissolved into palpable grief. Kirin had no defense against the abrupt change in her mood, or the intensity of her feelings; the tears simply came in a flood, unexpected, unbidden, and quite unstoppable.

David immediately recognized her reaction for what it was. Without hesitation or question, he went to his wife and held her, allowing her to vent her anguish without recrimination. Wordlessly, he stroked her hair and held her head in the hollow of his shoulder.

In his high chair, Casey fell strangely silent as he looked up at his parents, a faint expression of concern on his face.

He'd been conceived two years and four months after his sister's death. His parents hadn't meant for it to happen, and Kirin was terrified. She thought she would not survive a repetition of the events that snatched Amy from them. Tentatively, she suggested an abortion, but David's Catholic roots and his overriding desire for a family combined to help him stand against the idea. He convinced Kirin that in the absence of any logical or medical reason for such drastic action it would be a mistake they would long live to regret. The doctors swore that what happened to Amy wasn't genetic; it was random chance. There was no reason to think it would ever happen again. So the pregnancy continued, closely monitored.

It was a classic pregnancy, despite Kirin's anxieties, and culminated in the birth of a baby boy as acutely robust as his sister had been sick. The joy Casey brought to the Janacek home went a long way to supplant the pain of the past, except for those inexplicable moments, like this, when the past rose up in the shadows of Kirin's mind and assaulted her.

"I'm sorry," she said as control slowly returned. "I don't know why it happens to me. You'd think after four years..."

"Shhhh," he replied, continuing to stroke her hair. "Don't apologize. You have nothing to apologize for. It's all right that it happened today, and it will be all right if it happens again next week, or next year, or twenty-five years from now."

She pushed away from him and kissed him softly on the cheek.

"You know, Aunt Louise is so wrong about you," she said. "You're the best thing that ever happened to this family, to me."

He held her at arms' length and bowed his head in acknowledgment. "Thank you, ma'am. You going to be okay now?"

She brushed away the stray tears on her cheeks and nodded.

He glanced at the kitchen clock. "Then shouldn't you be getting ready for work?"

"I'm going in late this morning, remember?" she said. "The contractor we hired to do the new pantry is coming today."

He groaned. "So we're going to be shut out of our own kitchen for the next two months? Kiri, do we have to do this?"

"Yes, we do. And no, we're not. I do need the pantry space, sweetheart, and the work shouldn't bother us for very long. He's going to hang sheets of heavy plastic between the morning room and the kitchen when he's doing the dusty stuff, and he said he'd put up a temporary wall when he's working on the outside of the house so the flying and crawling things can't get in."

"Not to mention the heat and the rain," he said. "Do you really want to go through with this? The house is already too big for the three of us."

"We've had this conversation before," she said. "If it were only a matter of everyday living, I'd agree with you. Because of the friends we have and clients we have, we need a house like this to entertain properly, and that means enlarging the pantry."

"How often do we entertain?" he asked in exasperation. "Once every other month? We could rent a restaurant, we could rent the best restaurant in town, for God's sake, for what it takes to keep this place up and keep the improvements flowing. We don't *need* a bigger pantry. We don't *need* this big a house."

"This should be the last improvement," she said. Then she smiled sheepishly. "I promise."

"I sincerely hope so," he said with a shrug of capitulation. "I don't want to come home to any more projects."

"I said, I promise," she repeated.

"Okay. So what do you think of the contractor?"

"I liked him the two times I talked to him. He seems to know what he's doing. He's honest. He isn't exorbitantly expensive. And Mack told you he did excellent work."

"Probably saved them from a house fire, too, according to Mack. Found their wiring hooked up wrong and fixed it at his cost."

"That speaks well of his character," she said.

"And his business sense," David added. "It got him a recommendation for this job."

The doorbell rang.

"That's him," David said. "I'd like to hang out and gab with him . . ."

"I know," Kirin said. "Court beckons. Could you let him in while I get Casey cleaned up and out of the chair?"

"I can and will," he said. He took a long pull at his coffee mug and picked up the oatmeal-smeared English muffin. He looked at it a moment, wrinkled his nose, and set it down. "Maybe not," he thought aloud.

At the front door he was greeted by an intense-looking man in his midthirties. The contractor smiled cordially, extended his right hand, and introduced himself. "Good morning, Mr. Janacek, I'm Eugene Rickey."

SIXTEEN hours later, Rickey was sitting in his truck next to the chain-link fence guarding the forest of satellite dishes outside the studios on Gandy Boulevard from which Cynthia Diamond would emerge after the eleven o'clock news. The day had been busy.

He'd gone over the plans for the kitchen expansion with Kirin Janacek, and they had come to terms. It struck him as ironic that his daytime client was the woman who created Water Street Plaza, while the subject of his nighttime attention lived on Davis Islands, in the shadow of that very project.

Rickey had no trouble dividing his two lives, since he'd had a lot of practice. Like most serial killers, he led a normal life by day and became a deadly stalker by night. The metamorphosis in this case occurred when he grabbed a bourbon bottle and settled in front of the television in his living room as Cynthia Diamond began glittering up the six o'clock news. Later, as was becoming his habit, he took his bottle, got into his truck, and drove to the studio. He watched the eleven o'clock news on his portable television in the cab, then waited in the dark until she came out.

His plan was to ratchet up the chase a notch tonight. He would follow her out of the studio lot onto Gandy Boulevard and make certain she saw his truck. Then he would let her drive east to Bayshore Boulevard alone while he cut off on the Crosstown Expressway. He would race north and east and be in position at her house when she arrived from the other direction, so she wouldn't know if the gray truck parked across the street was the same one she'd seen on Gandy. Nor would she know if it was the same one that was parked across the street from her house two nights earlier.

Tomorrow night, he would vary the game again.

He loved the plan. His other victims knew no fear until, at most, forty minutes before they died. He would stretch out Cynthia Diamond's confusion until it became abject terror, until she was crazy with fear, until Opal told him it was time to move in and make the kill. It could go on for days. Or weeks.

Or Opal might decide it was time to move tomorrow.

DETECTIVE Lieutenant Ditmer O'Brien rubbed his eyes, burning from a night of reviewing computer printouts under the harsh glare of his desk lamp. He thought there had to be something he was missing, some piece of evidence so obscure he'd either forgotten about it or overlooked it. But he found nothing. The killer left no clues other than the ones he almost certainly couldn't hide, like blood type, DNA, and hair color, all knowable through his semen and pubic hair samples taken from the victim's bodies.

O'Brien kept returning to the nicknames, Shorty or Short Stuff, the gray or silver or white, or maybe light blue, Toyota pickup truck, and the knife, the seven-inch Schrade with the custom-made, abalone handle of many colors. They ought to tell the public about the nicknames and the truck and the knife. They always held back details only the real killer would know, details he would be asked to give up when he was caught to confirm authorities had the right man. But he thought they were withholding too much.

The decision about what to make public usually swung on the question of what the public needed to know for its own safety, and what might lead a citizen to recognize a friend or a neighbor as a suspect. So it was the MAIT task force quickly confirmed Marilyn Erlich was the serial killer's seventh victim. The task force also disclosed the strong evidence suggesting the killer had begun preying on more educated, upscale victims, to alert local women to watch carefully for repeated sightings or attention from men they didn't know and to report those sightings promptly.

But O'Brien believed, as they all did, that somewhere out in Hillsborough County was at least one woman who thought of herself as invulnerable, and who also happened to be exactly the type to trigger Shorty's fantasies.

They had to find him before he found her.

At midnight, O'Brien slammed his three-ring notebook closed and turned off his desk lamp. Three hours earlier, at the last MAIT meeting of the day, he had made his case for asking the question openly: Does anyone out there know a man with the nickname Shorty, or Short Stuff, who drives a light-colored Toyota pickup and owns a very special knife?

O'Brien could not have imagined that Britton would say no, or that Britton would come to think days later it was one of the worst decisions of his career.

10

It was eleven o'clock in the morning, and it was the devil's own definition of sweltering in west central Florida. The temperature already was lurking in the midnineties, unusually high morning readings, even for August. Ninety-three, ninety-four was generally as hot as it got in the afternoon, but forecasters said today the mercury would hammer ninety-nine for certain, and possibly top out at one hundred.

The higher the air temperature, the more moisture the atmosphere sucked up, which could save you a lot of money on steam baths, if you didn't mind taking steam baths dressed in business clothes. The humidity passed unbearable about daybreak and was streaking toward unspeakable. Huge thunderstorms with intense lightning, fierce winds, and hail were a virtual certainty toward sunset and into the evening. They would cool the air down a bit. But sunset was still eight hours off, and Cynthia Diamond thought the city and its residents might melt before then.

Lee Townsend assigned her to do a stand-up at a carnival on the campus of the University of South Florida. It was sponsored by several local service clubs, with the proceeds going to youth organizations all over Hillsborough County. Cynthia was grateful for the chance to go, even to a no-brain assignment like that, because it would keep her out of the center city, where the buildings and streets soaked up the heat and hurled it back with a ferocity that could knock the breath from anyone unlucky enough to be caught outside. There were several assignments on the daybook with outside locales downtown, and Cynthia was grateful for the chance to avoid them. USF had lots of grass and trees. If it wasn't cooler, at least it felt so.

When she and her crew arrived on campus, they surveyed possible spots for a story and settled on Wildman's Spook-Filled Fun House. It would make an entertaining story, Cynthia thought, if she wandered through the maze of crazy mirrors and fright gags by herself with a remote microphone and pretended to be scared and bewildered by it all. Then she could go through a second time with her camera and sound technicians and some kids who, she would say, were there to guide her and protect her from the monsters. And if the piece didn't turn out to be amusing, well, tough. Wildman's Spook-Filled Fun House was the only air-conditioned attraction at the carnival. That made it the only reasonable place to be.

Her soundman, Dick Tyler, set her up with a small remote mike clipped to her lapel, while her cameraman, Mark Munoz, scouted up some children to go through with her when she made the second trip.

The carnival sponsors cleared the attraction of other visitors temporarily to give the channel seven crew a chance to do its thing. Word spread that WFSC was on the carnival grounds, and a crowd gathered to watch, laughing and joking and generally getting a kick out of seeing a local television celebrity at work.

One man was taking matters more seriously. He, too, was getting a kick out of seeing the celebrity, but for entirely different reasons. Eugene Rickey had seen a teaser on the early morning news that Cynthia would be reporting from the carnival. Opal told him to check it out and go with his instincts. If the opportunity presented itself, he should crank up the pressure. So he called the Janaceks and told them he had to take a few hours to check some supplies for their project. He pledged to be at their home shortly after lunch. Then he made his way to the campus of the University of South Florida.

While others in the crowd watched the television crew prepare, Rickey slipped away, careful not to be seen, and slid into the fun house through the unguarded rear passageway usually used by those who had negotiated the maze and were coming out. Despite the midsummer heat, Rickey wore black pants, an overly large black T-shirt, and his heavy leather work boots with steel-reinforced toes. Once inside, he slid his fingers beneath his shirt. His lip curled slightly when his hand closed around the black ski mask tucked securely in the waist of his pants. He slipped the mask on and began working his way backward through the mirrors, knowing that very shortly he would meet Cynthia coming from the opposite direction.

Alone.

*   *   *

"CAN you hear me, Dick? How's the sound level?" Cynthia asked her soundman, leaning her head down toward the lapel of her rhinestone-studded dress where the wireless mike was attached by a small clip. She was about ten steps inside the maze.

"You're loud and clear, and the level's good," Tyler replied, yelling so she could hear him through the building's prefab walls.

"Okay, I'm on my way," Cynthia said.

She rounded a corner and sucked in her breath as her heart rate jumped into the aerobic range. Standing in front of her, reaching for her with slime-dripping gloved hands, was the most evil-looking clown she'd ever seen. She was reminded of Stephen King's horrific Pennywise in *It*, the only novel she could ever remember giving her nightmares. This creature was dressed entirely in bloodred clothing, except for its white gloves oozing half-congealed green mucus that steamed and sizzled when it hit the floor, as though it were eating its way through. The clown was wearing a bloodred jester's hat with bells that made a hollow, deathly rattle. The creature was done up in white face, and above his hugely grinning mouth, lifelike black eyes stared wide and glassy and humorless . . . utterly mad.

"Oh, gosh," Cynthia said with an embarrassed laugh. "This is enough to scare a lot of kids, let alone giving me the heebies for a week."

Slowly the mechanical clown backed into its hole in the wall, leaving with a high, metallic laugh as chilling as the first sight of him. Cynthia took three more steps into an open room and was greeted by the first vista of multiple misshapen images of herself.

"It would be kind of lonely in here if there weren't so many of me to keep me company," she quipped for the microphone.

It was then Cynthia realized how silent it had become. She couldn't hear any noises from outside at all, no barkers barking, no kids laughing, no music. It was downright spooky.

"Ouch!" she grunted as she walked smack into a mirror. It had looked like an opening in the maze. "Somebody could get really lost in here. Dick, I hope you can still hear me."

If the soundman answered, she couldn't make it out. There was no reason he should lose her signal, though, so she plunged on—right into the range of nine attacking snakes, each at least six feet long and fourteen inches around. They came to "life" when they were illuminated in a spot where there had been nothing but darkness seconds earlier. They hissed and flicked their forked tongues. They slithered along the ground and from the branches of trees that looked very real. They slid along her legs and shoulders. One even nuzzled in her hair. For several seconds, she stood frozen in place, unable to bring herself to move, so convincingly real were the creatures. She knew intellectually she was in no danger, that it was all mechanical fakery, but it didn't help. Each time she turned, there was another giant snake at her feet or in her face. A large green one with red eyes brushed her cheek with its tongue. She could feel panic growing, threatening again to overtake common sense. Modern technology made these horrors hugely more realistic than she remembered them as a child.

"Oh, ugh. Yuck," she said with a conviction that sounded as though she meant it, which, if truth be known, she did. "I'm not sure this is much fun if you're over twelve. I'd really like to get out of here."

The snakes retreated, and she found her way through several more halls of mirrors reflecting goofy images, like the Hubbell space telescope before it was fixed. A swarm of bats zoomed at her from the recesses of an eerie fake cave. As they swooped and darted, a few hit her back and head and the wing of one slapped her face. She described for the microphone what was happening and said she felt like Tippi Hedrin in the Alfred Hitchcock movie, *The Birds,* except there was no telephone booth nearby in which she could find temporary shelter. Eventually, she plunged on and stepped through an archway into the heart of the maze.

Her gasp echoed in the circular, vaulted room. The mirrors on every side distorted her image in bizarre, grotesque, frightening ways. One of them froze her for several moments; it made her appear to be melting. She made a mental note to ask the amusement's operator how mirrors were made to do that. The "why" was obvious. It was scary as all getout, building as it did on the fright gauntlet she'd already run and because she was beginning to feel isolated and out of touch.

What was that?

It sounded like shuffling feet. Or maybe it was another fright surprise coming to life.

"Mark, is that you?" she called out tentatively. "Dick? . . . Who's there?"

Suddenly her heart was pounding.

"Come on, guys, this isn't funny. Where are you?"

And then, in a mirror that bent her image in seven different directions, she glimpsed a dark figure, someone all in black, standing behind her.

She whirled, but there was no one there. If it was a gag, it was a damned good one. Too good. Too terrifying.

There! In the mirror where human forms appeared elongated and lumpy, she saw him behind her again. He was wearing black pants, a black T-shirt, and a black ski mask. He emitted a low growl from deep in the back of his throat. He sounded like a wild animal.

Panicked now, she turned again, and again he was gone. Desperately, she told herself it was a joke, part of the exhibit. And she desperately wanted to believe it. But she didn't.

She tried to swallow, but couldn't get saliva past her newly parched throat. She felt light-headed and slightly dizzy. Her eyes darted from mirror to mirror, but she couldn't find him. She was standing in the middle of the hall, completely open to his attack, if an attack were intended. Despite the cool brush of conditioned air against her face, she felt perspiration moisten her forehead and upper lip. The biggest chill in the room had just surged down her spine.

"Please, who are you?" she said in a voice that wouldn't reach much above a whisper. "What do you want with me? . . . Mark, where are you? Please, I need hel—"

Someone grabbed and immobilized her from behind, so suddenly she had no time to recognize he was there, so completely she hadn't even a split second to try to fight him off. He wrapped one arm around her, crushing her breasts, pinning her back against his chest, and jamming her arms at her sides. A hand covered her mouth, tightly enough to cause discomfort and effectively sealing off her ability to speak or call out. As an afterthought she tried to struggle, but she might as well have been fighting steel restraints. Her captor ripped the mike from her lapel and threw it into a far corner of the room. He had to remove his hand from her mouth to do it, but he was cat-quick and able to mute her again before she could scream. He jerked her head back so her right ear was close to his mouth.

"I'm here for you," he said in a menacing, guttural whisper she strained to understand. His voice was icy cold and palpably menacing. "We have business to attend to together, Cynthia, intimate business." He underscored his intentions by increasing the pressure against her chest enough to make her moan. "Your tits are hard for me, Cynthia. I knew they would be." He moved his arm around in a motion that kneaded her breasts viciously. She moaned again, in obvious pain, and tried to shrink from him. The pressure relented.

His hand slid down the front of her dress to her crotch. He pressed with incredibly strong fingers, trying to force the fabric to fold inward between her legs, but she resisted him by holding her thighs together tightly. He kicked the inside of her right ankle with a heavy, reinforced boot. The shock rippled along the nerves in her leg. She uttered a muffled cry and moved her leg enough for his hand to find its target. His fingers pressed upward with incredible power, the pressure causing her serious pain through several layers of clothing. She became light-headed again and felt herself sag. At the same time, she felt him press into her from behind and grind himself against her, his erection easily discernible through his clothing and hers.

"You're mine, bitch!" he hissed at her. "You need to be stripped and whipped and hurt real bad. And I'm the one who's gonna do that for you."

She heard herself whimper.

"You want it," he taunted. "I know how bad you want it. You can't wait to have me hurt you, to have me stuff myself inside you and make you scream. And you're gonna get it—soon. Not today, but soon."

At that instant, they both heard someone approaching, calling her name.

"Cynthia? Where are you?" It was Mark. He sounded alarmed. "We lost your audio after you said you needed help. Talk to us. Help us follow your voice."

Her captor eased the pressure between her legs.

"I'll be back for you, Cynthia," he promised in the same guttural whisper. The sound of it made her skin crawl. "You won't know where. You won't know when. But I will be back. Wait for me. And remember what I told you would happen to you when I return."

He released her then, and in the mirror across the hall, she saw him turn and head for the rear of the maze, toward the building's exit. In the blackness of the tunnel, he disappeared like vapor in a high wind.

MARK Munoz called 911, and both the university police and the Hillsborough Sheriff's Office responded quickly.

The operator of the fun house insisted on calling a doctor when he heard Cynthia's description of the way the intruder manhandled her. He offered to pay whatever medical bills there were. What he didn't want to have to pay were lawyer fees. His potential liability in this situation scared the bejezus out of him. The rear exit, obviously the way the intruder got into the maze and left it, was supposed to be manned at all times to make sure no kids sneaked in without paying. But the guard left his post to watch the television crew, which in turn left the operator with potentially big legal trouble. However, Cynthia assured him she was fine. She assured him she would see her own doctor if she came to think she'd been injured. The paramedic who responded with the SO said she appeared unharmed except for some

bruising and an elevated blood pressure, which, under the circumstance, was to be expected.

Ben Britton was notified as a matter of routine of the call from the
university and rolled on it, too. Any case of a woman attacked by a
stranger had the potential to be another piece of his puzzle. While
Cynthia was being checked by the paramedic, Britton talked to the
cameraman and the sound technician. They had already been interviewed by a school cop and the two sheriff's deputies who caught the
911 call, but Britton was part of the serial-killer task force and had to
interview them in that context.

"You think this mighta been that guy?" Munoz asked.

"I don't know," Britton replied truthfully. "It's not the way he's
worked before, but I've got to check out all the possibilities. I hate to
ask you to repeat your stories, but it's necessary."

"Yeah, sure, I got no problem with it," Dick Tyler said. "I tell ya, it
was really eerie when I heard her get scared. I don't mean scared of
the ghouls and goblins. I mean really scared, ya know? There's a big
difference. I had the headphones on, so I could hear what she was saying and keep the sound level right. At first, she was talking about the
maze and the scary things that jumped out at her, and then all of a
sudden she freaked. She called out for Mark and me a coupla times.
Then there was this loud pop and rattle—turns out that's when the
guy ripped off her mike and threw it away—and I didn't hear nothin'
else. Man, I didn't know which way to shit. Oops, sorry. I'm nervous
is all."

"I understand," Britton said with a smile. He turned to Munoz. "At
what point did the two of you actually enter the maze?"

"Soon as Dick heard her callin' our names, like somethin' scared her
for real. I told the operator to shut down the mechanical stuff and give
us enough light to find our way to where she was. Then we went in
after her."

"So you didn't see anybody inside the maze?"

"Nobody but Cynthia."

"Did either of you see anybody suspicious hanging around the
maze or coming out of it after you brought Cynthia out?" he asked.

"No," the soundman said. "I heard somebody say the guy mighta
went out the back, so he probably kept goin' straight down to the midway over there and lost himself in the crowd."

"Okay, gentlemen, thank you. The other detectives know how to
reach you, so I can get your numbers if I need to get back in touch. I
presume they've already requested that you turn over the audiotape?"

"They asked, yeah," Tyler confirmed. "Course I don't have the authority to give it up. But soon as we're done, I'll call the station from the van and start the request through channels. I don't expect there'll be a problem."

Britton drifted over near the two case deputies, who had just begun the interview with Cynthia Diamond. Thirty yards away, he saw university police holding back a growing number of print and broadcast reporters who, like Britton himself, had responded to the assault call on the sheriff's radio frequencies.

"How are you feeling?" one deputy asked Cynthia.

She sighed and attempted a smile. She didn't quite pull it off. "I'll be fine," she said. "I'm scared half to death, but he didn't do any serious damage."

"He threatened you?" the detective asked.

"Yes. He said he was my worst nightmare. He said he'd be back for me. And he, uh, he threatened to rape me."

"Can you tell us what happened, from the beginning, please?"

Cynthia did the best she could to recapture the incident, reconstructing it fairly well, although she didn't recall every word he had said. She described his clothes accurately. But she estimated his height at nearly six feet, an exaggeration victims often make as their imaginations inflate the memories of their assailants' proportions.

"Was there anything about him familiar to you?" the detective asked. "Anything that makes you think maybe you know him from somewhere?"

"No," she replied with a shudder. "Nothing."

"Is there anything about him you'd recognize if you saw or heard him again?"

"No, I don't think so. Just the voice, like I described it to you. But I don't think it's his real voice. It sounded strained, like he was trying to disguise it. He talked in sort of a hoarse growl. If frightening me was what he had in mind, he succeeded completely."

The detectives asked several more questions, uninterrupted by Britton, then excused themselves after extracting a promise that Cynthia would call them if she remembered anything else. They nodded toward Britton, recognizing him and why he was there, and left. Only then did the captain approach the television anchor, who was slumped in a borrowed chair. She looked to be under serious strain. He introduced himself.

"I think we've met before, Captain," she said. "But I don't recall the circumstances."

"We have, a few times," he confirmed, "but I don't recall when, either. Other murder investigations, no doubt."

She was studying him. "You're the head of the Heartbreak Killer task force now, aren't you?" she asked.

"Yes."

"Is that why you're here?"

"Yes."

"You think that's the man who attacked me?"

"That's what I'm trying to find out," Britton replied truthfully. "If you feel up to a few more questions, I'd like to get a little more specific than my colleagues."

"Sure," she said, almost eagerly.

"Did he have a weapon?"

Her brow furrowed as she considered the question. "You know, I don't think so," she said after a moment. "At least not one I saw. He grabbed me around the body with his right arm, and he had his left hand over my mouth. If he had a weapon, he must have kept it hidden."

"I know you didn't see his face, couldn't see his face, but did you get any impression of what his age might be?"

"Oh, gosh, young I suppose," she said quickly. "He was very strong. I doubt he was one of our old geezer retirees."

"Twenties? Thirties? Forties? Older?" Britton prompted.

"Toward the younger end, I think," she said. "His hand, the one he had over my mouth, was very hard, maybe callused, like someone who works at hard physical labor. That would explain his strength, too. I've never felt the kind of pain he caused when he forced his hand between my legs. He had to be really strong to hurt me that much."

Britton nodded. "Are you sure you're not injured?" he asked.

"I'm sure," Cynthia said. "I wish I could be more help, but I don't have a good sense of his age or his hair color or anything. I'm really sorry."

"That's okay," Britton assured her. "You're doing fine. One last question. You said he threatened to rape you?" She nodded. "Did he mention touching or harming any specific parts of your body? Like your arm or your leg, or maybe something internal?"

"You mean like my heart?" she asked. "It's common knowledge that your serial killer stabs his victims' hearts after they're dead."

"I can't confirm it," Britton said. "But if he said anything about what he planned to do to you, it might be helpful."

"He said he was going to stuff himself inside me. He also said he would strip me and whip me and hurt me real bad. And that's a quote."

"Whip you?"

"That's what he said."

"Okay, Miss Diamond. I think you've had all you need of this today. You want me to get somebody to drive you home?"

"Thanks just the same, but I'll ride back to the studio with the crew," she said. "I'm feeling better, and there's a day's work to do."

"Are you sure?" he asked. "An assault like this, you could get a little shocky later."

"Well, I won't be alone, and if I get to feeling ill, I'll go home," she said. "From what I just told you, does it sound like the man who attacked me is the serial killer?"

"No," Britton said with conviction. "He doesn't fit the pattern. For one thing, the Heartbreak Killer hasn't whipped any of his victims. But that doesn't mean the man who assaulted you isn't dangerous. I'd take some serious precautions if I were you."

"Oh, he was probably just somebody in the crowd who recognized me and decided on the spur of the moment to have a little sick sport with me. Everybody heard me say I was going into the maze alone."

"But everybody doesn't carry around a black ski mask in the middle of a Florida summer," Britton replied.

He thought he saw the blood drain from her face.

11

"So what have you got, Nick?" Ben Britton entered the MAIT command room, and the room grew quiet. For the detectives at work there, Britton's entrance focused all reality into the single, confounding mystery before them. It wasn't that they feared him—he had made it clear any number of times he knew they were doing their best—but he was their leader, and the lines of strain etched on his face were tangible reminders of their lack of progress. At that moment, their icy sense of failure was palpable.

Nick Estevez sat at a desk with his head cradled in his hands. Britton put a hand on the detective's right shoulder. "Anything?" he asked, knowing the question was rhetorical. If Estevez had anything, he'd be running around shouting about it.

Estevez let his hands fall to the desk. His dark complexion reflected his Spanish and Italian bloodlines, although, in Tampa, the combination wasn't considered a mixed heritage; Spanish and Italians alike called themselves Latins, and a comingling of the two ancestries was considered to change nothing and enrich both. On the streets of Ybor City and West Tampa, trilingual families were common, although some refused to use their English unless it was absolutely necessary. Estevez was trilingual, in fact. He didn't consider it a feat of any proportion; it was simply the way he grew up. At the moment, he gladly would have traded one of his languages for a month's worth of lost sleep. His normally deep olive complexion was shaded in the gray of fatigue.

"Nothing," the detective said. "Absolutely nothing." He turned in his chair and looked up at Britton. "You know, Captain, if I thought this guy was this smart, I'd flat quit the force. Quit. Walk out. I'd concede we're never gonna bust him." Estevez sighed. "He isn't smart, though. Hasn't ever been a smart serial killer I know of. Oh, brilliant killers, sure. Ted Bundy was brilliant. But not smart. This guy's not smart, either. But I'll tell you, he might be the luckiest sombitch ever walked this earth."

"I take it you're not having any luck with the trucks," Britton assumed quietly. "I don't suppose there are many light-colored pickups registered in the name of Shorty."

"Actually," Estevez said with a sigh, "there is one. Registered to a Shorty Powell, who lives in Hunter's Green."

"Didn't know they allowed pickup trucks in Hunter's Green," Britton said. "Just cars with stickers over $30,000."

"Well, they let Shorty in, and we checked the heck out of him," Estevez said. "Pillar of the community. School administrator. Wife. Three kids. Wife drives a Taurus wagon."

"Forget the references. Does he have alibis?"

"We checked his calendar on the dates of the Cipriano, Evans, and Erlich killings, and he was good on all three. Two school board functions and a piano recital by his ten-year-old daughter. Complete with witnesses. He's a saint."

"Saint Shorty. Sure," Britton said. He swiveled his chair toward the board with the names and pictures of the seven Heartbreak Killer victims. "How many trucks total meeting our description are registered within a three-mile radius of the fish-and-tackle place?"

"Sampson's? Not that many, if you're talking in relative terms. Eighty-seven."

Britton looked surprised. "Is that all?" he asked. "It sounds like a pretty small number for a fairly large territory, especially since we started with so many countywide."

"Yeah, but think about what's inside the circle," Estevez said. "Huge chunks of it are the Port of Tampa and water. Lots and lots of water. You got part of downtown, where there aren't a lot of residential addresses or the kinds of commerce that would have a use for pickup trucks. Your commerce is concentrated around Ybor City, plus Palm River and a little of Clair Mel. A little residential, too, but not much."

"You sound like you're ruling out commercial ownership."

"Well, I was, more or less," Estevez said, rubbing his chin. "Sampson Jones didn't remember seeing any business identification on the truck his customer drove. And the woman down in Gibsonton, who saw the pickup at Shorty's mother's trailer, said she didn't see any commercial advertising, either."

Britton shook his head and slouched down on a corner of the detective's desk. "Not all companies put their names on their vehicles. It doesn't matter, though. You've got good addresses inside the three-mile radius for eighty-seven Toyota pickups, so you assign teams of detectives and check out every one. You check them out at places of commerce, residences, wherever you find them. You interview the people who own them and the people who drive them. You pay special attention to the ones with toolboxes behind the cabs and maybe ladders in the beds. You also keep an eye out for light-colored Toyota pickups, even if they're only passing through. You stop them and check them out, too. And I want another team to start checking registrations from the Gibsonton area. The kid called Shorty is the best suspect we've got. Maybe he's come home. And do it fast. We're running out of time."

Britton stopped for a breath and a quick thought struck him. He snapped his fingers. "Wait a second," he said, slowly straightening up. "Wait a damned second. There might be an easier way to get at this." He pointed at Estevez. "Nick, hearing you talk about the school administrator must have thrown my mind in gear. What about school records? Why couldn't we identify this guy through his old school records?"

"Because we don't know his name," Estevez reminded his boss.

"But we know his address," Britton said, his eyes sparkling with renewed excitement. "We got it from the trailer park owner the night we were interviewing neighbors. Everybody says Shorty is in his midthirties. So we bracket thirty-five by as much as five years on either side and have the school system run its enrollment records for the ten-year period looking for that address. Why wouldn't it work? God knows we've been foiled at every other turn. I don't see what could go wrong with this idea."

"That's going back a long way," Hale said. "The records might not be computerized. That would mean going through every single one by hand."

"Then we'll do it. We'll give them the personnel. They won't have to lift a finger. All they have to do is show us where the records are. It's better than trying to run down every lousy Toyota pickup in the county."

Estevez checked the notebook in which he'd jotted down Opal Siefert's address, then spun his Rolodex, checking for a number. When he found it, he punched it into the console on his desk. Britton watched him conduct a subdued conversation with somebody at the other end of the line. There was a period where he didn't appear to be talking to anybody at all. When conversation resumed, the slump of the detective's shoulders broadcast defeat. Estevez replaced the receiver and turned to face his boss and his colleagues. Britton felt his heart sink.

"If we didn't have bad luck, we wouldn't have any luck at all," Estevez said.

"What?" Britton asked. "They can't do it? Why?"

"The school system's computerized records for Gibsonton go back seventeen years," Estevez said. "My friend did a quick run on the trailer's address and found no school registrations from that address in the last seventeen years."

"Like I said, we'll check the earlier paper records by hand," Britton said. "Get a team . . ."

Estevez interrupted. "That's not what I'm saying. The records from twenty to thirty years ago were computerized, too, but they don't exist anymore. That's what I meant about bad luck. The records were destroyed in the 1992 fire in the school administration building. If you went to public school in Gibsonton earlier than seventeen years ago, there's no way in the world you're ever going to be able to prove it. Unless you went there before 1955. For those years, there are still paper records."

The detectives sat and stared at each other in total disbelief.

Finally, Britton exhaled slowly. "You're right," he said, "this killer might be the luckiest sombitch who ever crossed our paths." He slapped his hands on his thighs, stood up, and tried to sound encouraging. "Well, get after the truck. And hope for a break."

"Yeah, well hoping for a break hasn't gotten us very far that I can tell," Estevez said, pushing himself to his feet.

"Then maybe tenacity will turn the trick, or the truck, as the case may be."

NOT every member of the MAIT team was having a bad day. Shortly after three P.M., Britton got a call from Dits O'Brien, the case review coordinator.

"Busy?" O'Brien asked.

"Why should I be?" Britton answered sarcastically.

"Well, with seven unsolved serial killings hung around your neck, some guys might think you had a pretty heavy workload."

"You only have a workload when you have clues," Britton replied. "We have wild hares to chase, but very few clues. Hence, unfortunately, I sit around and think a lot."

"You could burn out your brain, thinking too much. Can you take some time out from thinking and come over to the crime lab at TPD?"

"You'd have to have a good reason to get me out in this weather."

"What weather?" O'Brien asked. "It's summer for God's sake."

"It's very hot, and it's very humid," Britton said wearily.

"That's what I said, it's summer. Believe me, friend, it's a lot worse in Washington, D.C., and New York City, all that brick and concrete soaking up the heat all day and throwing it back at you. You're better off here. At least you got sea breezes."

"Hot sea breezes, maybe," Britton conceded. "Why do you want me over there?"

"It's a clue," O'Brien said.

Britton sat up very straight very suddenly. "Jesus, why didn't you say so earlier?"

"I couldn't, you bitchin' about the weather an' all. Besides, it's not a great clue, like it would be if I could give you the guy's name. I'd classify it as an interesting clue."

"On my way."

There wasn't much traffic between Ybor City and downtown Tampa at midafternoon, but Britton used the flashing blue light in the middle of his dashboard to move aside what vehicles there were. He pulled up at Tampa police headquarters in fewer than ten minutes.

Britton started to tell the receptionist he was looking for O'Brien, but the competent young woman already knew it. "In the lab," she said before he could speak. "He's waiting for you." Britton smiled and nodded.

He pushed open the door and stopped in his tracks. "Christ, Dits, I knew you took a nip now and again, but I didn't know your problem was this bad."

Lined up on a table were rows of liquor bottles, from the shot sizes the airlines favored to half and full pints. All appeared to have been opened and sampled.

"That's very funny," O'Brien replied. "I hope the city council will get as big a kick out of it when they find out I've charged off more than two-hundred dollars worth of booze to the police budget. Wouldn't the papers love it?"

Britton bent down to get a closer look at the collection. There were dozens of bottles, each one a different brand, or different proofs of the same brand.

"All this have anything to do with the sample I found on the floor in the dead doctor's office?" Britton asked.

"The very same," O'Brien replied. "You wanted the brand identified. I got sort of curious, too, so I've been helpin' the guys do the checks."

"Sacrificing your liver for the cause?" Britton asked, only in jest.

"Only way we could figure to get what you wanted was gas chromatography."

Britton looked up, startled. "I thought that was for blood analysis," he said.

"It is. But it's very versatile. Mostly, the lab techies use it around here to detect drugs in the blood and urine of their many deceased clients, but it's effective in almost any situation where you want a computerized analysis of chemical ingredients in a liquid."

"You mean you put in the bourbon sample and it replied, 'Old Grand-Dad'?"

"Um, no. But we put in the bourbon sample and got this." O'Brien held up a strip of paper crossed by lines and bars. "It's the chemical fingerprint of your sample. A distilling signature, if you will. Then all we had to do was find the matching signature. As you can see, the techs tested everything that might be bourbon or be mistaken for it: the real thing, sour mash, Canadian blends. At that, there was no guarantee of finding the right one, but we did."

"And . . . ?"

"Kite's Finest Real Kentucky Bourbon Whiskey."

"Never heard of it."

"It's distilled by Smithers and Boyle, the same people who make Old Oak."

"Now that's good stuff."

"Old Oak is, yeah. And when they wash out the wooden casks and squeeze out the dishrags, that's what they bottle as Kite's Finest."

"Not what I'd catch you drinking, in other words."

"You wouldn't catch me drinking any of it. I'm strictly a Scotch man. But if I were into bourbon, I'd give up the sauce before I'd let Kite's touch my tongue. This is the kind of stuff you buy when you're far more interested in quantity than quality and your funds are limited."

"It fits the killer's profile."

"True. But you can't alert all the liquor stores in Hillsborough to card every guy with brown hair who appears to be in his midthirties and comes in often to renew his Kite's supply. You'd spook him sure as hell. Or worse, somebody would tip the media to the Kite's vigil, and we'd have a circus on our hands."

"No, but we can send the killer's description along with the drawing we did from Sampson Jones's description to every liquor store in the county," Britton said. "I'll tell them to call us if they have a frequent Kite's customer who fits. Maybe we'll get lucky and find a clerk who knows his customer. If all else fails, we'll stake out the store until he comes back, although given the time pressure, I hope that isn't necessary."

"If you find him, don't touch his booze," O'Brien cautioned. "The stuff'll melt your teeth."

"You look like hell. What's the matter? That encounter up at USF still bugging you?"

It was Lee Townsend's way of expressing concern, of demonstrating he had a heart. But he came off the boor, Cynthia Diamond thought as she sat for the makeup attendant who was putting the final touches on her face and hair in preparation for the six o'clock segment of the *Evening News Show* on channel seven, WFSC-TV, the Eye on the Florida Sun Coast.

She had tried to minimize the assault. She asked, without hoping she would succeed, that her own station ignore the story in reporting the day's news.

Townsend flatly refused.

"It's been all over radio all day, and we've been teasing to it. We can't back away from it now," he told her. "And why would we? It's great ratings, sweetheart. A woman who visits a large percentage of Tampa Bay's living rooms everyday was assaulted, and people want to see her, to be sure she's okay, and to hear her story. You ought to love it. We'll sweep the ratings. And don't worry about being embarrassed. Max promises he will treat it very tastefully, nothing that should bother you at all."

"It will bother me to have to sit there on public display while he recreates something very horrible that happened to me today," she protested. "But you can't understand that, can you?"

"No, quite frankly, I can't. Now finish getting ready. You're on in twenty minutes. You're okay, right? You're not gonna crap out on me, are you?"

"I'm fine, Lee," she responded after a bit. "I'll be on the set on time."

"Oh? Then try to look like you're fine," Townsend instructed. "Except, maybe, while Max does the story about you. Then maybe you could put a sort of, well, you know, haunted look on your face. Wouldn't hurt the reading on the viewer-sympathy meter."

Cynthia threw him a withering look but said nothing. Lee didn't get it, and probably he never would. She had to quit letting him get to her.

She took a deep breath and felt her confidence return, and it stayed with her, right up to the first item on the six o'clock news.

"TAMPA Bay residents are bracing for another weekend of fear as regional police authorities admit to WFSC-TV they are no closer tonight to identifying and apprehending the serial killer terrorizing this area than they were last Monday when Dr. Marilyn Erlich was brutally murdered in her Carrollwood clinic. This killer's appetite for blood and his lust to inflict pain and terror know no bounds. Sources tell us the murderer's brutality and sadism have escalated with every killing, and they fear it will only get worse."

Max Clevenger, looking at once brave, resolute, and compassionate, was staring into the lens of the camera with the red light, ostensibly to inform and reassure the Tampa Bay region. But in fact, he was deliberately and wantonly jacking up the general panic to score ratings points. Cynthia felt certain the hype was a lead-in to her story, and if this was what Lee Townsend thought of as tasteful, she was going to spend the next few minutes in misery.

"Sources inside the MAIT team told me today new leads followed all week have taken them to a dead end," Clevenger continued. "And fears are mounting that the murderer has given up on prostitutes and disadvantaged women—the more typical and less-mourned victims of serial killers—and turned permanently to women who are better-educated and financially well off."

Out of range of the camera's eye, Cynthia stared at Clevenger in disbelief. Was it possible he was saying, and possibly meaning, that the lives of disadvantaged women were expendable, that it was only time to worry when the lives of teachers and doctors were at risk?

"The last two victims of the vicious killer were outstanding citizens of our community, and their loss is being profoundly felt," Clevenger intoned. Cynthia thought, quite correctly, *Oh, God, here come the heart-wrenching photographs from home.*

The first up on screen was the teacher. "Constance Evans," Clevenger continued, "just twenty-two years old, a kindergarten teacher in Brandon." Another picture. "Dr. Marilyn Erlich, thirty-two, a specialist in internal medicine in Carrollwood Village, studying to be a surgeon. Once again, police urge each of you women out there to be extremely cautious and on the lookout for anybody who might be following you. If you experience repeated sightings of the same man—whether you know him or not—if he's watching you for no apparent reason, get to a place where there are other people around and call the Hillsborough Sheriff's Office immediately. Until authorities catch this killer, the only thing the rest of us can do is to avoid making targets of ourselves. We'll have more on this breaking story at eleven." He paused, then he plunged ahead.

"We had a taste of the horror of assaults on women in our family at WFSC today," he said solemnly. "My air partner, Cynthia Diamond, was attacked while on an assignment on the campus of the University of South Florida. Cynthia was covering a wonderful event, a carnival whose proceeds go to help needy children. She was touring a fun house when a man she described to police as wearing all black, grabbed her, hit her, pinned her down, and tried to rape her."

What the hell is he talking about? Cynthia thought in horror. *That's not what happened at all, not even close!*

But Clevenger wasn't finished. "Her pleas for help were picked up by a remote microphone pinned to her dress, a microphone the assailant later ripped off and threw away. Before contact was lost, however, WFSC soundman Dick Tyler was able to monitor her plight."

No! Cynthia's mind screamed. *You have no right! You can't!*

But the next sound she heard was her own voice.

"Mark, is that you?" She sounded as frightened on the audiotape Tyler had recorded as she felt at the time of the attack. "Dick? . . . Who's there? . . . Come on, guys, this isn't funny. Where are you? . . ." She heard her voice became panicky. "Please, who are you? . . . What do you want with me? . . . Mark, where are you? . . . Please, I need hel—"

Seconds passed, then came the sound of the rattle of her remote mike as it hit and rolled across the fun house floor.

Cynthia was trembling. Part of it was a reaction to Clevenger's wholly distorted account of what happened to her at USF, and part of it was shock at hearing her taped words and fears just hours after she had lived the terrifying experience. She could not believe the utter audacity of the station to broadcast the tape, particularly without her permission—without so much as a warning of what was coming!

Clevenger turned to her, and she saw the camera pull back from his earnest face so both of them were appearing on television sets all across the Tampa Bay area.

Lee Townsend promised this wouldn't happen!

No, he hadn't, the bastard! What he'd promised was that Max would be tasteful. And I took his word as an assurance.

She cursed herself for being so naive. Clevenger didn't know the meaning of good taste.

"Horrible story, Cynthia, just horrible," Clevenger was saying. "You must have been frightened half to death. Do the police have any idea whether the attack on you is related to the attacks by the serial killer?"

Below the desk, out of sight of the camera's eye. Cynthia's hands were balled into fists.

"No connection," she replied curtly.

"And how are you feeling?" Clevenger pressed.

"I'm fine, Max. Just fine."

Cynthia made a decision not to extend the nonsense of the last three minutes one second more. She looked into the camera focused on her and said, "We'll be back after these messages."

As picture and sound faded, Cynthia turned on Max. "You son of a bitch!" she swore, not quite letting enough time pass for the sound technician to fade the audio entirely. Fortunately for the station, only the venomous, "You," got onto the air, along with a quick picture of her face pinched in anger. By the time a four-commercial package ran its course, the director had calmed Cynthia sufficiently to continue.

On her way home for dinner after the broadcast, Cynthia considered her options. She had given Max Clevenger the verbal pasting of his life when the broadcast ended, and he simply stared back with a look of uncomprehending hurt. He couldn't fathom what he had done to cause her reaction. She definitely planned a confrontation with Lee Townsend the next time she saw him, but it was Friday, and she wouldn't cross Townsend's path again until Monday. This was too serious to slide over the weekend. She decided she would call Lee at home right away, before she had dinner, and certainly before she returned to the studio for the eleven P.M. segment. She would vent all over him while the anger was painfully sharp.

Cynthia pulled into her garage and opened the car door to a withering blast of wet heat and the sharp crack of thunder. The station's meteorologist said weather radar was picking up huge storms over eastern Hillsborough moving west, with more storms blasting northwest out of Manatee and Sarasota Counties. All appeared destined to converge over Tampa very shortly. It was 7:30 in the evening, but with the sky over her home still blue and with the sun still up, the temperature hung stubbornly in the midnineties and the humidity in the seventy-five percent range.

She stepped out onto the concrete and whirled abruptly to face the street.

Someone was watching her.

The flash of a memory from the morning sent a cold shock along her nervous system, and she shivered despite the heat. There was no question the attack at USF had made her jumpy. Captain Britton assured her the assault was not the work of the Heartbreak Killer, but the assurance was little comfort considering the man in the fun house said he would be back for her later. And his description of what he intended to do to her . . . She shuddered again and pressed her thighs together against the memory of his hard hand.

Could he be out there now?

Slowly, she scanned neighborhood shrubbery, trying to see behind every leaf, for some sign that someone was there. But she saw nothing out of the ordinary. She breathed a deep sigh and turned toward the door that led from the garage to her laundry room.

She let herself into the house to a tumultuous welcome from her four-year-old long-haired dachshunds, a male and a female, brother and sister, Charlie and Mattie. They had heard the garage door go up and knew from habit their mistress was home to lead them on a predinner walk. Their need to relieve themselves wasn't nearly so great as their never-ending desire to eat. But they understood the quicker they got outside and did what was expected of them, the sooner there would be food.

The walk was uneventful, and Cynthia's sense of being watched was supplanted by angry thoughts of what she would say to Lee Townsend in the next few minutes. She decided to hold nothing back. If it cost her her job, so be it.

She prepared the dogs' meals of canned food and kibbles and set two identical bowls at the base of the refrigerator. As the two dogs pounced on the food, she scratched the two brown heads and smiled at their enjoyment. Her dogs gave the term "eager eaters" great new meaning.

She stood up, and her mind was torn instantly from the subject of Lee Townsend, from the memory of her frightened voice on tape, from her fury at Max Clevenger, even from her pets. What she saw hit her like a slap in the face.

On the refrigerator door, held by a yellow pineapple magnet, was a piece of nondescript white notepaper. Printed in red ink in very deliberate lettering were the words:

HI, BITCH!

THE HANDYMAN

WAS HERE.

There was no signature, but in the lower right-hand corner there was a crudely drawn heart. It was filled in with red ink, and dots, like drops of blood, trailed off the paper.

Someone, somehow, had entered her house and left the message. And Cynthia had no way to know if the intruder was still there.

12

The Tampa Police responded to Cynthia's frantic telephone call in less than three minutes. The 911 operator told her to hang up, leave the house, and go to a neighbor's until the squad cars arrived.

"Right," Cynthia said breathlessly, nodding her head furiously, "I'll get the dogs . . ."

"No!" the operator said sharply. "Forget the dogs. He doesn't want the dogs. Get out, and get out now. Do you understand me, ma'am?"

"Yes," Cynthia replied. "Okay."

She started for the access door to the garage and realized with heart-stopping anxiety she had left it unlocked. And the garage door was up. Was somebody waiting for her outside? Surely, he wouldn't try anything in the daylight.

He broke in and left the note in the daylight, didn't he?

She reached above the kitchen sink for the magnetic rack holding her utility knives and pulled down the longest one she found there.

With her weapon clutched in her right hand, she cracked the access door gingerly.

Nothing happened. Nobody yanked it open. Nobody tried to grab her.

Even as she rushed from the garage and sprinted across the street toward the home of Frank and Elaine Quinton, she heard the approaching sirens. By the time Elaine answered the door, the first police cars were sliding to the curb.

THE two TPD units responding to the call were joined by Ben Britton's unmarked car from the Hillsborough Sheriff's Office. When Britton first learned of the intruder report from Davis Islands, he saw no reason to roll on it. The neighborhood was within the city limits, and he had dismissed the assault on Cynthia Diamond earlier in the day as having no connection to the serial killer. Then Powell Reemer, the Tampa chief of police, alerted him to the nature of the note found on the refrigerator door, and Britton decided he and Nick Estevez ought to check it out. The serial killer had never approached a victim before striking, at least not that anybody knew. But a drawing of a red heart trailing droplets of blood touched a nerve.

Tampa officers completed a search of Cynthia's home and grounds as heavy winds and black clouds riven by crackling lightning strokes rolled up Hillsborough Bay. The officers determined the intruder was no longer around. Britton's arrival was followed closely by waves of news reporters, including the force from WFSC-TV, led by the intrepid Max Clevenger, who was still smarting from the tongue-lashing he had taken from Cynthia after the six o'clock segment. But she was in no shape to talk to any of them, including Max. Least of all, Max.

The excitement sent the dogs into a frenzy. When she returned from the Quinton's, Cynthia confined the dachshunds to her bedroom. It didn't quiet them, but it prevented them from escaping through open doors as the cops came and went.

The Tampa police interviewed Cynthia briefly, but deferred on the heavy questioning to Britton. He found her standing by the triple glass sliders leading from the family room to the lanai and pool enclosure.

"Long time, no see," Britton said, thinking too late that the words were an incredibly lame opening. But Cynthia turned to him and smiled.

"We really should quit meeting like this," she said, turning back to the view of the approaching storm. "This has been quite a day."

"Not one I suspect you want to relieve anytime soon," Britton agreed. "Feel up to a few questions? Or maybe I should say, a few more questions?"

"I will in a couple minutes, Captain," she said. "I'd like to pour a glass of wine to calm my nerves, if you don't mind."

Britton nodded, but he noted that instead of the refrigerator, Cynthia headed for the liquor cabinet in the dining room. It wasn't Chablis she got there, it was Scotch. The drink she poured looked to be at least three fingers. She retreated with it to the lanai beside the pool. It offered an eerie combination of views. From the west, it was washed in the reddish orange glow of a sunset sky. From the south and east, the sound-and-light show continued to advance. Britton guessed the storm would snuff out the sunset very shortly.

As Britton watched Cynthia, Estevez appeared at his elbow.

" 'Scuse me, Captain, you got a minute?" the detective asked.

"Not much more than that, or our victim out there will be in her cups," he replied, nodding toward Cynthia, who was sitting in a lounge chair, gazing across Hillsborough Bay, attacking the Scotch in small but steady sips.

"Maybe she's trying to create the courage to tell you she lied about an intruder," Estevez suggested. "Maybe she's wondering what she has to do to keep TPD from charging her with filing a false police report."

Britton frowned. "What are you talking about?" he asked.

"There isn't anything to suggest anybody broke in here," Estevez said. "Tampa cops checked out the house before we got here, and I rechecked everything myself. All the doors and windows are locked. There are no windows broken. There's no hole punched in the roof. There's no tunnel under the house to a hole in the floor. And the fireplace damper is closed, so even Santa Claus couldn't get in here. If somebody broke in, he can walk through walls. Or he has a key. But she told the Tampa blues nobody else has a key."

Estevez crossed his arms. "And that isn't all. The paper the refrigerator note was written on looks identical to a stack of notepaper by the phone over there. And right by the paper, there's a red felt-tipped pen. We'll have to have the lab check to make a firm connection, but I'm ready to bet a day's wages it's the pen that wrote the note that wound up on the fridge under the yellow pineapple magnet."

"Even so, it doesn't mean nobody broke in," Britton said. "Maybe he picked a lock and used what he found here to write the note. Don't forget to have the pen dusted."

"Already done, although I think we won't find any prints but the lady's."

"Because she wrote the note herself?"

"That, or because the burglar is our serial killer wearing gloves again. But probably she did it. None of this feels right. Why would the killer chance picking a lock in broad daylight, or what's really crazy, take time to lock up again when he left? Yet all the locks are locked."

"Maybe he's very good and very fast," Britton suggested.

"And I'm Elvis."

Britton shook his head. "She's not a fuckup," he said. "What motive would she have to make up a story like this and fabricate evidence? After what she went through this morning, she's more likely to want peace and quiet."

Estevez studied his feet and spoke softly, "Unless she made up this morning, too."

Britton snorted. He was getting irritated. "Oh, come on, Nick. Give me a break. The medics found bruises."

"I can bruise myself if I want to."

"That's ridiculous."

"Hear me out," Estevez asked. "I checked the detectives who responded this morning, and they haven't found a single witness who saw a man all in black coming or going from the area of the fun house. She had no visible injuries, except the bruises. The only real evidence is the audiotape, and it could have been faked, too. Flash forward to the present and, once again, no evidence to support the story and ample evidence to at least suggest she did this herself."

Estevez's scenario was punctuated by five or six lasers of lightning and a crash of thunder followed by rolling echoes.

"You think it's safe for her to be out there?" he asked, nodding his head toward Cynthia. "Storm's almost right on top of us."

"As long as she stays under cover, I guess so," Britton replied. "When the wind starts to blow the rain around, she'll come in." He paused, still weighing the possibility the attack and break-in were phony. "I've had dealings with this woman in the past. She seems reasonably bright and competent," he told Estevez. "I repeat my question: What's her motive?"

"Ratings," Estevez responded immediately. "I saw a story in the paper about her station trying to push up its news ratings. They're number two. They want to be number one. Can't think of a local story more on everybody's mind than the serial killer. Maybe she thought she could paint herself as one of his potential victims. A lot of folks would tune in to hear her talk about it."

"Christ, nobody would be so stupid," Britton suggested.

"I'd like to think not," Estevez replied. "But I'm old enough not to be quite so naive."

"You know, though, when I talked to her this morning, she recognized me as being from the task force," Britton recalled, thinking aloud. "She asked me then if I thought the man who attacked her might be the Heartbreak Killer."

"What'd you tell her?"

"I told her no, that nothing her attacker did—or at least what she said he did—fit the serial killer's pattern."

"So there you go," Estevez said. "Tonight she decided to get closer to the pattern. The red heart is a perfect touch. The killer's activities with regard to his victims' hearts seem to be fairly common knowledge."

"And what's the Handyman reference?"

"No clue."

Britton shook his head and sighed.

He thrust his hands deep into his pockets.

"I don't want to think you're right," he said. "Who's talking to the neighbors?"

"Tampa blues. I think they're finished, actually."

Britton glanced out at the lanai, where Cynthia had stopped attacking her drink but continued to gaze across the bay as the storm spread to the west.

Already, the lights on the opposite shore were gone, obscured behind billowing curtains of rain that pounded the roof and spanged off the flashing and gutters. The pool was caged with screening, and the wire mesh blasted the big drops into mist that hit the water in tens of thousands of overlapping ripples. Under the solid lanai roof, Cynthia continued to be unaffected by the uproar around her.

Britton would talk to her, but he wanted to know first what, if anything, the neighbors saw or heard during the afternoon.

"The neighbors saw zip," a young uniform said, consulting notes from his canvass. "A Mrs. Thomas Gillardy, who lives next door on the north side, said she heard the dogs bark briefly when she got home from work and walked to the mailbox about five-thirty. She looked over at the house, but didn't see anything unusual. On the other hand, she didn't expect to see anything since the dogs bark at anything moving in the street. She figured they probably were barking at her. Nobody else saw or heard anything."

"Oh, joy," Britton said. "Another tidal wave of clues."

It was time to talk to Cynthia Diamond, whether she was ready or not.

*   *   *

THE lassitude deepened the longer she sat in the lounge chair. The longer she remained still, the harder it became to move. It felt as though the earth's gravity had doubled, so deep was it pulling her into the cushions, squeezing her chest, and making breathing difficult. She no longer could raise her glass to sip her drink. Indeed, it was a strain to hold her head up; it would have been so much easier to let it fall back and to sleep. Even the growing storm would not have kept her awake. She wanted only to shut down consciousness and drift away from everything. The symptoms were diagnostic of withdrawal from trauma, and Cynthia recognized that, but the sensations were no less vivid for the understanding.

She had been violated. It was one thing to be sexually assaulted during a silly assignment in broad daylight; it was quite another to come home the same day to find a stranger had managed to force his way into your locked home and leave a threatening note to let you know he could get in again any time he chose. The two incidents were the work of the same man, of that Cynthia was certain. The bastard at the fun house said he would be back for her. And that's exactly why he came to her home, why he left the note, to prove to her how vulnerable she was. Cynthia shivered in the humid air and started as a blue-white slash of lightning struck the water just offshore. Thunder cracked at almost the same instant. She should go inside. But she didn't have the strength or the will to move.

The police were going to talk to her about the incident, and they weren't going to be sympathetic. A Tampa officer had already made it clear he doubted her story. They found no evidence of a break-in, he said, no evidence of an intruder. It looked as though the pen and paper used in the note came from her own telephone stand. Neighbors had seen and heard nothing. Did she want to change her story?

Nice question.

Why couldn't they leave her alone and let her go to sleep?

She heard someone open the glass slider between the lanai and the family room and felt his presence before she heard his voice. "Miss Diamond . . . Cynthia . . . It's Ben Britton. We can talk now, if you're feeling up to it." He had to speak loudly to be heard over the rain and intermittent rolling thunder.

She opened her eyes, although she didn't remember closing them, and looked up at him, saying nothing.

"Could we go inside?" he asked. "It's a little dangerous out here, and it's certainly noisy."

She smiled wanly and turned her head slowly from side to side against the pillow of the lounger. She had no intention of moving.

"Come on," Britton said, gripping her shoulders and gently urging her to her feet. "You'll feel better if you get up and move around a bit."

She let herself be led inside, clutching the remnants of her drink.

"I want to freshen this up," she mumbled, raising her glass.

"Later," he said, "after you tell me what you found when you came home this evening."

She burrowed into a corner of the sofa and went through it again. It was a strain to talk.

"And the first time you saw the note was when it caught your eye on the refrigerator door, after you put food down for the dogs?" he asked.

"That's right."

"Well, you know, it looks as though whoever wrote the note used the paper and pen beside your telephone in there." He nodded toward the family room.

"I know," she replied softly, her voice nearly drowned out by the rain pounding on the roof and the windows. "One of the Tampa police officers told me. Does it matter?"

"It might. I don't know yet." He paused. "Miss Diamond, do you have any idea what the reference to 'The Handyman' is about?"

"No."

"Have you had any workmen at the house lately? Any remodeling done? Painting?"

"No, nothing."

"Okay, is there any way into your house other than the doors and windows?"

"What do you mean?"

"Just what I asked. The Tampa police officers found all the doors and windows locked, except for the access door between the laundry and the garage, which you say you opened."

"I can't explain it."

"Maybe someone used a key to let himself in. Who else has a key?"

"Nobody," she said. "I explained it all to the police. I had all the locks changed after my divorce, and I haven't given a key to anyone."

"How about a neighbor?"

"I keep meaning to, but I haven't yet."

"Housekeeper?"

"No. She comes first thing Friday mornings and leaves before I go to work."

Britton frowned. "What about the door from the laundry to the garage?" he asked. "When you leave the house, do you always lock it?"

She thought a moment. "No," she said, "I don't think I ever do. The garage door has an automatic opener. Nobody can get in but me."

"Not necessarily," Britton said. "There are only a finite number of frequencies for garage door openers. There's an almost-perfect chance somebody someplace has an opener set to the same frequency as yours. He could open your garage as easily as his own, and if you leave the access door unlocked, he could walk right in."

"That's pretty far-fetched," she replied. "What are the odds against the person who wants to break in here specifically having exactly the right garage door frequency?"

Britton got up and moved over onto the sofa next to her. Even in the enclosed family room, it was difficult to hear normal conversation. Outside, the winds had picked up and were lashing the vegetation, and the rains were rolling across the property in undulating sheets. The water was coming down at a rate of about three inches an hour.

"It's a long shot, but we have to consider the possibility," he said. "What about the utility door, the one between the garage and the side yard?"

"What about it?"

"You keep it locked all the time?"

"Yes, I think so. I never use it. Is it locked now?"

"Yes."

"Then it's locked all the time."

"I want you to be certain of that, Miss Diamond, because, you see, the fewer hypotheses there are to cover how somebody broke in here, the harder it's going to be to believe your story. There's no sign of forced entry. There are no new footprints or scuff marks in the landscaping. Your dogs were heard to bark once, but it didn't go on long, and dachshunds are well-known barkers. Why should anybody believe you? Who's to say you didn't dream up this scheme as a publicity stunt and create the note yourself?"

She rolled her head back and forth across the back of the sofa, despair clouding her mind. "I'm not making it up," she said with tears of frustration filling her eyes. "What reason would I have for making it up?"

"I'm told you're in a ratings war," Britton suggested, his voice hard. He didn't like baiting her and didn't want to believe she'd made up the story and the clues. But he had to find out what she knew, and her mind was a thousand miles away. If it took baiting her to bring her back and get her focused, that's what he would do.

His implied accusation worked. Cynthia's eyes blazed behind the tears. "No way!" she insisted, as forcibly as she'd spoken since Britton arrived. "I'd have to be an idiot to do a thing like that. I'm *not* an idiot, Captain Britton."

"No, ma'am," he said. "No one said you were." Britton cleared his throat. "Miss Diamond, do you want to amend your story in any way? Is there anything you'd like to add? To change? You can do that now, and nobody will hold it against you. I'll see to that. Tell me now if the truth is a little different than you've been letting on. Once I leave this house, it will be too late."

"No," she replied. "There's nothing to change. I am telling you the truth."

The lightning was strobing almost nonstop now, and the thunder was cracking and rolling without letup. Britton stood.

"I'm going to leave my card on the kitchen table for you," he said. "I hope you'll call me if you remember anything else. Or if you need somebody to talk to."

She didn't respond.

He started to leave the room, but stopped in the middle of the kitchen. "By the way," he said over his shoulder, "you've got a truckload of media out front, including a crew from your station. You want me to let any of them in?"

Cynthia shook her head.

"I don't want to see anybody," she said.

She wanted only to sleep.

SHE didn't make it back to the station for the eleven o'clock news. Max had to manage on his own. He mentioned at the top of the show that she had the night off. There was no further mention of her during the half hour, no mention of the morning assault, no mention of the break-in she had reported at her Davis Islands home. Lee Townsend's obsession with ratings had deflated in the face of a possible police fraud by his top female anchor.

The competing stations mentioned it, gleefully, leading with word that Tampa police and Hillsborough Sheriff's deputies were expressing doubts about the reports of an assault on Cynthia Diamond at the University of South Florida that morning and a break-in at her Davis Islands house that afternoon. They stopped short of calling her a liar, but no listener misunderstood.

For her part, Cynthia slowly got drunk and watched the storm. She knew she should leave the house and check into a motel that would take her dogs. But the lethargy that set in earlier had overwhelmed her. She couldn't think of a place to go, couldn't concentrate on what to take with her, and couldn't face the prospect of driving around in the gale outside. She would consider moving out tomorrow.

Shortly after midnight, she was drunk enough to venture outside to walk the dogs, but she went no farther from her front door than the closest patch of lawn. It was still raining steadily, and the dogs finished their chores quickly, eager to get back inside where it was warm and dry. Then, with many of the lights in the house still blazing, Cynthia slid between the sheets of her bed. She recalled in her groggy state that she had intended to have a showdown this evening with Lee Townsend, but somehow the confrontation got overtaken by events.

Like Scarlett O'Hara, she thought, *I'll think about it tomorrow.*

Tomorrow is another day.

If I live until tomorrow.

Then, with her dogs snug against her legs, she passed out.

A FEW miles to the east, in his bungalow in Clair Mel, Eugene Rickey went to bed alone. He'd been disappointed at Cynthia's absence from the eleven o'clock news, but this minor letdown was more than offset by his certain knowledge of why she wasn't there. It pleased him. A lot of things pleased him.

In addition to spooking her unmercifully, he once again had reason to think his whole life had been pointing him in her direction, that he and Cynthia had been predestined to find one another. He could have stolen any number of things from Bud Westerly's fix-it shop while he worked there as a kid, but among the items he'd pocketed along with drivers and wrenches had been tension bars and sets of professional lock picks, including the equipment that made fast work of the Quikset key and dead-bolt latches on Cynthia's front door that afternoon.

The dogs had kicked up a fuss at his presence at first, but he bought them off with the treats he'd stashed in his pocket. He took care of the note and was out of the house inside five minutes, clean as a whistle.

It had been almost too simple.

13

The first sound of the telephone jangled from a deep well. It must be coming from somewhere outside, a neighbor's lanai, perhaps.

If the dogs hadn't stirred at the persistent ringing, Cynthia might have slept on until the caller gave up. But Charlie and Mattie started digging at the blanket, stopping only when Cynthia uncoiled from beneath the covers and reached out to her night table for the receiver. Her head, overloaded with Scotch residue, was pounding.

"Hello?"

"Cynthia? Lee Townsend. You all right? You sound terrible."

"I was sleeping."

"Well, get up, throw on some clothes, and come down to the station. You don't have to look pretty. I'm not sending you on assignment. Blue jeans will do. Hell, your bathrobe will do. Just get down here."

She boosted herself up on one elbow and looked at the clock. It was eight-thirty. She wondered why the dogs hadn't wakened her earlier to go out. Then she realized they might have tried and failed.

"It's Saturday, Lee," she said. "If you're not putting me on the street for something, why do I have to come down?"

"We need to talk," Townsend said sharply, "and it can't wait until Monday. An hour, Cynthia. No more than an hour."

It was more like seventy minutes later when she steered into the parking lot and signed into the building with the guard at the front door. She had indulged herself with three cups of coffee and four Tylenol. She felt barely human. When she reached Townsend's office, he was pacing in front of his large windows, gazing over grassy wetlands to a shore lined with mangroves. Tampa Bay lay beyond. The sun filtered through a thin haze of humidity left by the previous night's thunderstorms and danced off the water, dead calm in the still morning air.

"So I'm here," Cynthia said, strolling into Townsend's office and sitting without being invited to do so in the armchair across from the infamous bathroom that served as a changing room on modeling day. "What was so urgent?"

Townsend had his back to her and didn't turn around immediately. "Tell me what happened at your house last night."

"I figured that was it," she said. She was in no mood or condition to take a lot of crap from the news director, and she wasn't about to back down from her story.

"I went home, and I was furious. You told me to trust Max to be tasteful, and I believed you, and that was my big mistake. Max Clevenger wouldn't know good taste if it confronted him in a bright room and slapped him in the face. And then you let him use the tape from the fun house without my permission and didn't even have the common decency to warn me it was coming. You blindsided me live in living color, and I'll never forgive you for it. Maybe Max told you I dressed him down hard when we went off the air, and I'm not one bit sorry I did it. He had it coming. My plan was to call you at home to let you have some of the same treatment. You both behaved despicably. That was all I had on my mind when I walked into my house. So I didn't notice until I went to feed the dogs that somebody had left this sick note on my refrigerator. It was written in red ink. It said, 'Hi, Bitch! The Handyman was here.' It had a red heart drawn on it with red dots trailing off the paper, like drops of blood. I had no idea how anybody could have gotten into my locked house to leave the note. I was very scared. I called the police. It seemed the prudent thing to do. And frankly, Lee, I don't give a flying fuck how you feel about it. I know what the truth is, and I'm comfortable with it."

Sometime during her monologue, she'd gotten to her feet. She realized she was standing with her hands on her hips and breathing as though she'd just run three miles.

Townsend turned around. His face was blank. "The audiotape is the property of the station," he said emphatically. "You have no say in how it's used. Get that straight right now. Max asked if he could use it. He made a compelling case that it was an exclusive. I said yes."

"You said . . ."

"I did not lie to you. I don't think Max went overboard. And to quote you, I don't give a flying fuck how you feel about it. I'm comfortable with my decision. And that will end this topic of conversation right now. Understood?"

She glared at him without responding.

"I didn't call you here to talk about Max," he said, changing the subject abruptly. "I called you here to talk about you. The police don't believe your story about the note."

"I know," she replied. "And there isn't much I can do about it, is there? I already told you, I know what the truth is, and I'm comfortable with it."

"Evidently, there was no sign of a break-in. How can you explain that?"

"I can't," she said matter-of-factly. "Don't think I haven't tried."

Townsend took two steps toward her, his hands in front of him as if in supplication.

"Cynthia, the cops think you fantasized it, that you wrote the note yourself," he said. "There's even talk you faked the attack at USF. Or that if you didn't fake the attack at USF, it's what gave you the idea to fake the break-in at your house. They think you did it to hype our ratings, using this serial-killer thing. It took me two hours last night and another hour this morning to talk TPD out of filing charges against you."

"For what?" Her eyes flashed with anger.

"Filing a false police report. The call to 911 hauled a lot of manpower out to your house. They don't take these things lightly."

"Neither do I," Cynthia said defiantly. "Why would I try to hype ratings in the middle of August? We don't have sweeps weeks in August."

"The cops don't know that and don't care," he said. "All they know is what their logic tells them, and in this case, their logic tells them you were lying. They interpreted your unwillingness to talk to the media as confirming their suspicions."

"Why? That doesn't follow. I was exhausted. It was teeming outside. I wasn't in a mood to stand out in the storm and chat."

"The way they see it, if you'd really been scared of an intruder, you'd have left your house and gone to a motel to stay for as long as you felt threatened. That's the way cops think. Christ, it even seems logical to me."

"I was tired, Lee. I felt violated. I wanted to be left alone. I didn't have the emotional strength or the initiative to pack up and get out. It's a natural reaction. Everybody who's had a break-in goes through it. And I had more than a simple break-in yesterday."

"Cynthia!" Townsend sounded exasperated. "Even assuming a burglar managed to unlock one of your doors without leaving any trace, tell me how he managed to relock it when he left. And why would he want to?"

"To make me feel isolated and vulnerable," she said. "It's part of trying to frighten me. And it worked yesterday. Today, it's just pissing me off."

"Stop it!" Townsend ordered. "I won't hear any more of it."

"I don't see any reason to continue this conversation," she said. "I'm not going to convince you, and I'm sick of trying."

"You owe me!" Townsend snapped. "If it wasn't for me, you'd be in jail."

It was more than Cynthia could take.

"Am I supposed to thank you?" she challenged, her voice rising. "After what you did to me yesterday, you're lucky I didn't come in here and take a baseball bat to your head. That would be an appropriate gesture of gratitude, I think. You are a son of a bitch, you know it, Lee? A real live, genuine son of a bitch."

"And you're getting close to insubordination," Townsend replied.

"Aw, whatsa matter, Lee? You can deal it, but you can't take it?"

"Don't do this, Cynthia. You're upset and you're tired. Don't talk yourself into a hole you can't climb out of until you've had a chance to rest and think about it."

"I've thought about it all I need to," she said. "My opinion of you isn't going to change."

He decided to change the subject before she forced him to terminate her.

"Where's the note now?" he asked.

"What note?"

"The Handyman note."

"The police took it. They also took a blank sheet of paper from beside my phone and the red felt-tipped pen."

"Probably to use as evidence against you if they filed charges." Townsend paused, shaking his head slowly. "Okay, listen," he said. "I could—hell, I probably should discipline you for this." She started to object, but stopped when he raised his hands. "Not for making the police report. You say it happened. The cops say it didn't. I'm not going to decide who's right. But I would be within my rights to set you down hard for your attitude in here this morning and for making Max look foolish last night. You left him standing out in the grass with the grunts from the other stations like he was some kind of rookie cops reporter. People were laughing at him. That wasn't good for his image."

"Not knowing enough to get in his car out of the rain wasn't good for his image, either," she raged. Her life was on the line, and all Townsend could think of was Max Clevenger's *image!*

"It wasn't good for the station's image."

"Oh, come *on,* Lee!"

"Come on, nothing," he snapped. "You have a responsibility. You turned your back on it. I'm going to drop the subject. I won't raise it again. But you get off this kick right now, you understand? You're never to mention it again. If anybody asks you about it, even employees of this station, you say it was a misunderstanding. An unfortunate misunderstanding. You got that? And don't you forget, because if you persist, the consequences will be far, far greater than you're prepared to deal with."

"Are we quite through?" Cynthia asked.

"You understand what I'm telling you?"

"I understand what you're telling me. All too well."

"That better be the truth, doll. Now get outta here."

DURING the drive home, Cynthia tried to remember whether she'd had anything planned for the rest of the day. Her mind was blank, awash in seething anger toward Lee Townsend and Max Clevenger. She always regarded them with dull, droning irritation. But now, the emotion more resembled rage. Her feeling for the various police agencies that thought her a liar or worse was mounting indignation. She knew Ben Britton well by reputation and slightly in person, and she could recall nothing about him to suggest he would treat her situation so dismissively. And certainly, Britton knew her by reputation. Did he really consider her such an airhead that he could believe she would make up threats to her own safety?

As she pulled into her driveway, she was gripping the steering wheel so tightly her knuckles were white. She fought down a moment's dread that the intruder might have returned. His entry the day before had been at a time he knew she would be away. He could not have predicted her absence today . . . unless he was watching the house, something he would have difficulty pulling off in broad daylight with many of her neighbors working outside.

She let herself in through the laundry room access door, which she was locking now for the first time since she bought the house, and heard her phone ringing.

"Hey, I've been calling for an hour. I was worried about you. Where've you been?" It was Liz McCormick. She was agitated, and her words tumbled over one another, giving Cynthia no room to respond. "I heard what happened last night. At least I heard what you think happened last night. And I heard Mad Max's side and Lee Townsend's side, and they're really pissed off. And they say the police are really pissed off. Got calls from two of the other stations asking questions about you, but I refused to talk to them. I wouldn't know what to say. Some other people at the station got calls, too. What on earth is going on with you?"

Finally, she paused long enough for Cynthia to slide into the conversation. "I've been at the station this morning," she said. "Lee called me in and read me the riot act."

"What for?" Liz asked.

"Well, actually, I'm not supposed to talk about it," Cynthia replied. "Lee said to tell anybody who asked, including my colleagues, it was all a misunderstanding. So, officially, that's what I'm telling you. It was a misunderstanding."

"Was it? Is that the truth?"

"No, but you didn't hear me say that."

"You want some company? We could talk, and nobody would have to know about it. You're not expecting anybody today, are you?"

Cynthia thought about it. "No, I'm not," she said. "I'd like that."

"Be there in half an hour. Maybe we'll go to Ybor City for lunch to cheer you up. Carmine's, maybe, for black beans and yellow rice, or Cafe Creole for gumbo. Or someplace else. Your choice. Think about it."

Cynthia smiled as she replaced the receiver. When Liz got nervous or excited, she tended to ramble on. But her intentions were from the heart.

She turned away from the phone, and it rang again. It was probably Liz with something more she felt she had to say before the thought got away. Cynthia picked up the receiver.

"What else?" she asked with a laugh.

"Hello, bitch. I see you got my note."

Cynthia froze. An adrenaline rush kicked her in the gut, and she felt her heart leap. Bands of fear tightened around her chest, forcing her to breathe in short, shallow gasps, and her head began to swim as though she'd had too much to drink, although she still perceived the moment through the eyes of cold sobriety.

"How did you get my number?" It wasn't the question she would have predicted asking in this sort of situation, but it was something she wanted to know. How could this demon possibly have discovered her unlisted number?

"You've got a stack of bills piled up on that little table in the family room, including your phone bill, so I just helped myself," the man's voice responded. It was a young voice. It wasn't an unkind voice, but it wasn't friendly, either. It was flat. Cool. Unemotional. Unremarkable.

Terrifying.

"What do you want with me?" Cynthia asked tightly. "Have I done something to you? Is this a revenge thing?"

"I want your heart, my dear," the voice said calmly. "I want to steal your heart away. I'm a big, big fan of yours. I've watched you for a long time, for as long as you've been on television here. You sparkle for me on my television set. But I hate those crystals. They give me strange feelings. They make me have thoughts . . . of you . . . and me . . . and Opal . . ."

"Stop it!" Cynthia screamed. "Leave me alone! I am not going to let you run my life!"

"Oh, no? Think about me. Maybe I'm somewhere in your yard, or across the street, and I'm watching you right now. Maybe . . ."

She slammed the phone down and ran to the front windows. Where was he? She went to her dining room windows, which looked out across the front yard, but she saw nothing out of the ordinary. She moved to the living room and looked through the sliders, out over the pool. She couldn't see anyone out there, either, but there was a lot of foliage along the lot lines she shared with her neighbors. Could he be hiding in there, using a cellular phone to call her?

She took two very deep and ragged breaths. No, he probably wasn't anywhere around. It was another attempt to frighten her.

Or maybe he *was* out there, waiting for her.

She retrieved the same utility knife she had grabbed the day before, after she found the note on her refrigerator, and slid to the floor, sitting where she could see out the front and the back, waiting for Liz, waiting for the Handyman.

Who would come first?

Mattie and Charlie trotted in from the family room where they'd been sleeping and circled her, nuzzling her, sensing their mistress was upset and not liking it.

Absently, she reached out her hand and scratched their heads.

14

"Why are you even worried about it, Captain?" Nick Estevez asked earnestly. "You talked to the woman last night. There isn't much question she was lying, is there? Anyhow, TPD's pissed, and they don't care why you want to take possession of the note. Their message is, forget it."

Ben Britton started to reply, but was interrupted by Charlene Bradford, the forensic psychiatrist. "I missed something," Bradford said. "Why is TPD pissed? They get bad calls all the time. What's special about this one?"

"They think this was a deliberately calculated misrepresentation with manufactured evidence," Britton said. "Cynthia Diamond claimed the same man who assaulted her at USF in the morning broke into her house later, while she was at work, and left the note . . ."

"With the lovely bleeding heart logo," Estevez added.

"Yes," Britton agreed. "When TPD rolled, all the news organizations in town heard the scanner chatter and rolled, too. TPD was embarrassed."

"That's what I don't get," Bradford said.

"They hauled out a lot of manpower to a very pricey home in a pricey neighborhood in response to a call from a locally famous television personality," Britton said. "They might not have responded quite the same way to a note found on a fridge in an aging two-bedroom bungalow in West Tampa. Think about it."

Bradford's eyebrows rose and she nodded. "You got that right," she said.

"That's not all of it," Dits O'Brien added as he joined the small group. "A suit from the TV station called the higher-ups downtown, flexed some muscle, and pulled some strings. Said the station management didn't believe Cynthia's story either, but the entire news department's credibility would be shot if she got charged with a crime. Suddenly there's cold water all over an investigation that mighta got her slapped with charges for filing a false police report. You don't find strings that powerful lying around in the streets."

Bradford snorted. "You tellin' me there's people in TPD who actually believe the fiction there's one standard of justice for all: black folks, brown folks, red folks, yellow folks, white folks?" she asked, affecting a slight street accent.

"There are still idealists," O'Brien said with a shrug.

"Sound more like ostriches to me," Bradford replied, the smile on her face softening the sharp edge of her remark. O'Brien smiled back, appreciating both her point and the bluntness with which she made it.

"All this is fine, but it begs the question," Britton said, swinging back and forth in the swivel chair he'd appropriated from a nearby desk. "The woman insists the note is genuine. She insists she's telling the truth. She was unshakable, even in the face of massive official doubt last night. I don't want to take a chance she's telling the truth, and we ignore her, and we wind up with victim number eight on our hands."

"The fact the killer knifes his victims in the heart isn't exactly a state secret," Estevez said. "Her job keeps her close to the story. She'd know a detail like that. If she was trying to create a believable scenario, she might think to add a bloody heart to the note."

"Are you certain enough she's capable of something like that to ignore the possibility that she *is* telling the truth?" Britton asked.

Estevez frowned thoughtfully. "I don't know," he said. Then he added, "Would the killer try for somebody as visible as she is?"

Bradford pursed her lips. "He might. Who knows? Maybe this is his way of trying to end his nightmare and ours. Twice now, he's picked more dangerous victims, but he still gets away with it, and the police don't seem any closer to him than after Mabel Brown. So maybe he starts leaving clues, advance warnings. He might not even realize he's trying to help us. It might be a subconscious effort to get himself caught." Bradford thought a moment, then added, "Why don't we do a handwriting analysis on the note? If Cynthia Diamond didn't write it, perhaps we need to think again about her credibility. One thing I'm with Ben on, we don't want to dismiss her and find out later we made a tragic misjudgment."

"That's why I want TPD to give us the note," Britton said. "But they're bowing their necks."

"Why don't you let me ask," O'Brien offered. "After all, I'm one of them. They might not be as proprietary with me."

"We're all on the same side here," Estevez said.

"Oh, yeah, no question," O'Brien said. "But the brass hats are worried about image, so they're reacting wrong. When the SO comes in demanding possession of the note, they interpret it as you saying you're better equipped to handle the incident than TPD is in its own territory. I mean, that's not what you're saying, I know, but they think that's what you're saying. It might sit better if a fellow traveler does the asking. I'm one of them. I'm thinking it wouldn't hurt to be a little diplomatic."

"Go for it, Dits," Britton said. "I'm a big fan of diplomacy. Have a free and frank exchange of views. And clues."

Liz McCormick rang Cynthia's door chimes. Immediately she heard the two dogs barking inside. It had been only about forty-five minutes since she talked to her friend, and she expected the door to open quickly. When it didn't, she rang again. Still no response.

She looked in through the light beside the door and gasped. Cynthia was sitting cross-legged in the middle of her living room floor, staring at the front door with her eyes wide and a long knife clenched in her right fist.

"Cynthia!" Liz called through the door. "It's me. Liz. What's the matter in there, honey? Open the door!"

A moment later, Cynthia's face appeared at the light, and Liz heard the dead bolt lock slide back. She entered quickly and looked at the knife, which Cynthia still clenched in front of her.

"My God, what's the matter?" she asked, urgently taking her friend's arm. "Are you all right?"

Cynthia turned out of Liz's grasp and walked toward the family room. Liz followed, and Cynthia turned back.

"Lock the door, Liz," she said tightly. "Make sure it's bolted."

Liz, momentarily stunned mute, did as Cynthia instructed. Then she followed her into the house and sat next to her on the broad, flowered sofa. She waited for Cynthia to say something. When it didn't happen, Liz tried to open the conversation.

"What's wrong?" she asked. "You sounded downright feisty on the phone an hour ago. Now you look like you saw a ghost."

Cynthia swallowed hard and gulped down a deep breath. "Whoever is after me got my unlisted number," she said in a voice barely above a whisper. "He called right after you did this morning. He said he took the number off the phone bill over there when he was in the house yesterday. He's playing with me. He wants me to know how easy it would be for him to get to me. I'm scared to death, and I'm mad as hell. I don't want to leave my house, but I'm afraid even to walk the dogs after dark. And nobody believes I'm telling the truth."

"Why don't you start from the beginning and tell me everything? Don't leave anything out."

"How much of this have you told the police?" Liz asked when Cynthia finished.

"Everything, except the phone call today."

"Why haven't you told them?"

Cynthia held out her hands in a gesture of helplessness. "How can I? I don't have any proof that it happened. The answering machine didn't record the call. There were no witnesses. Claiming I've had still another threat I can't prove isn't going to help my credibility. Even Lee Townsend thinks I'm lying, Liz."

"Honey, if you feel you're in real danger, you can't *not* discuss it with the police. You have to tell them."

"I can't do it if it's going to cost me my job."

"And what if it costs you your life?" Liz shot back.

Cynthia dropped her head into her right hand with her elbow braced on the arm of the sofa. She thought for a minute and then spoke without raising her face.

"You know, Captain Britton said there's nothing about the way I was attacked at USF that followed the serial killer's pattern," she said. "And the serial killer didn't break into any of his victims' homes and leave threats before he murdered them." She sighed. "Maybe it's not him. Maybe I'm overreacting."

"You're not overreacting, Cynthia," Liz insisted. "You were attacked, your home has been broken into, and you've had a threatening call from a man who said he wanted your heart. Jesus, how much more proof do you need? You're being stalked by the Heartbreak Killer. It's real!"

It wasn't the right time for it, but phones rarely ring when it's exactly the right time.

Cynthia's head jerked up and she stared at the black instrument on the breakfast bar. She made no move for it. Liz did.

"No!" Cynthia pleaded. "What if it's him again?"

"Then you'll have a witness," Liz replied as she picked up the receiver. "Hello?"

"Is this Ms. Diamond?"

Liz thought the voice sounded friendly enough. "Who's calling?" she asked.

"Is Ms. Diamond in?"

"This is a friend of hers," Liz said.

"My name is Benjamin Britton. I'm a captain with the Hillsborough Sheriff's Office. I spoke with Ms. Diamond several times yesterday. I'm certain she'll remember."

"Just a moment, please," Liz said, covering the mouthpiece. She turned to Cynthia. "Benjamin Britton from the Sheriff's Office," she whispered.

Cynthia breathed relief. "Yes," she said. "I'll talk to him."

As she took the phone, Liz whispered, "Tell him about the phone call!"

"Hello, Captain," Cynthia said.

"Good morning. How are you feeling today?"

"A little rocky, frankly," Cynthia said. "I might have overindulged my fears last night. Or maybe what I overindulged was the potion I drank to relieve them."

"Understandable," Britton said. Cynthia could hear a smile in his voice. "I guess you were made pretty well aware last night that not everybody believed your story."

"Even the Scotch didn't shield me from the skepticism." She paused. "Uh, Captain, there's something else. And you're not going to like it."

"What's that?"

"The intruder called about an hour ago. When I asked him what he wanted from me, he said he wanted my heart."

There was a long moment of silence on the other end of the line. When Britton finally spoke, he chose his words deliberately.

"And what significance did you attach to that?"

"Let's not spar over the signature of the Heartbreak Killer, shall we, Captain?"

"Let's not, to be sure. I don't suppose you have a witness?"

"Only my dogs."

"And who's going to take the word of a loyal dog, huh?"

"This isn't funny, Captain."

"And you don't hear me laughing, Miss Diamond."

Britton paused.

"There is a way we could be certain about whether you or someone else wrote the note on your refrigerator," he said. "We could do a handwriting analysis."

"I wondered why nobody mentioned the possibility last night."

"Why didn't you?"

"I don't think I was up to suggesting much of anything last night."

"Would you be willing to give us a sample of your handwriting?"

"Of course. How will I get it to you?"

"I'll send someone by your house to pick it up."

"Do you want me to write something new, or do you want an old sample?"

"How about the grocery list that's hanging on your refrigerator door, and something new I'll have the deputy explain when he comes by. He can also take your statement about the phone call you received today."

"That would be fine," Cynthia said.

LIZ stayed with Cynthia for the afternoon and finally convinced her to pack a bag and the dogs and spend the rest of the weekend at her condo in South Tampa. Meanwhile, Britton found a handwriting expert on the criminal justice staff at USF, pulled him in from a bass fishing trip in Lettuce Lake Park, and had him brought to the sheriff's headquarters. His name was Philip Masterson, and he was powerfully curious about what sort of emergency would require the interruption of a Saturday fishing trip with his ten-year-old son.

Britton had the note left under the yellow pineapple on Cynthia Diamond's refrigerator door, as retrieved from TPD by a very resourceful Dits O'Brien. He also had Cynthia's shopping list and a duplicate of the refrigerator note written by Cynthia on the same kind of white paper with the same type of red felt-tipped pen as the original.

"What we need to know, as soon as possible, is whether any of these were written by the same hand," Britton said, pushing the three pieces of paper across an interview table to Masterson. "They don't look the same to my eye, but I'm not an expert."

"You want me to take an educated guess here, now?" Masterson said. "Or should I do a thorough job and take these back to my office?"

"Hmm, give us the educated guess now, and depending on what it is, we'll decide where to go from there," Britton suggested.

Masterson asked for some supplies, including a magnifying glass, a ruler, and some hard pencils, and bent to the task.

Half an hour later, he had a tentative conclusion.

"I'm relatively certain the grocery list and Handyman note number two were written by the same person, and it probably was a woman," he said. "They don't look identical because the grocery list was hanging on the refrigerator door while, I assume, the Handyman note was written on a table or countertop. Vertical handwriting doesn't always resemble horizontal penmanship, except in a few key diagnostic areas."

"Obvious only to an expert," Britton added.

"Well, yes, I suppose," Masterson said, somewhat self-conscious.

"What about Handyman note number one?" Britton asked impatiently.

"Different person," Masterson said. "Probably a man."

"Is it possible the woman who wrote the Handyman note number two also wrote number one and was trying to disguise the fact?" Britton asked.

Masterson frowned in thought, shaking his head very slowly. "I don't think so, Captain," he said. "There are too many differences."

"What about the same person writing one note left-handed and one right?"

"I'm certain that's not the case, no," the expert said.

Britton stood and extended his hand to Masterson. "Thank you," he said. "We might have to call on you later for a more thorough analysis."

"Happy to oblige," Masterson said. "Now if someone could arrange to reunite me with my son, we have a few bass left to catch this afternoon."

When that was accomplished, Britton sagged back into his chair and pulled the three writing samples close to him.

"So she didn't write it, after all," Estevez said. "Maybe she had a friend do it."

"Or maybe not, Nick," Britton said slowly and deliberately. "Maybe it's the Heartbreak Killer, and, if it is, he's just left us a handwriting sample. I, for one, am grateful."

Estevez stared at Britton for a moment, then shook his head.

"So what?" the younger detective asked in a tone blanketed with fatigue and pessimism. "We know his vehicle, more or less. We know his booze, for whatever it's worth. We know his weapon, his blood type, his DNA. We know his nickname. We have his description. We might have a handwriting sample. I repeat: So what? Where does all this information take us? Nowhere. We still don't have the slightest idea who or where he is."

"But we might know where he's going to be," Britton replied. "I want a discrete shadow on Cynthia Diamond twenty-four hours a day."

By the time he arrived home that evening, Ben Britton had begun to get seriously worried.

Dits O'Brien had been very helpful once again as a liaison between the Sheriff's Office and the Tampa Police and had arranged for the two departments to split the stakeouts of the television anchor woman's Davis Islands home. On Cynthia's days off, the daylight teams would appear variously as cable television, water, and electrical crews. She would be followed while she worked, shopped, re-created, and dated by undercover officers. The nighttime teams at her house would be in plainclothes and unmarked police cars, lingering in unlighted shadow areas of the neighborhood. But Britton had been unable to get Cynthia on the phone to give her the results of the handwriting analysis or to tell her she was going to get round-the-clock protection.

His sense of foreboding was ominous.

The first protective team on the scene reported the house appeared empty. There was no movement inside, ringing the doorbell elicited no barking from the dogs, and one officer, who peered through a window of the garage, said Cynthia's car was gone. They were ordered to stay put and wait for her.

Britton tracked down Chris Pappas, the station manager, to see if he knew where Cynthia was. Curtly, Britton thought, Pappas referred him to Lee Townsend. Townsend's demeanor also was cool until Britton informed him new evidence indicated Cynthia didn't write the note found on her refrigerator, that a man had written it. But Townsend said he had no idea where Cynthia could be found; she wasn't due back at work until Monday afternoon. Britton asked him to call the SO immediately if he heard from her. Townsend said he would.

When Britton arrived home shortly before eight P.M., the whereabouts of Cynthia Diamond still were unknown.

He resolutely refused even to consider the possibility that she'd been kidnapped and he was already too late.

15

"If you wear a rut in the carpet there, can I assume Sheriff Romano will pay to replace it?" Laura Britton asked her husband.

He looked at her, curled up in an oversized chair in the family room of their lakefront home in Lutz, in the northwest corner of Hillsborough County. She had a book open in her lap and a look of sympathy on her face. He shook his head, acknowledging his own impatience and his growing sense of dread.

"You said when the carpet wore out you wanted to replace it with hardwood floors," Britton reminded his wife. "So here I am, trying to help you out, and all you do is complain."

She got up and put the book down after marking her place with the cover flap. She put her arms around his neck. "I didn't realize that's what you were doing," she said. "It looked to me like you were pacing and worrying."

"Ach, silly woman," he said. "After all the years we've been married, I'd think you could tell the difference by now between pacing/worrying and pacing/wearing."

He kissed her forehead, disengaged her arms, and dropped onto the sofa. He let his head fall back and rubbed his eyes. His mind wouldn't let go of the thought of Cynthia Diamond. "Given what she's been through, you'd think she'd want to get home and locked up tight before dark," Britton said. He glanced at his watch. "It's almost ten-thirty now."

"Maybe she moved out, like all you cops said she should," Laura suggested.

"You'd think she'd have told someone."

"Who?" Laura asked, dropping to the sofa beside her husband. "From what I hear, nobody believes her story. Who would you suggest she call?"

"Well, me, for one," Britton said. "You'd think she'd want to wait around at least long enough to get the results of the handwriting analysis."

"Maybe she didn't feel she should have to provide that kind of evidence."

Britton nodded slightly. "Innocent till proven guilty?"

"In danger till proven delusional."

"You should have been a lawyer," he suggested, letting his head fall back again. He was silent a moment, then he asked, "What if she didn't leave of her own accord? What if he took her, and she's dead or dying right this minute?"

"Why would he take the dogs?"

"Maybe he killed the dogs and they're lying where they can't be seen from outside." He suddenly sat up straight and pounded his balled fists into his knees. "Jesus, I wish she'd show up!"

"What about a search warrant?" Laura suggested.

"It's still a bit early for a judge to agree to that," he said. "Besides, where would it get us? Even if we found two dog bodies and evidence of a struggle, we wouldn't have the first clue where to look for her."

"But if there are no dog bodies—geez, this is gruesome—and there's no evidence of a struggle, you could relax."

He put his arm around her and pulled her to him so her head was on his shoulder. "Judges don't approve search warrants to give individual cops peace of mind," he said. He yawned and let his head rest against his wife's. "This is nice," he said. "If I drift off, don't let me sleep more than three or four days."

"Why don't we go to bed?" she said. "It wouldn't hurt you to get some real rest."

"I won't sleep," he said.

"You could try. Even if you don't actually drop off, I've heard relaxed bed rest is eighty percent as good as sleep."

"I don't know anybody who could help me relax," he said, turning his head to her.

"Oh, I think you know at least one person," she said. "You'll remember who it is if you think about it real hard."

They made love slowly, and afterward, he held her until she fell asleep. Then he got out of bed carefully so he wouldn't disturb her and went to the den. By the light from the street lamp, he called his office. The cops on Davis Islands continued to report no sign of Cynthia Diamond and no activity at her house.

The deeper it got into the night, the more his certainty waned. He could no longer convince himself Cynthia was all right. Britton was convinced morning would bring the worst sort of news.

But Sunday morning brought no news, except from the stakeout team in front of Cynthia's house. They reported nobody appeared to pick up the Sunday *Times* or the *Tribune,* both of which had been delivered before dawn, tossed into her driveway. There was nothing further Sunday afternoon or Sunday evening. Cynthia was gone, and no one knew where.

Eugene Rickey, also unaware that Cynthia was away, pulled his gray truck onto the Davis Islands Bridge three hours after nightfall Sunday. He was alive with nervous energy. His hands danced against the wheel; his left foot bounced on its toes. He was headed for a special hiding place at the house on Riviera Drive, a place from which he would make his move when the television news star walked her dogs before going to bed.

Opal had told him it was time.

He parked his truck on the back side of the Riviera Drive oval, the side away from Cynthia's house, and cut through two lots, working his way toward his target. He very nearly burst into the open a scant twenty feet from the dark silhouette of a sedan at the curb, across the street and one door down from Cynthia's house. Was the car occupied? At first, he didn't think so. There was no movement, although the vehicle was parked as far as possible from the nearest streetlight, and it was hard to see much detail.

Wait! A flicker. Someone was in the car and had lit a match or a lighter. It went out quickly, but Rickey was certain he could see the orange glow of a lighted cigarette. So someone was watching her house. The license plate was canary yellow and depicted the five-pointed star of a sheriff's vehicle.

Rickey's heart was racing as he tried to decide what to do.

Did it matter that a deputy was watching the house?

He took a deep breath, fighting to calm himself.

He could afford to watch for awhile, from hiding. He slipped into his usual place in the shrubbery across the street.

It was the first time he noticed Cynthia's house was dark.

Could she be in bed already? It didn't seem likely.

More probably she was out.

But she would be home eventually.

"SHE has to be at work in the morning," Britton objected. "Surely, she'll be home sometime tonight, assuming she's able to come home at all."

"Her boss at the station says she doesn't have to be in until early afternoon, so there's no reason for her to come home tonight. The chief was adamant about it, Ben. He wants to save the overtime." The man on the other end of the phone was Ernest Osceola, deputy chief of the Tampa Police Department. Osceola was half Spanish and half Seminole Indian—Espaminole, he called himself in a self-deprecating way that belied his pride in both heritages. He was trying to explain to Britton why TPD Chief Powell Reemer didn't want to send a car to stand watch on Cynthia's home for the hours of 12:30 to 8:30 A.M. "We'd be guarding an empty house," he said. "She won't come back until daylight. Would you?"

"What we would do isn't relevant," Britton insisted.

"Look, if the SO wants to pull the shift, go ahead," Osceola said. "There's nothin' I can do about it, Ben. I already made the argument that we shouldn't pinch pennies at the risk of another killing, but the chief thinks we're safe for tonight."

"Damn," Britton swore softly. It was already close to midnight. He called Dits O'Brien, who'd taken charge of scheduling the protective watch, and woke him from a sound sleep. Britton explained the problem.

"Shit," O'Brien cursed. "Lemme see what I can do, Ben. I'll get back to you."

It was five after midnight when O'Brien called back. He had prevailed on two young deputies who were always hawking overtime to roll out and pull the overnight watch at the Davis Islands house. But both had been in bed, and there wasn't a chance they could get to the scene before 1:30 to 2:00.

"I'll take what I can get, Dits, and keep my fingers crossed about the rest. Thanks."

Britton called Osceola back and asked if the TPD cops could cover until the SO unit arrived.

"No can do, Ben," the deputy chief said. "My orders are to have those guys gone at twelve-thirty sharp. I'm sorry. But, hey, you're only talking an hour, hour and a half, max."

"Yeah, that's all," Britton said. "I hope none of us has cause to regret the window."

AT precisely twelve-thirty, the driver of the unmarked sedan fired up its engine, stoked its headlights, and headed away from Riviera Drive. Eugene Rickey, cramping in his crouched position in his palm blind, started when the engine roared to life. The departure was so sudden, so unexpected, he wasn't quite certain what to make of it. If they were cops on stakeout, then there should be another car taking the sedan's place any second. But there was no sign of one. Maybe the sedan was supposed to stay the night but got called away to something more urgent. He crouched lower, all of his sensing capacity on maximum. Was it a trick?

His breathing slowed to barely sustaining. He wished he had remembered to bring the bourbon bottle from his truck. He needed a drink in the worst way.

He waited for twenty minutes and saw nothing. He began to relax.

Another set of headlights washed Riviera Drive.

As the vehicle approached, a metallic, winching sound cut the stillness, and Rickey saw Cynthia Diamond's garage door start up. The light inside activated as soon as the door cracked open. Cynthia turned her Lexus up the driveway and steered it to the center of the two-car garage. She closed the garage door behind her before getting out.

Rickey rocked back on his haunches and stood up slowly. It was time to reposition himself across the street, close to Cynthia's front door.

THE dachshunds were bouncing up and down by the front door, forever creatures of habit.

"Yes, you're good babies," Cynthia assured them. "I love you both, but you're trying to con me, aren't you? You don't want to go outside again. You just went at Aunt Liz's. You're angling for more treats."

She looked at the door. She desperately didn't want to go outside alone at this time of night, which is why she had walked the dogs before leaving Liz McCormick's condo. Liz had invited her to stay, but it was a small place, one bedroom with a futon in the living room. Their hours were so different they couldn't help but end up disturbing each other if Cynthia moved in.

The dogs were growing increasingly agitated. She considered locking them in the laundry room for the night with some paper spread on the vinyl floor. But they would bark for hours, and she wouldn't get any sleep. They should go out. It was their habit at this hour.

It was probably safe enough. Anybody watching the house, waiting for her to return, surely would have given it up by now as hopeless for the night. Still, it paid to take precautions.

For the third time, Cynthia went to the kitchen for the utility knife that was rapidly amassing more time as a weapon than a cooking tool. The blinking red light on her answering machine caught her eye. There was a message from Lee Townsend asking that she call him when she got home. Well, the hell with him, she thought. He can cool his heels for the night.

There was a similar message from Max Clevenger.

Ditto.

She hooked up Mattie and Charlie to their leashes, clutched the knife firmly, and threw back the dead bolt lock on the front door.

"Okay, okay, calm down," she told the dogs. "You'd think you hadn't been out in half a day. You can't have to go that bad."

Cynthia opened the front door . . . and stopped cold. She saw nothing that screamed danger, but the sheer stillness of the street was spooky.

The dogs bounded outside as far as their leads would permit. They were used to going all the way to the front sidewalk and looked around in question when their mistress stopped inside the front door, which restrained them from going any farther than the portico.

Cynthia tried to set aside the prickle of concern crawling along the edges of her mind.

This is silly. Why am I getting all upset? There's nobody out there.

She took several tentative steps outside and glanced up and down the street. All the homes were dark. With the exception of the impatient dogs, nothing moved on Riviera Drive.

Creepy. There's not even a house with late company. It's like everybody's moved away. I'm all alone here.

Is somebody watching me?

She jumped at a sudden noise beside her.

. . . What's that? Who's there?

The tall hibiscus bush next to the porch shook suddenly and bent toward her, its branches reaching for her face. Cynthia gasped and scrabbled backward until her spine cracked painfully into the doorjamb. The dry rustle of hibiscus leaves sent a chill shock through her.

Oh, God!

No!

Got to get back in the house. Lock the door. Get the dogs in!

Hurry!

Oh, God, hurry . . .

". . . Oh, Charlie, get out of there."

One of the dogs had scooted into the landscaping after a neighborhood cat that liked to hang out waiting for unsuspecting geckos to come within range. The cat never killed the little lizards. She pounced on them, then let them go. And since she had no front claws, the reptiles were never in any danger other than being frightened to death—as Cynthia nearly had been at that moment—because a fourteen-pound dachshund impatient for his walk had gone rooting around until he got his leash tangled up with the shrubbery.

"Come on, you two," Cynthia said, bending to disengage Charlie's blue lead from the hibiscus. She was relieved of her immediate fright, but not of her vague sense of apprehension. "Let's get done and get back inside," she told the dogs.

Cynthia pulled the front door closed behind her but didn't lock it. She saw no need since she wasn't straying far enough from the house to lose sight of it. As she stepped onto the sidewalk, she tried to see inside the indigo shadows around her house and her neighbors' homes, shadows that could hide so many things. With every step she took away from the door, her apprehension mounted. There *was* someone out there. She *was* being watched. She felt certain of it.

She looked up and down the street, and it hit like a slap in the face: She was expecting to see a light-colored pickup truck.

Of course, why didn't I make the connection before?

The frequent sightings of the truck had to have a connection to the man who was threatening her. She hadn't tied the two together earlier because the encounters with the truck and the man never overlapped. But her subconscious must have registered the coincidence. Too bad it took so long for it to surface. She would have to relay the information to Captain Britton first thing in the morning. Instinct told her it was important.

She checked the street and again saw no sign of the truck. So why were the hairs on the back of her neck vibrating like a tuning fork pitched to detect danger?

She could hear the rasp of her breath, short and shallow. She could feel her heart pound against her chest wall. A vague sheen of perspiration covered her, causing her clothes to stick to her on this warm, close night.

A strong breeze off the water played tricks with the shadows created by the streetlights and the neighborhood vegetation.

Next door! What is that by the side hedge?

It was the cat, hunkered low, slithering after some prey, real or imagined.

Across the street! Somebody's coming this way!

There was no one there.

Behind me!

She whirled and confronted . . . an areca palm, its slender fronds rustling like dry paper in the wind. She was certain she'd heard something else, too.

"This is absolutely ridiculous," Cynthia whispered. She glanced down at the dogs, who were squatting in the grass next to the curb.

What had she been thinking, coming outside at this hour?

Why hadn't she accepted Liz's offer to spend another night?

She saw the two unopened Sunday newspapers lying in the driveway next to the lawn. She stooped and picked them up, and suddenly felt a presence.

Gripping the knife even more firmly, she came up ready. But no danger materialized.

The dogs were pulling her back toward the front door. Holding them tightly, Cynthia backed to the portico, carefully putting one foot behind the other, her eyes taking in everything on the street. Her breathing was faster, more shallow.

She couldn't escape the sense that the closer she got to the safety of her house, the more immediate the danger, as though whoever was out there would wait until the last second, the instant she thought she had reached security . . .

Quite abruptly, both dogs went on alert, staring into a thick stand of pittosporum that lined the garage wall to a height of more than eight feet. Mattie uttered a long, low growl and Charlie began to bark sharply.

There was someone there, partially concealed among the long waxy leaves.

He was moving out of his cover, coming toward her.

"Cynthia, I'm back," he rasped in a hoarse stage whisper.

She dropped the newspapers and reached a hand behind her, touching the cool brass of the front door hardware, aware of the knife still in her hand.

But he was only six feet away. She would never be able to open the door and drag the dogs in before he was on top of her.

And she had little confidence she could defend herself against his assault, even with the knife. She remembered his strength from the fun house.

She would have to drop the leashes and dive for her own safety, leaving Charlie and Mattie to fend for themselves.

She swallowed hard and started as a new set of headlights swept Riviera Drive, approaching quickly. It was a convertible. The top was down. The radio was playing too loudly for the hour, and she could hear the laughing voices of several people.

She saw the shadowy form turn and look toward the source of the intrusion.

Now!

Taking a deep breath, Cynthia pushed the door open and jumped through it, hauling the dogs in after her. Once across the threshold, she slammed the door shut, quickly double locked it, and ran for the darkness of the master bedroom.

Would he break in?

Did she dare call 911 after the last debacle?

She reached for the phone and stopped.

What about the rest of the house? Are all the sliding doors and windows locked?

With a throat so dry it bordered on sore, Cynthia raced from room to room, testing and retesting the windows and doors. All were secure. She drew the blinds, turned out all the lights, and stood in the middle of the family room, waiting.

The knife was still in her right hand.

This was her territory. If he came for her here, he would get as good as he gave.

She stood there for more than an hour, listening for any sound but hearing none.

Only then did she let herself move.

Only then did she fish a small flashlight from a catchall drawer in the kitchen and by its beam pour herself a triple vodka on the rocks. She carried the drink, the flashlight, and the knife to her bedroom, where she found Benjamin Britton's business card on her dresser. He had written his home phone number on the back.

She laid down the knife, picked up the receiver, and dialed.

16

Ben Britton took the bridge past Tampa General Hospital onto Davis Islands at fifty-nine miles an hour, and he would have stretched that out if the streets hadn't been wet with a gently falling mist. When he screeched the wide right turn off the bridge, he saw Nick Estevez in the passenger seat brace himself with his feet. And he heard Estevez mutter, "Lousy Florida driver. There's never a cop around when you need one."

"I'll get you there in one piece," Britton promised.

"That's a bet," Estevez replied.

Cynthia's call had caught Britton awake in his den, brooding about her fate. He caught the phone in mid-first-ring, before it could rouse anybody else in the household. He thought he might have yelped in relief when he heard her voice.

"Are you all right?" he asked quickly.

"I think so, but there's been an incident here."

"Where?"

"At my home. About an hour ago. Could you come over?"

"Yes, hang on a second." He put her on hold and called Estevez.

Britton didn't bother identifying himself when his sleepy partner picked up. "She's home and there's trouble," he said cryptically. "I'll pick you up in half an hour."

"Right," Estevez replied and hung up.

Britton returned to Cynthia.

"Where have you been?" he snapped. His cheer at learning of her safety was tempered by his irritation at the anxiety she had caused.

"I had to get away from the house for awhile," Cynthia replied, a note of bewilderment in her voice. "I spent the weekend with a friend from the station, at her condo. It's in South Tampa. I didn't leave town. And I didn't know anybody was looking for me. Except one person, of course, and I didn't want him to find me. Although he did."

"What do you mean, he did?"

"That's why I need to see you."

"I'll be there in less than an hour. Will you be all right that long?"

"Yes."

Britton sucked in a deep breath and let it out loudly, calming himself. "Before I hang up, check and see if there's a car outside your house."

She checked and said there wasn't.

"I expect one to show up there any minute," Britton said. "They're ours. We decided to put you under twenty-four-hour surveillance, for your protection. We had a little time tonight when we didn't have a car to assign to you, but that won't happen again."

"Then you believe me now?"

"Yes," he said. "You passed the handwriting analysis. The note on your refrigerator was written by a man."

"I think I told you that."

"Yes, I seem to recall that you did."

BRITTON'S car squealed into Cynthia Diamond's driveway, somehow having made the trip from his home to Estevez's to Davis Islands without killing anyone or damaging any property other than Estevez's natural tranquillity.

The stakeout had taken up a position a door down from Cynthia's house. Britton flashed his brights as he pulled in the driveway. The unmarked car switched its headlights on and then off immediately when the driver recognized the captain. Cynthia apparently had been watching for him and swung open the front door.

"It's good to see you in one piece," Britton said. "There were moments over the weekend when we had our doubts."

Cynthia showed them in, poured fresh coffee for everyone, and recounted her experience in the front yard earlier.

Britton excused himself and called in a crime scene team. When he returned, Cynthia said she had one more thing to report.

"What's that?" Britton asked.

"Someone's been following me."

"Since the attack Friday morning?"

"No, going back several days earlier. Tuesday or Wednesday, I think."

"What makes you think you're being followed?"

"Because I keep seeing this truck all the time—"

Britton and Estevez interrupted in chorus, "What truck?"

Cynthia was thunderstruck by the intensity of their reaction.

Britton put his coffee mug down and leaned forward, his elbows on his knees. "What truck, Cynthia?" he asked deliberately.

"Did I hit a nerve?" she asked, frowning with curiosity.

"What truck?" Britton repeated, more forcefully this time.

"A pickup," she said. "That's all I know about it. I don't know what make or year it is, what the license number is, or who drives it. I've never been able to see him, or her. I'm not even really sure about its color. Light is all I can tell you. It's white or silver or a pastel. I see it behind me sometimes when I'm driving home from the studio. I've seen it parked out in front of my house. I can't prove it's the same truck everytime, but they all look alike, and I feel in my gut that it's the same one."

Estevez was taking notes furiously. Britton was listening intently.

"Is there some reason you didn't mention this earlier?" Britton asked.

"I didn't make the connection earlier," she said. "The sightings never coincided with the threats. But outside tonight, when I was looking around for some sign of what was spooking me, I realized I was expecting to see this truck. That's when it hit me."

They questioned her closely about the truck, but she could dredge up no additional details. She was able to confirm the recollection of earlier witnesses that the vehicle had no obviously identifying decoration, damage, or printing on it.

Britton closed his eyes and squeezed them with his thumb and middle finger. Despite himself, he yawned.

"Sorry," he said. "You know, I understand why you didn't mention this earlier, but I have to tell you, if you'd remembered it Friday, I'd have believed your entire story without reservation, and so would every other cop in the city. And I'd have answered the question you asked me at the USF carnival quite differently."

"About whether the man who attacked me was the Heartbreak Killer?"

"That's the question," Britton said.

"You think now he was?"

"Very possibly. Probably."

"But you said it didn't fit his pattern."

"I'm beginning to believe," Britton replied, "this man is a chameleon."

THE twenty-four-hour protective watches over Cynthia Diamond would continue without interruption now. Powell Reemer, the Tampa police chief, personally called Ben Britton to apologize for his miscalculation Sunday night in pulling his men off the stakeout. He sounded truly miserable about the decision.

"It could have been tragic," he acknowledged.

"No blood, no foul," Britton replied.

"That phrase in this case is a little too apt for my comfort, I'm afraid," Reemer said.

They connected tracing equipment to her phone in case she heard from the intruder again, although Britton harbored no illusions about the chances it would work. The Heartbreak Killer had demonstrated his cunning too often to offer much hope that he would make a serious error and call from his home. Still, it was a chance worth taking.

Cynthia pledged to do whatever was necessary to help the police protect her. But she balked at taking a leave from her job.

"What am I supposed to do, stay locked up in my house while you hunt down every light-colored truck in the county, assuming it's from this county?" she protested. "I'm sorry, Captain. I'll do what you ask of me otherwise. I'll tell you every move I'm going to make. I won't try to elude your watchers. When I say I'm in for the night, I'll stay in. Furthermore, I won't go on the air with any information you tell me to hold back. But I will not stay off my job."

As it turned out, holding back information was easier said than done.

"What do you mean the cops don't want you disclosing details about last night?" Lee Townsend raged the next morning. "You don't work for the cops; you work for me, and you give up what I tell you to give up."

Cynthia stood toe-to-toe with her boss.

"I won't disobey a police order, and I won't further endanger my own welfare," she responded vehemently. "And don't you start threatening my job over it, either. I know what the Q-ratings are in this market, and mine is among the highest. You'd lose market share with me gone, and given what a slave you are to ratings, I don't see you letting that happen."

Townsend glowered at her. "We'll let Chris Pappas make that decision," he said, storming off to the station manager's office.

When the two of them returned together ten minutes later, Ben Britton was in Cynthia's office. He had dropped by ostensibly to check some details from the night before, but in reality, he suspected she might have trouble with her supervisors and came to lend support if she needed it. Cynthia made the introductions.

"I don't believe we asked to see the police," Pappas snarled.

"Let's pretend the police asked to see you," Britton replied with a stuck-on smile that looked just a bit too friendly.

"What do you want, then?" Pappas asked.

Britton explained his rationale for ordering Cynthia not to speak of certain aspects of her case. "We don't want to send the killer to ground or have him destroy evidence," he said, purposely being vague.

"What evidence?" Townsend demanded.

"That's just the point, Mr. Townsend. If we tell you, and if it gets out, the killer will know what we know. If we have an edge, it's knowledge of his patterns, his transportation, his methods. I'm here to see that edge protected."

"I won't accept that, Captain," Pappas said. "Cynthia has a responsibility to this station and to her viewers, and if she refuses to carry out that responsibility, we can always replace her."

Cynthia exploded. "And where do you think that would get you?" she demanded. "You still wouldn't have the information you want, but I'll tell you what you would have, one dandy lawsuit claiming discrimination, harassment, and intimidation. I'll throw in every damned complaint I can dredge up, including the sexual coercion that permeates the air around here like bad perfume in a closed room. I'll paint a crystal clear picture of what a stinking cesspool this place is and point my finger right at the noses of the two cesspersons in charge."

She turned to Townsend. "Oh, don't look so damned hurt. You look like a puppy that got whipped for peeing on the rug. You're over forty. Don't you think it's time to grow up and accept that the journalism you profess to practice isn't measured by overnight Nielsens alone, that access requires responsibility, and the public interest runs a little deeper than some godawful editorial at eleven twenty-four twice a week?"

She looked from Townsend to Pappas and back again. "For once, why don't you two use your heads and leave your genitals in your pants where they belong?"

Britton just stood and watched with his arms crossed, a half smile on his face and a sincere gratitude in his heart that he was not a target of Cynthia Diamond's anger. All in all, he thought, she made a pretty good speech. He could add only one thing, and did.

"I should also mention that if you persist in this ill-conceived pressure to get everything Cynthia knows on the air, thereby threatening our investigation and her life, I will charge you both with abetting a murderer and put my job on the line to see that you're prosecuted to the limit of the law," he said with quiet menace. "I don't really think I'd have a lot of trouble getting the state's attorney to go along."

Britton didn't know if he could really do that.

They key was, Townsend and Pappas didn't know, either.

AT the same time Britton pulled into Cynthia Diamond's driveway, Eugene Rickey was on the opposite side of Hillsborough Bay, pulling up in front of the Janacek house in Culbreath Isles with samples for some of the material going into their new-and-improved kitchen pantry. Rickey should have been exhausted. After the emotional letdown of his failure to capture Cynthia at her home, he spent the rest of the night analyzing what went wrong and what his next move should be. The prospect of working out still another encounter with her while she was under twenty-four-hour police guard should have been daunting, but it was exhilarating, a challenge he was eager to join.

David Janacek answered the front door.

"Good morning," he said with a warm smile. "You're right on time. I'm heading to work, but my wife will go over your samples. I'll go along with whatever she chooses."

"You gonna trust the two of us with your money?" Rickey asked, in a way it was obvious he was making a joke.

"Oh, it's Kirin's money, too," David said, loudly enough for his wife to hear, but none too seriously. "I trust her with it, although I'll tell you the truth, I don't know why we need this pantry project done at all."

"It'll be a showplace," Rickey assured him.

"It's supposed to be a *kitchen*," David said. There was no doubt the project was going ahead. Now it had become a subject of teasing between Kirin and David. "A kitchen is where you cook, eat sometimes, refrigerate, clean up. A showplace is where you invite people in to appreciate fine art. In my world, kitchens and showplaces aren't the same thing."

"But this is *my* world, and welcome to it," Kirin said, grinning as she strode into the foyer with Casey in her arms, his bib still around his neck. "I can't wait to see the samples."

"We need a place to spread them out," Rickey said.

"How about out by the pool?" Kirin suggested. "The long table should do, and it isn't too humid yet. I'll roll Casey's playpen out there so he can get some fresh air and be out of our hair until his nanny gets here."

"This is where I get off," David said. He reached for his son, and Kirin handed him over. David held the boy at arm's length and bounced him playfully. "You be a good guy, you hear me, and don't let Mommy spend your inheritance." Then he brought the giggling child to his chest, embracing and nuzzling him. "Your daddy loves you very much, little guy. Don't you dare forget it, or I won't let you have the keys to the car for a month."

Casey shrieked in delight, almost as though he understood the joke, and David handed him back to Kirin.

"Bye-bye, Casey," David said as he picked up his briefcase. "Bye-bye."

"Bah!" Casey replied, holding a hand in the air and opening and closing his fist, trying to wave but not quite getting it.

David kissed Kirin. "Love you, in spite of your projects," he said. He seemed not to care a bit about displaying affection in front of a total stranger.

"Love you, too," she replied. "I'll be heading for work as soon as we're though here. I've got a meeting at eleven about those infernal windows."

"Hope you get it solved this time," David said.

"No more than I do," she replied. "In a moment of weakness, I agreed to talk about the problem with one of the local television stations this afternoon. Oh, happy day."

"You going on live?"

"No, it'll be on the news tonight or tomorrow or whenever they have some minutes to fill."

David Janacek was laughing when he walked into the garage.

"What channel you gonna be on, Mrs. Janacek?" Rickey asked.

"Oh, gosh, I can never keep them straight, there are so many now," she said. "The woman interviewing me is Cynthia Diamond, the one who wears dresses with rhinestones in them."

"Oh, yeah," Rickey said, delighted to learn of another nexus between his two worlds. "That's channel seven."

"I think that's right," Kirin said.

She kissed Casey on the forehead and hoisted him to her left shoulder.

"This seems like a pretty nice family," Rickey observed, unasked. "Don't find a whole lot like you all."

"If that's true, it's a shame," Kirin said, walking toward the lanai.

"It's a shame, all right," Rickey replied. "You don't know how much a shame."

AT noon, Eugene Rickey slipped out and made several phone calls to Kirin's architectural firm and to channel seven, claiming in each case to be from the other company. He said he was checking on the final details for the interview, to be certain everyone was in the right place at the right time. The calls sounded innocuous to those with whom he spoke. But they yielded the information that Cynthia Diamond would interview Kirin Janacek outside, on the Water Street Plaza construction site, at two o'clock.

Rickey got there at one. He wanted to see the two women interact.

He saw the WFSC crew arrive, trailed by an unmarked, dark blue sedan whose two occupants were very obviously plainclothes cops. Cynthia stationed herself where she would stand for the interview, and the camera was set up accordingly. It would capture Cynthia's head from the left rear and Kirin Janacek almost full-faced, standing in front of the building she had designed. The two cops stationed themselves so they wouldn't lose sight of Cynthia. Kirin arrived, got her placement instructions, and the two women rehearsed what they would discuss. Rickey moved cautiously through the small crowd until he found a spot where Cynthia could see him if she happened to glance his way. He made certain he was not within the line of sight of either the cops or Kirin Janacek.

He actually found the gist of the interview interesting. Water Street Plaza was shaping up to be the prettiest project in downtown Tampa and a perfect waterfront counterpoint to the new aquarium and sports arena. Construction was ahead of schedule; some of the floors of the west building, referred to as WestWater, already were partially occupied. But for reasons nobody could explain, windows on the south side of the building, the side overlooking Garrison Channel, Harbour Island, and Davis Islands, had a tendency to shatter and crash to the ground. As a result, offices on the south side of the building, otherwise ready for occupancy, stood empty while engineers tried to solve the mystery. And the south grounds, intended to be an outdoor lounging and lunch area for workers in WestWater, were closed to all public use until the windows above could be convinced to stay where they were put.

"This isn't the first office building to have this problem, is it?" Cynthia asked.

"Not at all," Kirin replied. "The most famous, I suppose because it was the first, was the Hancock Tower in Boston years ago. But there have been a lot of examples since. They always get fixed. It's just a matter of finding what the right fix is."

"Do you have any clue at all about what's causing it?"

"We have several ideas we're working on with a specialist, I guess you'd call him a plate glass engineer, who's had past experience with this type of problem. We think it might somehow be related to the amount of heat baking the windows. The south side is exposed to the sun almost all day. But I don't want to speculate any further until we have a lot more information."

At that instant, Cynthia looked away from Kirin and moved her eyes across the crowd as she turned toward her camera to summarize the story and sign off. Rickey was staring at her intently, and he thought her eyes caught his for an instant and stopped on him before moving on.

From her point of view, the moment barely registered on Cynthia's consciousness. She was fully focused on Kirin Janacek and Water Street Plaza. The intensity of the expression on the face of the brown-haired man in the crowd caught her eye briefly and then was forgotten.

17

Cynthia and Liz McCormick sat in cushioned chairs around a glass table beside Cynthia's pool and sipped brandy as they watched the moon sparkle off the calm water of Hillsborough Bay. The lights of the South Tampa peninsula reflected warmly. Nature had provided a temporary respite from the violent weather of the previous few days. The humidity was low for August, the air temperature comfortable. Cynthia almost felt at peace.

She had tried to maintain a semblance of a normal life, but it was hard to do with two armed suits following her everywhere she went.

When she was looking at lettuce in the grocery story, they were examining endive. When she was selecting seafood, they were picking through pork. They were her entourage on assignment, her chaperon on social outings, her escort through shopping malls, her baby-sitter at home.

In the first few days, their presence was a comfort. But it quickly wore off.

Earlier in the evening, Cynthia had been able to feel the eyes of two detectives boring into her back from the lobby as she and Liz ate poached salmon with dill mayonnaise and hearts-of-palm salad at Maison Place. Cynthia had suggested they return to her home for coffee and brandy.

"The watchers will still be around, but at least we won't have to see them," she said.

On the lanai, Liz poured herself a generous drink, since she had no on-air duties until the next morning. Cynthia, who had to return to the studio for the eleven o'clock newscast, sipped more modestly. Conversation focused on a frequent topic between the two women: the obnoxious men of WFSC-TV.

"There's word around the office that you carved Chris and Lee new excretory orifices," Liz said with a giggle. "Tell me all about it."

"They were being outrageous," Cynthia said. "I simply gave them what they needed."

"Outrageous about what?"

"They insisted I go on the air with a lot of information the Sheriff's Office wanted to hold back. I refused and dared them to fire me. Captain Britton said if they forced me to divulge sensitive material, he'd press felony charges against them."

"I heard you threatened to file a lawsuit."

"The word might have crossed my lips."

"Boy, I wish you'd videotaped it. I'd give a week's pay to see the expression on their faces."

"I'll have to admit, it was pretty satisfying," Cynthia agreed.

"You know," Liz said with an admiring look across the table, "for a dizzy blond newsreader, you're a tough broad."

It was hours later, and Cynthia was in the deepest sleep, when the phone rang. When she was able to identify what was disturbing her, her first thought was for work. She would only be called in the middle of the night for some sort of disaster. She fumbled for the receiver and yanked it free of its cradle on the fourth ring.

"Hullo," she grunted.

"Hello, Cynthia. How are you?" It was a man's voice. Vaguely familiar.

"Who is this?" she asked, still groggy.

"You know who I am," the voice said. "I'm sorry to wake you in the middle of the night, but I have a question."

She was wide awake then, and she knew who she had on the phone. Captain Britton said if he called, to keep him talking as long as possible for tracing equipment now attached to the line.

"What do you want?" she demanded.

"I was just wondering about all this secret info your bosses want to get out of you but the cops want you to withhold," he said. "You can tell me. It will be our secret."

An adrenaline rush shocked her system. "What are you talking about?" she asked absently, trying to sort out in her sleep-clouded mind how the caller possibly could have heard the earlier conversation on the lanai about the confrontation with Lee Townsend and Chris Pappas.

"You know what I'm talking about. Think about it, Cynthia. You were just telling your friend Liz McCormick about it a few hours ago."

"Stop it!" she commanded. "Stop it right now!"

"Why? Do you want me to come over there and force you to tell? You think I couldn't do it? You think those two fat cops out front could stop me? Not a chance, Cynthia. I'd be in your house and out again with you before they had time to react. I could do it right now. You want to do it now, Cynthia? I'm ready to take you this very minute."

She swallowed hard, resisting the urge to slam the phone down.

"Where are you?" she asked, her heart threatening to pound through her chest, her hand sweaty against the telephone receiver.

"Look out any window. I'm there. I'm everywhere. I'm with you all the time. All you have to know is how to see through shadows. But I have to leave now. The police have had plenty of time to trace this call..."

She heard herself gasp.

"You're surprised I know? How little you give me credit for, Cynthia. Yes, I know your phone is bugged, so I'm calling from a safe place. But the police will come to this spot soon, and I need to be gone when they arrive. Wait for me Cynthia. We will meet again very soon."

"Wait!" she yelled, but the line went dead.

* * *

IT was nearly four in the morning when Britton arrived. Cynthia's conversation with the Heartbreak Killer was securely on tape. Now if they had a suspect, they could do a voiceprint comparison. And a DNA comparison. They would have the killer cold. But, alas, the growing body of evidence only mocked their lack of suspects.

Britton turned to the two police officers who'd been on duty outside Cynthia's house.

"You guys didn't see *anything?* No vehicles? Nobody on the street?"

Both shook their heads. "Nothing, Captain," said the older one. "Not even the neighbor's cat was out there tonight."

"So he came in here on foot, probably sneaking through yards and bushes and generally staying in the shadows, probably the same way he got into your shrubbery a few nights ago," Britton concluded, shaking his head. "He's a brazen bastard, I'll say that for him. He had to be hiding close enough to your lanai to hear your conversation."

"What are we going to do?" Cynthia demanded. "He could have shot me right then, right through the pool screen."

"Shooting isn't what he does," Britton reminded her. "But if you want, I'll assign a female officer inside the house with you."

"No!" Cynthia said adamantly. "I already feel like I'm living in a fishbowl. I guess he won't make a move with two cops sitting outside. Remember, when he attacked me the other night, your people weren't here."

"Don't remind me," Britton said.

"And I'll make a point to stay off the lanai."

"Keep the faith," Britton said. "We'll catch him."

Cynthia snorted. "Before he catches me, I hope."

18

"How're you gettin' along with the mess, Mr. Janacek?" Eugene Rickey asked as he came in the back door of the Culbreath Isles house on Thursday morning. "I'm trying to keep the dust down, but this is the beginning of the time when most of my clients think their houses will never be normal again."

"Well, then, my feeling this house will never be normal again is

right on schedule," David said, balancing Casey in his left arm as he
let Rickey in.

"I'm not workin' on anything else right now, so I can get out of your
hair pretty quick," Rickey said. "It shouldn't be more than ten days to
two weeks for the whole project and only a couple more days for the
dusty stuff. Could have it done sooner if I hired some help, but then I'd
have to vouch for their work, and I never met anybody else who could
come up to my standards."

"We'll survive," David said. "Felicia told Mrs. Janacek you work
hard every minute you're here and only took one break for lunch. My
wife and I appreciate your diligence."

"Felicia? You mean the kid's baby-sitter? I didn't know her name."

"I'm sorry, I guess we forgot to introduce you," David said. "Her
name is Felicia Encata. She's Casey's nanny. She's been with us since
he was born, and we're all very fond of her. In fact, we first found her
four years ago when . . ." His voice trailed off.

"Sir?" Rickey asked.

"Oh . . . just a memory," David said. "We had a child four years ago
who died about a week after she was born. We'd hired Felicia then to
be her nanny, but . . ."

"I'm sorry," Rickey said.

"Yes, well, Felicia told us then if we ever had another child she
wanted to come back, and she was as good as her word," David said.
"Casey's as precious to her as he is to us, and he's very precious
to us."

"He's a great-lookin' boy. Wonderful personality," Rickey said, ruf-
fling the child's hair. "He was very lucky to have been born into a
house like this."

"Felicia should be here any second," David said. "I'll make certain
you two are properly introduced, then I've got to get off to court."

"You're a lawyer?"

"So my business card says."

"What's your specialty?"

"Criminal law."

"Really! Ever represent anybody famous?"

"Infamous is more like it."

"No, really. Anybody real bad, like Bobby Joe Long?"

"The serial killer? No. Nobody like that. My clients are into endeav-
ors of a less violent nature. Of course, they're all innocent, but the
charges against them are for what we call white-collar crimes." David
was chuckling, and Rickey smiled.

"Yeah, everybody's innocent these days," Rickey said. "They're all just misunderstood. Come from bad homes, abusive parents, alcoholism, and drug abuse. Nobody takes responsibility for his actions anymore. Nobody stands up like a man and says, 'Yeah, I did it. Now whatcha gonna do about it?' Excuses. They all got excuses."

"You sound like a Republican, Mr. Rickey."

"Yeah? Well, I ain't soft on crime, whatever that makes me."

The front doorbell rang and there was the sound of a key in the lock. It was Felicia, who insisted on ringing as a courtesy, even though she'd long been welcome to let herself in.

Casey recognized the routine by now and began squirming in his father's arms and laughing. "Ah! Ah!" he repeated.

"That's all he can say of 'Felicia,' " David explained. "He calls her, 'Ah,' and he knows when she's due here."

"He likes her," Rickey said.

"It's mutual."

David introduced Eugene Rickey to Felicia Encata, handed Casey over to her, and left the house to begin his day. Behind him, Rickey began stripping sections of Sheetrock from the kitchen wall. He seemed to enjoy his work, singing softly as he went:

> *Hey, girls, gather 'round.*
> *Listen to what I'm puttin' down.*
> *Hey, baby, I'm your Handym-a-an.*

19

It began somewhere on a beach, on a Caribbean island, perhaps. Cynthia was dreaming that she lay asleep on the sand in the sun, dreaming. And in her dream of a dream, she was dreaming. It was like mirrors reflecting images of other mirrors, endlessly, down into time. There was nothing to the dream except the perpetual reflection of Cynthias lying on the sand in the sun. It was not the sort of dream from which one is easily extricated.

So the first flash of light and the window-rattling roar registered in Cynthia's dream-chain only as an oncoming thunderstorm. The second flash and bang began to draw her back, but it took the frenzied skittering of two panicky long-haired dachshunds across her bed-spread to draw her awake in time for the third explosion and report.

"My God, what's happening?" she mumbled as she ripped back the covers and raced to the window facing the direction from which the chaos came. She was wearing an extra-extra large Tampa Bay Light-ning hockey T-shirt that said "Kick Ice" and draped to midthigh. It covered everything, including her bikini underpants, so she had no hesitation about opening the vertical blinds to the world. She saw a white glow in the southern sky, but nothing more. And then there was yet another blast, creating a blinding light and a sound impact that shook the house and convinced Cynthia to retreat from the panels of plate glass.

She closed the blinds quickly, so if the window broke, glass shards would be contained.

There was a news story happening outside, and all her instincts told her to get to it. She always remained ready for something like this. She slept in a light makeup that wouldn't smear and would allow her to look acceptable, at least, to the television camera until she got time to break away and primp. And she was lucky with her hair. It would look all right with a quick brushing. She slipped into a broad-cloth shirt with a button-down collar, drew on some shorts, slipped into shoes, grabbed her cellular phone from its charger, and ran out the front door.

The first thing she saw were two deputies from the Sheriff's Office, standing by the open front doors of the sedan from which they'd been watching her house. They were facing south, the direction from which the explosions had come, and the driver was shouting into his radio.

"We need all available units! All available units! . . . Fire, rescue, everything!" Deputy Edward Bollen screamed. "It's Peter O. Knight! It's blowing all to hell," he said, identifying the small Davis Islands airport.

There was another flash and a fifth report that made their ears ring. Bollen's partner, Deputy Tungsten Philips, looked over his shoulder and saw Cynthia running up the sidewalk toward them. Ab-sently and appreciatively, he noticed she didn't appear to be wearing a bra. Then he remembered why he and Bollen were there in the first place.

"Ma'am, get back in the house," he yelled.

"I'm a credentialed reporter, you know that," she said. "What in blazes is going on?"

"Blazes is right," Bollen said. "It looks like the whole airport is blowing."

"Miss Diamond, please go back inside," Philips asked again.

"Are you kidding!" she said. "This is a big story, whatever it is." She stopped by the hood of the sedan and dialed her station's emergency number, which reached the overnight on-call crew. Ironically, the head of the crew this night was Mark Munoz, who had been her cameraman at the fun house the previous week. Cynthia filled him in quickly, and he said he was on his way.

"Ma'am, please, we've got to get over there and see what's going on," Philips said. "But we can't leave until you're back inside. It's not just you. It's the whole neighborhood. It's called crowd control."

Cynthia saw the other deputy was trying without great success to shoo curious and sleepy residents back inside their homes.

"You know who I am, and you know I've got the credentials to be on the scene of breaking news," Cynthia said stubbornly. "You've got to go. So go. I'm right behind you. Or I can be with you, if you'll let me ride in the backseat."

"At least we'll be able to keep an eye on her if she's in the car," Bollen said impatiently. "We can't wait any longer. Let's go, man!"

They put Cynthia in back—Philips put a hand on her head as she ducked through the door frame as if she were a suspect he was protecting—and he put his other hand lightly on the center of her back, just below the shoulder blades, to satisfy himself there was, indeed, no bra strap there. Bollen slapped a flashing blue light on the roof and they squealed off on a four-block race to the airfield. With every yard they drove down Lucerne Avenue, the sky brightened. Cynthia couldn't imagine what was burning so intensely. They swung hard left onto Martinique and the airport grounds. What had exploded, it turned out, were several of the small planes tied down on the field. The blasts had left them little more than piles of flaming rubble.

There appeared to be no pattern to the destruction. None of the five blazing aircraft was adjacent to another, although flying debris had done significant impact damage to planes parked close by. It looked like someone had ignited huge bonfires intermittently around the field, as though for some giant pep rally, except there were no sports teams, cheerleaders or fans, only the Davis Islands neighbors of the airport who were gathering on foot and in their cars, awakened from sound sleep as Cynthia had been.

Bollen was driving and talking into his radio simultaneously, calmer now, describing for his dispatcher what he was seeing. The emergency apparently was confined to destruction of property, he reported, and for the moment, at least, the explosions had ended.

Bollen braked the car and jockeyed it around so it blocked the two-lane airport road crosswise, in an effort to stop the curious from getting too close. The maneuver was largely symbolic. If anyone had really wanted to get by, it would have been no problem to skirt the sheriff's unit and drive in on the grass. But no one tried. This was a neighborhood of law-abiding citizens who respected orders from the police.

Bollen put the car in park, facing an isolated royal purple-over-white Cessna 210 tied down just inside the airport entrance. They could watch the fires from a safe distance through the driver's-side windows.

From the corner of her left eye, Cynthia thought she saw a new flash, although it registered with her as only a spark. She turned her head toward the windshield. There was a small explosion and the Cessna 210 burst into flame directly in front of them. The blaze began, she thought, under the left wing near the pilot's door and spread quickly. Then came a much larger explosion as the flame ignited the wing's fuel cells. The left wing, then the right, shattered in balls of white heat and simultaneous shock waves so violent they rocked the car. Debris was flying in all directions; the aircraft could not have been splintered more thoroughly by the swirling winds of a killer tornado.

"Get down!" Bollen hollered.

Cynthia saw a twisted piece of metal with a fireball on one end hurtling through the air directly at their windshield. She recognized it at the last second as a landing strut. The fireball was a burning rubber tire.

She ducked behind the seat, lying as flat as she could across the driveshaft hump in the floor. It flashed through her mind that the car could become her tomb; it was no match for the blazing missile hurtling toward them. She was breathing in short, fast bursts. She covered the back of her head with her hands, trying to remember what good that was supposed to do.

Almost instantly came a sharp, ear-piercing screech of metal scraping metal, then a heavy thunk. Glass shattered. The sedan lurched back on its haunches, then settled down again on all four wheels. She felt little pebbles of broken windshield rain down on her back and her bare legs and hands. And she felt heat. Fire was somewhere close by.

There was a shriek, long and loud, a combination of terror and pain. It was a decidedly human shriek, decidedly human terror and pain.

She rose to her knees as throat-clutching black smoke began to leak into the car. The scene in the front seat brought bile to her throat. The landing strut had crashed through the windshield and smashed into Bollen's chest. There was no chance he could have survived it. A long strip of burning tread from the tire had been knocked loose by the impact and it, too, had come through the windshield, covering Philips like a blanket from his chin to his knees. It appeared he'd been overcome by the flame and smoke before he'd been able to make even a cursory gesture to save himself. It was a grisly sight; she had to fight to keep from being sick.

While most of the smoke was escaping through the shattered windshield, enough filtered into the backseat of the car to irritate Cynthia's throat. She began coughing, and her eyes leaked steady tears. She scrabbled backward, scraping her bare knees on harsh floorboard carpeting, stiff from too many washings necessitated by too many bleeding and retching prisoners. She reached behind her and tried to grab the door handle. But there was no handle there, just a metal knob where the handle should have been. Of course! Police take the inside handles off back doors for prisoner security. Well, she was a prisoner, all right!

The fire was spreading now, beginning to envelop the front seat. In addition to choking on smoke, she was also gagging on the definite and sickening stench of burning flesh. Suffocation was an immediate danger. She had to get out or die!

She thought about trying to get over Bollen, about crawling over his left shoulder, opening his door, and sliding out headfirst. But the fire had reached his right hand, lying limp on the seat beside his body, and once his clothes caught, they would go fast. She might not have enough time to make it.

She'd about made up her mind to try it anyway when she heard a banging on the car door behind her. Then, miraculously, it opened, and several sets of strong hands began pulling her backward, out of the car to safety. One hand accidentally hooked the breast pocket of her shirt, tearing it slightly.

"It's okay, lady," a male voice said. "Gotta get out of here before the car blows."

"What about the two men in front?" a second voice asked urgently.

She was clear now, standing on the asphalt with the strong arms of two men supporting her. "They're both dead," she rasped between fits of coughing. In the near distance she heard the wail of multiple sirens. Help was on the Islands and headed her way.

"Come on, let's go," said the man whose arms were supporting her. "When the fire reaches the gas tank, it's gonna go, too. Let's get clear. Let's get you some fresh air."

She looked for the news team she'd called to the scene, but if it was there, she didn't see it.

Grateful to be alive and weak from shock, she let herself be led away.

"Maybe you should sit down and wait for an ambulence, Miss Diamond," one man suggested. Cynthia thought she recognized him as a neighbor.

"No," she said, still coughing but not as badly. "I'll be fine. I was on the floor most of the time, where the air was better. But I need to change. I'm going to have to do a broadcast, and I can't do it with a torn shirt. God, what a story! What do you supposed happened?"

"I don't know," the second man said. "But I recognized you. My wife and I heard you lived here when we bought our house."

"I'm glad that didn't dissuade you," she joked. She didn't recognize this person, but he had a kind face.

"Let me walk you home," he suggested.

"Don't you have a car?" the first man asked. He fished in the pocket of his chinos and came out with a set of keys. "Here, borrow mine. She needs to get back here quickly. It's too far to walk. It's the blue Buick Riviera parked just outside the gate."

"Thanks," Cynthia said.

"You sure you don't want to wait for the ambulance?" he asked.

"No. Definitely not," she said. "I'm fine."

They drove quickly north on Lucerne, involuntarily covering their ears as two squad cars and four pieces of fire equipment screamed by. Seconds behind the trucks were two ambulances and then two news units, including WFSC's. There was another explosion from the direction of the airport, and then still another. Cynthia couldn't imagine what had caused this much havoc.

"What street is your house on?" she asked, renewing the conversation with the man behind the wheel.

"Severn," he said. "We wanted a house on the water, but we couldn't afford it. Maybe we can buy up someday."

"You have me at a disadvantage," she said. "You know my name, but I don't know yours."

"Howard," he said. "Joe Howard. My wife's name is Ann. I'm in the ceramic tile business. She's a teacher."

"Well, I owe you my life, Joe," she said. "I was about to be burned alive inside that car, if I didn't die of asphyxiation first." Her mind flashed to the two deputies who'd died in the front seat, and she felt the hot sting of tears in her eyes.

"I'm sorry we couldn't save the other two," Howard said. "Were they friends of yours?"

"No," she said, "they were sheriff's deputies."

"I know," Howard said. "Tell me where to turn for your house."

"Right up there, left on Riviera, then around to the water side and halfway down."

They reached her driveway, and she thanked Howard for the ride.

"Why don't I wait while you change?" he suggested. "Then I can take you back."

"Fine, thanks. Come on in. I won't be a minute."

She tested the front door and realized she'd left it unlocked. A surge of apprehension flooded her mind, but she brushed it aside and felt grateful to have someone with her. Joe Howard followed her inside, setting off the dogs, who always reacted that way to strangers and were additionally jittery about the explosions and the smell of smoke hanging over their mistress.

"Charlie, Mattie, be quiet!" she commanded. "Hush!"

Both stopped yapping, but Charlie, his eyes firmly fixed on Joe Howard, began to growl, a low, urgent sound coming up from the back of his throat.

"Charlie, for heaven's sake. Stop it!" she ordered.

She thought she heard something snap, like rubber might. Then a second time. But it wasn't until she heard the front door close and lock that she half-turned toward her neighbor.

"I'm sorry about the dogs . . ." she began, but never finished the sentence. The man who helped save her life stood before her with a knife, an incredible, horribly beautiful knife with an abalone shell handle. He moved the long blade slowly in an arc, making no move toward her yet, apparently content for the moment to watch her watch him. His hands were encased in latex surgical gloves. The soft kindness was gone from Eugene Rickey's face, replaced by a set of hard, wild eyes over a cruelly grinning mouth.

"I told you I'd be back for you, Cynthia," he said in the same rasping whisper he'd used in the fun house and several times on the telephone. "And here I am."

"I don't believe this," she said so softly she might have been talking only to herself.

Behind her now, Charlie continued to growl. The dog had sensed in the man what she hadn't been able to see until it was too late.

"How . . . ?" she started.

"I did all this for you," Rickey interrupted. "And it was fun."

"Did all what for me?" she asked.

"The airport. The planes. All of it staged for you."

"Why?"

"To see how creative I could be in luring your shadows away from you," he said. "I couldn't return for you while your shadows were watching."

"The deputies."

"That's right. The deputies. I had to draw them away, and it worked, didn't it? I didn't intend to kill them, but it worked out fine. I'm good at what I do. I'm very, very good."

"Your name isn't Joe Howard, is it? You don't live here."

"Right again, on both counts. Smart lady. I like smart ladies. Opal likes smart ladies." At the mention of Opal, he gestured toward her with the knife.

Her mind was functioning with perfect clarity. She knew the nature of the menace she faced, although she couldn't possibly have imagined the lurid details of what he planned to do to her. She knew she had to keep him talking and pray somebody would stop by to check on her. There were several possibilities. When Mark Munoz got to the airport and didn't find her, he would ask around about her. Perhaps one of the other people who helped her out of the sheriff's unit would remember she had driven off toward home with a man none of them could identify. Or perhaps the Sheriff's Office, when they realized their two dead deputies had been her bodyguards for the night, would send another car. If she could only keep him talking and give them all some time.

"What do you think will happen when you don't return the car outside?" she asked.

"I'm going to return it," he replied quickly. "I'm going to knock you out, tie you up and gag you real tight, and drive you around to where my truck is hidden. I'll stash you on the floor under a blanket, then I'll take the car back to the airport, wipe my prints off, and give it back to the thoughtful owner. I'll walk back to my truck—you know my truck, don't you, Cynthia? You've been seeing it everywhere you look."

She felt herself shudder.

"The truck isn't far from the airport," he continued. "You and I will take it to a party. A wild party. I have some very, very special things planned, Cynthia."

She felt perspiration trace a thin line over her spine.

"That was a great show I put on up there, wasn't it?" Rickey asked. "Actually, it isn't over. How many explosions have there been? Did you count?"

She shook her head.

"Eight so far," he said. "There should be seven more to go. We want to have plenty of time to get away, so I had to arrange the party to keep the others busy for a long while."

Another blast shook the house and freaked the dogs.

He grinned. "Six to go," he said, "although it will be about twenty minutes until the next one goes up, and then a half hour, and then another half hour, and another, and another, and another." He held up his left hand and ticked off each upcoming blast with his fingers. "You want to know how I did it?"

"Yes," she said quickly. "I was wondering . . ."

"Timers," he said. "Dynamite and timers. One stick to an airplane, attached by duct tape to the skin under the wing tanks, set to detonate by a timer I designed and built myself. I placed them all two hours ago. I knew when they started to blow, the two deputies wouldn't be able to resist checking it out, even if it wasn't their jurisdiction. I figured when they left, I'd come in here after you, and we'd be gone by the time anybody came to look in on you. I didn't count on you going with them, although now that I think of it, I should have known you would. When I saw you get in the car, I ran to the field. Got there just in time to see the car destroyed. I couldn't let anything happen to you, so I helped get you out. And then you let me drive you home, even invited me in."

"Listen, Mr. . . . what is your name?"

"That's nothing you need to know. Think of me as the Handyman."

"Handyman? That's how you signed the note!"

"That's me."

"But why a handyman?" she asked.

He began to sing, grinning hideously and arcing the knife, moving toward her now:

> Hey, girls, gather 'round.
> Listen to what I'm puttin' down.
> Hey, baby, I'm your Handyman.

The voice had an almost tinny, mechanical quality to it. The words were sung with extreme pleasure but no joy, each syllable following the last with steady, deliberate, unimaginative spacing, like a metronome.

"No, wait, please," she said, moving slowly away from him. Her back hit a wall. There was no place to retreat further. "Please," she said again. She tried to gauge what chance she'd have if she lunged for the knife and caught him by surprise. Very little, probably. She was strong for a woman, but all the liberation and equal opportunity in the world couldn't change the fact that men have superior strength, and this man was stronger than most. But if she didn't try, she probably had no chance at all.

> *I'm not the kind to use a pencil or rule.*
> *I'm handy with love, and I'm no fool.*
> *I fix broken hearts,*
> *I know that I truly ca-a-an.*

She once heard you could kill someone with a blow to the nose. You use the butt of the hand to strike hard with an upward thrust at the point. It would drive cartilage into the brain. It was a deathblow. Was the story true?

"Tell me something about yourself," she said, thinking the words sounded trite. "Why do you do this? Do you know?"

"Oh, yes, I know," he said. But he didn't elaborate. He took another step toward her. And still that godawful song kept coming:

> *If your broken heart should need repair,*
> *then I am the man to se-e-e.*
> *I whisper sweet things, tell all your friends,*
> *they'll come runnin' to me-E-e-e.*

Beside him, Charlie growled again, long and low, and now Mattie joined him. For an instant, Cynthia was overwhelmed with grief at the thought that when this man kidnapped her, he would very likely kill her dogs. Strangely, that notion, more even than the idea of her own death, impelled her off the wall.

She sprang at him with her arms extended, one toward the hand holding the knife, one toward his face. She let all of her outrage at the situation propel her. She had only a split second to wonder why he made no move to sidestep or stop her. Her right hand grabbed at his left and the hasp of the knife. His right hand was loose at his side.

When he saw her jump, the hand balled into a fist. When she was in his face, he brought the fist up hard and accurately, catching her squarely on the chin. Her own forward momentum carried her into the blow, and she was unconscious before she hit the floor.

> *Here is the main thing that I want to say-ay-ay:*
> *I'm busy twenty-four hours a day.*
> *I fix broken hearts.*
> *Baby, I'm your Handym-a-an.*

He stood over her limp form in triumph. The rest would be easy.

He reached down for her arms and started the song again, from the top.

The dogs, now knowing full well there was danger, went crazy. Charlie raced at the intruder and leaped for the hand that struck his mistress. Rickey pulled it away in time, but the dog landed hard against his right leg at the knee and knocked him off balance. In trying to steady himself, he lowered the hand holding the knife.

From that side, Mattie took a cue from her brother and jumped at Rickey. She had better luck. Her strong jaws closed around his forearm, and when he yelled in pain and pulled away, her teeth raked him badly.

"Goddamn you fucking bitch," Rickey swore. He kicked at the dog. But Mattie was quick and dodged his boot.

While the man's attention was diverted, Charlie charged once more at the right leg. His teeth sank into the soft tissue behind the knee, and Rickey screamed as the dog tore a small hunk of flesh from the top of his calf muscle. Blood spurted from the wound. Rickey swung the knife called Opal at the dog's head, but Charlie ducked under a dining room chair.

Rickey dropped to one knee to go after the dog, but just as quickly Charlie and Mattie charged again, in unison this time. Charlie got a solid shot at Rickey's right biceps, while Mattie sank her teeth into his T-shirt. Rickey yelled again and jumped to his feet with Mattie hanging from him. He raised the knife to plunge it into the dog's back when Charlie hurled himself again into Rickey's right leg. Rickey changed the knife's direction, intending to bring it down and into the body of the male dog. Mattie began twisting vigorously and tore loose, dropping to the carpet with a sizable piece of red cotton cloth in her mouth. Charlie leaped away and almost made it. The point of the knife grazed his shoulder and he yelped. But he wasn't seriously injured.

Now the dogs were barking fiercely, and Rickey was reeling. The noise roused Cynthia, who raised her head and tried to sit up. Only a wave of dizziness stopped her.

"I should kill you, cunt, no fooling around about it. I should hack you to death, you and your fucking dogs," Rickey croaked at her. "Look what they've done to me." He was turning in circles in the middle of her living room, blood flowing down his left arm and right leg, deeply staining the light blue carpet. "Look what they've *DONE* to me!" he shrieked. The barking of the dogs and the keening sound of his voice was joined by the jangle of her telephone. Cynthia lurched to her feet and made a move toward the kitchen.

"No you don't, bitch!" Rickey screamed. "Stay away from there."

He made a run at her, but Mattie clamped her jaws around his Achilles tendon, then danced away and growled at him from a distance of seven or eight feet. He turned and looked at her in disbelief. On his other side, Charlie began growling again, too. And somebody was pounding at the front door.

Rickey, his eyes blazing with rage and panic, opted for a strategic retreat. He raced past Cynthia and through the family room. He unlocked and pushed open the sliding glass door to the pool area, slashed through a screen panel and rolled through the hole into the damp St. Augustine grass beyond.

Then he was on his feet and gone.

Another explosion ripped the night.

THE phone call was from Ben Britton, who'd been alerted to the assault on Peter O. Knight Airport and the deaths of two of his deputies. He was calling to assure Cynthia she hadn't been forgotten in the confusion, and a new team of watchers was on its way.

The pounding at the front door was Mark Munoz. When he was unable to locate his reporter at the airport and heard about her harrowing brush with death, he left someone else manning his camera and drove the four blocks to her house to be sure she was all right.

Neither Britton nor Munoz realized immediately the good fortune of their timing.

Two hours later, Cynthia was sitting in her family room talking to Britton. At one time, there had been no fewer than six detectives from the Tampa Police Department on the scene, too, but after delicate negotiations between Sheriff Romano and Chief Reemer, the Tampa cops had withdrawn and left the man in charge of the serial-killer investigation to question the latest victim. It helped sway Reemer that one of his own, Dits O'Brien, would be present. O'Brien showed up with Nick Estevez in tow.

A medical technician had examined Cynthia—she remarked on how the process was becoming a part of her routine—and pronounced her apparently fit but in need of closer examination at a hospital emergency room. There appeared to be no evidence of a concussion, he said, and her jaw wasn't broken. He suggested Tylenol for her headache.

The EMT also took a look at the cut on Charlie's shoulder, cleaned it, and pronounced the dog ready to fight another day.

"Who'da thought dachshunds would be capable of fighting off an intruder?" the young medic said in wonder.

"A lot of experts would tell you that," Cynthia said. "Pound for pound, they're said to be the best watchdogs around. Three different vets told me when I was looking for a dog that dachshunds would give their lives for their owner."

"Seems like one swift kick would finish 'em," the man said.

"You have to catch them first, and, as you can see, it's easier said than done," Cynthia explained. She sounded like a proud mother.

"I guess so," the EMT agreed. "This blood all over your house didn't come from the dogs. Looks like they tore the guy up pretty good."

After the medic left, Cynthia gave Britton's crew a full statement, starting from when she woke up in bed to the sound of aircraft exploding and concluding with the killer's escape through her torn screen. She also was able to raise their comfort level with the news that the latest of the explosions just minutes earlier should have been the last, if the killer was telling the truth about the number of planes he'd rigged with dynamite.

An all-points bulletin called a BOLO put out by the Tampa police within minutes of the end of Cynthia's ordeal failed to locate the assailant, although a team in one Tampa police cruiser racing for the airport reported seeing a light-colored pickup truck pass them headed away from Davis Islands as they crossed the bridge by Tampa General Hospital. It didn't register with the officers at the time, because it never occurred to either of them the destruction at Peter O. Knight could have something to do with a serial killer.

When Cynthia described the intruder's knife, including the fact that he referred to it by the name Opal, the three detectives exchanged glances. It registered with them again when she said he wore latex surgical gloves. When she described her assailant, they nodded, acknowledging her description fit what they already knew of the man.

"We'll get you together with an artist right away," Britton said. "The sooner you start working on a sketch of the man, the clearer your memory will be of what he looked like."

"Will it take long?" she asked.

"Shouldn't," Britton replied. "The process is faster than it used to be when they used pen and ink and sketch pads. Now it's all done on computers."

"Cynthia, did this guy ever tell you his real name?" Estevez asked.

She shook her head. "I asked him, but he wouldn't say. He admitted it wasn't Joe Howard, though. And he didn't live around here."

"Is there anything else, anything you've left out?" Britton asked.

She shivered and shook her head. "You suppose he'll come back for me?" she asked.

"If history is any judge, no," Britton said.

"What do you mean? He missed me outside the front door the other night, and that didn't seem to convince him to give up."

"But he never had a chance to confront you that night, to show his face and talk to you," Britton noted. "Tonight you actually escaped his assault. In other cases where intended victims escaped, the killers didn't try again. When a plan is foiled, the bubble bursts, and the fantasy ends. The guy wasn't after you because you're Cynthia Diamond, television news anchor. He was after you because you triggered something in him that made him want to strike out and torture and kill you in a very specific way. But you didn't let it happen, and that ruined his fantasy. And it creates one hell of a problem for us."

"What problem?"

"When it was you he was after, Cynthia, and we knew it was you, we could protect you, at least up the point where he set the world on fire. Now we think he's past you, which means he's on to somebody else, or will be very shortly."

"And you don't know . . ."

"Right," Britton said. "We don't have a clue who's next."

"How much of this are we going to put out? How much is she going to reveal?" Estevez asked Britton later, when they got to headquarters. It was barely five in the morning, but many of the team members had gathered after being alerted by O'Brien to the new and unsuccessful assault.

"We're going to agree here on what to say, and she's going to abide by our decision," Britton said. "Is Pete Sisko in yet, does anybody know?"

"Yeah, Pete's been here about an hour," O'Brien said. "He's already fielding calls from everywhere. Wire services, radio, early television. The *St. Pete Times* and the *Trib* people have been up dogging us all night. Having two deputies killed has added a whole new element to a story that's already pretty compelling." '

"Call the team in and let's talk about this," Britton said grimly.

Seven of them were there, including psychiatrist Charlene Bradford, but absent were Sheriff Romano, Jock Salerno, and Jerry Lowensdorf—thank God, there was no ripped and tortured body for the medical examiner this time, Britton thought. He briefed them.

"Miss Diamond just finished up with the artist and is headed home to get some rest," Britton said. "Her house is under guard, not so much because we think the killer will be back, but to give her some privacy for a while. Her phone is off the hook, and she won't talk to reporters or go on the air herself at least until noon. We arranged that for two reasons: She needed some time to pull herself together, and I wanted the opportunity to discuss with you exactly what information we need to let the public have and what we should withhold. She's agreed: What we don't want known, she'll keep to herself for the time being, although she's asked permission to be frank with her audience in acknowledging there are facts she's holding back at our request. I thought it sounded like a reasonable way for her to protect her credibility."

There were head nods and general murmurs of agreement around the room.

"I have some suggestions, all of which are open for debate," he continued. "There was a day last week when Dits suggested we go public with a description of the knife and the truck. I said no because I didn't want the killer to dump either piece of evidence. Now I'm reasonably sure it was, at least in part, the wrong decision. I'm not going to second-guess myself, but we need to consider the question again. Do we let the public have the truck and the knife and hope they strike a chord with someone who'll be bright enough to call us?"

More people nodded. Charlene Bradford frowned.

"The knife, yes," she said. "It's unique. It's the sort of thing somebody might not forget once they saw it, and if they saw it, they might remember who had possession of it and pass the information on to us."

"And what if he hears we know all about his knife—what is it he calls it . . . ?" Detective Dutch Hale asked.

"Opal," Britton replied. "After his mother, apparently. Opal of the many last names."

"Right," Hale said, grimacing. "Opal. Jeez. Unbelievable, naming a murder weapon after your dead mother. So what if the news stories spook him, and he dumps it?"

"He won't," Bradford said with assurance. "It means too much to him. It's a keepsake. He's killed seven times, nearly eight, with it. He's not going to get rid of it. If we publicize it, he might put it away somewhere, but he's not going to lose it. It will be there, somewhere nearby, when we find him. Trust me on this."

"Maybe," Hale agreed, although somewhat reluctantly.

"I'm not so sure about the truck, though," Bradford said.

"Why?" Britton asked. "You think he'd dump it." His words were more a conclusion than they were a question.

"I think your original reasoning was good," Bradford said. "I think he might."

"It belonged to his mother, too," Estevez reminded everyone.

"But there's no reason to think he's particularly attached to it," Bradford said. "A truck generally isn't a personal item, like a knife can be, especially if the man is a laborer. He would tend to look on a truck as something utilitarian, as opposed to a toy or a status symbol. And it's still the best beacon we have to him, even if there are a zillion out there. I don't think we should risk having the truck get away from us. I think putting out the knife and the artist's rendering is fine. Let the public chew on those awhile. Anybody who recognizes the knife or the picture won't need to be told the killer drives a light-colored pickup truck to make the ID."

Britton looked thoughtful. Then he slowly shook his head.

"I don't think so," he said, finally. "I think we give up all of it."

"Why risk losing him?" Bradford asked.

"Because we're desperate," Britton replied. "There are some things we have to hold back. Details of the murders, for example. But I think we should give the public every opportunity to help us nail this guy, and the sooner the better. I say we give them everything we've got: the sketch, the knife, the truck, the fact he's from Gibsonton, his mother, his choice in cheap booze, the whole bit. There has to be somebody left alive and sane out there who will remember Opal and be able to give us the name of her son. And maybe there's even somebody out there who can put a few of the facts together and come up with both a name and a current address. To protect ourselves on the truck, we'll notify all car dealers in the region to report anybody trying to sell or trade a pickup matching the description of his. We'll have the clerk's office watch for title transfers on private sales. This isn't the time to hold back. I don't want to risk another killing and then have somebody come forward and say, 'Gee, if you'd only told me about the truck or the bourbon, it would have clicked with me that I knew the man.' I don't think I could deal with that."

Britton sighed. "There's another reason, a selfish reason, to make it all public," he continued. "It will demonstrate to the citizens, and to the politicians, that we haven't been sitting on our duffs all these months cleaning lint hair from our navels while Rome burned. I really would like to get them off our backs for a little while."

"For what it's worth, I agree," Estevez said.

The others nodded, even Charlene Bradford. "You convinced me," she said.

"The newsies are clamoring to know if she was stalked," Sisko said. "What do I tell them?"

"The truth," Britton said. "We're all but certain she was stalked. It's par for the course with serial killers."

"How about the assault at USF?"

"It's already a public police report."

"The eavesdropping on her and her friend from the station, the McCormick woman?"

"That, too."

"How about the note on the refrigerator?" Sisko persisted. "The twenty-four-hour watch? What do we say about them?"

"What can it hurt to let it go?" Estevez asked. "A lot of people already know about the note. Confirming it can't hurt anything. Disclosing we had the twenty-four-hour watch posted on her, it all helps demonstrate we were paying attention and doing our jobs."

"Two dead deputies shows all too well we were paying attention," Britton said dourly. "Goddamn the son of a bitch!"

"So, basically, we're only holding back the details of the murders only the killer would know?" Sisko asked.

"And the exact contents of the refrigerator note," Britton said. "You can confirm somebody broke into her house and left a note on the refrigerator, but don't disclose what the note said or how it was signed. When we start getting kooks with false confessions, the contents of the note will be one of those defining pieces of information, like the details of the killings."

Sisko nodded again.

"I'll relay this to Ms. Diamond," Britton continued. "Pete, you take care of the wolf pack. Now let's go get this bastard!"

"We need to do it fast, Ben," Bradford said.

"I know," Britton replied and turned back to the others in the room.

"He's frustrated that he missed tonight. But it won't dissuade him from trying again. On the contrary, he's got a lot of pent-up anger and frustration, and it will drive him to find a new target. The chances are, people, he's going to strike very fast. We ain't got a lot of time."

PART
TWO

20

The panic swept over him in waves.

A sense of uncontrolled hysteria clawed at Eugene Rickey's mind and turned his throat to sandpaper, his heart into a jackhammer as he dashed across town from the established elegance of Davis Islands to the anonymity and safe haven of his modest home in Clair Mel. The speed limit meant nothing to him. Stop signs were barely reasons to slow down. The caution that was his hallmark was abandoned. The logic that had always helped him avoid detection was gone. He was driven by an urgency to get to his home and to cover up the dog-inflicted evidence of the act he nearly committed this night.

There would be no circuitous route along the Crosstown Express-way this time. He went directly over the Davis Islands Bridge to Bay Shore Boulevard, drove a few quick blocks to the Platt Street Bridge, turned north on Thirteenth Street, and ran a few red lights along the wholly deserted waterfront (he took time to feel a pang of recognition as he passed the Banana Docks where Linda Serruto had died), turned east on Adamo Drive to Twenty-second Street, ran south past Sampson Jones's bait shop, and across the causeway to home.

He coasted into his carport with his lights off and shut down the engine. His breathing was labored, and he let his head sag forward onto the top of the steering wheel. He slid his right hand over the vinyl covering of the passenger seat, seeking the cool surface of the glass bourbon bottle he'd left lying there. When he lifted it, he could tell it was empty by its lack of heft. He shook it slightly. No slosh.

Damn, but he needed a drink in the worst way.

He slipped out of the Toyota and closed the door without slamming it. The yards in Clair Mel were large by Florida standards, but there was no telling who might be awake and alert to the sound of a truck door closing in the middle of the night. If they hadn't been before, surely the police were looking for his pickup by now—Cynthia Diamond could have described it in some detail, although she had seen nothing to set it apart from hundreds of other Toyota pickups in the area. Still, he retained enough of a sense of self-preservation to realize the need to avoid drawing attention to this particular truck.

Without turning on any lights, he let himself into the house and felt his way to the liquor cabinet. He grabbed a bourbon bottle, noticing he had to reach deep into the shelf to find one, which meant he would have to replenish his stock before long. He took it with him to the bathroom, twisting the top and tearing the tax stamp as he walked. The bathroom's one window faced the woods and Delany Creek, and he could switch on the lights with the assurance no one would see. In the fluorescent illumination he took stock of his injuries. They weren't serious, but they were fairly bloody, and they were beginning to hurt. He opened the bourbon bottle and drank deeply from it, twice, before setting it on the toilet tank and gingerly stripping off his clothes. He would have to discard these, too, a pair of cargo shorts and a T-shirt. This murder business was playing havoc with his wardrobe. He sponged off the scrapes and cuts, treated them with antiseptic, and bandaged those still seeping blood.

He dressed in clean clothes, tore the ruined T-shirt into rags, and returned to his truck with his bourbon bottle, a small flashlight, and a bottle of enzyme cleaner. Inch by inch, he searched the seat of the vehicle, the driver's side door, the carpeting, the steering wheel, and gearshift for stains of his own blood. Fortunately, he found only three, and all were in areas covered with vinyl. He used shirt rags wet with the cleaner to scour the blood, and it came up easily. He went over each stain four times, to be certain he left nothing visible behind. If the cops ever went over the truck with Luminol, they'd be able to detect residual bloodstains, but even so, it was his blood. He could claim to have cut himself on the job.

With the help of the bourbon and the undeniable logic telling him he was safe, he felt himself relax, the tension slowly leaching from his shoulders and upper back. He had nothing to worry about. Nothing at all.

He took another drink.

Of course, he was going to have to find a way to cover the dog-inflicted cuts until they healed. Wearing long-sleeved shirts and long pants was not his idea of the way to work in Tampa in August, but if that's what it took, so be it.

He put the ruined clothes, as well as the sponge he'd used to doctor himself, into a plastic bag. He started to dump it in his trash barrel but thought better of it. It was early Friday morning. Trash pick up wasn't until Saturday morning. He didn't want to chance keeping the evidence around for more than twenty-four hours. He put the plastic bag on the passenger seat. He would dump it in the Janaceks' trash when he reported there for work in a few hours. Nobody would ever look in Culbreath Isles for a killer's bloody clothes.

Back inside with his bourbon bottle, Rickey sagged onto the sofa, overwhelmed by sadness. He ached to stop the killing. But he was helpless before Opal. He would always do what she commanded. He would do anything to gain her respect.

Even now, from his dresser drawer, she mocked him, reminding him over and over that he failed to plan for the dogs and couldn't find a way to kill them when they attacked. Two *dachshunds!* He had been overwhelmed by two *dachshunds?* What kind of a sissy lets himself be chased away from the woman he wants by two dogs no taller than the tops of his socks?

You are so weak, Shorty! You are so small! *How are you going to win the heart of a woman when your thing is no bigger than the thing on her little dog? You are* pitiful, *you hear me? Absolutely, pathetically* pitiful!

Depression wrapped him up like a blanket.

He took another long pull from his bottle.

He leaned back into the sofa and closed his eyes.

God, but he was tired.

So tired.

His head lolled back on the sofa, and he slept.

RICKEY slept, in fact, until almost noon on Friday, which was completely out of character for him. He was one of those people blessed, or cursed, by an ability to function on three to four hours of rest a night. He often tried to sleep longer, but once awake, his mind and body were ready to begin the day, and lying in bed only frustrated him. The occasions that broke the pattern were those following the murders. He would sleep nine to twelve hours, stirring several times during the period but never coming fully awake, overcome each time by a strong desire to lie back and sleep again. But he hadn't wanted it to happen on this day, not when he was supposed to be on a job. When Rickey came fully alert, hours late to the Janacek house, he feared the aberrant behavior might be noticed and rouse suspicions. He concocted a story and hoped it sounded plausible.

"I spent the morning at the lumberyard, trying to straighten out part of my order for this project," he told Felicia Encata, Casey Janacek's nanny, when he arrived at the Culbreath Isles house shortly before one P.M. "They got some of the stuff wrong. But it's straightened out now."

"Mister and missus wondered where you were before they go to work this morning," Felicia said. "Maybe you should call when you going to be late. Since they don't know you very well yet, maybe they worry you gonna tear up the house and then disappear."

Rickey smiled. "That's not going to happen, and they should know it from the job I did for their friends," he said. "I should have called this morning, but I was up and out of the house real early, probably before anybody here was awake. I'll explain to them when they get home tonight."

"You hear of terrible thing last night?" Felicia asked. Casey was occupying himself in his playpen on the lanai. Felicia glanced out to check on him every thirty seconds or so, but other than that, she appeared to have no pressing duties. She was in a mood to talk. "It was just a few miles from here, you know? On Davis Islands."

Rickey feigned ignorance. "I'm not sure," he said. "I heard something on the radio about an airplane blowing up, or something like that." He wanted to change the subject or, better yet, end the conversation altogether and get on with work. He had a kitchen wall to dismantle, and that was all he wanted to think about, not what happened on Davis Islands the night before. He didn't want to think of it ever again.

"The killer strike again," Felicia persisted. "He blew up many airplanes and tried to murder a television news lady. She is safe, but two policemen died."

"Oh, yeah, I did hear something about it," Rickey said, turning his back on the nanny. "It's a bad world out there," he added as he walked toward the kitchen.

"Oh, yes," Felicia said, following. "Missus, she is very upset this morning. Davis Islands is not far from here, and she knows the news lady. They have been on the television together some times. She say keep the doors and windows all locked all the time. She ask me to tell this to you. She say when you take out wall, you will have to find a way to make the house safe. You understand? You can do this?"

"Yes, I understand, and I can do it," Rickey said. "I planned to do it. I always do it."

"She is worried the killer may be close by," Felicia added.

Closer than she could imagine in her worst nightmare, Rickey thought. Then he began to hum his song.

*   *   *

ARMAND Romano was exhausted, and he looked it. He had personally assumed the sad duty of informing the families of Edward Bollen and Tungsten Philips about the deputies' deaths. He marveled that in his six years as sheriff, he'd had to make such a call only once before, to the home of a deputy shot and killed attempting to intervene in a bank holdup. At least there had been some bit of good come out of that incident. The holdup man was about to kill a hostage, a female teller. The deputy distracted the robber long enough for a sharp-shooter to blow half the robber's head off, but the deputy paid for his heroism with his life. Shit happens.

But not like this. Bollen and Philips had died so senselessly, sitting in their car, acting as a roadblock to prevent a bunch of sleepy rubber-neckers from wandering into an exploding airplane. There was no way to tell Bollen's parents or Philips's wife and eight-year-old son their loved ones died heroically. There wasn't anything very heroic about sitting in a car and getting taken out in a freak accident. At least Bollen's family could plan an open-casket service for him. Phil-ips was quite another story. There's nothing to do for a body burned black from the top of its head to midcalf but close the lid on the coffin and put it in the ground. He'd had to explain that to Philips's family. They'd taken it very badly.

So Romano was in no mood to hear Britton's assessment that the investigation probably was in worse trouble today because the police had lost the advantage of knowing where and at whom the serial killer planned to strike. But he listened to Britton explain it anyway, hoping for some divine inspiration on a new course of investigative action. None was immediately forthcoming.

"Sheriff, there isn't any sense of me candy-coating it for you any more than there's any sense of you candy-coating it for the public," Britton said, forcefully, in an attempt to head off a fight spawned by anger, frustration, and unrelenting political pressure. "I would strongly urge you to hold a press conference, and you've got to ham-mer home to women in this county that they are in danger, mortal and immediate danger, and we need their help. We need it now. Today. If you don't want to do it, I will, but it has to be one of us. It would be a more forceful message coming from you, and it can't wait until to-morrow."

"I'll do it, Captain," Romano said without a trace of enthusiasm in his voice. "I don't need to be reminded of my duty."

"Sorry, sir, I didn't intend any offense. I wasn't reminding you of your duty; I was volunteering to take some of the burden, that's all."

Romano nodded slowly. "I know, Ben. But you've got your own

burdens, and nobody shoulders them for you. I can't ask you to shoulder mine."

Britton thought Romano looked even more haggard than he felt himself. His deep-set brown eyes were puffy under beetle brows. There were streaks of gray in his black hair Britton didn't remember seeing as little as a year earlier. The creases in the sheriff's dark face had deepened, and the lines of his square jaw were softened by a new tendency to jowls. The job, more than the aging process, had done this to him.

Romano had the misfortune to take over the Sheriff's Office after the most popular man ever to hold it decided to retire. There's nothing tougher than following a great act, especially when the daunting task coincides with a serious upswing in high-profile crime that arouses the citizenry as well as government officials to demand solutions that don't exist in the real world. It didn't help, Britton thought, that Romano was facing a tough reelection campaign in the fall, and he didn't have a prayer of winning if the serial killer remained at large. Maybe it would be better for him if he didn't win. The job appeared to be taking years off his life.

Britton had watched Romano begin to bend under the weight of this job over the last eight years. Part of the problem was the sheer magnitude of the evolutionary changes in the county. Where it had once been predominantly rural and agricultural, a growing regional business center now blossomed and spread, its bedroom communities stretching north along I-75 into Pasco County and most of the way east along I-4 to the Polk County line and beyond.

Culture clashes were frequent and violent. Some who considered themselves part of the old Florida, particularly economically distressed whites in isolated pockets of aging houses or ragtag trailer parks, gloated that the Confederacy once reigned here because they believed wrongly this fact lent authority to their virulent racism. They resented the money and the power and the displacing influence of the newcomers, mostly northerners, who bulldozed old hunting fields and citrus orchards to make room for pastel stucco houses with tiled roofs, manicured lawns and landscaping, and caged swimming pools. These old-timers and their offspring protested with such vigor, it wasn't until 1994 that elected officials were able to muster the fortitude to order the Stars and Bars removed from the county seal. The battle was fought with words in official proceedings. But out on the fringes of the struggle, the war was carried on in more violent ways.

A black tourist from Brooklyn was kidnapped on New Year's morning in 1992, taken to a deserted field, doused with gasoline, and set afire by three pieces of white trash from the Midwest who'd settled in Polk County but ventured into Hillsborough that morning to take out their drug- and alcohol-fortified racial hatred on a quiet man whose crime was being out early to find a newspaper. Battered pickup trucks running without lights crept through newly suburbanized neighborhoods during the quiet post-midnight hours, the driver and passengers wielding tire irons or crowbars against the windows of new-model cars parked on the newly paved streets. Occasionally, a pet strayed from its neighborhood and was shot.

Nor was trouble for the Sheriff's Office limited to crimes by and against local residents. The tide of illegal aliens from Haiti and Cuba and Nicaragua and Colombia that inundated South Florida spread north, finding the county's western coastline an isolated stretch, ideally suited to the needs of those jumping off freighters and tankers as they slowed on their northward course for the Port of Tampa. By night the refugees swam and waded ashore at places with such exotic names as Cockroach Bay, Bahia Beach, the Kitchen, Hog & Hominy Cove and Bullfrog Creek, either to make their way invisibly into the general population or to be caught and turned over to immigration authorities. Until the Clinton administration put a stop to it in 1994, immigration inevitably and unfairly granted the Cubans political asylum, for this was federal policy, but sent most of the others back to their homelands where they were considered pariahs or criminals and often paid for their dashes to freedom with their lives.

For reasons no one fully understood, domestic violence was taking a huge toll on life and health in the county. And random violence grew with assaults and shootings at automatic teller machines and gunshots exchanged on the highways. Only a few years before, Tampa was declared by somebody to be the fourth most dangerous place to live in the nation, and as went Tampa, so went Hillsborough County. It all landed on Sheriff Armand Romano's shoulders, which were beginning to slump from the weight.

"Whyn't you go home and get a few hours' sleep?" Britton suggested. "If you really want to handle the presentation, we can schedule it for six, right in time to catch the news broadcasts. I can hold things together in the meantime."

"I don't need sleep any worse than you," Romano protested, his puffy brown eyes fixed on Britton. "Have Pete Sisko see if he can set up the dog-and-pony show for noon. I don't think we can afford to wait longer than that. And you might as well announce it as a press conference. That's what it'll turn into whether we want it or not."

The rush of information satisfied most of the newsies. But when one particularly obnoxious television reporter accused investigators of less-than-sterling detective work, Romano let his irritation get the better of his prudence.

"You know all this stuff about the suspect, but still you haven't been able to put a name to him," the reporter chided. "How many more murders will it take before you get some sort of positive identification? How many, Sheriff?"

"There's no question in my mind we're close to making a positive ID," Romano shot back defensively. "I already told you that. The extensive number of facts we have on the man should signal that. If you could manage to keep your big mouth shut and your rump in that chair and your mind and your ears in gear, you might hear me when I tell you these things. But you'd rather be jumping up and down, accusing us of shoddy police work and trying to get your mug more airtime so you can take home a fatter paycheck. Well, maybe I could get you more airtime if I threw your ass out of here."

The reporter sat down with a deep scowl on his face.

Oh, joy, Britton thought. *Another enemy.*

21

"It's the heat," Rob Gallagher said with a sigh of satisfaction. "That's all it is, the intensity of the summer heat."

Kirin Janacek leaned forward over the solid teak desk in her West Shore office, straining to catch the concept that apparently explained why large blue panes of glass kept shattering and falling out of their frames on the south side of Water Street Plaza West.

"I thought we'd always known that," she said to the chief engineer on the project. "I thought the mystery was why the heat had the effect it did and what do we do to stop it."

"I'm starting at the beginning," Gallagher said. "The glass expands during the day, under the glare of the sun, and it contracts at night when the air cools off, cool being a relative term this time of year, of course. In some of the panes—not all of them, but some, particularly on the south side—the expansion and contraction cycles—"

"Cause the glass to shatter," Kirin interrupted, eager to get to the bottom line. "How do we stop the cracks?"

"That's not it, exactly," Gallagher persisted, determined as usual to make his report at his own deliberate speed. He unfolded his lanky six-foot frame from a chair and moved to one of the window panels in the north wall of Kirin's Cypress Street office, spreading his long fingers and slowly waving his left hand over the glass surface, as if he were cleaning it. "Generally speaking, it's impossible to manufacture commercial glass so it doesn't have any cracks in it. It always has some. In good quality glass, like we're using, you can't see the flaws; they're microscopic. And they aren't normally a problem. But sometimes in Florida and other hot climates, like Texas and Southern California, and even in Arizona where the climate is considerably drier, they can cause trouble. The summer sun bakes the glass all day, and the humidity condenses on it at night, and the cracks tend to, oh, what's the word I'm looking for . . . ?"

"Spread?" Kirin suggested.

Gallagher shook his head vigorously. "They don't spread, not in terms of getting longer and more numerous, at least not in the beginning," he said. "They expand, or rather, they bloat. That's a good word for it. Bloat. They expand without spreading. Then at night, when it gets cooler, they contract to their original dimensions. This expansion and contraction weakens the structure of the glass eventually, and then the cracks can spread, or as you suggested, get longer and mate and make baby cracks. That gives us even more cracks to bloat, until, eventually, the glass structure weakens and breaks down completely. The pane shatters. We shower the ground with lethal missiles. And it's over."

"Wonderfully graphic description, Rob," Kirin said darkly. "Do we have to have all the panes replaced? Will the manufacturer stand behind them?"

"Well, he won't stand under them," Gallagher joked. He raised a rueful but genuinely amused smile from Kirin.

"Gallows humor," he explained. "Actually, it isn't as bad as replacing all the panes. We think that by covering the glass with a thin titanium film designed to reflect heat, we'll solve the problem. We can retrofit what's already been delivered and have the titanium factory-installed on future shipments, including all the panes we've been expecting for the east tower."

"Is this film like the stuff used to darken car windows?" she asked.

"The same."

"So instead of the beautiful blue windows overlooking the bay, they'll be gray-black?" Kirin shook her head firmly and sat back. "Damn! I don't like it at all. I won't accept it. It would spoil the whole effect. There has to be another way."

"No, no, it doesn't have to be dark gray," Gallagher said. "The contractor says it can be done in the same blue as the existing glass. It will have the effect of cutting some of the light into the south-side offices. And when the occupants look out, the world will look more, uh, more blue, I guess, than it really is. But the film will also deflect a lot of heat, making air-conditioning cheaper and the people in the offices more comfortable. That's an acceptable trade-off, I think."

"How will the buildings look from the outside?" Kirin asked.

"No different," Gallagher assured her. "Even with the titanium, the south-side windows will have the same appearance, the same color, the same gloss as the windows on the other elevations. It will be an exact match. The only difference will be that people outside the buildings will have a harder time seeing in through the treated glass on the south side than through the untreated glass in the rest of the building."

Kirin thought a moment and smiled. "Actually, it might help us lease those first- and second-floor south offices," she said. "There's going to be a lot of outdoor foot traffic on the south side. A few prospective tenants have rejected the space because they said they'd feel like they were working in a fishbowl."

"Not with the titanium," Gallagher said. "After the people outside get used to not being able to see in, they'll stop trying. The tenants on those floors won't draw a glance from the pedestrians. It'll work just like the stuff works on cars."

"And we know this will do the job?" Kirin demanded.

"The same solution has worked perfectly on other buildings with similar problems, so it should work fine for us."

"Any of those buildings been in Florida?"

"Several."

Kirin smiled. "Okay. I like it. Now what's it going to cost, and how much will it delay giving birth to this baby?"

Gallagher gave her an approximate dollar figure, adding that the contractor was willing to pick up half. "It shouldn't delay the project at all," he added.

"Well, I hate to spend any more money," Kirin said. "How much are we going to have to jack up leases to cover it?"

"The bean counters are crunching the numbers now, but best guess is we'd put ourselves on a five-year amortization by raising the prime space rates about thirty cents a square foot. It can be less if we expand our description of prime space to include the three top floors instead of two. Or we can increase rates and expand the prime space, too, and really make out."

"Really make out how?"

"At thirty, maybe thirty-five cents more per square foot over three floors—and that's just for the prime space still unleased in the west tower and all of the prime space in the east tower—we'll cover the expense out of the starting gate, and our long-term bottom line would tick up quite nicely, too, which wouldn't hurt my morale at all."

"I don't want the bottom line to tick up," Kirin shot back, an angry edge in her voice. "We're making out fine the way things are. I don't want rates to go up a penny a square foot more than necessary to cover this additional expense. And if it comes to pennies, I'd rather eat it than pass it through. We treat clients fairly, and it comes back in good to us."

"You're the boss," Gallagher acknowledged grudgingly. "The numbers should be ready late this afternoon, maybe earlier."

"Tell me something, Rob," Kirin said, her voice softening. "Shouldn't the glass contractor have been able to predict the breakage and head off this problem?"

"I guess they can't ever tell when it will happen."

"You know what I think? I think that's total bullshit!" Kirin shouted in barely controlled anger. "I'd bet you a week's salary they figure the cost of the titanium film into the original contract price. Then if this heat thing happens, and they actually have to apply the titanium, they magnanimously offer to pick up half the cost so they look honorable. In fact, they're not picking up jack, and they're sticking us for whatever the other fifty percent adds up to. It's a damned scam."

"Are you guessing, or do you know something?"

"I'm guessing. But it's a reasonable guess. I'd love to catch them at it."

"To what end?" Gallagher asked.

"What do you mean, to what end? The end that says we shouldn't spend more on this project than we have to. That we shouldn't charge tenants more than we have to. Don't forget, I'm not only the chief architect on this project, I'm one of the general contractors. It's my responsibility to watch for this sort of thing."

"We'd have to bring in somebody else to retrofit the glass. We'll wind up paying as much or more than if the original contractor did it, and we'll have the original contractor pissed off at us, to boot. Don't let your irritation overwhelm your better judgment, Kirin. That isn't like you."

"It isn't like me to let subs walk all over me, either, Rob." Kirin paused, tapping her pen pensively against the edge of the desk. "I want to talk to them about this," she decided aloud. "If a retrofit is necessary, they're going to pick up all the cost. They should have anticipated this, and I'm going to tell them so."

"And if they say no?"

"Then we'll have to rethink our position."

"And pay what they're asking?"

"Maybe strike a bargain."

"But we *will* do the retrofit, one way or another?"

"I suppose so," Kirin conceded. "It's better than risking the wholesale slaughter of our tenants in a hail of blue glass shards."

By the time she got home, Kirin had convinced herself she'd been jobbed by the commercial glass contractor, and her irritation was profound, so keen in fact she bristled when she found Eugene Rickey still cleaning up after the dissection of the kitchen wall where the new enlarged pantry would go.

"I didn't think you'd still be here," she said to the workman, taking Casey from Felicia Encata's arms. The child yelped and grinned and pulled his mother's hair. In dismay, Kirin surveyed the state of her kitchen. Rickey had moved all the furniture from the morning room into the dining room and had taken down most of a morning room wall, opening the house to the lanai. He covered the gaping hole with a thick plastic drape and tacked it to the ceiling and adjacent walls and anchored it at the bottom with a double row of cinder blocks. Finally, he'd nailed twelve two-by-fours vertically and horizontally across the plastic so even a strong wind coming in from the lanai wouldn't take it down.

Thinner plastic sheets were thrown over the kitchen appliances and countertops and over the floor, and a thin film of white dust from the ripped up Sheetrock had settled over everything. On top of everything, the house was stuffy and overly warm.

"And why is it so hot?" Kirin asked, turning to the nanny. "Is the air-conditioning not working, Felicia?"

"No, ma'am," the young woman replied. "It's working, but it's turned off."

Rickey hurried to explain. "This is the worst part of the job, Mrs. Janacek," he said apologetically. "There's no way to rip out wallboard without making a mess. I turned the air off so the system wouldn't carry white dust through the ductwork and mess up the whole house, not to mention clogging up your air filters."

"Does it have to stay like this all night?" Kirin asked.

"You can turn the air back on most any time," Rickey said. "I finished pulling the wall down more than two hours ago, so the dust has had plenty of time to settle. Now, I can either leave this be for the night, or, if you want me to, I can roll up the dustcovers and take them with me, shake 'em out somewhere where the dust won't make a difference. Then at least you'll be able to use the kitchen tonight. This is the end of the dirty part of the job. I do all my carpentry work outside, so you won't get sawdust and grit in the house."

"We have to be able to use the kitchen," Kirin said, "if for nothing else than to have a place to handle the baby's food."

"No problem," Rickey said. "You'll have your kitchen back in half an hour. I'll clean up the floor for you, too, so you won't track white dust in on your carpets."

"I appreciate your consideration," Kirin said. "But what about the hole in the wall? Is that safe? The incident on Davis Islands last night was too close for comfort."

"That's why I put so many boards across it, ma'am," Rickey said. "Somebody'd play hell getting through there without making a racket to wake up the dead. There won't be any bugs getting in, either. There are no gaps. The plastic isn't as good an insulator for the air-conditioning as your wall was, but it'll only be this way for the next few days. I promise."

Kirin smiled the regretful smile of someone who'd gotten deeper into a situation than intended. "David's going to hit the roof when he sees this," she said to Felicia.

"Then I'd better get it looking as good as possible as quick as possible," Rickey said. "I don't want to be the cause of family grief."

"You taking Casey with you, missus?" Felicia asked. "If you tend to the baby, I can be helping Mr. Rickey with the cleaning up, so it get finished quicker."

"That's very sweet of you, Felicia, thank you," Kirin said. "I'll go and get my bath, and I can look after Casey."

"If we finish before you, I be seeing you next week, then," the nanny said.

"And I'll be seeing you tomorrow," Rickey said.

"I hope you can get started earlier," Kirin said. "I'd like to have most of the mess gone by dinnertime tomorrow."

"I'll do the best I can, Mrs. Janacek," he replied.

KIRIN luxuriated in her bath, one of those big oval jobs builders refer to as garden tubs, and, indeed, this one fit the description. Two large windows filled with glass blocks flooded the bath nook with morning and early afternoon sunlight, nourishing the dozen live plants on the deep tiled shelf serving both as a windowsill and bath accessory ledge. The tub had fourteen water jets capable of blasting away the worst aches and cares of the day, but Kirin had them operating at their lowest setting, producing a very gentle, almost subliminal, massage effect. She reclined against the white fiberglass, her head resting on the edge, and she used her right foot to adjust the thin stream of hot water falling from the faucet. Every once in a while, she'd curl her toes around the drain lever and let a little water out, to make room for new. Keeping the bathwater just hot enough for maximum relaxation without letting the tub get overly full was a delicate balancing act. It was something that had to be practiced.

Casey sat in a small, mesh playpen outside the door of the main bath, where Kirin could see him and watch his play. The simple act of watching him entertain himself seemed to drain the tension from her neck and shoulders.

God, but she'd been touchy today, first with Rob Gallagher, who was only doing his job, and then with Felicia and with Eugene Rickey. She didn't know why she was so irritated at seeing the kitchen torn up. She knew it was part of the process. This was the eggshell breaking stage of the creation of a master omelet.

Perhaps she was irritated in preparation for the irritation she feared she would feel from David when he got home and saw the mess. And maybe, once again, she was feeling the pangs of guilt at making their grand home, a place with which David already was uncomfortable, more grandiose still. She needed more pantry space, but maybe not this much more. Well, this would be the last project; there were no other improvements she could think of, except one landscaping replacement job that could wait a year and couldn't really be called an improvement project. It was more like a maintenance job. The kitchen might upset David, but he would get past it. He always got past his irritations. Kirin envied him his equilibrium and tried diligently not to take advantage of his easygoing nature. Perhaps the kitchen wouldn't look too bad by the time he got home. Eugene Rickey had promised.

She snuggled down deeper into the warm water and tried to shut down her mind. She pushed the kitchen work out of her thoughts first. Then she dismissed the shattering blue glass at the west tower. The next thing to go was all thought of any part of the Water Street Plaza project. Perhaps she cleared out too much. She had just closed her eyes to doze lightly for five minutes when suddenly the memories that had struggled all day to cross the borders of her consciousness rose and overwhelmed her. If truth be told, it was the approach of these memories that prompted and fed her irritable mood all day. They were memories of Amy, and the recollection that had her daughter lived, today would have been her fourth birthday.

Tears leaked from beneath Kirin's closed eyelids, flowed down her cheeks, and dropped onto the tops of her breasts where they dipped below the surface of the bathwater. Then the sobs came in crashing waves without end, first convulsing her chest, then wracking her entire body.

From his playpen, Casey sensed something wrong with his mother and stopped playing with his toy clown. His cooing slowly subsided, and he sat and stared at the woman in the bath, the beginnings of a look of bewilderment and concern on his soft baby face.

Rickey and Felicia had finished cleaning up the kitchen and left the house by the time David Janacek arrived home. He knew his wife was at home because her car was parked in the garage. But she didn't respond to his calls to her. Nor could he find Casey.

When he finally thought to check their bedroom, what he found hit him in the stomach like a balled fist.

There, in the bathroom, he found his wife in wretched agony, sobbing softly and curled into the fetal position in a large tub of slowly cooling water.

22

Eugene Rickey spent the evening thoroughly agitated. He paced his living room and drank. He tried to watch television, but the effort only raised his level of nervous energy. By force of habit, he tuned in the early news on channel seven, and there she was, Cynthia Diamond, sparkling as ever, perhaps a bit more restrained than usual, tired looking around the eyes, but there in her usual chair beside Max Clevenger, not even missing a day's work after nearly losing her life. The sight of her focused his attention on the pain in the heavily bandaged wounds her damned dogs had inflicted. He entertained a thought, as he had the night before while he was still in her house, about doing away with all of them: Cynthia Diamond, the dogs, even the cops, if new ones had been assigned to protect her. There would be no ritual, no rape, no work for Opal this time. Perhaps a shotgun blast to each head. It would be easy. It would be satisfying.

It would be stupid.

And it wasn't what Opal commanded him to do.

It would prove nothing but that a shotgun is mightier than flesh.

Opal had other things for him to prove. And he had to move quickly.

But where?

How would he find the special person she selected for him next? He'd always had confidence she would lead him to the right woman; indeed, he didn't recall ever thinking about it before this. But now he wasn't sure. She had not taken his failure on Davis Islands well at all. She would punish him for it, but how?

He paced his living room, flipping through channels. Everywhere, it seemed, local stations had preempted network reruns to air special reports on the Heartbreak Killer, complete with another computer sketch of what he might look like. The new likeness wasn't much better than the first one. Rickey figured the original had come from the fat guy who sharpened Opal for a while. Rickey recalled he'd laughed out loud when he saw it. It looked so little like the way he saw himself that it was worse than useless. Nobody appeared to have made the connection between him and the picture, either. He never saw anyone eye him suspiciously, never felt as though he were being watched. Now there was a second one, probably provided by Cynthia Diamond. The face was too puffy, the hair too long, the eyebrows too thick, the chin too pointed, the nose too blunt, the ears too large. Way too large. It also made him appear too dark and too hard around the eyes and mouth. Perhaps, in the heat of the assault, she'd seen the hardness in him, but no other living being had ever seen him look like that. All the rest was garbage. The two computer simulations together would create more confusion than illumination. Of that Rickey was certain.

They had some sketchy facts about his truck. A Toyota. Light-colored. What the hell good that would do them he couldn't figure. There must be thousands fitting the description.

What worried him more was the police had a good description of Opal, although they either didn't know her name or weren't giving it out. Television showed depictions of what a Schrade inlaid with abalone might look like, and this likeness was much more like Opal than the two drawings were like him. He tried to think who besides the bait man and Cynthia might have seen Opal or might be able to tie the knife to him. He couldn't recall ever showing her to anyone; his relationship with her was too private. Assuming he kept Opal out of sight until she called to him again, it should be safe to keep her nearby.

He took a fresh bottle of bourbon from his stash and noticed again he was getting low. He would go booze shopping on his lunch break tomorrow. He closed and locked his house, put the bottle under the passenger seat, and took off east, toward Brandon, where he had found the young schoolteacher. Perhaps if he confined his initial search to places where he'd had success in the past, he would have success again.

As he wheeled onto State Road 60, a bustling strip of franchise burger joints and upscale bars, he began to hum his song. Absently, he rubbed the denim of the jeans pocket where Opal rested and watched.

"All right, girl," he said to himself. "It's time to get it on again."

RICKEY tried just about everything.

He stopped in a Burger King and had a cup of coffee, spending forty minutes pretending to sip at it as customers came and went. Many were young, families out for a big Friday night at the fast-food restaurant. Some were teenagers. Some were working people, like him, stopping for dinner on the way home. Nobody particularly caught his eye.

He stopped for a drink in the overflowing bar at Outback Steakhouse and watched patrons get increasingly tipsy as their waits for tables expanded toward two hours. One woman, about thirty Rickey guessed, was wearing a lot of jewelry that caught the lights and sparkled, but it wasn't doing anything for him this night. He was having trouble concentrating. His mind kept wandering from the task at hand to the confrontation with Cynthia Diamond and the dustup with Kirin Janacek. He had to force himself to watch the women in the crowd closely, but as they came and went, he felt nothing. He left after three drinks, feeling a growing urgency to find his next target. He wouldn't settle for anyone. Opal wouldn't accept that; indeed, she wouldn't permit it. But she didn't seem to be helping him much, either.

He cruised a sports bar and found himself getting caught up in a televised exhibition football game between the Tampa Bay Buccaneers and the Pittsburgh Steelers. Tampa Bay was holding its own, but the announcers expressed little confidence at the outcome of the regular season. There were women in the bar. They held no appeal for him.

He tried a singles bar out toward Valrico, but he tired of the scene after half an hour and two hits from women who repulsed him.

He tried an Irish pub and found himself in the middle of a darts competition that attracted dozens of men. The few women in the place sat at the bar looking sullen and drinking Newcastle Brown ale. It was nearing midnight, and the only eyes that made contact with Rickey's over the pints of malt were glassy and uninteresting.

It was nearly one A.M. when Rickey pulled into his driveway. He sat and sucked on his bourbon bottle for several minutes, wondering if he was trying too hard. You couldn't force these things. They either happened or they didn't.

Just because they hadn't happened this night didn't mean they wouldn't happen tomorrow.

23

It was Saturday, but Eugene Rickey was at the Janacek house at 8:30 A.M. He normally worked jobs like this on Saturdays, even Sundays if the client wanted him to, and he was especially eager to get into the Culbreath Isles kitchen and get it past the messy and dusty phase before either or both of the Janaceks completely lost patience with the process. He thought Mrs. Janacek might have come close the day before. Today, he supposed, Mr. Janacek would be home, too, and he was the one who had little patience for the project in the first place. Better to get it cleaned up as early as possible and get on to the detail work that wouldn't interfere so much in the family's daily routine.

When Kirin Janacek opened the front door, she was holding a mug of coffee. Her feet were bare. Her hair was hanging straight and wet. She had been for a morning swim. She was dressed in a short lime green terry robe barely covering her backside. It was tied in the front by a strip of terry fabric and loosely closed over a brightly hued single-piece bathing suit. At the bustline at least, it emphasized one of her best attributes. Although he couldn't see under the robe at the bottom, Rickey made a silent bet with himself that the legs of the suit were cut high on the sides. Most observers would have thought, quite rightly, the suit made Kirin look good, and Kirin made the suit look good, a thoroughly happy circumstance. But Eugene Rickey didn't look at women that way. He considered the suit's design downright exhibitionist. And that made the woman wrapped inside it nothing more than a whore.

She ushered him in with a smile, then put a hand gently on his arm to stop him from walking straight back to the kitchen.

"Mr. Rickey, I want to apologize for yesterday," she said sincerely. "I think I was a little abrupt with you when I got home, and I'm sorry. I had an altogether rotten day at work, and I was wrestling with some very painful personal matters. I was snappish. The mess isn't your fault. I knew it would be this way for a few days. I had no right to be annoyed, especially since you said you would stay and clean up as best you could, and you did."

"That's all right, ma'am," Rickey said. "Nobody likes having their house tore up, even when they're expecting it. I'm going to lay the concrete floor today. Tomorrow I'll do the exterior walls and the roof, and I should have the worst of the project, the messy parts, finished up by the end of tomorrow night. There's a chance we can get it all done by the end of next week if the weather doesn't kick up and delay the outside work."

"Thank you, that sounds wonderful," she said, and took her hand off his arm.

She walked in front of him toward the kitchen. Although she was moving naturally, making no attempt whatever to be alluring to him, Rickey thought she was deliberately swinging her hips in a way to turn him on. He hated that. Opal used to do it for the men she brought into their trailer. Inevitably, the male *du jour* would lean forward and grab a handful, and Opal would giggle and pretend to be surprised by the physical attention. The liquor would begin to flow, and soon after, Eugene always knew, his humiliation and Opal's sexual promiscuity would begin.

He shook his head sharply to dislodge the images. This was no time and this was no place to be thinking about those things. This was one kind of business; the other was another kind of business. The two were not to be mixed, not under any circumstances.

He forced himself to think about the difficulties he would have the following week: tiling a concrete floor in a space huge for a pantry but confining for manual labor, and getting a perfect fit and finish on the three sets of louvered bifold doors he would put on the front of the

pantry. They were always a bitch to size and hang straight, and
the fact there were three sets—six doors—on this job made it all the
more complicated. He dreaded the prospect.

They passed by the dining room. David Janacek was feeding his
son. Rickey had to smile, although the sexual provocation of Kirin
Janacek had left an emotional bad taste on his mood. The lawyer had
the day's newspapers spread out over the table, and other newspapers
spread on the floor, under Casey's high chair, to catch whatever the
toddler chose to drop, throw, or spit from his perch. So far, the papers
appeared to have captured a toy and something that looked like a
half-eaten piece of Zwieback. The thin slice of overly dry toast looked
sort of whitish and soft at one end, as though Casey had gummed it to
death before discarding it.

"Good morning," Rickey said to him.

"Morning," David grumbled, his concentration focused on spoon-
ing cooked cereal into a small reluctant mouth with several new front
teeth.

Rickey could see this would be a swell day. Maybe Janacek would
leave the house, go to his office to catch up on some work. Or the golf
course. All big-shot lawyers in Florida played golf. It was supposed to
be a nice day for it until the typical afternoon thunderstorms boiled
up. If Janacek would get lost until midafternoon, he'd come home to a
nearly normal kitchen, which presumably would put him in a better
mood.

As if she'd been reading Rickey's mind, Kirin asked her husband,
"What's your tee time?"

"Nine-fifty," he replied. "Guess I'd better get a move on."

"What's the rush? That's over an hour from now."

"I'm supposed to meet Mike Annunciello for coffee in the grill. He
said he wants to talk about the Guyetti case."

"You say it like you don't believe it."

"I don't. Why would the deputy state's attorney want to discuss an
open-and-shut murder case with the defendant's lawyer on a Saturday morning? They've got Guyetti cold. He doesn't even pretend to be
innocent. Only thing to decide is how far to plead the case down to get
it off the books and out of the courtroom. We can do that in five minutes on the phone during the week."

"So what does he really want?" Kirin Janacek asked from the
kitchen as she poured herself another cup. "Mr. Rickey, you want
some coffee?" she asked as an afterthought.

"No, ma'am," Rickey replied as he laid out his tools. "I've had my
fill this mornin'."

"He wants money," David said. "What else?"

Kirin smiled. "You going to give it to him?"

Her husband shrugged. "I don't know," he said. "We're sure as hell not going to get any political return on it. He isn't going to survive the primary, and even if he does, he won't win the general, not running as a Republican, not against a Democrat who's held the seat since the invention of dirt. It's a pipe dream for him, that's all. An ego trip. Who's going to vote seriously for a candidate for Congress who's never held any elective office anywhere before, not a legislative seat, not even a local position like state's attorney or city councilman?"

"On the other hand . . ."

"On the other hand, this defense lawyer doesn't want to get on the bad side of a man who can make life tough on the lawyer's clients," David conceded. "It's a joke, but I'll probably cut him a check of some sort and think of it as a cost of doing business. You know, there ought to be a way to write off these contributions as business expenses, because that's what they are."

"I wouldn't advise trying it," Kirin said with a laugh.

"You wouldn't bring me a file in a cake if I went to prison?" he asked.

"And set a bad example for Casey? Not on your life. You do the crime, you do the time."

He got up and went to her and circled his arms around her waist. "You ought to learn to be nicer to me," he said gently.

"And if I don't, big boy?"

"I'll wear my golf cleats home and walk all over your expensive carpets."

They laughed, and he kissed her lightly on the forehead.

For his part, Rickey made a point not to look at them, although he heard every word they said. He couldn't help but compare this ostensibly happy home to his wretched life growing up. But how happy were they, really? There was a dark side to their lives, that was apparent. Rickey had seen it when Kirin Janacek displayed her wares for him. He wondered how many other men she'd done that for. How many had taken the bait? Did her husband know? Did he know his wife was a cock tease and a bitch and very likely a whore, just like Rickey's mother had been? In his mind, Rickey bet not and then, once again, he tried to push the thoughts away.

Why didn't Janacek haul his ass to the golf course like he said he would? Whyn't he stop pawing his wife and get out and leave the mother with her baby and the workman with his project? Rickey deliberately dropped several of his tools, hoping the clatter and his grunt of irritation would break their romantic spell, and it worked.

"You'd better get on to your political summit," Kirin told her husband. "I'll clean up."

"You going to the office, then?" he asked.

"Probably, for a couple of hours anyway, to figure out what I need to haul back here so I can work at home next week."

David looked surprised. "I didn't know you were going to do that."

"I really have to," she said. "The redesign of those two floors at WestWater is falling too far behind schedule. This is the only place I can avoid distractions and get the project done."

"Can you manage today with Casey?"

"Sure. I'll take him with me."

"You'll be hauling a bunch of stuff from your office to the car."

"Not all that much. I brought a lot of it home last night. Casey will be in his stroller. I can pack the floor plans in there with him. It might even keep him from crawling out and testing his walking legs. He's doing it now every chance he gets. Have you noticed?"

David grinned. "Yep. He's getting the hang of it. It won't be long." Then he added, "I feel guilty going to play golf when you're going to work, although not so guilty that I'm going to offer to stay home."

"And I don't want to change places with you," she said. "Writing big checks to political campaigns gives me hives. It's manly work."

He left to get dressed. She plucked Casey from his high chair and carried him out to the lanai for some fresh air.

As she left, Rickey started to sing.

> *If your broken heart should need repair,*
> *then I am the man to see-e-e.*
> *I whisper sweet things, tell all your friends,*
> *they'll come runnin' to me-e-e-e . . .*

That night, Rickey stayed at home and got drunk. He was too tired to go out prowling the streets for a new victim. At least that's what he told himself. The fact was, he'd already selected one, but he wouldn't acknowledge it to himself yet.

He didn't want it to be Kirin Janacek. In his periods of sanity, Rickey told himself she had not been displaying for him in the front hallway of the Culbreath Isles home at all; it's impossible for a woman at her level of beauty to move without looking alluring, especially in a form-fitting bathing suit. And why shouldn't she wear a suit like that in her own home, or out in public, for that matter? She definitely had the body for it, and it wasn't as revealing as a bikini or those hot dog vendors along the highways who wore thong suits with the thin fab-

ric of the suit bottoms tucked into their ass cracks so they might as
well be wearing nothing at all. What was the Janacek woman supposed to do, go for a dip in loose-fitting Levis?

But the lucid moments were becoming more infrequent. Rickey was
slipping fast into a state of transfixion. He had been able to think of
nothing but Kirin Janacek since he left her house at five o'clock. While
he'd been there working, he appeared to function normally, but he
was working by rote. He appeared to be concentrating on two-
by-fours, but he was seeing her face, her breasts, her ass. And he was
imagining what he would do to them. He concocted fantasy after fantasy about the ways he and Opal could cut her up and cause her pain.
He tried briefly to think how he could get her alone; it would be more
difficult to do since she lived with a man and a baby, and during the
week there was the added barrier of the nanny. But she said she'd be
working at home all next week. That presented some interesting options.

But it was a problem for later. It was a problem Opal would tell him
how to solve.

For now, while working at Kirin's house and while getting drunk at
home on his own sofa, the killing fantasies carried him away. They
were everything to him. They gave purpose to his life.

24

Ben Britton tried to remember his last day off. It had been only eight
days earlier, actually, although he had spent that day stewing about
where Cynthia Diamond had disappeared to, even as he tried to concentrate on celebrating his older son's birthday. Not a very restful in-
terlude, all in all. And since then, the days and nights of work on the
Heartbreak Killer case had dispelled whatever modicum of rest the
day off afforded him and run him even more deeply in arrears on
sleep. The weekend just past—the last three days, when you factored
in Friday—had been particularly intense.

Two FBI specialists in Washington and one from the Florida Department of Law Enforcement in Tallahassee had worked the weekend by computer and phone with Dits O'Brien, futilely scouring na-

tional and state records for something, anything, that would be a lead
to the killer. There was no doubt in their minds, or in the minds of
other experts the MAIT team was consulting, that the killer's next attempt would come quickly, as soon as a suitable target could be
found. And the hunt for a suitable target no doubt was in serious
progress.

"Everybody agrees with Charlene," Dits told Britton during a brief
retreat from cyberspace on Saturday morning. "As soon as our guy
can find someone, he'll move. The only thing buying us time is the
killer's looking for more mature, more sophisticated targets, and
they'll be harder to locate and isolate. On the other hand, one of my
buds in Tally thinks maybe the guy'll get so desperate, he won't care
about the social status of the next victim. He might take out a prostitute or a homeless kid just to get his confidence back. In case you
hadn't noticed, this isn't a pretty picture I'm painting you here."

"I noticed," Britton said sourly.

He asked Dutch Hale to check for female victims who might have
been killed anytime on Friday or since. Anywhere in Hillsborough
County. And for good measure, just in case, check Pinellas, Manatee,
Polk, and Pasco, too. Hale said he'd get right on it.

But here it was Monday morning, and only two women had been
killed in the region in the past seventy-two hours. Both were domestic
violence cases, perps identified and in custody. No ornate knife involved in either case. One had been a straight shooting. In the other,
the guy had run down his common-law wife because she borrowed
his new truck and put a ding in it in a very minor accident. The weird-
ness of it was that he used his new truck to kill her. It was dinged
now, but good. Bumper askew, grill destroyed, hood pushed in, windshield smashed, window frame bent. It would be in the shop a long
time, but not as long as the guy would be in the Florida state prison
system. What a world!

The paperwork facing the MAIT team was getting outrageous.
Tips were coming in to the Heartbreak Killer hot line from all over the
region—from all over the state, for that matter. People resembling the
killer and his profile were spotted almost simultaneously in Jackson-
ville and Miami, in Ocala and Orlando, in Sarasota and Sebring, in
Pensacola and Naples and Tallahassee. Around Tampa Bay, he was
seen everywhere, in a string of sightings adding up to 373 in less than
three days. And each report had to be checked out.

"Guy gets around," Nick Estevez said.

It was an impossibility of time and human resources for the Hillsborough Sheriff's Office to check every report, in and out of its juris-

diction, even with the assistance of the Tampa Police. So help was requested and readily received from surrounding police agencies, and
every report was followed up. Some were nothing more than possible
sightings called in by witnesses who wouldn't give their names. Each
of those drew a cruiser and two officers to check out the report, although the check might involve nothing more than having a good
look around the area of the sighting. Of the 373 reports, 41 resulted in
police interviews with real people. Two men were brought in for questioning. Neither was held for long. Four people called in to report a
neighbor was the killer. Twenty-seven people turned in relatives.
Three women turned in their husbands. One man turned in his wife
who was, he said, a lesbian transvestite quite capable of dressing as a
man and killing another woman when roused to anger. But he
couldn't explain how his wife could commit rape, complete with genuine semen.

None of the tips came close to a match.

And still the calls kept coming, generated in large measure by a
media blitz in which the daily papers, every day, radio and television
stations, every hour, hammered home how critical it was to find the
murderer who might be driven to strike again quickly. Private detectives and rent-a-guard agencies reported business booming as companies hired protection for their female employees and customers walking to and from their cars, and women who could afford it hired
individual guards for themselves. Requests for off-duty police to patrol shopping mall and supermarket parking lots went off the scale,
and most had to be turned down because all available cops already
were on overtime working their regular jobs.

The area was mobilized and frantic, yet the investigation was dead
in the water. Britton felt cornered, totally at the mercy of an anonymous madman who seemed able to strike at will and disappear into
the shadows so completely that he might never have existed. Except
for the dead and bleeding bodies he left behind.

"I'm going home for lunch," Britton told Estevez. "I haven't had a
chance to talk to my wife in a week and a half. I want to make sure our
kids still live with us."

"Take your time, boss," Estevez said with a sympathetic smile.
"We know where to find you if anything brea—"

"Cap'n, Cynthia Diamond's here to see you," Dutch Hale interrupted.

Britton nodded. "Okay," he said. "Tell her I need forty seconds to
call home and talk to my wife, then send her in."

Laura Britton feigned irritation at her husband's delay. "Reheating

Spam sandwiches can ruin them, you know," she chided. "And here I went to great pains to cut the stuff real thick, in slabs, on raisin bread with grapefruit marmalade, just the way you like it."

"I'll make it up to you, sweetheart, if it's the last thing I do, as it might very well be," he promised. "What are we having with the Spam sandwiches?"

"Turnip green tofu salad with castor oil vinaigrette."

"My favorite. I'll be there quick as I can."

He was still chuckling when he set the receiver in the phone's metallic arms and looked up. Cynthia Diamond was standing in his doorway. She looked dissipated. Dark circles ringed her eyes and her skin was pale and flaccid.

Britton stood to greet her, his smile replaced quickly by a mask of concern. "Miss Diamond," he said with a nod. "Come in. Sit down. Are you all right?"

"Yes. No." Cynthia shook her head. She remained standing, her hands washing each other nervously. "I don't know. I heard you say the killer probably won't be back after me since I got away once, but I don't think I fully accepted it. I can't sleep. I can't eat. I'm having trouble concentrating at work."

Britton rose from his chair, walked around the desk, and took Cynthia by the elbow. He guided her to the sofa, and they both sat. He was turned slightly toward her and took her hands in his. She smiled at him weakly.

"I think you have to take into account that only a weekend has gone by since a totally deranged maniac tried to kill you," he said, speaking softly, so the words sounded less frightening. "Now, unless you're one of those women deranged maniacs try to kill regularly, then it's probably not an experience you've grown used to. Therefore, it would be my judgment that you need to give yourself a lot of time to get past this."

"I know that in my head, but in my heart . . ." Her voice trailed off.

"Do you want protection? I'm sure I could arrange for it for a while. Not forever. But the budget can stand the strain until you're feeling a little more confident."

"No!" she said emphatically. "I'm the reason two decent cops are dead already. I'm not—"

"Stop it!" Britton interrupted sharply. "You've got to get past that part of it right now! You are not the reason the deputies died. They died in the line of duty, and their duty was to protect you and other citizens. They weren't assigned to you because you're a famous local celebrity. They were assigned to you because you were the target of a killer we want desperately to catch. If you think you were singled out for special favors, it's a conceit you haven't earned. The Hillsborough Sheriff's Office wouldn't have cared if you were in a steno pool. You still would have gotten round-the-clock protection."

She continued to look miserable.

His voice grew more gentle.

"Give yourself some time," he said.

She exhaled a long, shuddering sigh and appeared close to tears.

"I remembered something else," she said softly. "It was so weird."

"About your assailant?" he asked.

She nodded.

"He sang to me," she said.

"He *what?*" Britton was every bit as incredulous as he sounded.

"He sang to me."

"Hold on a second," he said. He went to his office door. "Nick, step in a minute, can you?"

Estevez appeared immediately.

"Now, tell us about this singing," Britton said.

"The what?" Estevez asked, but Britton held up a hand for silence. "Go ahead, Ms. Diamond," he said.

"The guy's coming at me with that horrible knife, and he starts singing," she said. "It was so scary. He was smiling this really nasty, pasted-on kind of smile and singing the song real slow, almost like a dirge. It totally freaked me out."

"Was it a song you recognized, or something he was making up as he went along?" Britton asked. Estevez was taking notes furiously.

"Oh, no, I know the song," she said. "It's an old pop song. I used to like it. Now I don't think I'll ever hear it again without getting the hinks. It's called 'Handyman.' "

" 'Handyman,' " Britton repeated almost breathlessly. "Dear sweet Jesus."

"That's the way the intruder signed the note on the refrigerator," Estevez said. "I never made the connection. It never even occurred to me."

"Not to anybody," Britton recalled.

Cynthia continued. "He was singing the words very carefully, like it was some part of a ritual or something. It was really, really creepy, a guy coming at me with a knife and singing an old pop love song."

"We ought to get the lyrics, see if there's some clue in them," Estevez suggested.

"I've got it on a James Taylor CD at home," Britton said. "I'll get it when I go for lunch." He asked Cynthia, "Is that all you remembered?"

She nodded. "I think so," she said. "I think that's all there is to remember. He sang to me before he knocked me unconscious, and maybe that's why I forgot it for a few days. I remembered it in a nightmare that woke me up early this morning. That's the real reason I came here, not to cry on your shoulder, Captain."

He smiled warmly.

"I don't mind you crying on my shoulder, Cynthia," he said, meaning it. "But whatever guilt load you're carrying, you need to let it go."

She stood and extended her hand.

"I'll work on it," she promised with a firm shake. "But I suspect it's not going to be as easy as it sounds."

THERE was nothing in the lyrics of "Handyman" to provide any obvious clues for Britton or Estevez. They gave a copy to Charlene Bradford, who pored over them for hours, but she couldn't find anything, either. It was something for Dits O'Brien to add to his cyberspace hunt for a computer link to the killer's identity.

The song and the fact of its singing became items, along with the contents of the note and the gruesome details of the murders, that would be held in confidence until the killer was caught.

Beyond that, "Handyman" held no meaning for anyone.

EXCEPT Kirin Janacek.

The song was about to drive her crazy.

The man who was remodeling her kitchen sang it constantly. She didn't want to hurt his feelings by asking him to stop, but she was quickly reaching the limits of her tolerance for it.

She was working this Monday in the den she and David shared as an in-home office. It was large enough to accommodate two desks and two computer systems, an indulgence they wouldn't have needed had they been able to resolve a years-long, good-natured dispute and settle on a single computer brand. He favored Macintosh; she would use anything as long as it was IBM-compatible and spoke MS-DOS. Each was intractable, although the need for dual systems was more complicated than mere personal choice. Both computers were extensions of the systems in their offices, connected across town by modems and dedicated telephone lines separate from their personal number and their home fax number.

"I remember the good old days," David had mused on the day they completed installing the in-home office setup.

"What good old days?" she asked.

"When two adults living under the same roof could make do with one telephone number," he said. "When I was growing up, it was a really big deal if the teenagers in a house got their own phone. Now the only things that don't have their own phones are the potted plants. Life was a lot simpler when I was growing up."

"You're beginning to sound like an old fogey," she told him with a playful chuck on the arm. "Did I tell you the ficus in the living room asked for a private line?"

"No," he replied. "And I was born an old fogey. I thought you knew that."

On this day, Kirin was structuring some redesign work for the electrical and communications systems in WestWater to accommodate a client whose office would consume two entire floors and who had some very special technical requirements. Working with her design software at home, where her staff would be reluctant to disturb her, she'd get the job done a lot faster. Still, it probably would take the entire week to finish the project.

Felicia was there to look after Casey, although Kirin took a long break to play with her son and feed him lunch.

He was sitting in his high chair at the kitchen table, deciding whether to take a chance on the cooked carrots, when Eugene Rickey began singing "Handyman" again. Kirin thought she must have heard it three dozen times already. And when she wasn't listening to her contractor sing it, she was hearing it on an unstoppable repeating tape loop in her head. She turned toward the new pantry area to plead for a respite, but saw him there in deep concentration as he studded up the new interior walls. Her objection to his choice of music was quickly overtaken by awe at the speed with which he was progressing on the job.

The new rebar-enforced exterior cinder block wall was up and covered in new stucco. The roof had been extended to cover the addition and tiled to match the preexisting construction. Working fourteen-hour days, Rickey had accomplished all this over the weekend when, he said, there was less likelihood of a building inspector happening by and stopping to inquire about building permits and other assorted bureaucratic nonsense. The interior work would be slower, Rickey said, but still he anticipated finishing by the end of the next weekend. When he completed the studding, he would do the electrical wiring, then the insulation, the Sheetrock, the floor tiles, the bifold doors, and, finally, the painting.

Kirin had no idea how the man was able to do so much so quickly and with such quality workmanship, but she felt certain he was driving himself to spare David as much disruption as possible. It was an exceedingly thoughtful attitude, and she decided she could put up with the song for a week if it helped Rickey work.

Meanwhile, Casey had decided the cooked carrots probably weren't life-threatening and was reaching out for the spoon, grunting in an effort to reunite his mother's divided attention. Kirin grinned to see it. She shoveled a mouthful into the maw.

"Can you say, beta-carotene, Casey?" she asked. "Can you say anti-oxidant? An-ti-ox-i-dant? No? Well, maybe next week. I guess we should master "mama" and "dada" first."

When lunch was over—Kirin indulged herself with a container of Dannon cherry-vanilla yogurt that she shared with her son—Felicia volunteered to clean up.

"You go back to work, missus," she said. "I will wash up, and then Casey and I will play for a little while until he is ready for his nap. You don't worry about anything."

"I never do when you're here, Felicia," Kirin said kindly. "I don't know what we'd do without you. You're the glue that holds this house together."

Felicia giggled and blushed. "I don't know what that means, but I think it's good, yes?" she asked. "It is good to be glue?"

Kirin patted her shoulder. "Very good," she said sincerely. "Very, very good."

WHILE Rickey had appeared deep in concentration as he nailed two-by-fours into place, he'd been paying very close attention to the lunch in the kitchen. He was taking care with his work, but a part of his mind was considering other possibilities.

If the nanny would go away, he could take the bitch this very afternoon. Maybe the Hispanic chick would leave when the baby went to sleep. No, probably not. She would want to be there the moment the child awoke to change him and keep him from getting fussy. When *was* the woman alone, with or without the kid?

The nanny got there in the morning before the husband left for work and her stay frequently overlapped his arrival home at night. If no opportunity presented itself today, perhaps tomorrow, or the next day. Rickey had heard the woman say she'd be working at home all week, and the time was certain to come when Felicia would have to run an errand, or the woman would go out and give him the opportunity to follow and take her and . . .

Opal had let him know she was ready anytime, at the first opening. She, too, was eager to get on with it. The woman was asking for it. Over the weekend, she'd practically lived in that provocative bathing suit, not even bothering to wear the jacket when she was out by the pool and sometimes leaving it hanging open when she came inside. Today, she was wearing shorts that barely covered her ass cheeks— he thought—and a cotton shirt tied up at the midriff, directly under her breasts. She was trying to entice somebody; you could practically see her nipples hard behind the fabric.

In fact, she was wearing white tennis shorts with a perfectly appropriate three-inch inseam and a bra under her shirt. But Eugene Rickey would see what he wanted to see. He would see the images that drove his fantasy.

He thought about what he could do to those breasts, those nipples. He would destroy them, destroy the rest of the parts of her body she used as enticements, too.

He would strap her down to her bed, make the bindings real tight and . . .

Stop it!

Not now.

Don't get aroused yet.

There's nothing to be done for it now, so stay calm.

Stay coolheaded.

Stay focused.

But stay ready.

25

They met first thing Tuesday morning in Sheriff Romano's conference room at the request of State Attorney Jock Salerno, a mainline thread in the political fabric of Hillsborough County. Salerno was in his second term as the chief prosecutor, well-entrenched and popular enough to win almost any office he chose, but he always chose the law. It was his passion, and he was very, very good at it.

His conviction rate was a little over ninety-four percent, the best by far in the entire state, and he was obsessed with reaching the ninety-five percent mark, something no Florida prosecutor had ever achieved. He worked toward that goal by holding his staff to exceptionally high standards of evidence and preparation. Occasional losses were inevitable, especially when juries were involved; even the best prosecutor couldn't always prevail over the quirkiness of human nature.

Because of Salerno's style, there was a lot of turnover in his office; many a young prosecutor couldn't meet his exacting standards or wouldn't bother to try. But he had a solid core in whom his complete faith was justified regularly, and he had no concerns about leaving day-to-day matters in their hands while he helped out on the MAIT team. Salerno told friends what he wanted more than anything in his long career was to be responsible for ridding the world of the Heartbreak Killer. If there was a way to avoid committing the man in favor of hauling him before a jury that would sentence him to death, Salerno vowed he would find it. It was not his intention to let this one get away on some sort of insanity or diminished-capacity defense.

Neither the police nor Salerno had yet switched to Handyman as a moniker for the serial murderer. They'd been calling him the Heartbreak Killer since the previous spring, early April to be exact, when Ruskin prostitute Christina Samprezze had died under circumstances both bizarre and similar to her colleague, Mabel Brown, the previous February. At that point the Sheriff's Office began to believe it had two victims and one killer. The fact that both had punctured hearts prompted a now-forgotten author to coin the nickname, Heartbreak Killer. It stuck, and it was a hard habit to break. But more importantly, the MAIT members didn't want to risk using the Handyman designation in public, where they might be asked to explain it before they were prepared to release information on its significance.

But how they referred to the killer wasn't the topic of the meeting. The only thing that mattered to Salerno was the strength of the evidence on which he would base a case.

"Are there any fingerprints at all?" he asked. "I won't have any trouble getting DNA admitted into evidence; it's solid in Florida courts. But what if I get a defense attorney who went to school on the O. J. Simpson case, or a box full of jurors sick of hearing about the subject because for months, every time they turned on television or opened a newspaper, there was some O. J. commentator blathering on about the credibility or pitfalls of DNA? Or worse, what if they think they don't need to listen to me because watching the Simpson trial made them experts on the subject? Give me the irrefutable fingerprint everytime. It's got a long and happy history, ordinary people can look at two prints side by side and see the similarities, and there's never any question about the quality of the evidence or its handling and possible contamination."

"Much as I'd like to, I can't do it," Britton said flatly. "Lord knows the crime-scene units have tried. But he doesn't leave prints. He's been using gloves from the get-go. Jerry has tried to raise prints from the bodies, we've searched all the crime-scene areas looking for the gloves, hoping to raise prints from the inside. Nothing."

"Why would women go anyplace with a guy wearing plastic gloves?" Salerno wondered. "They would ask questions, it seems to me."

"Well, the early victims were prostitutes," Romano reminded him. "They go where the money is, and the more kinks a guy has, the more they can charge. I doubt they saw the danger signs for the dollar signs."

"More likely, he didn't put gloves on right away," Lowensdorf said. "He knocked out all his victims at some point. All he had to do was wait until they were unconscious, until he actually had to touch them to tie them up and position them the way he wanted. The victims had no way to predict it was coming."

"And he didn't make any mistakes at all?" Salerno asked, incredulous. "He didn't touch anything, not one single thing, before he pulled on the latex?"

"There wasn't much at most of the crime scenes that would hold a print," Lowensdorf said. "They were all outdoors until the Evans woman."

"There were tons of prints around the apartment workshop where she died," Britton said, "but who knows if any were the killer's? We lifted all we could find, so when we catch the guy, we can determine if he was ever there, but that's all his prints would be good for. Same with the doctor's office. We got some from the Davis Islands house, too, but Ms. Diamond said she heard the guy who attacked her pull on the gloves as soon as he walked in the front door behind her, and he was still wearing them when he left. He didn't touch anything with bare hands."

The prosecutor drew a deep breath and pursed his lips. "So, we depend on DNA and hope for a jury that hasn't been so sensitized to it they're ready to puke."

"Or acquit," Britton added. "I guess a lot will swing on how good a job you do finding out how potential jurors feel about DNA. That's assuming you ever get to trial. I don't think there's a chance in hell he could pass a competency hearing."

"I'll get him to trial, Captain," Salerno replied with conviction.

Lowensdorf sighed deeply. "Jock, you and me, we've been having this DNA discussion for ten years," he said. "When are you gonna accept that DNA isn't one iota less reliable than fingerprints? Not one iota. We never have any problems with it in Florida courts."

"*I* already accept that, Jerry," the prosecutor said. "It's the juries I worry about. No matter how good a job we do probing their attitudes about DNA during selection, once the trial starts we can have a tough time getting them past the reasonable-doubt threshold with DQ-alpha."

"Seems to me when that test says you've got ninety-three chances out of a hundred a match is from the same person, you're well past the reasonable-doubt threshold."

"Not if I'm the defense lawyer, especially in a capital case," Salerno said. "I could make a jury buy a seven-percent margin for error."

"But we'll have more than the PCR-DQ-alpha," Britton said. "The lab's running RFLP on all our samples. We've got perfect matches in the Brown, Samprezze, Isabel, Serruto, and Cipriano cases. Hair and semen all from the same man."

"On each one of them, even using RFLP, there's still a one-in-one-million margin for error," Salerno said stubbornly. "And that's if the lab handled all the samples impeccably. You know as well as I do that isn't often the case. It's simply indisputable fact: Fingerprints remain the only identifier where there's no margin for error at all. None. End of argument."

"Not the end of the argument," Lowensdorf said. "A one-in-one-million chance for error is minuscule, and when you've got results coming up the same in five cases, you pretty much eliminate even that sliver of doubt."

"And we have results still to come in the Evans and Erlich killings," Romano added. "Assuming more matches, that makes seven murders where the DNA evidence gives you the same result. How much more do you want?"

"I'm not going to be prosecuting five cases," Salerno said. "I'm not going to be prosecuting seven. I'm going to have to pick one, and it will be one of the last two. A jury's a lot more sympathetic to the prosecution if the victim is respectable. And I would throw your own words back at you: the RFLPs aren't back on either of those cases yet, so we have no idea what we're going to be looking at."

"For God's sake, Jock!" Sheriff Romano was beside himself. "Look at how he butchered those women! Escalating torture. Escalating mutilation. It's the same guy, getting worse by the case. The DNA results won't be any different."

"I'm not going to make that judgment without the results," Salerno insisted. "What lab are you using for the tests?"

"Same one that did the first five, Conlee MacFarland in Jackson-ville," Lowensdorf replied.

"What kind of record do they have handling samples?" Salerno asked. "Any foul-ups, contamination problems, lost samples?"

Lowensdorf shrugged. "They're human," he said. "Shit happens. They're good as any."

"Not good enough," Salerno objected. "You put a hotshot defense lawyer in front of the jury, like Janet Songee or David Janacek, and you're gonna have a panel that wouldn't believe your Conlee MacFar-land if they said the sun's gonna rise in the east tomorrow."

Salerno started to rise from the table.

"What the hell do you want us to do?" Lowensdorf asked in amaze-ment.

"Get me fingerprints, dammit," Salerno growled. "And no more vic-tims. Please!"

EUGENE Rickey was strung out tight as a high-C piano wire.

It had never been difficult for him before to keep his two lives sepa-rate. He could be Eugene Rickey during the day and pursue his other interests as the Handyman at night, slipping from one persona to the other as easily as most people change shoes. But never before had he been in a situation that forced him to work all day under the same roof as the object of his nighttime fantasies. He'd just get to concentrating on the drywall he was nailing up and mudding when she'd walk by him in the same kind of shorts she was wearing the day before, shorts that made her look more naked than dressed in his eyes. Then he'd get angry and lose track of where he was, lose his train of thought and generally lose control of himself. He seemed to have contracted a per-manent case of the jitters.

For one thing, Opal was getting more insistent that he move against the new woman, punish her for her indiscretions thoroughly and horribly and without more delay. Yet there was no opening for him, no access to her.

Had she been going to work every day, he could have tried to take her in her car, as she arrived in the garage of her building, or as she left for home in the evening. But she was working at home all week, and by the end of the week, his project for her would be done, and he would be out of the house. He thought he might have to wait until the following week, when she resumed her normal routine. But he couldn't. The urges were too strong.

If she would go out on an errand, he could follow her and take her when she arrived, but she wasn't running errands. The groceries were being delivered from a posh market called Simon's that catered to the wealthy of South Tampa. No other shopping was on the schedule.

If the nanny would go away, take the baby to the doctor or something. But that wasn't happening, either. Felicia Encata spent her days playing with Casey, feeding Casey, changing Casey, taking Casey into the den for visits with his mother. She came in the morning before the husband was gone and left in the evening after he was at home.

If perhaps, one night, the husband was late. That would work. But David Janacek was always home by six.

He counted on opportunity presenting itself by chance. He already knew where he was going to take her to ensure their privacy. There was an abandoned house on an abandoned farm south of Brandon he could use. There was no one around for miles. And under cover of darkness, nobody would spot his truck. Getting from her house to the farm would necessitate keeping her unconscious and out of sight for the half-hour drive, but that was doable.

The problem was it was already Tuesday.

He was running out of options.

And Opal told him he was running out of time.

26

The window of opportunity opened on Wednesday for Eugene Rickey.

But leading up to it, he had spent a miserable night of drinking and fantasizing and trying to placate Opal, whose shrill voice pounded his head demanding to know:

When?

When?

WHEN!?

And he couldn't tell her.

Why didn't she help him? Why didn't she find an opening for him, guide him, show him what to do? That was all he needed. A chance. She should be helping. It was her duty. She was his *mother,* after all!

When he finally went to bed shortly before midnight, his sleep was fitful and filled with nightmares. When he woke at six A.M.—something his body clock arranged automatically on a daily basis, whether he wanted to get up or not—he was poorly rested, which only added to his jitters and feelings of desperation.

He was standing in the new pantry in Culbreath Isles, bleakly trying to develop a plan to draw out the finishing work in the hope that more time would increase the chances for him, when he heard Kirin Janacek call to Felicia Encata, who was entertaining Casey in the family room.

Rickey moved to the pantry door, feigning an inspection of molding he installed the day before, and strained to hear Kirin's voice.

"I'm going to have to go out for a few hours this afternoon," she said. "I'll be leaving about two-thirty, and I don't know exactly when I'll be back. It could be as late as four-thirty, even five. Does that pose any problems for you?"

"Not at all, missus," Felicia replied. "I made no plans to go out today, although I did make an appointment to have my hair done tomorrow, if that is all right."

"No problem at all," Kirin assured her. "I wouldn't normally go out today, either, except the television station that's taken such a keen interest in my buildings found out we've solved our window problem and asked me to do another interview on the site. It will be a big public relations boost, a way of letting people know the building is okay."

"You can fix window pop-out?" Felicia asked, and Kirin laughed. The young Cuban woman had a wonderful take on the English language and its idiom. She was self-taught and proficient enough to have earned her American citizenship and a bachelor's degree in fine arts at the University of South Florida. Kirin had seen some design flair in her. When Casey was no longer in need of daytime tending, or when Felicia got tired of the job and wanted to move on, Kirin thought she would try to tempt her into taking some sort of job in the architectural firm, something that would help her develop professionally and linguistically. The young woman had a marvelous work ethic, so the rest would be relatively easy.

"Yes," Kirin said, "we can fix the window pop-out. And I'm going to tell people so on the television news."

Rickey was pumped. This was it. The woman was going out by herself in her car. She would be driving from her house to the Water Street building complex and then back again. He would stop her and pick her up along the route.

But where?

If she was leaving the house at 2:30, it meant the interview probably was at three. He thought it unwise to stop her on her way to the building project. That would make her a no-show for the interview. Given how jittery the community was, someone certainly would raise an alarm, and he didn't want anybody to start looking for her right away. It would be better for a couple of reasons to grab her on her way home.

She'd spend, say, an hour with the reporter, maybe another hour poking around the site—he knew from personal experience no contractor could ever be on the scene of his or her work and not take time to admire and critique it—and it would be rush hour by the time she headed back to South Tampa. Perfect. He could approach her as she left the buildings on the pretext of having a design change or some sort of paperwork for her to look at right away. She would follow him to his truck. He would knock her out, shove her in, and be off. He would have to do it quickly and cleanly so nobody would notice.

It would be after 5:30, maybe close to 6:00, by the time he got her secure in the abandoned farmhouse, the last building she would ever see. Soon thereafter, it would begin to go dark, and the area around the farmhouse would be completely deserted. His truck wouldn't be exposed for long. Yes, taking her after the interview was the better course. It meant less time he had to keep her quiet before he could began his night's work and more time before anybody realized she was missing and began a search for her. The nanny had only a vague idea when to expect her home. If his luck held, nobody would get suspicious until her husband arrived and began asking questions.

By that time, it would be way too late to find either Kirin Janacek or Eugene Rickey.

He began to write a mind script for getting her to his truck and making the capture. It was like choreography, he thought.

A dance of the dead.

"KIRIN! It's good to see you again," Cynthia Diamond gushed when the architect approached the entry arch to Water Street Plaza. It wasn't Cynthia's habit to be effusive, but after she remembered the details of the song the Heartbreak Killer sang to her, and after she unloaded those details and more on Captain Britton, she felt enormously better. Not healed, but rid of a lot of nightmarish baggage that had been cluttering her mind.

She had slept better the night before and awoke actually looking forward to the new day. She was beginning to believe the consensus that the killer wouldn't return for her. While she remained cautious about her movements and carefully made sure to have people around her when she went out, she no longer looked over her shoulder every ten paces or hesitated before passing a recessed doorway or started at every loud noise.

The two women shook hands.

"It's good to see you, too, Cynthia," Kirin said. "Especially after what you've been through. How are you doing?"

"I'm getting better," Cynthia said. "You don't get over something like this overnight, but I'm making progress in putting it behind me. I don't jump out of my skin anymore at the harmless things that go bump in the night."

"I wouldn't call what you encountered harmless."

"Well, no, not then. But the police are sure he won't be back. Sometimes, things that go bump in the night are nothing more than things that go bump in the night, like the house settling or a dog falling off the bed."

"Doesn't sound to me from what I read in the paper like your dogs are that clumsy," Kirin said. "I suspect the local sale of dachshunds is soaring."

Cynthia sighed and took Kirin's arm, leading her toward the spot where they would sit to do the interview.

"It was remarkable," she said. "It was like the dogs were working together; each one knew what the other was going to do. It was like they had a plan." She shrugged. "I won't ever understand it. I'm just very grateful for it and grateful they weren't seriously hurt in the process."

EUGENE Rickey had briefly gone into a kind of alarmed shock.

He parked his truck in an alley next to an abandoned, fire-gutted building on Gunn Street, just north of the rising towers of Water Street Plaza. He was delighted at his luck. Nobody would see him take the woman there.

Rickey was walking toward the towers when he spotted Cynthia Diamond walking with her left arm through Kirin Janacek's right. They were talking it up and giggling like two old college chums. It hadn't occurred to Rickey until that moment that the Janacek woman's interview might be with Cynthia Diamond, although it came back to him that it was Cynthia who interviewed her before. Small world, he thought.

Too damned small.

The coincidence of their meeting on the very afternoon that would be Kirin Janacek's last on earth was too eerie to dismiss. Was it an omen? If so, was it good or bad?

Could Cynthia tell the Janacek woman anything that might tip her to him? Anything that would put her on her guard when he approached her later? Cynthia surely retained a mental image of what he looked like, but would she be able to convey it to Kirin? If the police artist's sketch was the best she'd been able to recall his features, he had no worries.

Rickey decided there was no way Cynthia could adequately warn Kirin, and he relaxed marginally. He still had to be very careful to stay out of the line of sight of either one of them. He could imagine Kirin turning around and exclaiming, "Oh, there's the man who's redoing my kitchen," only to have Cynthia reply, "Oh, you mean the one over there, the one who tried to kill me?" No, that wouldn't do.

He looked around until he spotted Kirin Janacek's white Mercedes. That was where she would return eventually, and he needed to be able to approach her as she walked toward it. He looked for a suitable spot from which to watch for her and picked a moderate-sized live-oak tree, nearly twenty feet high, planted as part of the green space around the Water Street project. He leaned against it as inconspicuously as possible.

He saw the women stop in front of the newly completed portico of Water Street Plaza and sit on a large stone bench. The interview was about to begin, apparently. Rickey didn't want to appear to be staring, so he turned his attention to the water, his head at an angle where he could see the women from the corner of his left eye. He was satisfied he appeared to be a casual stroller who'd stopped to admire the view.

The interview took only ten minutes, but after the camera and sound technicians packed up and left, the two women continued to chat, eating up time. That was good.

It was 3:50 when they got up. Rickey made a bet with himself. Would they say good-bye at that point, or would Kirin submit to an urge to take a look around her project, as he would have? What actually happened surprised him. The two women entered the WestWater building together.

It made Rickey nervous. The sooner the Diamond woman was gone from the scene, the better he would feel. He couldn't relax as long as there was any danger she might spot him or say something to Kirin Janacek that would connect the man working at her house to the killer.

He was confident neither had happened so far. His attack on Cynthia was recent enough that if she spotted him in the area, she would at least appear agitated. She might even flee. If the Janacek woman were suspicious of him, she would be headed for home as quickly as possible to collect her infant son.

But as they disappeared through the front door of the building, the women were chatting and laughing. No angst there.

Where were they going? If Kirin was giving Cynthia Diamond a tour, they might chance to look out a window facing his tree and spot him. He moved farther away, behind the spot where Kirin parked her car. Now he was far enough away that he probably couldn't be seen at all and certainly couldn't be recognized.

It was a good forty-five minutes before the women emerged, still chatting and walking easily, without tension. Rickey sighed in relief.

They stopped beneath the portico, and he saw Kirin Janacek point toward her car. Then *both* women began walking toward it.

No! Rickey's mind yelled, although it sounded to him as if it were Opal's voice. They can't be leaving together. That can't happen!

But they remained side by side, moving steadily closer to the white Mercedes. When they were within fifty yards of it, they paused, shook hands, and parted. Cynthia walked off at a right angle to the route to Kirin's car, and Kirin approached him alone.

This is it!

Rickey took a step toward her and raised his hand to get her attention, very much aware of the weight of Opal in his right pocket.

It's our time, Mama! It's our time again. I'll win her heart for both of us. You'll see how good I am at this thing with women. I've showed you before, and I'll show you again, and maybe this time you'll be convinced.

A voice from behind the woman broke through the spell.

"Kirin! Kirin, wait a sec! I forgot something."

It was the Diamond woman, and she was walking fast, coming straight at Kirin Janacek, who stopped and turned around. More importantly, Cynthia was walking straight toward the Handyman. She was looking down, trying to avoid tripping on the construction detritus littering the street. If she looked up and focused just beyond Kirin, she would see him!

Got to hide, Opal!

Where can we go?

Quickly!

Rickey turned and walked away, back toward the abandoned building where his truck was hidden. It was just for a millisecond, but he thought as he turned he had made eye contact with Cynthia, and he thought he saw her eyes widen in recognition. He dared not turn back to see. His jaw clenched and he felt the muscles across his upper back and shoulders tighten as he waited for the scream that would prove she had both seen and identified him. When it came, he would run. He and Opal would get in the truck and go.

Where?

It didn't matter.

Away.

Far away.

And fast.

Oh, God, it was nearly five o'clock. Rush hour. He could get caught in traffic, maybe cornered by a police helicopter.

He had to get out of town fast. Which route would carry the least traffic?

The Crosstown Expressway! It would take him due east to I-75, where he could head south, toward Naples. There was never any traffic to speak of headed south on I-75 this time of year. Too early for the snowbirds to be returning for the winter. . . .

But there was no scream.

There was no sound of recognition at all.

The only sounds were his work boots crunching old gravel.

When he reached his truck and stopped by the door, he heard only silence.

KIRIN Janacek saw none of this, since she had turned her back on Rickey when Cynthia called her name. What she did see was the newswoman look up and stop abruptly, gazing with a hint of fear on her face at something over Kirin's shoulder. By the time Kirin turned to see what had startled Cynthia, Rickey was already around the corner of the burned-out building and out of sight. She turned back to the newswoman.

"Is something wrong?" Kirin asked.

Cynthia put a hand over the center of her chest and took a deep breath.

"For a moment, I thought I was looking at the man who attacked me," she said softly.

Kirin spun around again, but there was nothing to see but an empty, weedy vacant lot and a crumbling old building.

"Are you sure?" she asked Cynthia. "We should call the police. I have a phone in my car."

Cynthia laughed nervously.

"No," she said. "I'm certain it wasn't him. For the last few days, every man I see who's built like him and even vaguely resembles him has done this to me. In my heart, I guess I expect to see him, so I see him everywhere. The police say he won't bother me again, and I have to believe it. They're the experts." She paused and stared at the vacant lot. "Still, when it happens, it has a way of unnerving me."

"No kidding," Kirin said in complete sympathy. "It's unnerved me just seeing it happen to you. Want me to walk with you to your car?"

Cynthia smiled bravely.

"Thanks, but I'll be fine. I have to get past this sooner or later," she said, sounding as though she really believed it. "I forgot to ask you if you've set a date for the formal dedication of the project, now that the window problem is solved."

"Not yet," Kirin said. "We want to get the titanium film in place and make sure it works before we actually let tenants move into the south offices. It won't be long, though. A lot of the suites are ready for occupancy, and I have to say, some of us are eager to begin collecting rent."

"You'll let me know?"

"Oh, sure. Absolutely."

"Great. Thanks."

"Will the interview be on tonight?" Kirin asked.

"I don't know, to tell you the truth," Cynthia said. "Depends on the crush of other news. By the end of the week, for sure."

"Sounds good."

Cynthia turned to go.

"You take care of yourself," Kirin called after her.

"Always," Cynthia replied.

Kirin unlocked her car and got in, relocking the doors securely.

She turned the ignition and the big V-8 engine roared to life, its power giving her a great feeling of security.

She put the car in gear but kept her foot on the brake, glancing one last time at the beat-up old building at the edge of the vacant lot.

Something about it made her shudder.

RICKEY was leaning heavily against the door of his truck, trying to regulate his breathing so he could hear somebody coming after him, if anyone did.

He thought at one point he could hear the two women talking again, but he couldn't make out their words or be certain it was them. Then he heard a car door slam and an engine fire up, and he caught a glimpse of the back of the Mercedes as it turned onto Franklin Street and headed north. He couldn't tell how many women were in the car, but it had to be Kirin driving, and if Cynthia thought she spotted the man who tried to kill her, it was a dead certainty she wouldn't be lingering alone in the vicinity. She most likely was gone, too.

That had been too damned close.

"I'm sorry, Opal," he said in a whisper.

"Give me another chance.

"Please."

When Kirin Janacek returned home, she was surprised to find Eugene Rickey gone.

"I thought he was trying to finish up here by the weekend," she said to Felicia Encata.

"He didn't say where he go, missus," Felicia replied. "He say it was an important errand."

"And he'll be back tomorrow?"

"I'm sure," Felicia said. "He is very dependable, no?"

27

Eugene Rickey bit his lower lip nervously as he stood in line at the checkout counter at his local liquor store, two quarts of Kite's Finest Kentucky Bourbon Whiskey wrapped in his left arm. He'd run out the night before, draining the last drop in the house before the eleven o'clock news, while he was still sober enough to know he'd had too much to drink to drive safely to a place where he could buy some more.

So he polished off what was left of an old bottle of a cheap Canadian blend, which tasted thin and sweet, but it did the trick and put him down for the night, albeit once again into a fitful and nightmarish sleep that again left him feeling unrested.

In the morning, he found he didn't have enough cash to buy his usual case of Kite's, and he had no intention of writing a check for the stuff, not with the police broadcasting the fact that the serial killer's whiskey brand of choice was Kite's Finest. Writing a check with his driver's license number appended, as any store certainly would require, would leave too clear a paper trail to his doorstep. So he picked up two bottles, the cost of which he could cover from his cash on hand, figuring they were sufficient to last through to Friday, the day he always went to the bank for money to run on through the following week. Friday was tomorrow, after all.

Then he had second thoughts.

Slipping out of line, he snagged a third bottle. It would leave him a little short in the lunch money department, but he would survive. He needed the booze worse than he needed food. If he got a chance to grab the Janacek woman today or tomorrow, he would require extra alcohol to get through the experience. He'd keep the liquor hidden in his truck, in case an opportunity arose to bag his prey. He didn't want to get his captive in his truck and have to stop at home to pick up his bottles. No, sir. Better to keep them close by at all times.

Semper paratus, baby!

"How're ya doin'?" the clerk asked him when he got to the register.

"Fine," Rickey replied, not eager to be engaged in conversation. But this was a regular clerk, and he recognized Rickey as a regular customer. Conversation was difficult to avoid.

"Yeah, you're my big Kite's customer," the clerk said. "I was tryin' to remember the other day, when the cops said that Heartbreak Killer guy drinks Kite's. You don't look like a killer to me." He laughed dryly.

"Right," Rickey said.

He saw the clerk eyeing him closely.

"What?" Rickey asked.

"This," the clerk said, shoving a piece of paper across the counter.

Rickey had only to glance quickly at the paper to see it was a copy of the two artist's depictions of him based on Sampson Jones's and Cynthia Diamond's descriptions. He hadn't thought them very good depictions when he saw them on television, but maybe, if the clerk made the connection, they were better than Rickey gave them credit for.

"Just tryin' to figure out if it looks like you," the clerk said. But he said it with enough of a laugh that Rickey decided the man had already concluded his customer and the killer were not the same man. Nonetheless, Rickey thought, when he needed more booze he'd find himself another store, preferably well away from here.

"It's not me," Rickey said flatly.

"I know," the clerk said. "Still, you might wanna switch your brand till this thing blows over, you know, so nobody mistakes you for this guy."

"Right," Rickey said. "I'll consider it."

Rickey paid cash.

· "What's your name?" the clerk asked casually as he made change.

"Why do you want to know?" Rickey asked.

"Cause you're a regular," the clerk replied. "I like to call our regular customers by name. Makes doin' business a little more personal."

"When I want my booze business personal, I'll tell you," Rickey said. He hoisted the paper bag into his arms and left.

As soon as he was out the door, the clerk called to a colleague standing nearby.

"George, quick, get that guy's license number," the clerk ordered.

"What?" George asked. "Why?"

"Just do it, dammit," the clerk said.

George peered through the glass doors, up and down the parking lot.

"Don't see him," he reported.

"Well, go outside," the clerk said. "Come on, be quick, before he gets away."

George poked his head out and surveyed the lot again."

"Nope, nothin'," he said. "What's the problem?"

"I'm callin' the police," the clerk said.

GEORGE wasn't able to spot Rickey's truck because Rickey parked on the road beside the store, not in the lot out front, in case this very situation arose. As he pulled into traffic, he saw George poke his head through the liquor store doors and look futilely for the vehicle driven by the last customer. But George was looking in the wrong place.

Rickey grinned as he drove away, figuring that the clerk would probably call the police now, and there would be a third bad artist's sketch of him added to the file. Well, he wouldn't be back to this store, so fuck 'em all. They had nothing they didn't have before.

Sometimes he thought he was too lucky to live.

THE liquor store clerk was able to give Ben Britton and Nick Estevez precious little new information, although he was able to corroborate details supplied by both Cynthia Diamond and Sampson Jones, the bait-and-tackle dealer. He could not confirm his anonymous customer drove a light-colored pickup truck, however. But the guy did bear a vague resemblance to the man in the police artist's pictures.

"His nose is a little shorter than the picture on the left, and maybe the mouth is a touch wider than the one on the right," the clerk said. "And the eyes, this guy's eyes were set closer together, closer than either of the pictures make them out. Make the hair a little fuller on top and a little longer in the back, and you got 'im."

"Taken together, those changes could make a big difference in his appearance," Estevez said.

"Hey, maybe it's not the same guy, I dunno," the clerk said. "But you guys asked us to watch for a customer who looks something like this and buys a lot of Kite's. My customer looks something like this and usually buys Kite's by the case. Either he has a lotta parties or he's a boozer, big time."

"What would be your guess?" Britton asked.

"As to what?" the clerk asked.

"Party animal or boozer?"

"Boozer. Big time. Although he doesn't have the look yet. Still young."

"How young?"

"Hard to say exactly. Skin's real tan, so it probably makes him look older than he is. I'd guess maybe early to midthirties. More like midthirties."

"Height?"

"Umm, under six feet. Maybe five nine, five ten."

A match.

Britton and Estevez exchanged a glance that spoke volumes to each other but meant nothing to the clerk, whose curiosity was growing by the question.

"So?" he asked. "Is it him?"

"I don't know, sir, but I'm going to get you downtown with the police artist. You can make whatever alterations will make the sketch look more like your customer. Then we'll take the composite and circulate it with the first two."

"Think it will help catch him?"

"You never know."

"I get off work at three. Can I come down then?"

"No, it has to be now. Before the details you've got stored in your mind begin to get fuzzy."

"But I can't leave George here alone. That's against store rules."

So Britton called the store owner, who lived in Riverview, and fortunately found him at home. He explained the situation.

"I was coming in at noon anyhow," the owner said. "I'll come over now. I'm only ten minutes away, if you don't mind waiting that long."

Thus arrangements were made to free up the clerk who would, as it turned out, give investigators their most accurate portrait of the killer.

But by the time sheriff's deputies had a chance to compare the artist's rendering to the flesh-and-blood subject, it would be way too late.

28

There was no way, Eugene Rickey knew, to string out the pantry job beyond today and tomorrow. Friday and Saturday. Two days to get his hands on Kirin Janacek the easy way, from the inside of her home.

Two final days.

Close-out time.

He was going mad with anxiety. Opal was hounding him constantly now, demanding he take immediate action against the Janacek woman, requiring her son to obey her, threatening to give him the whipping of his life if he failed her expectations.

"I'm *trying*," Eugene said to thin air as he drove toward Culbreath Isles on Friday morning. "Can't you see, I'm trying?"

He thought he felt his backside smart. He had regressed twenty-five years. Once again, he was bent over, hands on his knees, his jeans and briefs down around his ankles, his own belt biting into the flesh of his bare butt. Opal was wielding the belt and laughing and scolding him: "You're never gonna be able to fuck anybody with a thing that small. Maybe a good whippin' will make a man of you." The belt hit him again and again, until his thin backside was burning from his waist to his knees.

"Ma! Please stop!" It was his own voice, a quarter century later, in real time, pleading with his dead mother on a very different level. "No more, Ma! It hurts. Ple-e-e-ase!"

Tears were streaming down his face, and he had to blink his eyes to keep his view of the road clear.

He heard himself whimper, and that angered him and brought him back to the present.

By the time he reached the Janacek house, he was composed.

At least outwardly.

* * *

Rickey had picked up the pantry shelving on his way, and it took him the better part of an hour to bring it all into the Janacek kitchen. It was reflex with him, so he rarely noticed it, but he had started singing his song when he first arrived at ten and hadn't stopped since. It was beginning to wear even on the normally placid disposition of Felicia Encata.

"Why does he have to sing that same song alla time?" she asked Kirin Janacek, who had taken a break from her design work to play with Casey, who'd grown increasingly fussy as the morning progressed. Kirin wondered if perhaps he was catching a cold.

"I don't know," she replied. "It's been driving me crazy for days. I almost asked him to stop once, but I didn't want to hurt his feelings."

"I don' wanna hurt his feelings, neither, but I don' think I can listen to that song anymore without screaming," the nanny said with uncharacteristic vehemence.

Kirin smiled at her. "Look, Felicia, he says tomorrow is his last day. He's going to hang the shelving and put the doors on today, paint tomorrow, and he's gone. We can handle it for two more days, don't you think?"

"Honest, I don' know, missus," Felicia said.

"Well, if it gets to the point where you want to hit him, take Casey back into the nursery and close the door. Then you won't be able to hear him. I can't hear him when I'm in the den, so I know the nursery will be a safe haven."

"Thank you, missus," Felicia said. "I think I might do that."

It occurred to Rickey sometime after lunch that the architect and the nanny were in different rooms and that the nanny had the baby's door closed. An adrenaline rush made him tingle. Should he take a chance and get this done now?

He could enter the den where she was working, on the pretext of showing her the same design idea he had planned to show her the day before, when he wanted to lure her to his truck. When he got close enough, he would pop her hard on the point of her chin, and she would go out, like the rest of them had. Then all he had to do was drag her through the family room sliding glass doors, across the lanai and down the driveway to his truck.

The last part would be tricky, and risky if a neighbor should look out. Better he should pull his truck in, over the grass to the door of the cedar stockade fencing, and load her unconscious body. There was still a chance of a neighbor seeing, but not as great a chance as if he dragged or carried her down the driveway.

It could work.

Every fiber of him screamed, *Yes!*, but Opal gave him a quick, firm, *No!*

What if the nanny came out of the nursery during the process and began screaming her head off? What if the neighbors did see? This had to be done where there was virtually no chance of anyone witnessing it.

But time is running out!

No chance of witnesses, unless you want to kill them to keep them quiet. What's another killing or two to you?

No. I don't want to kill the nanny, or a neighbor. There's no sense in it, no satisfaction.

Then wait until she's alone.

She's never alone!

Of course she is.

When?

Watch for the time. It will come.

Later the same afternoon, it did.

DAVID Janacek arrived home shortly before three o'clock, just as Rickey started on the last of the pantry shelving.

"I wasn't in favor of doing this project," the lawyer told him, "but it looks great. We're going to be very happy with it."

"Good," Rickey said, adding in his mind only, *but you aren't going to be very happy with me when I finish with your bitch wife.*

"David, I thought I heard your voice. When did you come in? Did you fire yourself?"

Kirin Janacek entered the kitchen as Rickey thought of her.

Her husband took her in his arms and kissed her forehead.

"Just got here. Nobody's been fired," he replied. "I thought I'd come home, see if you and Casey would like to spend the afternoon with me, have dinner at some exotic restaurant, and spend the night together. An entire evening with just we three. Felicia probably wouldn't mind getting off early, either."

She pulled slightly back from him as a sly grin enveloped her face.

"Which, translated, means you're offering to spend this evening with your family because you're going to spend the weekend away."

"Not *away* away," he said. "And not the whole weekend. Just one afternoon."

"Which one?"

"Sunday. If you don't mind."

"Where?"

"On the golf course."

"Of course. Why did I ask?"

"If you've got plans . . ."

"No plans," she said. "Well, actually, now that you mention it, I'm wrapping up the floor designs for the Tomasen Group's offices, and I wouldn't mind taking them down to my office Sunday to double-check the modifications against the real, live blueprints."

"What about the future president of the United States?" David asked.

"The kid? I'll take him with me like I did last weekend. He'll be fine. He found lots of new things to get into."

"You sure, honey?"

"Positive. Since you've actually learned to play golf, you should keep at it so your game doesn't slide. Use it or lose it, isn't that what they say?"

He leaned in toward her ear and whispered, "They say that about lots of things, but we should probably wait until the nanny and the contractor are gone."

She shook her head. "You *are* bad," she said. "But we'll discuss that later, too."

THE Janaceks decided against doing anything too fancy about dinner. They gave Felicia the rest of the day off, and it was too late to get a baby-sitter, so wherever they went, Casey would come along. That meant finding a place with a short wait for a table, prompt service, and experience with young children.

"How about Paulie Rome's?" David suggested.

"On a Friday night?" Kirin asked. "Can we get in?"

David called. They got in.

It was a short drive down to the Westport area, a bayside warehouse district rapidly going trendy as a pocket of boutique shops and restaurants became established. Casey was strapped snugly into his car seat in the rear of David's Ford Explorer. The car radio was playing soft rock oldies. Kirin and David rode in silence, comfortable in the warmth of each other.

They had just entered the warehouse district when Kirin heard the first strains.

"Oh, no," she groaned. "I can't stand it! Not even the real thing."

David turned and looked at her in complete bafflement as she turned off the radio.

"What brought that on?" he asked.

"That song," she said. "I can't stand listening to it anymore."

David wasn't sure which song his wife was referring to—he'd been thinking about a case and only half listening to the music—so he turned the radio on again. "What's the song?"

He was able to identify it immediately.

"James Taylor. 'Handyman.' That's a great song." He looked at her again in amused disbelief. "I thought you were a big James Taylor fan."

"I am," she said. "Please turn it off."

He did.

She explained the aversion she and Felicia had developed to that particular James Taylor hit as performed by Eugene Rickey.

"That's pretty funny," he said. "Why didn't you say something to him, so he'd stop, or sing something else for awhile, or do a medley?"

"We didn't want to hurt his feelings."

"What about James Taylor's feelings? You just blew him off."

She looked at her husband and grinned.

"I doubt he'll ever know," she said.

EUGENE Rickey left the Janacek house shortly after David arrived. The germ of an idea was growing in his mind, and he had to get to the city planning office before it closed. Buying what he needed was an expensive proposition, and the clerk wasn't particularly happy about his demand so late in the day for a copy of a large and complex file of blueprints. But Rickey was adamant, and the clerk relented.

He had stopped on his way downtown at an ATM, and he paid cash for the documents. Then he picked a liquor store at random, one he'd never patronized before, and bought a case of Kite's without so much as a curious glance from the store clerk. Now he had fifteen bottles in all, plenty to get him through his plans for the weekend and many days thereafter. He shouldn't have to buy anymore until the news frenzy over Kirin Janacek's death died down.

He drove home and turned on the six o'clock news. The Diamond woman finally aired the interview done two days earlier with the chief architect of the Water Street Plaza project. Rickey listened intently. When it ended, he cracked the seal on a new bottle of Kite's and opened the plans for the WestWater building.

He was feeling high even before he took his first drink.

Opal had been right. Patience was its own reward.

The woman would be alone with her baby in her office on Sunday. Her husband would be on the golf course. The nanny was off. It was perfect. Absolutely perfect.

There would have to be something super special about this one. It had taken so much time to set it up, and coming on the heels of so much disappointment on Davis Islands, this one would have to be spectacular. He didn't have to rush his plans. He could take time and savor them. He had tonight and all day Saturday, while he was fitting and painting the pantry doors. And Saturday night. Plenty of time to come up with a plan worthy of the all the trouble he'd been through. This new idea he had showed great promise.

When Sunday came, he would be ready.

He loved Sundays.

Bloody Sundays.

29

On Sunday morning, Eugene Rickey awoke even earlier than usual. He wanted to rehearse his plan again to be certain it had no hidden flaws, carried no unnecessary risks. When he had satisfied himself, he would set it in motion. There was no time to waste. He figured he had at least two hours of work to do at the site he'd chosen before he summoned her there, and he didn't want to be rushed. When you rush, you make mistakes.

After hours of poring over the WestWater blueprints, he understood that pulling this off would take all of the professional skills he had mastered over the years, but he relished the challenge, and if it worked as he planned it, it would be glorious.

He had been able to fill in the only additional details he needed from an overheard conversation at the Culbreath Isles house the day before, where he finished the pantry project and collected the balance due him.

What exquisite timing. He got his information and his money, too.

While he was putting on the final coat of paint, he heard the husband complain about his 1:20 P.M. tee time on Sunday. He said he wasn't looking forward to playing during the hottest hours of the day, although it wouldn't take as long to play the eighteen-hole round since there wouldn't be as many people on the course. Who, after all, plays golf in Florida during the afternoon of an August day?

"Well, you could put it off for a week and make your reservation earlier, so you get an earlier tee-off," Kirin suggested.

"I don't think so," the husband said. "None of the other guys thinks it's a problem. I'll just shut up and sweat. I might even need an extra beer when we're done. But you knew I'd think of that, didn't you?"

So the plans were set. The husband would go to his club about noon and grab a sandwich there before his game. The woman would eat something at home and feed Casey and go to her office. Rickey figured she wouldn't arrive before 1:00 or 1:30. He would set his plan in motion at precisely 2:00 P.M.

At the strike of that hour, the world would become his.

It was shortly after noon Sunday when Rickey arrived at a deserted Water Street Plaza. He circled the buildings twice, drinking in every detail of the exterior of the place. The WestWater Tower was farther along in construction and occupancy than EastWater. Most of the higher floors of EastWater were still open, without the blue-tinted glass that gave the project its distinctive look. A few of the floors at WestWater were already partially occupied, and all the floors were fully glassed in, with the exception of conspicuous points on the south side where plywood sheets covered holes created by missing glass panes. He heard the architect say in the television interview the problem had been fixed. But the architect didn't know everything.

It would happen again at least once, because Eugene Rickey would make it happen.

Satisfied he knew all he needed to know about the exterior of West-Water, Rickey circled the project again and pulled up to the entrance of the ten-story parking garage, located between the two towers. A metal lattice door blocked entry. Beyond it, Rickey could see the security office, occupied by only one man.

It was just as he suspected it would be.

Rickey got out of his truck, carefully hiding his face from the security camera trained on this location. The cameras probably fed video-tape machines, and he didn't want a pictorial record of this day falling into police hands. He pushed the call button on the building's exterior wall. He heard no sound, but he saw the security guard look up from his bank of video monitors.

The man, who Rickey judged to be in his fifties, pushed himself out of his chair, opened his office door, and approached the metal lattice gate.

"Help you?" he asked.

"I have an appointment to meet one of the general contractors here at two o'clock, to talk about fixing the windows on the south side of the building," Rickey said.

The security guard glanced at his watch.

"You're plenty early," he said.

"Well, I thought maybe I could go up and have a look at the situation before she got here," Rickey said. "Might cut some time off the meeting so we can both get home to our families."

The guard shook his head.

"Is it Mrs. Janacek you're meeting?"

Rickey nodded.

"I don't recall seeing an appointment for her on the calendar today."

"She had me paged yesterday," Rickey said. "I returned her call and we set this up. She probably never thought to let you know."

"Well, let's see if we can get it straightened out," the guard said, turning his back on Rickey. "I'll put up the gate for you so's you can drive in. No sense standin' out there bakin' in the sun. It's a scorcher, isn't it?"

From inside his office, the guard triggered the door, and it rumbled upward and onto tracks set tight against the ceiling. Rickey pulled in and stopped beside the guard office, again taking care to hide his face. He stopped the truck before its license tag was exposed to the security camera and mentally patted himself on the back for thinking of it.

Perfect! Just perfect!

He fished in his pocket for a latex glove and quickly pulled it on his right hand. Then he reached around behind himself and pulled his weapon from his belt.

The guard's back was to him. He was looking at a clipboard, which he picked up as he turned around to face the visitor.

"I'm sorry, mister," he said, "but I don't . . ."

His voice died in midsentence when he looked up and saw the man he'd just willingly admitted to the building holding a ten-inch butcher knife in a hand sheathed in a surgical glove. The knife looked cheap but none the less deadly for it. The man's face had hardened and his eyes had gone stone cold.

The guard tried to reach for his gun, but his right hand was full of clipboard. It wouldn't have mattered, anyway. Rickey was too quick. He took two long steps forward and brought the knife up, into the guard's abdomen just below the sternum. Three inches of the end of the blade penetrated the guard's heart, and he immediately sagged toward Rickey, his eyes wide in terror and frozen in death.

Rickey sidestepped the body and let it fall to the concrete floor on its back. It was a virtually bloodless killing. When the heart pump quit, there was nothing to force blood through the wound. Rickey left the knife where it was, embedded in the guard's chest. He'd bought it at a grocery store because he had no intention of soiling Opal by asking her to make this kill. But he had no further use for it now.

Rickey felt some urgency. Assuming the dead guard came on at 6:00 A.M., his relief would appear at 6:00 P.M. and find the body. Rickey had to be done with Kirin Janacek and gone before then. There was plenty of time but none to lose.

He stepped over the dead legs and to the office door, pulling a second glove onto his left hand and keeping his face down. He hit the button that lowered and locked the lattice gate. Then he moved his truck to the rear of the structure, taking a route that avoided exposing it to the security cameras. The overhead lights were off for the weekend to save electricity. Only the security lights on the walls were on. He parked in deep shadow where the truck wouldn't be seen by human eyes or security cameras.

He returned to the office and pulled the guard's body to a back wall, out of the way, and helped himself to the dead man's keys. He rummaged through the pockets for the wallet. When he found it, he searched until he found the thick laminated card he was looking for and slid it into a hip pocket of his blue jeans.

He was running on autopilot now, certain of every move, smooth, almost mechanical in his actions. His facial muscles were set, his eyes clear and hard.

He took a deep breath and heard Opal tell him to keep calm. For the first time he could ever remember, she didn't call him Shorty. She called him Handyman, and it made him proud. It was who he would be forever. In that moment, the Handyman persona overtook and overwhelmed Eugene Rickey. Eugene Rickey died in the same small office as the security guard. And for the Handyman, every semblance of sanity was gone.

He sat in the guard's chair in front of the computer/video console. State-of-the-art. The woman was probably familiar with every facet of it. He didn't have much time to catch up, but he didn't need much.

The security surveillance was typical. There were two large banks of black-and-white television monitors and one small one. Each of the two towers was covered by a large bank; the parking structure was covered by the small one. Each of the large banks had thirty-two monitors, one for every floor. The small one had ten screens, one for each level of parking. The pictures on each monitor rotated every five seconds. Depending on how many cameras were on each floor, it took about a minute to do a complete security scan. Then the rotation began again. The operator could override the automatic sequencing and hold a view from one camera, or he could set them up as they were set up today, in a holiday/weekend configuration in which a camera only came on if the sensor behind the lens detected movement. The camera then stayed on until the operator satisfied himself nothing was amiss and shut it down.

The bank of view screens for EastWater hadn't yet been activated because the building was still completely vacant. The video cameras probably hadn't even been installed on most of the floors, especially those still open to the elements. But there were tenants in WestWater, and its bank was operational, as was the system for the parking structure.

Two garage monitors displayed live pictures. One camera had been triggered when he drove his truck to its current parking position, but there was so little light, the image on the monitor was nothing more than a vague shadow. He could have activated the ceiling lights right from where he sat, but darkness served him better and would for the rest of the day. The other monitor was showing a picture of the security office. It had been triggered by the motion of two bodies inside. The Handyman had been careful to keep his face averted.

However, all of the monitors covering the WestWater Tower were blank. Nobody was in the building. The Handyman switched them to the weekday configuration of sequential rotation and watched for a few minutes. It was very dull viewing, confirming that but for him and one dead body, the Water Street Plaza complex was empty.

Some other time, it would have been a kick to play around with the security surveillance, but not this day. There was work to be done and the whole system would crash, anyway, when he cut the building's power and destroyed the emergency generators.

Better yet, he thought, shut it down now. He didn't want to have to worry about it anymore. There was about to be too much else on his mind. He hit the power switches for both the WestWater Tower and garage boards and watched the active screens flicker to black. Then he shut down the video cameras. WestWater now was his to do with as he chose, whenever he chose, without fear of detection.

He turned next to the elevator system. The computer display showed him the service status of the tower's seven public and two freight elevators. Both freight haulers were out of service. Public elevators one, two, and three—the low-rise cars stopping only at the first fifteen floors—and four, five, and six—the high-rise cars that went to floors sixteen through thirty-two—also were down for the weekend. The only active elevator was seven, the one car servicing all floors. It was at a standstill at the lobby level.

Had car number seven been moving up, it would have appeared in the computer simulation to be riding on a column of red. When the car was going down, the column was green. There also was a readout of the weight inside the car and an extrapolation of the probable number of individuals inside. He couldn't be certain how this particular system was set up, but in most similar systems with which he was familiar, the total weight was divided by one-hundred fifty pounds. Any pounds left over were assumed to belong to someone in need of a diet. It was amazing how accurate the estimates were most of the time. He wanted car seven to remain active. He would need it for a while.

Next, he located the emergency electrical disconnect for West-Water, four red buttons, each about four inches in diameter, each controlling electrical power to a single quadrant of the building. Hit one, and power would be cut to one-fourth of the structure. Hit them all, and all power would be gone. The system was called a fireman's service disconnect because it eliminated the risk of electrocution from hosing water around live wires. But it could be used in any emergency. It was even going to play a role in a madman's personal mission.

He left the disconnect alone for the moment. He would deal with it later from a duplicate panel in the electrical closet.

Since the telephone service to WestWater was supplied by a private telecommunications company, it needed an on-site power supply to work. Shut down power and within minutes the telephone system would go down with it, as long as the battery backups were disabled, something he planned to take care of soon.

There were public phones in the lobby. He could disable those quickly and easily.

Satisfied he had everything he needed from the security office, the Handyman walked out and closed the door behind him. It locked automatically.

He looked back in through the glass to be certain the guard's body was out of sight. It was.

Using the security guard's master key, he left the garage by a service door connecting the parking structure to the ground level of the WestWater Tower. He located the mechanical room that housed the backup electrical generators. He would visit them later.

In the telephone room, he cut the wires to the battery backups for the phone system. In the electrical closet, he took out the fire-alarm system. He made a mental note to remember to destroy its battery backups, located on every fourth floor.

The master key admitted him to the lobby. It was interesting how few keys were on the ring, how few it took to provide complete access to a modern high-rise building. One key worked all the doors to service areas, one to the building's front doors, one to the security office, one to the garage door, and one master provided access to every office in the structure.

The lobby soared to thirty feet, at least, and was done in handsome blue marble. It was carpeted in Williamsburg blue with mauve highlights. The elevator doors were bright brass. The lighting was subdued. Even the two public telephones, set in hidden alcoves on both sides of the lobby, were on burnished wood desks with straight-back chairs. With sharp, powerful tugs, he dislodged the receiver cord from one phone, then crossed the lobby and treated the second phone with the same rudeness.

He wondered if setting the phones in alcoves didn't create some security risk, blocking callers from public view. Then he saw that each was guarded by its own security camera, neither of which had an iota of power now. He looked up at the one above him, grinned broadly, and gave it the finger.

"Fuck you, you're blind," he whispered.

He strode to elevator seven. The doors were closed, as he expected. There was an "Up" call button, but it was deactivated on weekends and before and after normal weekday business hours. The heavy laminated call card he had taken from the dead security guard was his ticket to ride.

He inspected it briefly then waved it in front of the call buttons. Deep inside the wall was a strong proximity sensor capable of reading the coding through concrete and activating the elevator for the cardholder. If the holder was a tenant, the code would tell the elevator to what floor the tenant should be delivered. The tenant could not override the command. Thus other tenants on other floors were protected from possible intrusion by unauthorized visitors. For the same reason, stairway doors were kept locked, although once the electrical-power systems went down, the doors would unlock automatically.

The call card he possessed had no limitations coded within it. Security personnel had access to every floor. The elevator sensor instantly recognized the signal from an authorized user.

With a muted *bing,* the car doors pulled back smoothly. He elected to start at the top and work his way down.

The roof was designed to be an observation area, with panoramic views of the Tampa area and the bay. He walked around the perimeter and had to acknowledge it was breathtaking. The city sparkled quietly under the hot, midday sun and the water glinted invitingly. He'd read somewhere that when the roof was finished, it would be a garden with real trees, shrubs, and flowers, and concrete tables and benches where tenants could take in the view or lunch.

The garden wasn't ready yet, however, and the roof remained off-limits to everyone but personnel working there, according to a large sign on the door. It would be nice when it was finished, he thought, although he smiled at the notion of trying to eat a bag of potato chips under conditions that would exist most days. Right now the hot breeze was blowing at fifteen miles an hour or so, enough to launch an entire potato chip bag, if caught right. There probably were plans for some sort of shielding to cut both the wind and the chance of anybody using the roof as a takeoff point for suicide.

The rest of the roof contained standard-issue technology. The giant cooling tower purred within its housing, and the four-foot wall around the roof was studded every twenty-five feet with air terminals—commonly called lightning rods—the visible tips of a system designed to provide a harmless metallic path to the ground for the enormous discharge of electricity transferred by the region's powerful lightning strokes.

The air terminals were connected by copper cables to structural steel columns and served as down conductors, carrying the lightning's charge to the ground. From there the cables traveled beneath the surface to ground plates, large squares of flat metal buried a minimum of twelve feet from the building's foundation. The plates dispersed the current benignly, preventing damage or injury. It was a variation on technology that had been around for centuries, and nothing had been found to work better. It might be the only system that would continue to work when the building's power supply was shut down, since nothing about it was electrical.

The Handyman concluded there was nothing on the roof he needed to carry out his plan or that the woman could use to help her make an escape.

It was time to find the perfect place for the endgame.

He stopped on each floor, using the master key to unlock doors as he went. He disabled the battery-powered fire-alarm backups as he went. But his main mission was to find a suitable office for the job he'd come to do. He had to be able to tie the woman down. A nice conference room with a big table would be acceptable, and he found several from which he could choose. He made mental notes about their locations and continued searching for something that would be even more special.

He found what he wanted on the twenty-second floor.

When he stepped into the messy elevator lobby and looked around, he recognized the location instantly as one of the two floors the architect had stayed home all the previous week to redesign for a single tenant. He had a sense of what he would find in the open expanse of unfinished space, and indeed it was right there. Four heavy, industrial sawhorses were standing in a square formation, and resting on top of them was a massive sheet of thick plywood. It would take a crew of men to carry the wood panel; one woman lying on it, lashed to the sawhorses beneath, would never be able to move it.

How wonderful, he thought. How absolutely perfect.

Now he could get on with the preparations.

He proceeded down the flights of stairs until he was back in the parking garage, making no effort now to hide his face, for there were no active surveillance cameras to watch him. He took a large black duffel bag from the bed of his pickup. It was heavy enough that he listed left when he swung it over his shoulder. There was a lot of gear inside.

He headed for the mechanical room housing the emergency generators.

There were four of them, all identical. Radiator-cooled, diesel-fueled.

They were basically big engines sitting on vibration isolators with gigantic mufflers mounted above them. He had no problem finding the fuel pumps. To the lines extending from each, he attached collars filled with an acid that would eat through the lines, severing them, within a matter of seconds. The openings from which the acid would flow were sealed with small amounts of black powder connected to igniters that would be activated by a radio signal. He had made certain there was only enough black powder on each collar to break the acid seal. He didn't want to create explosions and chance starting a fire.

He was proud of his ingenuity. At the push of a button from anywhere within a city block, the Handyman could blow the seals and free the acid. Starved of fuel, the emergency generators would swiftly become useless. That would take care of any escape by elevator.

Timing was critical. He had to lure her to the twenty-second floor, then get to the basement to shut down the electrical systems at the fireman's disconnect panel. That would activate the emergency generators. Next, he would take the elevator back to the twenty-second floor and then, by radio signal, kill the generators. They would be stranded together. When he finished his day's work, he would get out of the building by the light of his flashlight, gingerly descending twenty-two stories to the lobby and finding his way back to the parking garage. He would use the security guard's keys to unlock the metal lattice gate and raise it manually. That was likely to be a bitch. The thing looked very heavy.

The woman would pay for making him work this hard.

Now all he had to do was set the trap and bring her to the appointed place.

He checked his watch. 1:40. Good timing. She had probably just gotten to her office.

He hauled his bag of goodies to the elevator and rode up to the twenty-second floor. The temperature was high, in the low nineties, at least, since the uncompleted area wasn't being cooled and the August sun was intense. He could tolerate the heat. And it might make the whore sweat more. He remembered with pleasure how much it hurt the bitch doctor when her sweat leaked into her wounds.

He took an assortment of ropes and bungee cords from his bag and put them on the floor at what would become the top end of the plywood bed. Then he found his hammer and his glass cutter. He chose the window exactly opposite the plywood and carefully tapped the inner pane until it crumbled into ten thousand harmless glass pebbles and exposed the blue outer pane. He had to stand on tiptoe to reach the top, but with a little effort, he managed to make a cut all the way around. Now a solid shove would break the glass free and send it plunging to the ground.

But it wasn't time yet.

He had to alert her first.

He rode the elevator up a level, to an occupied floor, and let himself into an office. He sat on a corner of the secretary's desk and dialed Kirin Janacek's office number. No answer. *Damn!* Was she running late?

Maybe she simply wasn't answering the phone, preferring privacy. Well, he had her cellular phone number, too. He'd called it up and jotted it down one day when she had the phone charging in the kitchen.

She answered on the second ring.

"Mrs. Janacek?" he asked.

"Speaking," she said.

"This is John Fraser, the security guard at Water Street. I'm sorry to bother you, but we just lost another window down here. No serious damage and nobody hurt, but I'm sure it's not what you wanted to hear on a Sunday."

"Not on a Sunday or any other day. Did it fall from the south side?"

"Yes, ma'am. Just like the others. This one popped out of the twenty-second story."

"The twenty-second floor, huh? Great. That's one of the floors I'm working on right now . . . John? Did you say your name was John?"

"Yes, ma'am. John Fraser. It's my second day on the job. But I've been briefed about the window problem. I also heard you thought you had it solved."

"We haven't had a chance to implement the solution, yet, more's the pity. Look, I'm at my office. It's going to take me a few minutes to pack up everything. I should be there in less than half an hour. And I guess I'd better call the police."

"I've already taken the liberty of doing that, ma'am," he said. "Hope you don't mind."

"Not at all. Keep things calm till I get there."

"Yes, ma'am," he said, but the phone at her end had already gone dead.

It had begun.

30

Kirin Janacek was considerably annoyed on several levels. She was all settled in, ready to complete the revisions for the twenty-first and twenty-second floors of WestWater, and Casey was napping peacefully. Now she had to put the revisions on hold and try to move her son without waking him. He would be unrested and cranky. And what was she supposed to do with him while she climbed around the twenty-second floor? It was one of the pitfalls of being both the chief architect and the general contractor on a project like this. She couldn't simply draw the pictures and diagrams. She had to be on-site when problems cropped up, too. And she was getting tired of chasing broken windows.

On a shallower, public-relations level, she worried about television viewers and prospective tenants who had seen her latest interview with Cynthia Diamond, in which she said a solution to the window failures had been found. Although Kirin made it clear the windows hadn't yet been retrofitted with the protective film, how many people would remember that? How many others might think in the aftermath of the latest failure that she had been covering up a problem that still existed? She would try to reach Cynthia the next day and make the point clear again.

At least no one had been hurt. Thank goodness for that.

Kirin shut down her computer, locked her door, and carried Casey in his combination car seat/carrier down to the white Mercedes parked in the garage of the Cypress Street office building. She strapped the carrier down and marveled that her son didn't stir. The sleep of the innocent. It was wonderful and welcome.

"You just stay in the Land of Nod for another hour or so," she whispered to him, bending into the car to kiss his forehead.

"Mommy's had enough grief for one day."

THE Handyman returned to the twenty-second floor and walked to the window he had precut. He peered long and carefully at the ground, making absolutely certain nobody was below where they might be hit by falling glass. Satisfied the area was clear, he spread his gloved hands out as far and up as high as he could on the panel and gave a short, hard shove. He heard a sharp cracking sound and thought he felt the left side of the glass give a little, but the window stayed in place. He shoved again.

This time he felt both sides give. One more push should do it.

Be careful.

Now!

The blue glass panel gave in a single piece. The top edge fell outward first. When the ice-blue sheet was parallel to the ground, the bottom edge came free, and the glass sailed for a moment before nosing over. It was too heavy and too lacking in fundamental aerodynamics to float on the air currents for long.

He followed the panel's descent all the way to the ground and watched it explode into thousands of fragments. He held onto the window frame for support, taking care not to cut himself on the sharp glass edges that remained clamped in. There was only a three-foot wall beneath the windows, and he could easily have pitched right over it, hurtling to his death on a bed of blue glass shards below. But that, he knew, would not be his fate.

The wind was whistling in—he could see typical thunderheads beginning to build to the east, portents of yet another afternoon rain. His eyes were beginning to feel dry and scratchy from the breeze, so he moved back from the opening and blinked until he produced soothing tears. He moved to the next window, where his view of the ground was just as good and he was less conspicuous. He didn't want to be peering out when Kirin Janacek arrived and looked up. She might or might not recognize him at this distance.

That she would come around and look at the broken glass and then look up to the empty window frame on the twenty-second floor he was most certain. She would do that even before she came upstairs. It was simple curiosity.

And then there she was, standing amid the remains of the window in blue jeans and sneakers. He thought he saw her shake her head in frustration, and—yes!—she glanced up at the gaping hole in her building, just as he predicted. He felt his pulse ratchet up a bit with excitement. And he gave himself a mental pat on the back. Did he understand human nature, or what?

He saw she was lugging the baby in his carrier, and he smiled. He'd forgotten about the baby. He heard her say she would take the child with her to the office, but it had slipped his mind. Now he had two of them in his sights.

"Well, doesn't *that* open up some interesting possibilities?" he said softly to himself.

When he saw her start for the building's front door, he took a powerful flashlight from his duffel bag, let himself into a stairwell, and walked down to the unfinished twenty-first floor. If he stood right by elevator number seven, he would be able to hear the *bing* when the doors opened one story above.

It was easy to predict what would happen next. She would call for John Fraser, and getting no reply, she would go over and examine what was left of the broken window. She might see that the frame still contained the edges of the missing double panel. It might even cross her mind that the blue glass had been cut. But that was all right. It would ensure she would stay put until somebody came along to answer her questions.

The noise of the wind would probably cover it, but there was at least a chance she would hear the elevator leave the twenty-second floor to pick him up on the twenty-first. If she did, that was fine, too. She would think it was off to pick up his alter ego, the security guard, wherever he was in the building.

The rest would only serve to confuse her more.

And the more she was confused, the more vulnerable she would be.

KIRIN opened the building's front door using a duplicate of the same key in the possession of the Handyman. The door relocked automatically when it closed behind her. She used her all-access card to call the all-floors elevator, and she set Casey's carrier on the floor while she waited for the car to arrive. The baby still slept soundly.

The floor panel indicator said the elevator was coming down from twenty-two. John Fraser was probably up there, waiting for her.

She wondered briefly where the police were. Fraser said he'd called them.

With no damage to anyone else's property and absent personal injury, they probably weren't in any hurry. And why should they be?

The car arrived. She picked up Casey and stepped inside.

The elevator doors closed and the car started up.

THE Handyman stood close to the twenty-first-floor doors of elevator shaft number seven, listening intently. He heard the car arrive on the floor above him and calculated when the woman would get off and when the doors would close. She would be looking now for the security guard, perhaps walking toward the open window frame.

He felt a visceral thrill that his plan was proceeding exactly as designed. He could feel her just a floor above him, sense her confusion and perhaps just a hint of apprehension.

He felt an excitement in his lower abdomen and fought it down.

Not now, he told himself. In time.

He pressed the elevator call button. The car came almost instantly. He rode to the lobby, let himself through the security door, and walked to the electrical closet. In this phase of his plan, he had to work quickly, before the woman got suspicious and moved to leave.

He let himself into the room and hit the four red buttons on the electrical service disconnect. Instantly, the room was thrown into darkness. Fifteen seconds later, the emergency generators kicked in. That was fast, he thought. In most commercial buildings the kick-in delays were longer. The quicker the kick-in, the more expensive the system. Many hospitals, where power was a matter of life or death, had the delay down to ten seconds. Very sophisticated buildings housing sensitive computer systems had delays of milliseconds. You could get all the speed you were willing to pay for, but ordinary commercial generator customers usually didn't buy superfast technology because they didn't consider it necessary.

The generators in this building were racehorses, all right. He not only could hear their rumblings through the wall, he could feel their vibrations in the floor, right through the thick rubber soles of his shoes. Building code required only that they provide enough juice for low-level emergency egress lighting, a one-foot-candle level of illumination in the halls and stairwells, as well as illumination of red EXIT signs. One foot-candle wasn't much, considering seventy foot-candles is considered proper reading light. These generators were capable of far more than that. They had been built to operate the elevators, too, and perhaps even the air-exchange system.

But they wouldn't for much longer.

Using the emergency lighting, he found his way back to the lobby. He felt a small wave of relief when he found the all-floors elevator still waiting for him. It meant she hadn't yet become suspicious, or at least not suspicious enough to make a run for it.

Once in the car, he altered his plans slightly. He rode only to the twenty-first floor, electing to walk up the last flight. He would use the rear stairwell, which would bring him out on the opposite side of the twenty-second floor from where she likely would be standing, and he could observe her for as long as he liked before making his move.

He stepped out of the elevator car and took the radio transmitter from his pocket. He pushed the white button, imagining how it looked as the black powder fired and opened the acid collars on the generator fuel lines. He fixed his eyes on the elevator status light, waiting anxiously for it to go out, a signal that the generators were down.

Five seconds passed.

He could feel his breathing, shallow and fast.

Ten seconds.

The light remained on.

Fifteen seconds.

Something had gone wrong!

Damn!

Did he have time to go back downstairs and cut the fuel lines by hand? He doubted it. The woman would grow tired of waiting soon and leave to find the security guard on her own. He'd designed this plan specifically to save time so that wouldn't happen.

Damn!

At the nineteen-second mark, the elevator status light flickered and died. This and all the other elevators were now useless.

He breathed a huge sigh. It occurred to him then why the process had taken longer than he anticipated. Once the fuel lines were severed, the generators continued to operate until the fuel beyond the line breaks was exhausted. Naturally, that took extra time.

So all had gone well.

The building was now totally without power and phone service.

He was in complete control.

And as yet the woman would have no way of knowing. On the unfinished twenty-first and twenty-second floors on this Sunday afternoon, there were no lamps, computers, or pieces of machinery suddenly powering down. There wasn't even a change in the perceivable lighting. It was only 2:30 in the afternoon, and the sun, even tempered by the blue-tinted windows, was bright and reassuring.

She didn't know yet that anything was wrong.

She didn't have the vaguest idea of the fate coming up the stairs to meet her.

31

Kirin set Casey's carrier on the floor, away from the wind, and turned back to stare again at the huge window frame, an expression of complete puzzlement on her face.

What in the hell had happened here?

This wasn't what she should have been seeing, what she saw at every other occurrence of glass failure. This was too even, too perfect, too . . .

Deliberate?

The word screamed in her mind and sent a chill through her, despite the hot, wet breeze coming through the gaping hole.

Gingerly, she ran a finger along the raw edges of glass still clamped in the window frame, as if tactile contact with the surface would somehow convey to her what had happened. There was no question; this was *not* a matter of heat-induced failure.

But why would anybody want to do this on purpose?

What end could be served with this sort of malicious mischief?

Where was the security guard? Where was John Fraser?

Probably came to the same conclusion she did and went off to find the idiot who did this.

A tingle hit her at the back of the neck.

That can't be right.

If he went off looking for the glass cutter, why was the elevator on the twenty-second floor when she arrived?

Maybe Fraser realized, too, that this was deliberate and had gone after the culprit. Maybe he had taken the stairs.

But . . . no.

He wouldn't look in the stairwells. The person who destroyed the window would have no access to stairs. You needed a key to get in.

Unless somebody turned in a fire alarm, in which case all locks opened automatically.

But there was no sign such an alarm had been triggered.

To possess a stairwell key, you had to be a member of the building's security force or maintenance staff. They'd all been screened meticulously before they were hired. None of them would do something like this. At least not in theory. No, she decided, nobody who worked for Water Street could be responsible for this.

So why would Fraser take the stairs if the person he was looking for couldn't use them?

She had to find Fraser.

She peered through the gaping window frame to see if the security guard was below, where the glass landed. She saw no one.

Then something happened.

It was so subtle, she wasn't certain what she'd felt.

Leaning against the window frame, she sensed the building's vibration through her fingers. It was faint, so subtle, it was almost subliminal. Anyone else would have noticed nothing. But this building was her baby, and she knew how it felt, how it lived, and how it breathed.

And she knew how it vibrated.

And now the vibrations were gone.

She paused for a few seconds, to be certain of her conclusion.

It was true. The vibrations had ceased.

And then they were back.

But they weren't right.

The building seemed to shudder before the new vibrations evened out and subsided slightly. And she was sure the vibrations didn't feel the same as they had. She couldn't have described the difference, but she was as certain it existed as she was of her name.

Something was very wrong at WestWater.

Something more sinister than vandalism was at work here.

Suddenly, she was frightened.

THE Handyman depressed the latch gently and pulled open the back stairwell door to the twenty-second floor. He thought he heard the latch click faintly. Since it was barely audible to him, there was no chance the woman heard it, not over the rush of the wind coming through the empty window frame. Still, he thought, he would be doubly careful when he closed the door.

This was to be a surprise party, after all.

All his senses were on full alert as he stepped out onto the bare concrete floor and scanned the area. He saw no one.

But he heard the wind.

And far off in the distance, he heard the thunder rumble.

He let the door slide closed behind him, keeping a light grip on it so it didn't slam.

He peered through the elevator lobby area, and there she was!

Again he felt the pressure in his groin.

She was leaning with her back against the building's exterior wall, her hands shoved deep in the pockets of her blue jeans, her eyes fixed on the floor. There was an unmistakable look of worry masking her face.

At her feet, her baby stirred in his carrier, slowly waking up.

The woman saw it, too. She knelt on the floor and fumbled in the small case attached to the carrier. She came up with a bottle that appeared to have a dark yellow juice in it; apple juice, perhaps, to fill the baby's stomach until it was time for a regular meal. She laid the bottle at the bottom of the carrier and pushed her right hand up under the baby's blanket.

"Well, it's not the best time, and it's not the best place, but when you're wet, you need to get dry," she said to the child.

The Handyman pulled back out of her line of sight. She was actually going to change the kid there on the floor. He guessed he could wait to confront her until that was done. No sense having a squally, pee-soaked child distracting him later.

After five minutes, he peeked around the corner again. A used diaper, some baby wipes, and a small shaker of talc lay on the floor. She was finishing with the fasteners of the new diaper and cooing at her son, who was giggling back from his carrier. She tucked him in and offered him the bottle, which he accepted hungrily. She placed the used diaper in a washable, zippered sleeve and stowed everything in the case.

Then she stood up, glancing back once again at the empty window frame. She placed her hand where it had been before and shook her head slightly. A frown creased her forehead.

It was time!

He stepped forward.

Her back was to him. She didn't hear him coming over the noise of the wind.

When he was a dozen feet away, he stopped.

"Hello, bitch!" he spat at her. "The Handyman has come for you!"

*   *   *

THE sound of the harsh voice created a cold knot of fear in her gut.

She turned to confront whoever it was and was astonished.

"Mr. Rickey?" she asked, suddenly tentative. "What are you doing here?"

"I'm here for you."

Her frown deepened. He didn't sound or look the same. The man standing before her had a much harsher voice, much harder eyes. But it was the same man, her kitchen contractor, of that she was certain.

"I don't understand. Is something wrong with the pantry? How did you even know to find me here? And how did you get in? How did you get up here?"

The questions were building in her mind even faster than she could put them to words. And she felt as though she were screaming to be heard over the wailing of the wind.

"Don't you know?" he asked.

She shook her head and looked at him quizzically.

"Know what?"

"Who I am."

"I thought you were Eugene Rickey."

"Not anymore. Maybe not for a long time."

She frowned and pulled back slightly, although she was already close to the wall. "You *are* the man who did our kitchen improvement, aren't you?" she asked.

"I resemble him, don't I?"

She shrank from him.

"You're frightening me, Mr. Rickey. Why are you doing this?"

"You're going to be more than frightened, bitch!" His voice sounded metallic, hollow.

Reflexively, she reached down for the handle on the baby's carrier. Blissfully unaware of the danger confronting his mother, Casey sucked happily at his apple juice.

The Handyman ignored the child. He backed away from the woman, toward the sawhorses and plywood sheeting.

"Come over here," he said. "I've got something to show you."

She stayed put, her left hand fumbling in her pocket for her keys. She didn't know what was going on, but she knew she had to get away. If he came for her, the longest key on her ring could make a weapon. She'd heard that, anyway. She hoped she didn't have to find out.

"There's a security guard around here," she said. "He'll be looking for me."

"John Fraser? You're lookin' at him."

Her eyes went wide.

"What?" she gasped.

"I'm the one who called you. I'm the one busted out the window behind you to get you up here. I did all this for you."

"But there *is* a security guard on duty," she said hopefully.

"Was."

"What do you mean?"

"I mean was. There *was* a security guard on duty. He's not on duty here anymore. He's standin' watch now at the pearly gates."

"Oh, God," she breathed. "Dear God."

"Come over here," he commanded.

"No," she said, so softly he didn't hear her over the wind noise.

"Come over here," he commanded again. "Now!"

"No!" She grabbed Casey's carrier and backed toward the elevators. "Stay away from me," she screamed.

He laughed at her and stood still beside the plywood bed.

"You aren't going anywhere," he said confidently.

"Just stay away," she repeated.

He held his hands wide and shrugged. "If you say so, for the time being, anyway," he said. "But I think you'll find you and I are stuck here together."

Holding the keys at her side, she backed into the elevator area. She reached for the button to call number seven, then saw with a shock that the lights behind the call buttons were out and the floor-indicator panel over the elevator doors was dark.

This was the change she felt in the building's vibrations. He had shut down the power and the emergency generators had come on automatically.

But the elevators were backed up by the generators. They should have continued to operate.

Unless . . .

"Power's all gone, even emergency power," he yelled over the wind. "There's no escape."

If he had this planned to such a degree, he probably disabled the phone system, too, she thought. And she'd left her cellular on the front seat of the car. Less to carry, she'd figured.

Wonderful. Brilliant reasoning.

The stairs!

She had to get to one of the stairwells. Without power, they would be unlocked.

She started to pocket her keys and paused. She should keep them ready in case she needed to get into a specific office where there might be a weapon or a good place to hide. Or in case she had the opportunity to use them as a poor substitute for brass knuckles.

She closed her hand firmly around them.

"Where are you?" he called harshly. "You might as well give it up. You can't get away."

"I can sure as hell try," she whispered to herself.

She grasped the knob on the door to the front stairway.

Please be unlocked. Please!

In the movies, the door would have jammed. But this was real life, and sometimes in real life you get lucky. The door opened smoothly.

She fairly dove through, dragging Casey along, and jumped down the first stairs. Then the door slammed shut, and she was pitched into total blackness. There were no emergency lights to guide her, and she was twenty-two stories from safety.

The first hint of despair crossed her mind.

Surely, he would be right behind them.

32

When he heard the sharp clank of a stairwell door closing, his gut clutched. He knew he had badly miscalculated.

He started after her and paused. Which set of stairs did she take, front or back? And did she go up or down?

She wouldn't go up. She would fear narrowing the possibilities for places to hide. She would know he could drive her up and trap her eventually on the roof.

No, she would go down.

Unless she knew he would reason that way. In which case, she might go up.

Stop it!

She doesn't have the time to think in circles. She's frightened and desperate. She will operate on instinct alone. She will go down.

What he couldn't let her do was get all the way down and into the lobby. Then she was out, and he was finished.

How far would she try to get? All the way at once, or down just a few flights at a time?

She should realize she couldn't outrun him. There was no light in the stairwells. He had the flashlight and could move quickly; she was burdened by darkness and a baby.

He eased open the door to the rear stairway and squeezed through quickly. He let the door partially close behind him.

He held his breath and listened.

She couldn't have crept down more than two or three floors in the pitch-black, not dragging that awkward baby carrier. He thought he might be able to hear something, but he didn't. No footfalls, nothing scraping the walls. She would be easier to track when the baby got hungry or uncomfortable. He recalled the kid had an excellent set of lungs.

She must have used the front stairs. He tried them.

Almost as soon as he stopped on the landing to listen, he heard it. A soft sound from the child, like he was playing with something and speaking to himself. It was faint, no more than three floors below. Maybe four. He could have caught up with them in a moment. But he preferred to scare the shit out of her for a while to get back at her for trying to run.

He filled his lungs with air.

"I know where you are, bitch, and I know where you're going!" he screamed loudly. "I'm going to give you a head start to make this game more fun. Then I'm coming for you. As you will see in the end, there is no escape."

He heard his voice echo off the block walls and reverberate up and down the stairwell shaft.

And he heard the baby scream.

Must have scared the kid.

Well, scream all you want to, little man.

Lead me and Opal straight to your mama.

THE realization of who he was came to Kirin with absolute clarity as she backed away from him on the concrete of the cavernous twenty-second floor. The knowledge actually made the task before her easier to define. There would be no trying to bargain with him, no trying to talk some sense and sanity into his head. There was only running, trying to outthink and outmaneuver him. The alternative . . . was too grim to consider.

My God, he was working in my house just a few hours before he attacked Cynthia Diamond! He first came to my house right after he killed the doctor in Carrollwood Village!

She remembered the news reports about what he had done to the victims he killed.

She had to manage an escape, somehow, for more than just herself. What might this madman do to Casey if they were captured?

If it came to that, she would be prepared to offer herself and whatever he chose to do to her for the life of her second child.

But she knew she would have no way, no leverage, to hold him to the bargain, assuming he'd even make it.

So it couldn't come to that.

She couldn't let it come to that.

She would beat him.

She thought she had never experienced such total darkness.

It seemed thick enough to create resistance as she tried to pick her way carefully and silently down the stairs, holding the rails and her keys with her left hand, gripping Casey's carrier with her right and trying not to knock it into the wall or trip and pitch forward over it.

She found herself sliding one foot in front of the other and, when it hit air, gently stepping down, scraping the back of her heel against the riser to be sure she didn't step out too far. Then she repeated the process with the other foot.

Take it slow! Don't rush. Don't make a mistake.

There were twenty steps to a flight. Each flight had a landing halfway down where the steps reversed direction. She counted each step as she went; when she got to ten, she knew she had to make a 180-degree turn.

She could feel cramps begin to tie knots in her thighs.

She put the pain out of her mind.

He had a flashlight.

She had seen it in his hand when he first confronted her on twenty-two. So he would be able to make faster progress down the stairs than she could, even if she hadn't had Casey with her. She would never get all the way to the lobby before he caught up with them. So she would have to find a place to hide.

She hugged the wall and passed the door to the twentieth floor. She felt the door handle hit her in the back as she slid by. Like the one above, this floor was unfinished and wide open. She needed to find a finished floor, a place with offices and closets.

Think, Kirin!

What's the status here?

Nineteen is partially done. Everything from eighteen to fifteen is completely done, but nothing below fifteen.

She had four floors from which to choose.

Four floors on which to save her life or lose it, to save her son or lose him.

She passed the door to the nineteenth floor.

Did he know which floors were fully or partially occupied? Probably. He knew everything else about the building.

Would he anticipate her attempt to hide on a fully occupied floor? Again, yes, probably.

So which to choose?

Not the first or the last. One in the middle. Sixteen or seventeen.

She passed the nineteenth floor.

And the eighteenth.

Far above her, she thought she saw a ray of light penetrate the blackness.

He was in the stairwell!

And then she heard him scream.

And Casey screamed.

And there was no choice left. He was coming.

She would begin her stand at the seventeenth floor.

HE stopped in the middle of the flight between the twenty-second and twenty-first floors.

As quickly as the baby's scream began, it ended.

The woman must have left the stairs, let herself onto a floor.

Which one?

The odds favored a finished one. More places to hide.

He consulted his memory of his tour of the building earlier.

There were four floors completely finished. The first one she would come to was eighteen. She might not want to take the first one, but his challenge could have forced her to be less picky and take what she could get.

But what if she'd gotten down farther than eighteen? If he started by searching eighteen, and she was already below him, she could slip back into the stairwell and make it to safety before he knew she was gone.

Better for him to start at fifteen and work his way up. He would check both stairwells every few minutes as he searched each floor. There would be less chance of her getting by him that way, especially with the baby spooked now. Once the baby started crying, it would be hard to stop him. Once he got hungry, there would be no stopping him.

Fifteen it is.

The struggle was joined.

He told himself to be quick about it.

THE corridors of the seventeenth floor were nearly as dark as the stairwell. The only light coming in was filtering from two offices at opposite ends of the floor where glass brick had been used instead of solid walls fronting the hallway. There was no emergency lighting, no illumination of the EXIT signs, nothing but the little bit of daylight seeping through.

She tried to read her watch, but couldn't. It must be after three o'clock by now. There were probably three more hours of useful daylight by which she could make her way around the finished floors. After that, an hour or so of dusk before the city lights began to come on. They wouldn't be of any help to her, not way up here. If she hadn't escaped by then, or been rescued, she likely would be dead.

Or wishing she were dead.

She shuddered and turned her attention to Casey, who continued to cry softly.

She picked him up and rocked him, singing softly to him, and she could feel him begin to relax. It wouldn't last, she knew. Nor would he be willing to stay in the carrier forever. He was fully awake and ready to play, blissfully unaware of the danger surrounding them.

He tried to push himself away from his mother's arms, and she confined him again to the carrier, strapping him in. He keened in opposition to enforced inactivity and struggled to get out. She stroked his head and tried to soothe him. He would have none of it.

She didn't have time to do more.

They had to move.

She used her master key to unlock office doors, scouting them quickly for hiding places.

There was nothing that gave her any confidence.

She relocked each office as she left. No sense telling the killer where she had been. Let him take the time to look for her.

When she'd evaluated half the floor, she came to the understanding that perhaps hiding here wasn't a good idea after all. If she sealed herself and her son into an office, and he found them there, they'd be cornered. If they were going to hide, she would have to find a place that would remain secure for hours, long enough for David to get home from the club, to miss her, to realize she wasn't at her office, and to begin looking for her, maybe to call the police and ask them to mount a full-scale search.

She couldn't think of any place in the building providing the level of security she needed. There were no secret doors or hidden chambers.

Would David actually call the police? If he did, would the police take a missing-person report before Kirin had been gone for twenty-four hours? She thought they usually insisted on waiting at least that long.

In the current climate of fear, they might be more inclined to act faster. But even if they did, would anybody, the police or David, think to check this building complex and find her car parked on the street?

All the possibilities seemed so hopeless.

Panic began to constrict her chest. Her breathing was fast and shallow.

Calm down, Kirin! You're going to hyperventilate.

You've got to think calmly. If you're going to get out of this, you've got to save yourself. You can't count on anyone riding to your rescue. The bottom line is tough: If you panic, you and Casey are both dead.

Where could they go? The killer had access to every place she did. And with a flashlight, and unburdened by a baby or the need to maintain quiet, he could move farther and faster.

She had to find a way to get past him and feel her way to the lobby.

But where was he?

She might open a stairwell door and find him standing there waiting for her.

But he could only cover one at a time.

The odds were as much in her favor as his in terms of choosing.

She turned the knob on the door to the rear stairwell.

She held her breath and pulled it open slightly. All she saw was pitch-dark.

She slid into the stairwell, holding the door in position just short of locking, and listened.

Silence.

She let the door close fully and began to feel her way down again toward . . .

What?

WHEN the door closed and clicked, she heard it.

He *saw* it.

He had just entered the seventeenth floor from the front stairwell and had worked his way around the elevators to the escape route she chose.

He had her!

All he had to do was slip into the rear stairwell behind her and follow wherever she went.

She was making her last run.

KIRIN didn't think so.

She had spotted the vague wedge of low light that penetrated the stairwell above her when he entered from the seventeenth floor.

So he knew where she was.

But she knew where he was, and he didn't know that.

He had figured her to do go down rather than up.

And she would have preferred to continue that course.

But the situation required her to ignore what she preferred and act to survive. That was her only responsibility now.

She would start down, but then she would reverse her course.

If she could get to the front stairwell, she would start back up.

She could make the crossover without being spotted on the fourteenth floor. The entire elevator lobby, including access to the two stairways, was encircled by a floor-to-ceiling plywood barrier. A computer software design company was taking the whole floor and doing most of the finishing work with its own people because its executives took no chances competitors might send someone over to pry into what was going on. The only way to get beyond the plywood was through a temporary door always kept closed and padlocked.

She could let herself out of the rear stairwell without any light leak betraying her. Then she would go to the front stairwell and begin to climb.

If only Casey would remain quiet until she got safely onto the fourteenth floor.

WHEN she reached the door, she paused and briefly tried to massage the cramps from her legs. She prayed she hadn't lost count of the floors.

No, she was sure. She had come down three flights of steps from the seventeenth floor. Six changes of direction, two for each flight. This was right. This was fourteen.

But something didn't feel right.

He had let himself into the stairwell above her, but she had seen nothing of his flashlight and heard no steps descending after her. And he hadn't called to her again.

Was he coming in silence and darkness?

That would be foolish and unnecessary.

Was he trying to increase the terror?

If he was, it was working.

The sweat was trickling down the center of her back and dampening her face. Part of it was from exertion. Most of it was from fright.

She could feel her pulse pounding in her temples and her heart thudding in her chest.

Her heart . . .

Didn't the papers say he mutilated his victims' hearts?

Don't think about it!

For God's sake, keep your mind on what you're doing.

She didn't have time to indulge her fears, anyway. If he was coming down behind her, she had to move.

Now!

She pulled open the door to the fourteenth floor and launched herself through it, swinging Casey's carrier through after her.

SHE stood there, her breath coming in spasms, and let the door close behind her so gently it made virtually no noise.

She blinked. If there was any light, her eyes would become accustomed to it shortly.

But nothing happened. It was as dark as she thought it would be.

She called up a mental image of the elevator lobby and placed herself in the picture. With her back to the door, she was facing west and standing on the north end of the floor. She had to walk around to her left to get between the elevator banks, then cross over and work her way along until she faced east at the south end of the floor.

With no light at all, it would be tricky to avoid getting turned around.

She pressed her back to the wall and inched to her left.

One step. Two.

On the seventh step, she reached the corner.

She stopped.

Remember to breathe.

She slid her shoulders around the corner, pressed her back to the wall once again, and stepped to her left. And again.

She felt the indentation in the wall behind her, the brass doors to elevator number four.

So far, so good.

She continued to her left until she came to the next set of doors: number five elevator. Now she was roughly in the center of the elevator lobby. All she had to do was walk straight across it to the doors of elevator number two on the other side.

She took a deep breath and stepped out, a hand stretched out in front of her. She was completely and utterly blind. She had her key ring circled over her thumb and was probing the darkness with her fingers.

Casey began to whimper.

"Sssh, honey," she said. "It's all right. We're going to get out of this. Mommy's going to get us home safe and sound."

She reached down to stroke his head, took another step forward as she did so . . . and ran into something . . . someone! She felt the stiff hair.

It grabbed her.

She screamed and pulled back and heard her keys clatter to the floor.

Casey screamed.

She tried to fight her assailant and realized he . . . it . . . was giving her no resistance.

What the hell?

She felt for it and found a mop. And a broom.

Her breath was coming in great gulps now, and Casey was crying. She felt around the thing she'd run into long enough to realize it was a cleaning cart carrying mops and brooms, rolls of toilet paper, paper towels, and soap refills.

What the hell was it doing on the fourteenth floor?

The floor had no occupants.

But it did have working bathrooms being used by the service personnel putting the offices together for the tenant.

What a *stupid* place to leave a cleaning cart!

She considered briefly that there might be containers of solvents or cleaners on the cart that would make useful weapons against the killer who stalked her. Ammonia to the eyes could be a huge deterrent. But even if she found some, how would she carry it around? She had Casey in one hand, and she had to keep her keys—where had they fallen?—in the other. She refused to put anything so toxic inside Casey's carrier. The fumes, the danger of a leak, were dangers too great to dismiss. Besides, if the killer was close enough to hurl a chemical at him, he would be close enough to snatch it from her as she took it from under the baby's blanket.

No, it wouldn't work. She shouldn't waste any more time thinking about it.

She calmed herself and stooped to soothe her son. His crying now was out of both fear and hunger, and he wouldn't be comforted. His apple juice bottle was still there, and when she shook it, she heard it slosh. There still were several ounces left, she judged.

"Just a little while longer, Casey, I promise," she cooed. "Be a good boy and be quiet. *Please.* For just a little while longer, and then we can go home, and you can have ice cream."

Whether the child understood the term was doubtful, but she thought she heard him giggle. She offered him the apple juice, but he rejected it, heaving the bottle aside. She heard it whack on the concrete floor and roll away. She dared not try to find it for fear of losing her bearings, if she hadn't already.

She had to find her keys.

She kept the cleaning cart directly in front of her while she felt around on the floor.

Her fingers touched the jumble of metal and she picked it up.

She stood and hoisted Casey, felt her way around the cleaning cart, and moved forward, her fingers outstretched, feeling for the opposite wall.

She touched something metallic and cool.

Brass.

Elevator doors.

She had made it to the other side of the elevator lobby.

She pressed her back to the elevator doors and began inching along to her right. She passed elevator number one and reached the corner. All she had to do was get around it and take a half dozen steps to reach the door to the front stairwell.

We're going to make it, Casey. Hang on, kid.

As quietly as possible she pulled the door open.

A strong beam of light hit her in the face!

It stunned her eyes!

She stumbled backward, away from the dazzling brightness.

It moved to underlight a man's face.

She screamed as an adrenaline bath shocked her system.

He reached out quickly and put an iron grip on Casey's carrier. She was pulling at it, but he wouldn't let go.

"No!" she screamed. "Give me my baby!"

"You want your baby?" he asked in a voice full of cruelty. "You'll have to come and get him. You'll have to come to me and beg me to let him live."

"No! Oh, no, *please!*" She screamed again. She felt herself start to cry and could do nothing to stop it. She felt Casey's carrier slipping from her grasp, and she heard the baby screeching in terror, sensing his mother's own, no doubt. "Please! You don't understand. I can't lose him. I can't! Don't hurt my baby!"

"It isn't your baby I want to hurt," he said nastily. "It's you. But I can't handle you both on this stairwell, so I'm going to leave you here for now. If you want to see your son alive again, you're going to have to come back to the twenty-second floor for him."

With a strong tug, he succeeded in dislodging the carrier from her hands.

"Please! I lost a baby once. Don't do this to me. I couldn't take it again. I'll do anything!"

"Then come to me and beg for your baby's life. I'll be waiting for you on the twenty-second floor. If you don't come within the next hour, the baby goes out the broken window. I don't think he could survive a twenty-two-story fall. Do you?"

She started to protest from the bottom of her soul, but never got the words past her lips.

He smashed the flashlight hard into the point of her chin.

Her head snapped back, and the last thing she saw before she hit the floor was the light beam dancing crazily off the plywood walls around her.

33

David Janacek hung the telephone receiver back in its cradle, the unanswered ring still droning from the earpiece.

"Kirin isn't home yet, so I guess I've got time for that drink," David said to the man to whom he'd just lost fifty-five dollars on the Palma Ceia golf course.

"I'll buy," Jock Salerno offered graciously. "After all, I've got some extra cash on me."

"Yeah, tell me about it," Janacek replied sarcastically. "My wallet feels a little light."

They walked together through the clubhouse toward the bar.

"Speaking of light, we're losing it fast today," Salerno said. "Must be one heck of a series of storms coming in."

"You can see it right here," Janacek said, stopping before a television set someone had tuned to the Weather Channel. On the blue screen, the forecast said the chance of rain was seventy percent during the afternoon and eighty percent during the evening, diminishing after nightfall. The radar of central Florida painted strong storm cells in yellow and red embedded in vast fields of lighter rain painted in green.

"Pretty good odds of rain, and pretty mean-looking storms," Janacek said, and Salerno grunted in agreement.

Along the bottom of the picture, a red strip was detailing a severe thunderstorm warning. It covered all west-central Florida and marine interests along the shores of Tampa Bay and the Gulf Coast. One line of huge cells was rumbling northwest from Avon Park. Its leading edge had already penetrated Hillsborough County. It was expected to join with another line of intense storms traveling due west from Plant City. Both systems were moving at fifteen miles an hour, a pretty good clip, and were expected to dump heavy rain on most of the region, the warning said. The rain would be accompanied by high winds, intense lightning, and hail. Tornadoes were a possibility. Marine warnings were up.

Janacek whistled softly.

"I'd feel better if Kirin and Casey were safe at home," he said.

"They'll be fine," Salerno assured him. "Kirin won't take any chances, not with the baby. I know her better than that."

Janacek smiled. "That's an absolute certainty," he said.

"She's probably planning to ride it out at her office," Salerno said. "Why don't you give her a call there? Be sure she knows what's coming."

But Janacek got no answer at Kirin's office, either. He dialed her cellular phone and got a recording saying the owner wasn't available at the moment.

He reported the results to Salerno.

"Is that odd?" the prosecutor asked.

"No, not really. If she's still at the office, she's probably deep into work and isn't answering the phone. It's been known to happen before. Or she's on the way home and forgot to turn the cell phone on. That happens about fifty percent of the time, particularly when she's preoccupied. I'm sure she's fine."

"Then let's find us some tall gin-and-tonics before I die of thirst," Salerno suggested.

Janacek smiled and followed along into the bar, but in the back of his mind, a nugget of apprehension began to grow.

34

The sharp report of thunder was the first thing that penetrated Kirin Janacek's consciousness. Thunder and pain.

And then a stab of terror.

How long had he given her?

An hour. One hour!

How much time had she lost, lying unconscious on the concrete?

She struggled to sit up, her jaw throbbing, her head aching. She must have cracked it on the floor when she fell.

The first thing she had to do was find her keys again.

The next was to find a weapon.

She thought about going back to the cleaning cart, but what if she searched it for a solvent and came up empty? She didn't have that kind of time to waste.

That Eugene Rickey meant it when he said he would kill Casey she had little doubt.

That she would do everything in her power to stop him was a dead-bang certainty.

She got lucky early. The heavy key ring had fallen at her side. She found it quickly. She pulled herself to her feet, swayed with dizziness for a moment, then willed herself steady and felt for the door. She let herself through it.

She mounted the stairs slowly, and vertigo engulfed her again. The first thing she had to do was find out what time it was.

It was about three o'clock, probably a little after, when she and Casey escaped from him on the twenty-second floor. That probably would have made it close to four when he caught up with them and snatched Casey.

So she had until roughly until five to locate her son.

She let herself onto the fifteenth floor, squinting against the expected assault of light, but it was nearly pitch-black.

My God, is it that late already?

Is it too late?

But the blackness was explained quickly. Through small spaces between the office doors and their frames, she saw the brilliant flash of a lightning stroke, followed almost immediately by the crack and thud of thunder rolling over the building and making it tremble.

She found the office master key and let herself into the door nearest the stairwell.

Through the exterior windows, she could see the eastern sky ablaze.

A leading edge of low, ominously black clouds, several miles wide, was advancing on the city. It hurled lightning bolts singly and in clusters, creating thunder that didn't end. There was enough light for her to read her watch.

It was 4:42.

If her calculations were right, she had eighteen minutes to get to her son. Eighteen minutes to save Casey.

Eighteen minutes until a madman hurled her child into the angry sky and to his death.

A sob choked her, and she struggled against a surge of panic.

A weapon!

She had to find a weapon.

She searched the desks frantically. The best she could come up with was a long, stainless-steel letter opener.

It would serve as a stabbing weapon if she could get close enough to the killer to use it. But he had a knife.

Was it possible there was a gun around? So many people owned them now.

The secretaries' desks were unlocked but yielded no guns.

What about the executives who worked here?

She tried the doors to their offices, but they were locked.

Damn!

She didn't have a passkey to the interior doors.

And it didn't make sense to break a door down unless there was some certainty of finding what she was looking for on the other side.

She gripped the letter opener firmly and tried some other suites on the floor with the same results. Where she could get access, there were no weapons. Where there might be weapons, she couldn't gain access.

So that was it.

Armed only with a letter opener, she would confront the man who threatened to kill her son and vowed to kill her.

There wasn't really a lot of choice, was there?

She let herself into the stairwell again and began the slow, laborious climb up seven flights of stairs to the twenty-second floor.

35

"Jesus, will you *look* at that?"

Jock Salerno was finishing his gin-and-tonic, standing by a set of windows looking to the south and east, directly into the teeth of the storm system overtaking Tampa.

"That's awesome," he added.

He turned to David Janacek, who was standing at his elbow.

"We ain't gonna be goin' any place in the immediate future," he said. "How about another splash of juniper juice?"

"Don't mind if I do," Janacek replied. "I hope Kirin gets home before this hits."

"She's fine, David," Salerno insisted. "She's a big girl. Relax."

They got their drinks and took them to chairs near the picture windows.

"Welcome to Tampa Bay," Janacek said as multiple strobes of lightning split the blackened sky. "With storms like this, we might as well be living on Venus."

Salerno was pensive.

"We might all be safer there," he mused. "Especially the women."

Janacek regarded him for a moment. Beneath the golf-course tan, the prosecutor looked tired.

"This serial-killer thing got you down?" he asked.

Salerno nodded.

"I'll tell you, David, although I don't want it repeated outside this conversation, right?" Janacek nodded. "We thought after he missed the Diamond woman, he'd come back with a vengeance. It would have fit the pattern for this sort of killer. When a victim gets away, he strikes again, hard and fast, to get his confidence back."

"But there's been no sign of him?"

"Not a peep. Not a sighting. Not a threat. We don't know if he's gone underground, or if he's stalking somebody but hasn't been able to isolate her to take her yet. The waiting, the uncertainty, are playing havoc with everybody's nerves, especially the cops. I've never worked with a more frustrated bunch in my life. They've tried everything. They've invented new things to try. Nothing works. Nobody can get a make on this guy."

"But you'll know him for sure when you get him?"

"Oh, yeah, easy. We've got blood type, DNA, all a match from killing to killing. I wish we had fingerprints. I'd rather have fingerprints than DNA. But he doesn't leave any. Even without prints, we won't have a problem, though. We'll make him hard and cold."

"You holding back anything interesting?"

"Details of the killings, you mean? Yeah, a good deal of that. And some of it is so bizarre and far-fetched, nobody but the killer could possibly know."

"Like what?"

"You know I'm not supposed to say."

"I'm trying to make conversation here, not collect gossip. I figure for my fifty-five dollars, you owe me more than a couple of drinks."

"Well, this guy apparently likes to sing to his victims."

"How would you know something like that? From Cynthia Diamond?"

"Exactly. He started singing to her right before her dogs attacked him. It freaked her."

"That *is* weird," Janacek acknowledged. "I didn't know there was such a thing as a medley of songs to kill by."

"No medley, at least not for Cynthia Diamond. Just one song. It's an old pop hit called 'Handyman.' But that's top secret, David. I shouldn't have even mentioned . . ."

But David Janacek had stopped listening. A cold knot had formed at the top of his stomach and threatened to crush his chest as he searched his memory frantically.

"Handyman." That was the song Kirin had turned off in the car Friday night.

What had she said about it? Their contractor sang it all the time, until she was absolutely sick of it. Couldn't stand to hear it, even by the artist who made it popular.

Coincidence?

No!

Janacek's mind screamed at him.

It fit. All the clues fit!

The cops were looking for a light-colored pickup truck. Eugene Rickey's was light gray.

The police artist's sketches. David had looked at them long and hard once, trying to get behind the man's eyes, trying, as a lawyer, to get into his head. Professional curiosity, then. Now perhaps a matter of life and death. It wasn't too much of a stretch to put Eugene Rickey's face beside those sketches and see the resemblance.

"Oh, shit!" Janacek spit out the expletive so forcefully it startled Jock Salerno. Several other patrons of the bar stopped their conversations and turned to look.

"David? What the hell's wrong?" the prosecutor asked sharply. He thought his golfing partner looked white to the eyes.

"I know who he is, Jock!" Janacek said in a hoarse whisper. His hands were shaking and a light sheen of perspiration beaded on his upper lip. "I know the Heartbreak Killer."

Janacek had leaped from his chair, his eyes wide, his breath coming in short gasps.

"God help us, Jock, he's been working in my house for weeks! He's after Kirin!"

36

At the ferocious heart of the summer thunderstorms, the streets of Tampa came awash with water and cops.

Blue-over-white units from the Tampa Police Department, green-over-white units from the Hillsborough Sheriff's Office, and yellow-and-black units from the Florida Highway Patrol crisscrossed flooding streets in search of Kirin Janacek and her son. Three TPD units wailed to a stop in her driveway and six officers, none of whom gave a second thought to the downpour or the dangers of the lightning, sprinted to the house. Two went to the front door. Two more went around behind. The two remaining began a search of the grounds as water built up in the grass flooded into their shoes.

Four units, including an unmarked car carrying Benjamin Britton and Nick Estevez, raced to Cypress Street. They found Kirin's office locked. The weekend watchman let them in. Kirin signed into the building at 1:52 but she hadn't signed out, and the watchman said he didn't see her leave. But that wasn't unusual. People often forgot to sign out, he said, and he was probably away from his desk when she left. There was no one in her office now, at any rate.

Britton was preparing to leave when David Janacek and Jock Salerno showed up in Salerno's car. They were still in golf clothes, and they were soaking wet.

"Anything?" the prosecutor asked cryptically. It was he who placed the alerting call to Britton that set the citywide hunt in motion.

Britton shook his head. "Nothing. No sign of them. TPD reports the same at the house."

"Have they been inside to look?" Salerno demanded.

"Yes, a neighbor let them in," Britton said. He turned to Janacek. "Are you the husband?"

"Yes." He could barely raise his voice, hoarse with fear, above a whisper.

"Where else might she have gone?" Britton asked. "Friends? Relatives?"

"No!" Janacek replied. "She was coming here to work, and then she was going home. She wouldn't have changed her plans without letting me know."

"But you've been on the golf course all afternoon," Britton snapped. "She had no way to reach you there, did she?"

"She'd have left a message at the pro shop. They'd have given it to me when I finished the round. If it was an emergency, they'd have sent somebody out in a golf cart to find me."

"And if her plans had changed, you're certain she'd have called?"

"If it was important, or if she thought the change was going to delay her getting home, yes. That was . . . is . . . her routine. She's done it before."

"But not this time."

Janacek hung his head. "No," he said softly. "Not this time."

"Well, she got here, but obviously she isn't here now. She isn't at your home. And there's no sign of her car between here and there, at least so far." Britton squeezed David's arm hard enough that he winced. "I need options, Mr. Janacek. And we might not have much time."

Britton could see David Janacek was plainly panicky. His hands opened and closed into fists and he was having difficulty standing still.

"Focus, Mr. Janacek," the detective said. "Focus. Think! Where else could your wife have gone when she left here?"

"I don't know!" Janacek insisted. "Goddamn it, I don't *know!* She was coming here to work on the Water Street project. But she didn't plan on visiting the site. At least she didn't say anything about it when she left the house. I don't think she'd have taken the baby there, anyhow. There wasn't any reason for her to go there. All she had to do was update some computer files with new specifications she'd drawn up last week at home."

"Water Street is a place to start," Britton said.

He turned to Nick Estevez barking orders.

"Nearest units to Water Street Plaza, tell them to look around. Fast. Remember, white Mercedes. They find it, I wanna know yesterday!"

KIRIN'S hand rested on the release bar that would open the front stairwell to the twenty-second floor. She could feel perspiration soak her clothes. Part of it was the exertion of climbing seven flights of stairs with a concussion, part of it was the closeness of the air in the stairwells where there didn't seem to be enough molecules of oxygen to feed her body's needs. But most was the mental strain.

She could hear thunder even through the heavy metal door and felt the building vibrate with each clap. They were coming one on top of another; as fast as one rumbled into the distance, another and another replaced it in a cacophony that must be terrifying Casey, she thought.

She pressed her ear to the door and listened intently.

And breathed a huge sigh of relief.

She could hear Casey crying at the top of his lungs.

Thank God!

How could she have let this happen to him?

Well, it was going to end.

Now!

She pushed through the door and was slapped in the face by a warm, wet wind, blowing—no howling—through the gaping hole the killer had made in the side of her building.

There were no lights that she could see.

What had she expected without power?

Perhaps battery-operated lanterns. Didn't the Heartbreak Killer want to be able to see his victim suffer as she died?

Casey!

Her mind called to the child when a brief respite in the lightning and thunder brought his screams to her ears more clearly.

She held her ring of keys in her left hand with the longest key extending between her index and middle finger. It might be of some use as a weapon if she could get a clear shot at the killer's eyes. In her right hand was the letter opener, held low but anchored in a fist, pointed upward, ready for a thrust. Perhaps she would get a chance to use it before he saw it. The details of what he would be able to discern between the strobes of lightning would be limited at best.

She walked slowly through the elevator lobby, toward Casey's cries. He sounded so afraid. She longed to hold him and stroke his head and reassure him that everything was all right.

Her mind flashed back to the crib in the hospital, to the beautiful baby girl whose external looks were perfect but whose internal flaws would kill her. How she had stroked Amy's head and reassured her everything would be all right. And how it wasn't.

Tears began to stream down Kirin's face.

Angrily, she blinked them away.

She needed to be able to see everything.

To think without distraction.

To react to . . .

He grabbed her from behind, snatched her right arm at the wrist, and twisted it up and behind her until she yelped in pain. He'd been waiting somewhere behind her, knowing she would move for her child.

She cursed herself for not anticipating that.

She felt him prying the letter opener from her hand. The more she tried to resist, the more upward pressure he put on her arm. It felt as if it were about to pop from the shoulder socket.

He ripped the would-be weapon from her grasp, the second arm-wrestling match she'd lost to him this day.

"And just what do you think you were going to do with this?" he asked harshly. "I don't think you were expecting mail on a Sunday, now were you?"

While his concentration was focused entirely on her right hand, she spun around and hammered him in the abdomen with her left. She felt the key protruding from between her fingers punch through fabric and skin, and she thought she felt the warm wetness of his blood against her fist.

He screamed in surprise and pain and smashed his fist into a place just below her sternum.

She heard her breath whoosh from her lungs and felt fire in her chest. She fell to both knees, desperately fighting off unconsciousness, gasping like a fish thrown up on a riverbank.

She had barely started getting her breath back when she heard him yelling curses at her.

"You fucking bitch!" he hollered. "You cunt!" She thought he sounded curiously as if he were about to cry. "Whadda you think you're doing, huh? You gonna kill me with a key? You stupid whore! You stinking bitch! You're gonna pay for this. You're gonna pay good. I'm bleeding like a fucking stuck pig, you fucking bitch!"

He was standing over her now.

"Please!" she heard herself whimper. She hated herself for doing that.

In a flash of lightning, she saw his body lurch as he threw the letter opener across the vast open space on the floor. She heard it clatter on the concrete at the far end of the building. Then he bent over and wrested the keys from her other hand and threw them away, too.

"You won't have any need for them anymore. You won't be leaving this floor again, at least not alive," he hissed. "God, I'm gonna make you suffer for hurtin' me. Opal's gonna really make you suffer. She's thinkin' up whole new things to do to you, you whore!"

She looked up and saw close to her face the silhouette of his fist and a knife.

"Have you met Opal?" he asked. He waved the knife slowly in front of her. "No? I didn't think so. Opal, meet the bitch. Bitch, meet Opal." He paused, then shook his head. He said, "First impressions mean a lot, and Opal says she doesn't like you. Opal is a good judge of character. Women she doesn't like usually come to a bad end."

In the lightning flashes, she could see the knife's hideous length, its razor-sharp blade and gleaming blue-green hasp.

How many women had this knife killed?

She couldn't stop her mind from imagining the enormity of the damage it had inflicted on other women's bodies, and the scope of the horror was almost hypnotizing as he passed the weapon back and forth before her face.

She forced herself to shake off its effect.

"Let me go to my son," she pleaded. "Let me hold him. He's frightened."

"Of course he's frightened, bitch! You shouldn't have brought him here. You had no business doin' that. This isn't anything for a kid to see. You've abused him, just like you abused me. I'm going to see you pay for it with your life."

She stared at him in disbelief.

Why was he accusing her of abusing him? The wound she made with the key?

Somehow, she didn't think that was it.

"You're insane," she said softly. Over the noise of the storm, he didn't hear her.

She stumbled to her feet and started for Casey, but he grabbed her hair and pulled her back, slamming her against an outer wall of the elevator shaft.

He slapped her hard, with the back of his hand, across the left cheek, and she gasped. Her mouth filled with the metallic taste of her own blood.

He got in close to her face. "You go where I *tell* you to go," he spat at her. She smelled the reek of alcohol on his breath and recoiled from it. If he saw her reaction, it didn't faze him. "You do what I *tell* you to do," he continued. "You disobey me, and your punishment will be a lot more painful. You understand?" He shook her. "*Do* you?"

Casey was shrieking now.

She didn't reply, but turned toward the baby.

"Please," she asked again. "He needs me."

"I need you, too," he said. "I need you worse. Maybe I should make it so the kid doesn't need you anymore."

He began backing away from Kirin, toward the carrier where Casey cried and struggled to free himself from the belt holding him in.

"I can make it so he never needs you or anyone else again," the killer said.

Another memory of Amy flashed through her mind and triggered an emotional overload.

Another enormous flash of lightning originating in the evening sky directly above their heads allowed him to see her hands fly to her face and let him read her lips when she screamed, *"NO!"* But the crash of thunder came even before the sound of her voice could travel across the twenty feet now separating them.

He reached down and undid the strap confining Casey. He grabbed a handful of the boy's shirt and began to haul him out of the carrier.

Then she was there in front of him, challenging him.

She threw her body across the boy, wholly unmindful of the knife posed above her back. She was not going to lose Casey. She had lost Amy; she would save Casey at any cost.

"Leave him—"

The rest of her desperate words were drowned out by the monstrous roll of thunder that accompanied another lightning stroke.

The man released the child and grabbed for the mother, hauling her a few feet from her baby. He reached under her arms and forced her to stand, ready to propel her backward toward the waiting plywood bed.

"You're not going to interfere with me again," he said, his mouth pressed to her ear. His boozy breath reached her nose again and turned her stomach.

But she wasn't prepared to give up and struggled mightily to get free.

He plunged the knife into the back of her right leg.

She screamed and crumpled like a rag doll suddenly bereft of its stuffing.

He was laughing horribly now, backing once again toward Casey.

"Since you're not gonna cooperate with me, I'm gonna throw him out the window," he called to her. "That will be your punishment for disobedience. I had planned to let the kid live, but I've changed my mind. His blood will be on your hands and your soul."

She was dragging herself across the floor after him, leaving a trail of blood smearing from the leg dragging uselessly behind her.

He was not going to kill her child!

She felt the spray of rain blowing through the hole in her building. It ran down her face into her eyes, but she didn't take time to wipe it away. She had to get to the killer before it was too late for her son.

She would push Eugene Rickey through the open window. He could stab her as many times as he wanted, but he wouldn't stop her. If he dragged her through after him, so be it. At least Casey would be alive.

The child, meanwhile, having recognized his mother when she came to him moments earlier, was sobbing and struggling to find her and the comfort of her arms. He used all his strength to push himself over the edge of his carrier, a trick not exactly new to him.

He got himself into a kneeling position, then pushed himself to his feet, using the carrier for support. In the now-continuous flashes of lightning, he saw his mother crawling across the floor to him, and his crying began to subside.

He thought she was playing with him.

His face was wet with tears, and his clothes were soaked by rain, but a hint of a grin creased the corners of his mouth.

He started toward her, taking shaky, halting steps.

His first steps.

He didn't see the man backing toward him, toward the hole where the window had been, until it was too late.

The dark figure suddenly loomed over Casey and startled him. His tenuous balance slipped and he fell—forward, as fate would have it.

One of the strange things about human anatomy is that even a light tap behind the knee can cause the leg to buckle. Casey tumbled into the back of both of the man's knees, and both of the Handyman's legs buckled together.

He gasped and grunted as he lost his balance and reached out to grab for something to stabilize himself, even as Casey reached out for him for the same reason. The baby's little fist snagged and held onto the cloth of the Handyman's pant leg.

The Handyman's left hand grabbed a stainless steel delivery pipe that was part of the building's sprinkler system. His body, head, and right foot slammed against one of the building's structural steel columns, directly on top of a copper grounding cable that was part of the building's lightning suppression system. The cable ran the length of the column, from the roof to the ground.

At that precise instant, the raging storm fired five simultaneous salvos.

One struck a tree on the campus of the University of Tampa, one hit a tree at the DeSoto Park Playground, one hit an unoccupied thirty-eight-foot sloop docked at the Davis Islands Yacht Club, one struck Landmark Tower on Jackson Street, and the fifth hit West-Water Tower's roof.

The two trees were destroyed, and the yacht exploded. The lightning protection system at the Landmark building worked perfectly, carrying the surge to the ground. The system at WestWater would have worked perfectly, too, but for the human body in simultaneous contact with a grounding cable and a steel water pipe.

A single stroke of lightning can carry a charge equal to one billion volts of electricity, and the bolt that hit WestWater was every bit that powerful. The lightning suppression system converted it to current, and the surge coursed ten floors down. It would have continued to the ground, but when it reached the twenty-second floor, the human body became its path of least resistance.

The current exploded into the Handyman's body through his right temple. It coursed down his neck, across his chest, and out both arms to his hands. It ripped through the vital organs in his torso, short-circuiting the electrical patterns of his heart. It continued down through his intestines and his groin to his right leg. It blew out a hole in his ankle and arced, ironically, to the copper grounding cable, where it benignly completed its journey to the ground.

It was as if a large electric stove burner had been left on high for six months, and all the heat generated in that time were focused on a human body for a millisecond. Some of his clothes caught fire. Water in his body's cells boiled away in an instant, and his skin burned black. His brain, his heart, and most of his internal organs were cooked. His testicles burst. Sparks danced off the tip of the blade of the knife he called Opal, and it was seared by fire to the palm that gripped it, its gorgeous abalone shell ruined by the heat.

In one brutal irony of timing, the Handyman died.

And at long last, Eugene Rickey found his peace.

37

The patrol car dispatched to WestWater Tower found Kirin Janacek's Mercedes immediately.

Every police vehicle within the city limits went on full alert. The building was surrounded, the area awash in blazing red, blue, and white lights.

Despite the weather, a police helicopter transported a crack assault team to WestWater and dropped the men onto the roof. They let themselves onto the top floor and waited, tense and alert, for further orders. Their helicopter darted away just as the lightning bolt that killed the Handyman exploded from the sky.

One ground unit immediately spotted the broken window shards on the ground and radioed to everyone else on the frequency that the pane apparently had fallen from the twenty-second floor.

"If somebody reached Kirin about that, it would have gotten her here right away," David told Salerno and Britton, shouting to be heard over the raging storm.

Ben Britton stormed through the lobby door. Estevez and Salerno followed him in, as did David Janacek. The cops had ordered him to stay in the car, but he would have none of it. They didn't have time to argue.

The unlocked front doors were a warning to Britton that the building was without power.

He issued orders to Hale.

"Get into the utility rooms and get the power on whatever way you have to," he shouted. "I want the elevators and lights back now!"

He refocused on Detective Bobby Brown.

"Is that assault team down?" he asked.

"Down and already in the building, on the top floor, awaiting orders," Brown said.

"Tell them to divide up," he ordered. "I want half of 'em to start a floor-by-floor search from the top down. I want the other half to go directly to twenty-two. We'll start a floor-by-floor from the bottom up. And tell those guys, for chrissake, try not to shoot each other, or us, in the dark. Now *move!*"

Brown brought his radio to his mouth.

Britton spun around, looking for a familiar face. He found Dits O'Brien. God only knew how Dits got there.

"O'Brien," he bellowed, "I want a dozen men in the lobby and another dozen out back by the garage exit. This guy is *not* getting past us, understand?"

O'Brien nodded.

"Okay," Britton said to the combined group of cops around him. "Divide up into two teams and hopscotch each other. Nick Estevez will lead one and take odd floors; I'll lead the other and take even. Let's go!"

It took the first TPD team only minutes to find what they were looking for.

Eugene Rickey was dead, his blackened body rigid on the floor, rivulets of rain sliding down creases in his charred skin. Smoke actually curled up from four places on the corpse, but it dissipated quickly on the breeze.

Nearby, Kirin Janacek was bent over the prone body of her son.

Just before the deadly lightning stroke, Casey had grabbed Rickey's pant leg to break his fall and was clutching the fabric when the charge surged through the Handyman's body. Because the infant wasn't in direct contact with Rickey's flesh, he didn't receive the full impact of the current.

Nonetheless, he got a big enough shock to stop his young heart.

As soon as Kirin had been able to crawl to him, she put her ear to his mouth. He wasn't breathing. Desperately, she began administering infant cardiopulmonary resuscitation.

Kirin, weak and faint from emotional strain, excruciating pain, and blood loss, was working on adrenaline.

Come on, Casey. Breathe!

A desperate calm had infused her.

There was nobody else around.

If her son was going to live, she would have to make it happen. There was no sense fretting about it. The future was in her hands.

She tilted Casey's head back and tipped his chin up to open his airway and prayed that would be enough to restart his respiration.

Once more she put her ear close to his open mouth and her right hand on his chest. If he'd begun breathing again on his own, she couldn't hear it over the noise of the wind. But she didn't feel any breath on her ear and she couldn't feel any expansion or contraction of the tiny chest under her hand. What she could feel was the banging of her own heart in her chest, her neck, even in her head. If only she could pass some of that life to her young son!

She covered his nose and mouth with her mouth, ballooned her cheeks, and forced some air into his lungs. She felt his chest rise and fall. That was good. But when she put her ear against his mouth again, she felt nothing. She breathed for him again. And again Casey failed to begin breathing on his own.

Ignoring the fire in her leg and dizziness brought on by concussion, blood loss, terror, and fatigue, she repositioned herself over the boy. With a strength she didn't know she had, she tore away the clothes covering his chest and arms and felt for a pulse in the brachial artery on the inside of his right upper arm. There was none. Without any available light, by feel, she located the midpoint directly between his nipples and placed her third and fourth fingers on his chest half an inch below that spot.

She began compressions at a rate she hoped would approximate the recommended one-hundred per minute and breathed into Casey's mouth at the same time.

Five compressions, one breath.

Again.

And again.

The exertion was increasing her dizziness. She refused to let herself pass out.

She hoped she wasn't compressing so hard that she risked breaking his ribs or his sternum.

Then she remembered what her instructor told her when she took the infant CPR course after Casey was born.

Don't worry about broken bones or injured organs. Get his heart beating. Get him breathing. At least we'll have a live little boy to take into surgery later.

She felt the brachial artery again.

Nothing.

She took several deep breaths to steady herself and began the compressions and the breathing for Casey again.

Her pain was a red haze of agony overlaid by a black blanket of fear.

She wouldn't give up.

She would never give up.

Compressions and breathing.

Come on, Casey! Breathe!

Please, God, let him breathe!

That's how they were found by the first unit from the Tampa Police Department to burst onto the twenty-second floor.

The group leader quickly assessed the scene and lifted his radio to report. Another rushed to Casey's side to relieve an obviously exhausted Kirin.

But as he reached them, the child began to cry, a loud, gasping, keening screech of terror.

It was music to their ears.

The officer bent over and laid a hand on Kirin's shoulder.

"Looks like you saved his life," he said. "Why don't you let me take over? Give us a chance to help you both."

She looked up, tears glistening on her face.

"Will he be all right?" she asked desperately.

"You were here when it happened?"

"Yes. I started CPR right away."

"Then he should be fine. Good as new. Kids his age come through lots worse without a sign anything ever happened."

Laughing and crying simultaneously, Kirin collapsed on her back on the floor.

It was over.

The killer was dead.

Her child was alive.

She was alive.

She lay still, feeling the rain wash over her and cleanse away her terror.

Then suddenly—with eerie abruptness, the cops would remark later—the storm spent its fury and abated, and the sky began to clear.

38

Casey was discharged from the hospital the next day, fit and happy and happily unaware of the bruise in the center of his chest or the reason for it.

Kirin was held for three days. Doctors didn't want to take a chance with the concussion. They also were concerned about her leg. Rickey's knife has sliced deep into the sartorius muscle and nicked the femoral artery. She wouldn't be permitted to go home until it was clear both were healing without complication.

With the serial killer dead, Benjamin Britton was in no great rush to debrief his witness. He decided to let Kirin get some rest before taking her statement.

She felt well enough to discuss the ordeal the following morning.

David stood beside her bed, holding her hand tightly as she recounted the terror of the previous day. Halfway through her account, a nurse wheeled in Casey in his stroller. He was ready to go home. After several futile attempts to get out of the straps confining him so that he could test his legs again, the little boy gave up and concentrated on his newest toy, various widths of brightly painted wooden doughnuts on a post. When they were put together in the right order, they formed a red and yellow clown.

"The end is a jumble to me, Captain," Kirin Janacek said. "The only time I could see anything was when the lightning flashed. It was like one of those old horror movies where the actor knows the monster is out there moving toward him in the storm, but he can't see him except when the lightning strikes. I saw Casey take a couple of steps toward me at the same time Mr. Rickey started to back up toward the baby carrier. I didn't see it, but I sensed the two of them would bump into each other if their paths didn't change. The first thing I actually saw after that was Mr. Rickey falling and Casey falling and both of them reaching out for something to grab onto. Then there was a bright flash and a huge clap of thunder. After that, it was really dark and really quiet. That's when I smelled it."

"Smelled what?" Britton asked.

"It was horrible. Sickening. The smell of burning flesh."

David spoke up for the first time since she'd started her story. "Don't think about it, Kiri. Put it out of your mind."

"That's a little difficult," she said looking up at him with a smile. "It's not the sort of memory you lose quickly, like, you know, what you had for breakfast yesterday."

She turned back to Britton.

"Anyhow, I was terrified the lightning had hit Casey. Then there was another series of flashes, and I saw Mr. Rickey's body, or what was left of it. And I saw Casey. He was lying real still, but I could see he wasn't burned, and that was a big relief. The only thing I could think about was getting to him. I guess you know the rest."

Britton nodded. "That was quick thinking on your part. The doctors say Casey's fine."

"Thankfully," Kirin breathed.

"He's a tough little guy, and I think he gets it from his mother," David said.

Kirin squeezed his hand.

"You might be interested to know we searched Rickey's home last night and found all the evidence we need to close this case," Britton said. "He had souvenirs of each one of the killings sitting on his coffee table or tacked to his living room wall. His truck fits the description we got from three witnesses, and we found a couple of bottles of Kite's Finest inside. That's the cheap bourbon we found at the scene of Dr. Erlich's murder. And the knife he used to stab you matches in every detail what we know of the serial killer's weapon."

"It's too bad he had to die," Kirin said softly.

David was horrified. "Surely, you're joking," he said.

She glanced at him with a grin and a line from their favorite movie. "No, I'm not joking," she said. "And quit calling me Shirley."

She turned back to Britton. "I didn't mean I'm sad about his death. But it seems like after all the pain and suffering he caused, there would have been some catharsis for all of us in seeing him stand trial."

"The state attorney feels the same way," Britton said. "He wanted nothing more than to prosecute the son of a bitch. Pardon my French."

"You're both dreaming," David said. "He'd have been evaluated and committed. He wouldn't have done a day in prison."

"Spoken like a sharp defense lawyer," Britton said. He stood. "Well, I have all I need. Thanks for seeing me so promptly, Mrs. Janacek. I hope you're up and around soon." He handed her his card. "If there's anything you need, give me a call. If you find you have trouble shaking this thing—and that would be a very common reaction, nothing at all to be ashamed of—we have a crack psychiatrist on our investigative team who would be more than happy, I know, to help you restore your equilibrium."

"I'll remember that, Captain. Thank you."

LATER that day, Britton told his wife, Laura, he had changed his mind about retiring.

"With the citizens out there solving the tough crimes for us, my life should get a lot easier," he said with a grin.

"And just when I was getting used to the idea of having you home for lunch," Laura joked. Then she grew serious. "I think you should still consider leaving. Police work, especially homicide, takes its toll. Eventually, it comes time to move on."

He kissed her forehead. "Okay, I'll think about it," he promised. "Maybe tomorrow I'll think about it. Today, I'm going to relax."

THAT same afternoon, and during the two afternoons which followed, Cynthia Diamond visited Kirin. At first there was a temptation to fall into one another's arms and cry with relief, like two battle-fatigued soldiers who've prevailed together in a deadly firefight. Instead, they just talked. Theirs was the world's smallest sorority, populated by the only two victims who'd lived through an encounter with the Heartbreak Killer, aka the Handyman. They were able to share emotions they couldn't share with anyone else. They grappled with the question of why they were spared when so many others died. A survivors' bond developed quickly between them, and from that a friendship that would span several decades. They were able to sort out what was important in their lives and what wasn't, what inconveniences and annoyances were just that and no more, and what it was truly important to fight for.

After the second day of conversation with Kirin, Cynthia returned to WFSC-TV and demanded a meeting with Chris Pappas and Lee Townsend. She laid out her grievances in no uncertain terms and said if their conduct toward her and the other women at the station didn't improve immediately, she would go to the EEOC and file a formal complaint charging sexual harassment. They wouldn't dare fire her, she reminded them, because of her high profile in the biggest story in town and because she would lay bare all the station's dirty little secrets to the two local newspapers.

Pappas sputtered something about not giving in to blackmail, but relented when Cynthia promised to waste him professionally and made him believe she was capable of it. Townsend insisted he didn't realize his actions had offended anyone and was prepared to try to mend his ways. Cynthia promised to let him know immediately if he strayed from his vows.

Pappas left the meeting furious with what he regarded as Townsend's timid response. A wall developed between the two that resulted five months later in Townsend's dismissal. Pappas offered Cynthia the news director's job, but she said she preferred to remain on the air. However when Pappas himself was fired three years later for putting a move on the station owner's sixteen-year-old daughter, Cynthia was offered the top job, and she took it. Through some brilliant programming and news coverage decisions, she copped the number one spot in the market for WFSC-TV before the end of the calendar year.

DAVID pushed open the door between the garage and the kitchen and helped his wife negotiate the step with her crutches.

"Welcome home," he said.

"It's good to be here," she said. "Could we go out on the lanai? It's a beautiful morning, and I'd like to feel the sun."

She settled onto a lounger. Casey went into his playpen. David sat in a rocker. They were silent for nearly ten minutes.

"Something very important happened to me at WestWater that day," Kirin said softly, finally breaking the quiet. David turned and looked at her, but he said nothing. He sensed it was important to let her tell the story at her own pace.

She took a deep breath.

"I found out there are some things in this world I can control and a lot more I can't," she said, staring straight ahead of her at the glistening waters of Tampa Bay. "I learned it's important to take command of the things you can change. And . . . and it's just as important not to beat yourself up over the things you can't."

"Amy?" David asked.

"Amy," she said with a firm nod. "There isn't anything I wouldn't offer to restore her life and give her health, but I don't have anything like that. Nobody does. That's not my fault. It's not your fault. It wasn't even Amy's fault. It just happened."

"That's right," he said.

"The first night in the hospital, I thought about how I'd brought Casey back. I was nearly unconscious myself, but I took command and changed something it was within my power to change. That was good. And for the first time I can remember, I could think about Amy, and how I couldn't change any of that, and I didn't fall apart."

She looked over at her husband. "I think that's progress, don't you?"

David got up and moved to his wife's side, bending to kiss her gently on the forehead. "I think that's great progress," he said. "I love you."

"I love you, too, darling. And I want to apologize."

"You have nothing to apologize for."

"Yes, I do. The pantry project. Maybe this whole house. I know how much they bother you."

He sat down again with a sigh.

"I've been thinking a lot about the pantry, too," he said, "but not in the way you think. I was wondering how it was going to be for you, living in a house where Eugene Rickey will be a presence everyday. I thought maybe we should have the work torn out and done over, to get rid of his memory, his aura."

She grinned in amazement. "You'd do that? That's quite an offer, considering how tight you are with a buck."

"I wasn't kidding," he said. "Or we could sell the house and build a new one. I wouldn't even argue for getting off the water or into some place smaller or cheaper. It could be even grander if you wanted. As long as you're comfortable."

"That's really sweet," Kirin said genuinely. "But I'm comfortable right here. Just the way we are. Besides, I plan to spend a ton of money at Simon's Market stocking that pantry. And I plan to enjoy the hell out of it."

"You're sure?" David asked. "Maybe if we painted the doors a different color . . ."

"David! The pantry is wood and metal and tile and paint. It's not Eugene Rickey. There are a lot of reasons I'm going to have a difficult time forgetting the Heartbreak Killer, and a pantry is the very least of them."

"If you say so."

"I say so."

She put an end to the discussion by closing her eyes. "I'm going to take a nap now," she announced. "Will you watch Casey?"

"Absolutely."

For the next two hours, Kirin Janacek slept soundly.

And her dreams were good.